Richard Salsbury is a novelis
writer based in the south of E
Flash: The International Short-
World Wide Writers, *Portsmouth News*, the Fairlight Books website and on BBC Radio. His debut novel, the darkly comic thriller *Mute*, was published in 2023. He is the website designer for environmental writing project *Pens of the Earth* and one of the editors (along with his wife) of their anthology *Wild Seas, Wilder Cities*. He also plays the guitar and brews his own beer.

www.richardsalsbury.com

Praise for *Mute*:

'Quite simply one of the best three or four books I've read this year ... an original, compelling and beautifully written page turner.' Steve Sheppard, author of *Bored to Death in the Baltics*

'Superb. As intelligent as it is gripping.' Loree Westron, author of *Missing Words*

'Runs with a richly dark humour that makes it a joy to read.' David Clensy, author of *Prayer in Time of War*

'So clever.' Hayley Sale www.myloveofreading.com

'So many layers ... it had me utterly engrossed.' Patrice Gotting @prdgreads

'I stayed up way too late finishing this last night.' @donnareads03

ALSO BY RICHARD SALSBURY

NOVELS:
Mute

AS CO-EDITOR:
Wild Seas, Wilder Cities

Gifts of Anger

Richard Salsbury

R Salsbury

First published in 2025

Copyright © 2025 Richard Salsbury

The right of Richard Salsbury to be identified as the author
of this work has been asserted by him in accordance with
Section 77 of the Copyright, Designs and Patents Act 1988.

All rights reserved. No part of this publication may be reproduced,
stored in a retrieval system or transmitted, in any form, or by any means
(electronic, mechanical, photocopying, recording or otherwise) without
the prior written permission of the publisher. No part of this publication
may be used to train artificial intelligence technologies or large language
models without prior written permission of the publisher.

This is a work of fiction. Names, characters, businesses, places, events
and incidents are either the product of the author's imagination
or used in a fictitious manner. Any resemblance to actual persons,
living or dead, or actual events is purely coincidental.

www.richardsalsbury.com

ISBNs:
Paperback: 978-1-7394794-2-8
Ebook: 978-1-7394794-3-5

A CIP catalogue record for this book is available from the British Library

Typeset by the author in Adobe Garamond Pro,
Myriad Pro and Source Code Pro

Cover design by The Art of Communication: book-design.co.uk

Printed and bound in the UK by Biddles Books Ltd, King's Lynn, PE32 1SF

For Heg

1

THE NIGHT AROUND ME throbs in time with my stride. The limbs of the trees that line the road remind me of blood vessels, or the tiny, branching passageways of the lung. At this edge of town the sparseness of the street lights makes everything indistinct. I try to reduce my pace from the relentless pounding it has been since leaving my parents' house two minutes ago. The evening is in ruins. Home is only fifteen minutes away, and I'm craving the privacy of my room and a few slugs of vodka to take the edge off.

My brothers; ah, my dear, beloved brothers. Their conversation at the dinner table had been like a pincer movement. Do Zach and Alistair do this out of malice, or just stumble into it by habit? It hardly matters. The evening had been dominated by Zach, smug at the prospect of flouncing around on TV again, while the rest of us struggle to hold down real jobs. 'I expect you all to watch me,' he said. 'I'm flying the flag for the Griffin family here.' He made himself sound like an ambassador, rather than what he really is: a game show contestant on some two-a-penny Freeview channel. And then Alistair had felt the need to discuss Iraq, and how the amount spent on the war had made Britain more vulnerable to the ongoing global financial crisis. Why does he never talk about the thousands of people who have died? Why does everything always have to be about money? I had to challenge him on it. Bingo: instant argument. Just add wine.

And although I've managed to walk away before wrecking the evening for everybody, I've only left in a physical sense. In every other way I'm still there, still arguing with them. Families, eh? Can't live with them, can't slaughter them and bury them under the patio.

I look up from the pavement and, yes, the outside world still exists. At the bend in the road is one of the few other houses in the vicinity, almost as large as my parents' place, white and ruthlessly rectangular, the sort of house estate agents refer to as a 'cottage' in order to soften its ugliness. I glance through the gap in the surrounding wall and see a man crouching down at the front door, picking the lock in the glow of the security light. My pace slows, and after a few more steps I've stopped. Did I just see that? I press my back against the rough flint of the wall. Yes, the snapshot is still clear: the long hair and leather jacket, hands at eye height as he fiddles with the door mechanism.

I take another step, just the one. So, I'm going to walk away again, am I? Twice in one evening seems a bit too much like cowardice. I don't know who owns this house, but am I really going to stroll on by while someone goes through their stuff, trampling all over their lives for a bit of drug money? Fishing out my mobile, I stab at the tiny plastic buttons and end up with four nines. It's a new phone and I fumble to find the delete key.

Wait a minute. Let's get this straight: I'm seething, I'm on the brink, and I'm going to phone the cops – who have always made me nervous – to report a crime when I don't even know for certain that one is taking place.

I lower the phone. My breath is coming too fast. I can see it fogging in the cold air, short-lived and luminescent from the light of a street lamp. I have to step back, take stock, the way Dr Nylund told me. I close my eyes, but a scene immediately plays across the inside of my eyelids: me pushing my chair back from my parents' dining table and retreating to the sanctuary of the toilet while the others finish the lamb, oblivious. I open my eyes to banish the images.

Leave it. Just leave it and go home.

Maybe the guy at the front door is the owner. He might be struggling to get his key into the door after staggering back from Foley's wine bar. On the other hand, if he is a thief, he's not going to wait around for me to make a decision. He's going to be half a mile down the road with his pockets stuffed full of jewellery. I know how Zach would react. He'd walk past, thinking it was bad luck; just one of those things. Unless it happened to him, of course. Then it would be bang out of order.

Well, I'm not Zach.

I peer round the corner to see the porch is now empty, just as the security light times out. Why is nothing ever simple? The windows of the house are dark, the night silent except for a faint rustle of leaves. This is one of the last properties on the outskirts of Strathurst before the town begins in earnest. It's expensive, but without the luxury of being isolated in woodland like my parents' place. He can't have left – the walls are over two metres high and topped with broken glass, and I'm pretty sure I'm covering the only exit. Which means he's inside, illegally or otherwise. I'm hoping for the former; if I prevent a burglary, at least I'll have salvaged something from the evening.

If the door isn't shut then he must be turning the place over and hoping for a quick getaway. I need to get closer, see if the door is ajar. I switch my phone to silent before pocketing it – a sudden blast of Muse's 'Supermassive Black Hole' isn't going to do me any favours. The gap in the flint wall has mounting posts but no gate, leading onto a sea of gravel that stretches all the way up to the house and double garage. I don't understand this fad for hard landscaping. What's wrong with a modest pathway and lots of nice, quiet grass? The gravel crunches underfoot as I take my first steps. I approach from an oblique angle, not wanting to trigger the light, but I'm sure I'm going to be blinded by it at any moment. Where is the sensor mounted?

About halfway across the ocean of stones, I get the proof I need: there's a slight breeze and I see the door move. I bloody knew it. I reach into my pocket for the phone. From inside I hear a thump and a wordless shout. The door opens and the leather-jacketed thief comes tearing out. Light floods us both. Like a cartoon burglar he has a bag slung over one shoulder: a green canvas sack pulled shut at the top. He runs straight for the road, footfalls splashing, the bag bouncing against his back.

'Shit,' he says as he sees me, but it doesn't slow him down. He's past before I can recover from the shock. My eyes re-focus on the face of a white-haired man wearing a bathrobe and slippers. He steps onto the porch, and just before he becomes a silhouette haloed by the light, I see his mouth is a rectangle of outrage, stuffed full of teeth.

'Thieving bastards!' he yells.

I open my mouth to explain, but I stall as he lifts his arm above his head. He's holding a fire poker, an iron rod that glints as he swings it. Animal instinct takes hold. I turn to run, but slip on the stones and end up on all fours. As I go down, I catch sight of the thief going through the entrance and turning down the hill. The old man will be close enough to bludgeon me within seconds. To get some traction, I dig both hands and feet into the gravel, pushing off in a headlong stumble, bursting onto the pavement in a scatter of stones. My momentum carries me into the middle of the road before I can turn down the hill. Thank God there's no traffic. The whistle of the wind sounds in my ears as I accelerate, aided by the downward slope and the grip of good, hard tarmac. Glancing round, I see the old man standing next to the flint wall, accepting that he's not going to catch anyone.

'Come back for something else,' he shouts. 'I'll crack your bloody skulls open!'

My attention shifts like cross hairs to the thief, who is already halfway down the hill. He glances at me and turns back to concentrate on running. He's a tall guy, and not built for it. But these aren't ideal conditions for me either. I'm wearing my one and only pair of formal leather shoes – nothing but the best for Mum and Dad – and my coat is acting like a sail. I grab both sides in one hand to minimise the billowing and start to gain on him.

The sack. I'm having that. He'll abandon it if I get close enough. Then I can return it to the old man and explain that I'm nothing to do with this. Job done.

At the bottom of the hill the housing estates begin, with pavements on both sides and more regular street lighting. He veers to the right and into a gap between two rows of houses. The path splits in a T-junction at the end and he goes left, hoping to lose me. But I'm too close to be thrown off. Up ahead of him the alley ends in a wall of greenery and fencing.

'Drop it!' I yell, now there's nowhere left for him to run. But no: he finds a sparse bit of hedge and goes crashing through into someone's back garden. Something catches at the sack, spinning it round. I go straight through after him, holding my arms up in front of my face for protection. Thorns catch at my sleeves, and I'm through.

A wrought iron gate by the side of the house leads back onto the road, but he heads straight for the fence instead. A sturdy brick barbecue borders the patio. He mounts it with two quick steps, puts his free hand on the fence, and vaults straight over. Without giving myself a chance to think about it, I follow him, using the same footholds. Two metres above the ground, as I clear the wooden slats, I see him in the neighbouring garden, veering past a kid's climbing frame as he heads for the garden gate. I hit the ground running. I'll be on him when he has to slow down to deal with the gate. But on his way past the climbing frame, he reaches out and pulls it straight into my path. I try to sidestep, but I've built up too much momentum. My legs stop dead as they hit the frame. I hinge at the waist, and my forearms slam into the steel. The pain is like a camera flash going off in my head. I look up to see that he isn't bothering with the gate latch: he's tall enough to swing one leg over the top bar, then the other, and he's off. It's like a taunt.

I accelerate again, jumping the gate like a hurdler. He's crossed the road and gone down Nettlecombe Lane, but I notice a looseness in his limbs. He's tiring, and I'm making up ground fast. His mistake is to head down The Willows, which he should know, if he'd bothered to look at the street sign, is a cul-de-sac. He skirts the uninterrupted wall of housing and, seeing no easy route out, he raises one hand above his head, as if calling for a pause in a tennis match. He slows to a stop, watching me to make sure I do the same. I leave a few metres between us, but block his exit from the street. The only sound is of us both breathing hard.

He was supposed to drop the sack. Why has he chosen to let me catch up rather than abandon it? Why, now I think about it, have I been chasing a thief who's prepared to injure me, so I can return some goods to a man who wants to brain me with a length of iron? I hate this feeling: the plummet into doubt. He coughs a couple of times, clearly not used to the exertion, but he looks entirely prepared for a face-off. And why wouldn't he be? He's a burglar. He could have a flick-knife in his pocket, even a gun. He might be the sort that reacts like a wild animal when cornered.

He was supposed to drop the fucking sack.

After recovering his breath he straightens, regarding me with eyes so big they seem to bulge out of his head. His face, slick with sweat, is long and lumpy. I re-estimate his height at a full two metres, and he's broad-shouldered too – a giant. There's a bit of a gut on him, but that doesn't mean I fancy my chances if it comes to a fight. He takes a couple of steps towards me and I stifle the urge to step backwards.

'So,' he says with a grin, 'did you enjoy that?'

2

IT'S AN ODD QUESTION, and I don't know how to answer without betraying my fear, or provoking him, or admitting that what I've just done is utterly reckless. He, on the other hand, looks completely relaxed.

'Why did you come after me?' A Yorkshire accent. 'I know you're not related to the old man.'

I did it because, like the man said, you're a thieving bastard. I don't say it out loud. I'm alert for the two quick steps forward that will put him in punching or kicking range.

'A have-a-go hero?' he suggests.

'You're surprised someone would try and stop you?'

'I'm delighted,' he says.

'Give me the sack and I'll let you go.'

He laughs at my audacity. 'Very good,' he says, and immediately his mirth disappears. 'I can't do that.'

I hold my mobile out to one side so he can see it.

'What have you got there?' His eyes go wide. 'A detonator?'

Bastard. He knows how little I've got to bargain with.

He waves a hand. 'Put it away. The police won't get here in time to catch me. And anyway, once I show you what's in the bag, you won't want to call them.'

I hesitate, cursing myself for the display of weakness, and pocket the phone. He swings the bag off his shoulder and holds it out, one hand grasping the neck, the other supporting it at the bottom. 'Want to see what I've got?'

'Empty it there.' I point to the ground in front of him.

He up-ends the sack. Balls bounce off in all directions – footballs, tennis balls, soft foam balls. Due to the camber of the road, they end up settling against the kerb. He shakes the bag to show there's nothing else inside, and grins. 'Confused?'

He interprets my silence as a yes.

'The guy who lives in that house, Slater, could give Scrooge a run for his money. Shackleton Park backs onto his house, and kids lose balls in his garden all the time. He doesn't return any of them. I've already been round his house and asked, perfectly polite, but the grumpy sod told me it was tough cheese; they were his now. So ... I took them back.'

His story is plausible. The house does back onto the park.

'You don't believe me,' he says.

I shrug, a pathetic gesture. I don't have a better explanation, just a suspicion that the real reason hasn't occurred to me yet.

'Huh,' he says, a percussive sound, then starts to pick up the balls and put them back in the sack. 'I don't blame you for being cynical. It's the media does that to people: "There's a psycho round every corner. Thieving, drug-crazed immigrants stalk our streets." Not very helpful, is it? Tell you what: meet me at the park tomorrow, ten in the morning, and I'll prove what I say is true. Broad daylight. Plenty of other people around.'

'And you expect me to believe you'll show up?'

'Of course.'

'What guarantee have I got?'

'Because I've given you my word.'

'Which is worth?'

'Hey, don't push your luck.'

I clench my teeth. He's offering me a way out that won't seem like completely backing down. It's the best I'm going to get.

'Okay, then. Ten o'clock.'

He finishes rounding up his booty and says, 'I reckon I'll be off, then.'

I stand aside and gesture with an open hand. I should be grateful that a trip to the hospital isn't on the cards.

'Bloody good chase,' he says in parting. 'I nearly had a friggin' heart attack.'

—

'All right, Olly?' mutters Jodie, my landlady's daughter, as I walk in.

She's in her customary position: slouched on the sofa in front of the TV, feet on the coffee table, curling a blonde lock around one finger. She doesn't turn her head; she has a psychic talent for knowing who's entered the room, a skill that allows her to indulge her appetite for trash TV without interruption.

'Hiya.' I shed my coat and release my feet from what have definitely proved to be my least comfortable pair of shoes. I sigh and slump in one of the armchairs – a big, pink, chintzy thing that epitomises her mum's taste in home furnishings. On the TV, a bunch of dolled-up fashion victims are gathered in a circle, looking down at a corpse on a rug. They nudge each other and giggle while a presenter gives them instructions.

'What's this?' I ask.

'Celebrity Crime Scene.'

These are celebrities? I don't recognise any of them. A woman with impeccable hair tries to dust for fingerprints on the victim's denim jacket while the others call her a dozy cow.

'It's not as good as last week,' Jodie says, but makes no effort to change the channel. 'Oh, that reminds me: how did it go?'

Given the evening's profusion of excitements, this is not an easy question to answer.

'Come on,' she says, 'is your brother gonna be on telly again?'

Ah, that. 'Yes, he is. Another game show.'

'When's it on?'

'Tuesdays, nine o'clock, FizzTV.' Zach had drilled this nugget of information into our brains. 'It starts next week.'

'And? Go on.'

'It's called *Obedience*. The contestants have to do a bunch of horrible tasks, and whoever makes the worst job of it gets voted off by the viewers. Oh, and there's a second phone-in to decide what tasks are set for the next week.'

'Cool.'

'Even cooler,' I say, with an irony I suspect is lost on her, 'is that he's going to be called ZG from now on.' He had pronounced it the American way: Zee-Jee. 'He's re-branded himself.'

I envy her ability to accept this without question, without an accompanying stab of irritation. Zach will do anything to get noticed. Still, we had all promised to watch him, just as we had for that singing programme he was on. He had set the tone for the evening as soon as I arrived. I'd found him in the garden, bouncing up and down on the old trampoline which had been sitting there, unused, for years. It reminded me of the old Zach, pre-showbiz – the brother I grew up with, shared my stuff with, got into trouble with. When I asked what he was doing, he said with a laugh, 'Checking for paparazzi.'

Yeah, not quite yet, Zach. 'You're nuts,' I'd said.

'That's what you love about me.'

And five years ago, yes, he would have been right.

—

The bath water is hot enough to strip the skin off lesser mammals and I'm wallowing in mountains of foam. I use this much bubble bath so that if Jodie or Moira wander in – which is possible, since the door lock is broken – they won't see my dick. I throw Jodie's yellow plastic duck, Dudley, into the tub and watch him disappear among the bubbles. What a day.

Dinner at my parents' is like Russian roulette, each bullet an argument. It's also mercifully infrequent now Zach and Alistair have moved further away. Mum does her best for us, getting out the posh cutlery and those burgundy napkins I didn't even know they owned until we'd all left home. She spends hours cooking. I told her once that she didn't have to go to all this effort, but she said, 'Not make an effort when my boys are coming home? Don't deprive me of that.' It's generous of her, given that she has no shortage of reasons to despise me. She can't have forgotten the time I was arguing with Alistair and swept her favourite china plate off the mantelpiece with one of my wilder gesticulations. Or my last physical fight with Zach, more than three years ago, over a girl who didn't have the slightest interest in either of us. Mum had found us in the garden, Zach trying to ward off the blow that would give him a second black eye.

I managed not to boil over tonight – shame has taught me a thing or two over the years – but Zach's insistence that fame is the pinnacle of human achievement and Alistair's throwaway comment that Obama is 'proving to be a bit of a disappointment compared to Bush' kept the cauldron bubbling nicely. Dad probably hadn't meant to make things worse when he asked me, 'So, how's the job at SMC?'

To a man who co-founded his own company and spent twenty years making it a success, a job is a sacred thing. It's who you are. He's offered employment to all his sons but only Alistair, the archetypal daddy's boy, has taken him up on it. Zach and I would rather gouge our eyes out than become intellectual property lawyers.

I had speared an asparagus tip with my fork as I said, 'SMC let me go.'

It had just the effect I anticipated. I could feel the shift in atmosphere, people pausing in mid-mouthful, then trying to continue as if nothing had happened. They were already imagining the worst. *He must have punched a colleague, screamed abuse at his manager*. And yet, when was the last time I had lost my temper with any of them? They would always jump to these conclusions about me. Always.

I glanced around the table as I munched, but none of them would meet my gaze. I relented and told them the rest. 'They let all of us go. The whole department.'

I was surprised not to hear a collective sigh of relief. I wanted to say, 'See? You're wrong about me. I've got so much better and you just can't see it.'

'I thought SMC were doing okay,' Alistair ventured.

'Yeah, they are. But they've decided to outsource to India.'

'Bastards,' Zach muttered.

'They flew the new team over to Britain so we could train them, and that was it. "Thanks for everything. Here's your P45."'

Alistair's mouth dropped open. 'You're joking! You had to help these … people take away your job?'

'I got on fine with these *people*, actually. They're a good bunch. It's my manager who sold us down the river.'

Zach said, 'So you pulped his face, right?'

'Zach!' Mum hissed.

'No,' I said, 'I asked if he was being shipped out to India too. He shook his head, and I said, "Are you sure?" He didn't look too happy about that. I asked him if he was scared of the people he'd betrayed, now they had nothing left to lose.'

Zach said, 'So *then* you pulped his face?'

I felt a surge up my spine, something chemical, potent. I put my cutlery down and wrapped my fingers round the edges of the chair. If Zach knew the effect he was having on my adrenaline levels, would he still have done it? I glared at him but he was looking at his plate, toying with his food.

'Relax,' he said without meeting my gaze, 'I'm just messing with you, bro.'

'So you're looking for a job now?' Dad said.

'No,' I managed. 'I found a position at Caduceus Technologies, working in support. I started last Monday. It's different to programming but, you know ... not a problem.'

It was supposed to be the happy ending, smiles all round and a toast to the victor, but all I got from Dad was a nod. To me, finding another job in a recession was a success story, but the long silence swallowed my achievement. I wanted him to say something. Anything. But I knew he wouldn't.

'Well done, mate,' Zach said. 'I know how hard it is getting a job these days ... which is why it's so great that I've got through the selection process for this game show. It's another one by WTF Productions. I think they're taking a bit of a shine to me.'

Aaaaand we were back to Zach and his TV career. Enough. Enough of this. I pushed my chair back and retreated to the loo. Sitting on the toilet seat, head in hands, I tried to rein myself in, but hearing Zach from the dining room, regaling them with his TV exploits, I knew I was too close to the precipice. Just one more nudge and I'd be watching myself destroy the evening for everybody. So I decided to take Dr Nylund's advice and save us all from the ordeal. I slipped out the front door, unnoticed, before Mum served up the white chocolate brioche.

I scoop up a handful of bathwater and splash it over my face. I've got to stop thinking about this. Dudley watches me, bobbing from side to side with disapproval. I flick him in the head, sending him spinning off to the far end of the bath.

There's something I'm missing about that thief. Nobody goes to that sort of effort for some old balls. Perhaps they were signed by someone famous. No. Perhaps they were a distraction and his jacket was stuffed full of valuables. But then why would he have bothered to steal the balls at all?

I slide further down into the bath and push my toes up through the foam. By doing this, I put pressure on my arms and I can feel a tenderness where they hit the climbing frame. I pull them out of the water and wipe the suds off. There's no more than a hint of red. Typical. To see this I have to look beneath the parallel white ridges climbing all the way up my forearms. Another good reason for using lots of bath foam.

I haven't cut for two months now. The impulse hasn't gone away, but I'm not going back to that, I'm just not. If I think that the guilt and shame of this evening is strong, I have to remind myself how I used to feel after slicing my arms with a razor blade. It brought a fantastic sense of release, but it was hardly a solution, and ultimately just caused a fresh set of problems. At least the climbing frame bruises were sustained while trying to do the right thing.

I get out of the bath, pull the plug and towel myself dry. Once I'm up in my room, I pull the loft ladder up and close the hatch. When I'd first looked around the place, the loft conversion was only half-finished, but while Moira apologised about the lack of a staircase, I saw it as the perfect way to maintain my privacy. I'd been living with my parents again after splitting up with Kerry, and I needed my freedom; Moira needed to rent the room out and make some cash. The arrangement suited us both. I've helped them out with a few bits of DIY, like the shelving I needed for my legion of books and CDs. In return she takes a bit off the rent.

I chuck my clothes onto the heap in the corner and flop onto the bed. I'm lucky to have a place like this. It's a modest Victorian semi, with just about enough space for the three of us. By contrast, my parents' house has six bedrooms – which is five more than they need now their sons have left home – plus every convenience and comfort. But it's this place, up in the eaves, that feels like home. Neither Moira nor Jodie has ever seen me lose my rag, and as a result they assume I'm normal. They cannot know how much this means to me.

My mobile is on the desk next to the PC keyboard, watching me innocently. I won't phone any of my family – what the hell would I say? – but I can't resist checking for missed calls and texts. It's probably not a good idea so soon after I've managed to calm down, but I have to know.

There's nothing. I can't tell if I'm relieved or disappointed.

3

MY PHONE READS 10:10 and I'm beginning to feel like a mug. I'm sitting on a bench with my hands stuffed into my pockets, and now I've been here for a while, I'm feeling cold. It's halfway through October, and I'm still wearing my thin summer coat. A low roof of cloud threatens rain.

This park is smaller than the Queen Victoria Playing Fields across the other side of town. It has only one marked-out football pitch, currently in use by the Sunday youth league. A bunch of teens tear around the grass to the barked commands of their coach, who seems to think he's directing a battle. Across the other side is a small lake with ducks and a few trees, where a woman walks her dog and a young couple snog their way around the perimeter. Closer to my bench is another, impromptu game of football, with half a dozen younger kids using upturned bicycles as goalposts. To get enough space for their pitch they've had to set up near the flint wall that marks the edge of the old man's property. It's not hard to see how balls could end up in his garden. Of course, that still doesn't mean the burglar was telling the truth. It could just be a useful cover story.

So, how much longer do I wait? He could be watching me from the cover of the trees, chuckling at my gullibility. I fold my arms in an effort to trap some more warmth. If I was on the move like everyone else in the park I wouldn't be feeling the chill. The younger kids are having a great time. Most of them have grass stains up their legs, the result of sliding kicks that are more for show than actually scoring goals. If the Sunday league coach was overseeing this bunch, he'd crush all that grandstanding out of them, because the game they're playing isn't proper football; it's something of their own making. I find myself hoping none of them ever decide to join the league.

10:15.

My plan was to meet up with Kerry this morning, but I texted to say I wouldn't be able to make it. She said it was fine; we'd catch up some other time. To be honest, I'm lucky she still agrees to see me at all. I put her through a lot. As soon as we moved in together, the arguments had started. I always won, if you can call reducing your girlfriend to tears winning. After we were over as a couple, when I was at my worst, I wanted to hear about her going under the wheels of a bus. Pretty damning proof that she was right to chuck me. Weeks later, when she phoned to say there was no chance of us getting back together, but she'd like to see me anyway, I wondered what the hell the point would be. But she was right. I no longer have to deal with the things about her that drove me up the wall: her lazy fatalism, her unrestrained spending, the deranged bull terrier she loved more than she ever loved me. Meeting up every few weeks for a chat or a movie, I've rediscovered her as a friend.

Another glance at my phone and I decide this is pointless. Maybe Kerry's still up for a coffee. I stand and head for the gate. In case he's watching, I try to look like I don't give a damn. And there he is, striding straight towards me. He's wearing that same leather jacket over a huge white fisherman's jumper and loose-fit blue jeans. The canvas sack is slung over one shoulder.

'See?' he says. 'I'm a man of my word.'

Having made up my mind to leave, I'm not sure I want to go through with this any more.

'Take a seat.' He gestures at the bench I've just vacated, as if I might not have noticed it. 'I want to show you I'm on the level.'

I sit. He's about to join me on the bench when the kids spot him and go nuts. Their football rolls off across the grass, abandoned, and they all run towards him. He holds up a hand, bringing them to a halt so sudden it looks like they've struck a force field. He swings the sack off his shoulder, reaches inside and produces a single red and white football. At the head of the rabble is a skinny kid with a bright orange sweater. His mouth drops open, revealing a gap between two big front teeth.

'You got it!' he says, grabbing the ball as if it might not be real.

'Uh-huh.'

'Wicked!'

'And all the others.' He empties the rest of the balls from the bag and there are more coos of amazement.

'Play a match with us, Uncle Trib,' Orange-Top says, and his friends chime in.

'Not this week,' he says. 'Too much to do.'

They look crestfallen, until he knocks the ball out of Orange-Top's hands and makes a dash for one of the bicycle goals. They spring into action, but instead of tackling they pile onto him, attaching themselves to his arms and legs, leaping onto his back. He keeps the ball going, groaning under the weight, until he can take no more and collapses. They smother him, cackling like monkeys. One of the kids hooks the ball out from under him and takes it away. With the ball safe, they release him. He brushes the grass off his jacket and says, 'Next week I promise you a proper match.'

'No – now!'

'Tell you what,' he says, taking out a pen and a dog-eared diary, 'I'll book you in for next Sunday.' He finishes writing the entry and stabs a full stop.

'We want you to play now,' Orange-Top whines.

He taps the diary twice on the boy's head. 'Next ... week.'

The kid slumps, like a puppet with its strings cut, and dawdles back to his mates. 'Uncle Trib' comes over to the bench and sits down next to me.

'The one I gave the ball to,' he says, 'is Adam, son of a friend of mine. He's a great kid.'

So, he's not really an uncle. At least not to Adam.

'The red and white ball is his favourite,' he continues. 'His dad bought it for him when he had flu, a kind of incentive to get better. Thanks for turning up, by the way. I didn't want to leave you with the impression I was your standard burglar. Name's John Tribbeck, but everyone calls me Trib.'

I hesitate, but it seems petty to withhold my name. 'Olly Griffin.'

In daylight and up close, he looks far less threatening than he did last night, the unusual shape of his head more a case for sympathy than fear. In the dark, everyone's a phrenologist.

'I forgot to congratulate you,' he says.

'For turning up?'

'No, for coming after me last night.'

'Why?'

'Because it was the right thing to do.'

'It would have been if I'd caught you with a bag full of jewellery.'

'No, no, no. It doesn't matter that you were mistaken. It matters that you were drawing a line in the sand. It was a statement of your beliefs and a demonstration of your willingness to act on them.'

'Huh.' I turn to watch the kids. 'Sounds impressive. I didn't realise I was doing all of that.' But he's grasped something fundamental about me that's eluded other people, even my own family, for years.

We're silent for a moment. Orange-Top shoots for the goal, but the ball bounces off a bike tyre and returns to hit him on the forehead. His mates laugh as he staggers comically, arms shaking, before falling over.

'Just a practical point, but shouldn't you have waited until the old man was out of the house before going in?'

'I thought he was. He's usually out late on a Saturday evening and there weren't any lights on. The idea is that he'd come back home and the balls would just have disappeared. There's no way I'd have gone in there if I knew he was in. Even an old git like Slater doesn't deserve that. We scared the shit out of each other.' He laughs at the memory of it, a short bark. 'Luckily I'd already found the balls in this little cloakroom and he'd conveniently put them all in a garden bag. All I had to do was sling it over my shoulder and run like buggery.'

'What if he goes to the police? He got a good look at you.' And me.

'And says what? They weren't his in the first place. And do you think the cops have enough free officers to put onto the Case of the Missing Balls?'

'You did steal his bag,' I point out.

'Oh, I'll be dropping that off tonight.'

I raise my eyebrows. 'You're going to break back in so you can return his property?'

'Safer to just leave it on his porch, I think.'

'So this whole thing was planned out beforehand?'

'Of course it was. It wasn't some spur-of-the-moment thing. I wasn't robbing him.'

'No?' His defensive tone makes me feel I can push harder. 'You didn't pocket anything else while you were there? Something small and valuable?'

He jerks round to look at me. 'No, I did not!' He's more

wounded than angry.

I don't reply; I don't even face him. This is a trick my dad uses – if you don't speak or react, the other person feels obliged to fill the silence.

'I shouldn't be surprised you don't trust me,' he says. 'It can't have looked good from your point of view. What were you doing on Slater's property anyway?'

'I was just walking by and I saw you picking the lock. I was going to call the police, but I never saw you go inside. I had to be sure you were really robbing him.'

'Wow. Bad luck on my part, then.'

'So,' I ask him, 'you're in the habit of doing things like this, are you?'

I expect him to say 'no, of course not', but instead he fixes me with a stare, long and direct. I turn and stare back. It was an idle question, but the longer his pause stretches, the more interested I become in his answer.

'I'm peckish,' he says. 'How about you? I know this great little café.'

4

SINCE LAST NIGHT'S FACE-OFF everything has reversed. I now have the upper hand. He wants something from me – forgiveness, or understanding, or a promise not to call the police – and it's my right to bestow or withhold it as I see fit.

I've never really noticed the café before. It's on a road tucked behind the pedestrianised bustle of Broad Street, between a hairdresser's and an antique shop, neither of which are open. A flaking wooden sign, black text on white, announces it simply as 'Sumi's'. A bell rings as we go in. Most of the space is taken up by a cluster of round tables. Two couples sit, eat and chat. The counter has racks of food behind glass, like a delicatessen. There are baguettes, quiches and cakes, but also a range of Indian finger food. Although it's only a quarter to eleven, breakfast seems a long time ago.

'You've got to try the samosas,' he says. 'And the pakoras. In fact, it's pretty much all good.'

From a room behind the counter a woman in a sari appears, beaming, her greying hair tied back in a bun.

'Hello, Trib,' she says.

'Hi, Sumi. How's business?'

'Oh, I struggle on. What can I get for you?'

He picks out a substantial plate of delicacies.

'These are quite high in fat, you know,' she stage-whispers. 'Most people would order one or two. All things in moderation.'

'Except your food, Sumi. I can't help myself.'

She turns to me. 'He's such a flatterer, isn't he?'

I smile, polite but non-committal.

'Anyway,' Trib says. 'I'm ordering for both of us, if that's okay by you.'

I nod, then wonder why I shouldn't be ordering my own. Too late now. While Sumi is adding up the order on the till, he mutters, 'If I pay for this, would you take it as a friendly gesture, or a bribe not to tell anyone what happened last night?'

'Depends which it actually is.'

'A friendly gesture.'

'Okay.'

'Ace. That's what I like to hear.'

He pays and we sit in the far corner with the stacked plate between us.

'Dig in,' he says. 'I would say I'll race you, but that wouldn't be fair.'

It's delicious. The spicy stuff isn't just a vague wash of chilli heat, like my attempts at Indian food at university. Sumi clearly uses fresh spices rather than just chucking curry powder at it.

'So, what do you do for a living, Olly?' Trib asks.

'Computer support.'

'Wife? Girlfriend?'

I give him a direct look.

He grins. 'I know what that means: "None of your business, but no, I haven't."'

'You didn't tell me about your line of work.'

'Security consultant.'

'So that's how you got into Slater's house.'

'Principled *and* smart,' he says round half a samosa. He points the other half towards me. 'I'm beginning to like you.'

I roll my eyes. 'Oh, puh-lease.'

He laughs. 'Am I being too liberal with my praise?'

'You're acting like we're best mates. I don't know the first thing about you.'

He spreads his crumb-encrusted hands and says, 'Then ask me a question. Anything.'

'Well, you still haven't answered the one I asked you in the park: what have you done other than nicking those balls?'

'I'm 31 years old. I've done all kinds of other things in my life.'

'You know what I mean.'

He chooses this moment to pop in another generous mouthful, so I have to wait until he's finished chewing. He hums elaborately in appreciation and gestures for me to eat something else.

'Before I tell you,' he says, 'I need to ask you something.'

I let out a sigh. 'So, you're not going to answer? Happy to just string me along?'

'All right, no need to get narky. The straight answer is yes.'

'Yes, what?'

'Yes, I've done things other than nicking the balls. Lots of things. Missions, I call them.'

The word seems designed to give them an air of legitimacy. 'Give me an example.'

'Okaaay …' He thinks for a moment, and I wonder what sort

of feat he's trying to recall, the most impressive or the least incriminating.

'There's this guy who runs a garage on the east side of town, just behind the leisure centre, and he used to do work on cars that didn't strictly need to be done. Sometimes it was just replacing spark plugs or brake pads. Sometimes it was a lot more.'

'That sort of thing does happen.'

'Which makes it right?'

'No, but you don't have to get involved. It's a matter for the police.'

'That's the problem, though, isn't it? You could go to the police with something like that, but proving it isn't easy. It boils down to your word against his. The whole thing gets mired down in paperwork and court hearings and it's a big waste of everybody's time. Now don't get me wrong, I've got a lot of time for the boys in blue, but don't you think their resources are better used catching murderers and arsonists and international drug rings?'

'You're still taking the law into your own hands.'

He leans forwards. 'So you think all things immoral, no matter how small, should be trusted to an overstretched, underfunded police force?'

He phrases it in a way that makes it difficult to contradict. 'It's still wrong.'

'Depends on your point of view. Legally it might be wrong. But if I act in an effort to save my fellow car owners from being fleeced, then am I not doing something morally right?'

'Okay, potentially,' I allow. 'Depends what you did.'

'Well, this guy drives a BMW 7 Series, a car he can afford as a direct result of having ripped off other people. So I mock up a letter on BMW-headed paper saying his car's been recalled for a minor safety issue and it'll be picked up, checked out, and returned to him on the same day. So I turn up at his house, collect his car and take it to Guildford. It really is a lovely car to drive. Once there, I park it in a short stay car park, do some shopping, and take the train home. His car gets towed away and he has to pay to get it released, as well as getting a stern lecture from the authorities.'

'For real?'

'For real. In the glove compartment I leave a note saying, "Unexpected costs are such a drag, aren't they?"'

'But you're giving him evidence of what you've done.'

'Ahh, that's the beauty of it: if he goes to the police with the note, he throws suspicion on himself.'

'Aren't you worried he might bump into you in the street and recognise you?'

'Oh, there's no chance of that. I dyed my hair blonde and wore a fake moustache.'

Either this guy is living in a dream-world or he's the most audacious person I've ever met.

He grins like a kid caught with his hand in the sweet jar. 'Brilliant fun, it was.'

I shake my head. 'That's batshit.'

'This isn't just for kicks,' he says. 'Think about the guy's reaction. He's doing something wrong, and he knows someone's onto him. He has no way to fight back. So, what does he do?'

'He stops?'

'Yes. And he did.'

'Haven't you ever been caught?'

'Of course not. I'm careful. I plan meticulously.'

This rubs me up the wrong way. Out of the two of us, how come I'm the one that's spent a night in a police cell? 'So, you're a vigilante?'

'Ah, I never use violence,' he says. 'Rule number one.'

'Not even if there's a convenient climbing frame you can chuck at someone?'

'Okay, okay,' he says in a pained voice, 'that was just meant to slow you down.'

'Right.'

'I thought you might beat the crap out of me if you caught up.'

Me beat the crap out of him?

'The point is,' he says, 'I never intentionally hurt anyone.'

'But it might happen, given what you do.'

'Well, there's an element of risk to everything. You endanger someone if you ask them to drive round your house, don't you? They might end up in a horrific car accident. Look, you chose to chase after me. I could have been a murderer on the run. The point is, you can't let fear stop you from doing what you believe in.'

'It's your duty to punish the wicked?'

'Oh, you make me sound so holier-than-thou! You've got to act according to your principles. People put up with so much crap. They whinge and moan, but they never *do* anything. It's always someone else's responsibility: the police, the council, the man next door.'

'And your "missions" are the best way of taking responsibility?'

'Not always. Some things are best left to the police, obviously. But if you're selective and creative and thorough, yes, it works. You can tell a man he's doing something wrong and he'll just tell you to eff off. But *demonstrate* he's doing something wrong, or show him what might happen as a result of his actions, and you might change his mind. Especially if you don't give him any chance to argue with you.'

'There was nearly an argument last night. Between a fire poker and your head.'

'Yeah,' he muses. 'It wasn't supposed to be like that. The idea was that the balls would just disappear, and he wouldn't see the point in hoarding them any more. To prevent someone from going into his house again, he'd take the easy option and throw the balls back into the park.'

'But,' and here I put the boot in, 'you didn't plan thoroughly enough.'

He nods in a slow rhythm. 'There's a first time for everything.'

'So, why have you gone to the effort of explaining all this to me?'

'Because you came after me when you thought I was a burglar. You want to do the right thing.'

'Doesn't everyone?'

'God, no. Not at all. Most people are too uninterested, too afraid. Whereas you've got bollocks.'

What I've got is a towering sense of frustration at the state of the world. What I've got is the ability to lash out when I get pissed off and make a dick of myself. Why would he think this is something to be proud of?

'So,' he says, 'what I'm getting round to is ... I wondered if you wanted to, erm ...' He looks around at the walls, scratches the back of his neck. 'You know, help me out with a couple of things. It's just an idea.'

My jaw drops. 'You want me to help you steal footballs from rich men's houses?'

'Oh, there's plenty more can be done. You've no idea.'

I have to admire his lunacy. A crusade against the injustice of the world has its appeal.

'I'm sorry,' I tell him, 'you've got the wrong man.'

'Really?' he blinks his owlish eyes.

'You sound surprised. I mean, come on. I've only witnessed one example of your work, and you cocked it up.'

'I got the balls back,' he protests.

'Sorry. I've got enough to be dealing with.'

He looks deflated, as if he expected me to leap up and down in my eagerness to get into trouble.

'At least do me one favour,' he says. 'Don't change. Don't stop trying to do the right thing. I respect you for that.'

It would be easy to dismiss this as more flattery. The truth, though, is that I'm not used to such naked praise. I make a gesture halfway between acknowledgement and dismissal because I don't know what to say. The plate between us is empty, so I'm not even able to hide behind another mouthful of food.

'Well, I won't keep you,' he says. 'I'm sure you've got things to do. Hope you enjoyed the food.'

'Yeah. Cheers.'

He offers me a hand and we shake. I'm not surprised to find his grip firm.

—

I've given up trying to read my copy of *Brighton Rock*. Jodie's incessant channel-flicking has seen to that. While I could hardly be less interested in the dross that glides across the screen, it's enough to distract me. I don't know why I try to read while she does this. An attempt to be sociable, I suppose, instead of reading alone in my room.

She often does this, searching for a programme to watch, but never staying on one channel for more than a few seconds. She cycles through them endlessly, searching, searching … If there's nothing to watch, why doesn't she turn the sodding thing off? It's one of those Sunday afternoons, grey and wet and dull, but surely she can find something more interesting to do. I once asked her if she ever read instead of watching the telly. 'Read a book?' she'd snorted. 'What am I, still at school? Nah. Books are for you intellectuals.' And with that last word, her scorn had swerved into a kind of compliment. None of my family would ever accuse me of being an intellectual.

I toss the book down and sigh. Moira's *Daily Express* from yesterday catches my attention. Not exactly my choice of paper, but the headline lures me in: 'Fat Cat Gets the Cream'. Robert Xavier-Walters, the CEO of ExaWatt, has been ousted by his shareholders and received a £4 million golden handshake for his trouble. And this is after the company has shed 1,500 jobs and seen a nose-dive in its share price. They've chosen a particularly smug picture of him to accompany the story.

On the TV there's a burst of Beethoven's 5th, quickly subjugated by a voice-over: 'Sound Bite Classics: the best bits from over a hundred famous classical tunes, seamlessly blended together into one great double-CD mega-mix!' A couple of bars of Chopin. 'Give yourself a shot of culture with Sound Bite Classics! Out now.'

I imagine Trib out on another moral odyssey tonight, making a hash of it and getting picked up by the police. I can see their impatient disbelief as they bundle him into the back of a squad car and he tries to explain himself: 'No, I'm on your side. Don't you see?' If I want to get him into trouble, all I have to do is find Slater's phone number and tell him the thief is returning tonight with some of the evidence. So why did Trib tell me he was going back there? Another screw-up, or an inappropriate level of trust in someone he barely knows? Difficult to tell. After all, his perception of me changed from risk to recruit in less than a day. And why was he so surprised that I refused his offer? He didn't exactly make it irresistible. If Trib thinks I'm not doing my civic duty then he's wrong. I give money to charity. I vote. I argue with Zach and Alistair.

The front door opens and a moment later Moira appears in the lounge with two bulging Morrisons bags.

'All right, you two?' she says. 'Busy, I see.'

I offer to give her a hand with the shopping.

'No, I'm fine, thanks. *Hello, daughter.*'

'Yeah, yeah. All right, Mum.'

It's funny how different they sound. Jodie could have stepped straight off the set of *EastEnders*, while Moira has retained her Dublin accent, despite having lived in England for over 25 years. She skims over 't' sounds like a flat stone across water. It isn't right that such a beautiful voice should so often be used for arguing.

Moira puts her shopping down and says to Jodie, 'Did you give him the …?'

'Nah. Forgot.'

'What's this?' I ask.

'Useless girl,' Moira says, prompting a sneer of irritation.

She ducks into the kitchen, returning with a takeaway food container which she hands to me.

'Your mum dropped it off while you were out this morning.'

Even before I take the lid off, I know what's inside: a slice of white chocolate brioche.

5

MERE DAYS AFTER I'd started working at Caduceus we had been shunted out to a Portakabin with only our computers and each other for warmth. By winter we'll all be icicles. In addition, the floor creaks and flexes underfoot and the acoustics are boxy. It's not something you'd expect to matter, but when I pointed it out last week, everyone agreed – the place even *sounds* cheap.

I say hi to Andy and Dom as I walk in, then, 'Bonjour. Ça va?' to Steph.

'Don't ask,' she says. 'I have been here since seven o'clock. I have more work now than when I started.'

Caduceus has recently bought out Peterson Medical, and Steph has been given the unenviable task of integrating their systems with ours.

'It's ridiculous that you should have to do all this on your own,' I tell her. 'You should complain.'

'To who? Jane? You know she will not accept anyone questioning her authority.'

'How about her manager?'

'Ah, Olly. So naive! You have not been here long enough to see it.'

'See what?'

'They are like one big club, the managers. They get together and beat their chests and say, "We are the important ones! You will not question us!"'

I'm trying to make the best of this new job, and that means suppressing my natural suspicion of management. Not easy when my colleagues keep trampling over the tiny green shoots of hope.

'Watch them in their meeting at three o'clock this afternoon,' says Steph. 'You will see. Look at how many days they have off for "management training". Holiday, more like. They are a bunch of wankers.'

I shouldn't laugh, but it sounds so funny with a French accent.

She dips her head. 'I got the expression right?'

'Perfect.'

Steph is about ten years older than me, with blonde hair caught up artfully in a grip and thick-framed, ultra-chic glasses that sit above finely sculpted cheekbones. Her voice is so husky I thought she was putting it on at first.

'Jesus,' Dom drones, staring at his monitor. 'Even my eyeballs are cold.'

'Do you mind?' says Andy. He has a zero tolerance attitude to blasphemy, the result of having a Baptist minister for a dad.

'Oh, God. I forgot.'

Andy slaps his biro down on the desk. 'You do this deliberately, don't you?'

'Sorry. Hey, look on the bright side: you won't have to put up with it any more once my jaw freezes shut.'

At first I thought their arguments were going to make work difficult, but although Andy is uncompromising, he's quick to forgive. I think Andy and Dom actually like each other, although they'd rather dance naked through the streets of Strathurst than admit it. Steph finds their spats more irritating than I do.

'Dom,' she says, 'if you promise to be quiet until lunch, I will give you this.'

She holds out a bulging blue hot water bottle. Dom is like a snake before the charmer.

'I filled it two minutes ago,' she says. 'It is hot.'

Dom slides across the floor on his chair and strikes. The water bottle goes onto his lap, then he wheels himself under his desk and presses his thighs upwards, curling over the source of heat. We've asked for an electric heater, but Jane says there must be no unnecessary expenditure in these 'challenging times'. We said it was very much a necessity, but she doesn't see things that way. In the meantime, we use other tactics to keep warm. Last week Dom installed a protein folding program on all three of his computers. The intensive processing causes the PCs to get slightly warmer, and as a bonus, there's a tiny chance one of them will help find a cure for cancer. This seems particularly appropriate in a medical company, but we've all agreed not to tell Jane about it.

Steps sound on the tarmac outside, and the door opens to reveal our glorious leader. Jane is hard-faced and habitually unsmiling. The ends of her bob curl in towards her chin like two scythes.

Shut the door. Shut the door!

'Hello, team,' she says, surveying us. Her eyes fall on me, because I'm still wearing my coat. 'Oh, come on, Olly. It's not that cold.'

Not if you're only stopping for two minutes. Any longer and it begins to leech into your bones. I take my coat off anyway; I'm still on probation with this job.

'How's the integration work going?' she asks, finally closing the door behind her.

Steph sighs. 'There is so much of it.'

'But we sized the work. What's the problem?'

Steph says nothing.

'Come on, speak to me,' Jane says.

Steph shrugs in a manner suggesting she's already tried, but that Jane wasn't listening.

'I can give Steph a hand,' I interject.

'Not until you've completed the firewall testing,' Jane says.

'It's done. Finished.'

'Excellent,' she says, sounding a little surprised. And well she might, because I'm lying. 'In which case I've got another job for you. The director of engineering wants to set up an internal website with details about his staff: their skills, work history, that sort of thing.'

'But surely ... I mean, Steph's work affects the whole company.'

Jane frowns. 'Olly, this is the *director of engineering*.'

Right. Might there be some brownie points in this for our Jane? Because I'm pretty sure the director of engineering won't be thanking little old me when the work's done.

'I'll send you the details, Olly,' Jane says. She turns to Steph. 'You'd better come with me so we can discuss the schedule.'

They leave for the warmth of Jane's office. I can see Steph keeping a lid on her frustration but Jane sees nothing. She has a very strong sense of denial. She's selectively blind, selectively deaf, and, in the case of our frigid work environment, oblivious to temperature too.

I turn to Andy and Dom. 'Can you believe that?'

'Yep,' they say in unison.

Dom says, 'None of it will matter once we're dead.'

'Right,' Andy says, clapping his hands together, 'since Steph's having such a hard time ...' From his desk drawer, he produces the IT Workers' Solidarity Coffee Box, which in another life was the box for an Ethernet router. He slides it across the desk towards Dom and says, 'Come on, stump up, you miserable git.'

I expect Dom to complain, but he drops in some coins. I follow suit and Andy finishes off the whip-round. Later it will be used to buy Steph a latte from the coffee shop. It's the least we can do.

—

In the afternoon I bump into Steph by the photocopier.

'How was the meeting with Jane?'

She makes a sound like a horse exhaling. 'I sit there for an hour, and at the end nothing has changed. No extension to the deadline. She just fiddles everything to fit her precious schedule.'

'You told her you need more time?'

'Of course. But this means I now have to listen to all the reasons I cannot have more time. Which – you guessed it – takes up more of my time.'

I would have put up more resistance. Or at least I like to think I would. And then I imagine an hour sat in front of the immovable brick wall that is Jane. You either argue and lose or sit there and take it.

'I really don't know how you put up with that cow.'

'I tell her my position. She ignores me. I switch off and nod my head. I wait for her to let me go.'

This is a scenario I have to avoid at all costs, because I won't be able to take Steph's stoic attitude. My heart rate increases just hearing about it.

She cocks her head to one side, 'There is one thing I do not understand about this morning. You have not finished the firewall testing, have you?'

'No, I bloody haven't,' I mutter. Then, remembering this is my team leader, I add, 'Are you annoyed?'

'Not at all. It was sweet of you to try to help. You have managed to fit in here so well. I am assuming, of course, that you are not looking for another job already.'

'No, I'm not. Things were no better in SMC. At least Jane hasn't tried to outsource all our jobs to India.'

'Olly,' she says, 'I was thinking … would you like to come out with a few of us on Wednesday next week? My friend is doing a gig at The Crown.'

'Yeah?'

'She is a singer and guitar player. Very talented. If there was any justice, she should be famous.'

'Who else will be there?'

'My husband – we have a babysitter – Andy and his wife Nigella, Dom, a few other friends.'

'Are you sure this is Dom's sort of thing? I mean, it does

involve going out of the house.'

'So cruel! No, he will probably not enjoy it, but we can try to broaden his horizons. There is a strict ban on talking about work.'

'An excellent idea.'

'And after, everyone will pop back to our house for a little of my husband's apricot wine and my home-made mignardises. So, you will come?'

'Yeah, I'd love to.' At the very least I'll find out what mignardises are.

—

Perhaps Steph didn't literally mean I should hang around the Building 5 conference room for the end of the managers' meeting, but that's what I end up doing. Their voices are too muffled for me to tell what they're talking about, but there's a lot of laughter. At the end they exit in a gaggle, Jane among them, wielding aluminium laptops so thin you could chop vegetables with them. Once they're gone, I pop my head into the meeting room. There's a coffee spill on the table, perfectly flat and reflective. Three empty boxes of doughnuts and several cardboard cups are strewn around. It looks less like the detritus of important decision-making than a college canteen after a food fight. The secretary with the immaculate grey hair comes in. Seeing the mess, she tuts and starts to clean up.

'It wasn't me,' I tell her, like a guilty schoolboy.

'I know,' she sighs.

I give her a hand tidying up and she thanks me. Back at my desk I check Jane's calendar entries. Steph's right: every month, regular as clockwork, there's a management jolly at a golf club or a castle or a posh hotel. There goes the money for our heater. I flop back into my chair. So, this job is going to be no better than my previous one. Why is the world so full of people like this? How can we let them be in charge of anything when it's so clear they're only in it for themselves?

These are not new thoughts for me. Ever since my school days

I've known that seniority and responsibility are two completely distinct concepts. The frustrating thing is that they *should* go together, that they *can*. I'm reminded of the time Dr Nylund asked me whether I had a problem with authority.

'You bet I have,' I'd said. 'People are in power because they've got huge egos. And they want power so they can demonstrate their superiority. It's an endless circle. Most of the politicians and businessmen and celebrities we're supposed to look up to are horrible people. I mean, is there anyone who doesn't hate the bankers? We put these people in positions of power and influence and wealth, and they shit on us.'

'You are maybe thinking of …' he calmly consulted his notes '… Mr Lambert, your old headmaster?'

'Well, of course I am. Look what he did.'

'And would you include your father among these people?'

I opened my mouth to fire another broadside because I'd always carried a big brick of resentment concerning my dad and how little attention he had paid to his sons. He never reacted to anything we did. He had even remained stony-faced when Zach and I, at the ages of fifteen and sixteen, had returned home pissed out of our minds and vomited on his brand new hall carpet. But that wasn't what Nylund had asked, and I couldn't recall a single instance where my dad had used his authority inappropriately. In fact, maybe that was my problem with him: he had more time for his staff than he did for his own family. At a party, his secretary, squiffy on G&Ts, had told me what a great man he was to work for. And I remember him giving up a Sunday to help a colleague out with some unspecified personal problem. Yes, I'd have preferred it if more attention had been reserved for me and Zach, but could I honestly claim he'd abused his power as a company director? I've never thought of him the same way since.

—

My parents are still on my mind when I get home, and I realise I have to phone them and clear things up after Saturday's dinner. I sit on the bed with my back to the wall, take a deep breath and hit the speed dial. Dad answers.

'Hello, son. I'll pass you straight on to your mother.'

And that's that. To be honest, I prefer it this way. Mum's easier to talk to.

'The brioche was really good,' I tell her.

'Thank you.' There's a pause. 'I'm sorry about your father. He's a bit distracted at the moment.' This is one of her typical peace-keeping manoeuvres. She'll defend any member of the family against any of the others.

I ask her how the piano lessons are going. Her grade six exam is at the end of the month, and she's planning to do a couple of recitals afterwards.

'Thank you for coming to the meal,' she says. 'I know it's not always easy for you, but I do appreciate it. I worried all night after you left. And then I dropped off the brioche and you weren't there, and I thought you probably just wanted to be alone for a bit. I hope you won't boycott any future invitations. We are a family, after all. If it helps, I could get your father to tape Zach and Alistair's mouths shut.'

This sounds like a wonderful idea, though a little impractical. 'Won't they have to eat intravenously?'

'Soup it is, then!' she says, and I laugh.

She becomes more serious. 'You will come again, though, won't you?'

'Of course I will.'

6

FOR HIS FIRST CHALLENGE, Zach has to eat sheep's eyes.

Jodie, Moira and I have gathered for the momentous first episode of *Obedience*. I've been dreading it, but ever since I mentioned it to Jodie she's insisted we all watch it together. Seeing Zach on

TV is a novelty for her – one that wears off soon, I hope.

'That's him?' she says, as the contestants gather round a bowl of the boiled eyeballs. This is the part of the show where they give a preview of what you're about to see, a tactic to stall the trigger fingers of inveterate channel-switchers.

'Yep,' I sigh, 'that's him.'

Zach looks nothing like he did on Saturday. He's wearing ripped jeans that end halfway up the calf, a waistcoat punctuated with acid-house smileys and a shirt with more ruffles than a bullfighter's. His hair sticks two fingers up at the law of gravity: it's streaked with blue and green, and shoots out from the back of his skull like a peacock's tail. At the front, a fringe like a blackout curtain sweeps across his face, obscuring one eye. He's given up stereoscopic sight for the sake of fashion.

'That's your brother?' Jodie is clearly struggling to believe that two such different creatures could have sprung from the same womb.

'I'm afraid so.'

'You should be proud of him, being on TV.'

'Maybe I would if he was on *Mastermind* or presenting a documentary.' I ponder both of these blissful scenarios for a moment.

'You've got to start somewhere,' she chirps.

Yeah, I bet John Humphrys began his career just like this.

The title sequence features frenetic dance beats, littered with orchestral hits – music that screams, 'Be excited! Be excited!' The set is designed like a dungeon, all flagstones and rusting iron, but lit incongruously with multicoloured neon. The lights pulsate and the camera swoops in on an archway. The host of the show – Nat, according to the subtitle – swaggers through it. He wears an immaculate suit and is flanked by two blondes in school uniforms: pleated skirts, straining white blouses, and half-undone ties. Nat holds a whip which he cracks at the camera to enthusiastic applause, before sending his assistants into opposite corners of the studio, where they climb into cages and pout from behind bars. I hear the sound of a thousand feminists exploding.

Nat turns to the audience and spreads his arms in welcome. He has hair like yellow plastic and an I'm-shagging-your-wife grin. He outlines the format of the show and it's pretty much as my brother described, with a £20,000 prize for whoever survives to the end. Nat explains that the first task will be to eat three boiled sheep's eyes. Then he introduces the contestants, one by one, asking them their name and a bit of background detail, so we can form some vague emotional bond with them before the torture begins.

When he gets to Zach, he asks, 'So where do you get a name like Zee-Jee?'

Zach is nonchalant. 'It's my handle.'

'Well, let me just say I'll be delighted to "use your handle", ZG.'

A whoop of lascivious delight from the audience.

'Is that going to be one of the challenges?' Zach asks innocently. An even bigger whoop.

'I can tell you're going to be trouble.'

'Lord have mercy,' Moira says from the corner. 'It's like a *Carry On* film.'

'Shush, Mum,' says Jodie.

Their sofa is plump, but right now I wish it had even deeper stuffing. Then I might disappear into it completely, subsisting on whatever stale crisps and bits of biscuit I might find there until it's safe to come out. I glance at the clock. There's another 25 minutes of this.

Nat doesn't look overjoyed that Zach might be stealing the limelight. 'So tell me, ZG, have you ever eaten anything like this before?'

'To be honest, it doesn't look too different from my mum's cooking.'

What an arsehole. I manage not to say it out loud, though only just.

'I'm kidding,' Zach says, 'my mum's a great cook.'

I don't know why I'm surprised. This is how Zach is these days: anything to get noticed. And of course, it works; the audience are lapping it up. None of the other contestants can match Zach's wit or cockiness, although another couple of them try before being trumped by Nat, who steers a course between the innuendo of Graham Norton and the steely edge of Anne Robinson. The 'schoolgirls' come out of their cages to set each contestant up with a glass of water and a plate with three sheep's eyes. Are these a delicacy somewhere in the world? Nat isn't saying. Heaven forbid that the show might accidentally be educational.

Zach shows no hesitation. He throws each one in, chews and swallows, without even appearing to consider what he's doing. He remains stony-faced while the audience give vent to their queasiness, then he knocks back a glass of water and even manages to smack his lips with relish. The other contestants show varying degrees of fortitude. Lanky surfer and walking O'Neill advert Ryan eats them as fast as Zach, with no sign of displeasure at all. Antonio chunders into a strategically placed bucket. Gemma from Cornwall struggles to even touch the things, and refuses point-blank to eat any. She'll make up for it, she says, in the remaining challenges. As Nat is announcing the end of the first task, Zach strides up to the bowl and chucks another eyeball in his mouth, prompting an 'Oooh' from the audience.

Moira says, 'I'm going to leave you to it,' and gets up from the sofa.

'Mum!' Jodie protests. 'It's his *brother*.'

'Yes, well, my commiserations to you, Olly.'

'God, Mum, you've got no sense of fun. I like him. He's a lot better than that creepy Nat guy.'

Moira leaves anyway. There's always housework to do, and for once I envy her – right now, a frenzied bout of hoovering could be the most blissful activity in the world. But I promised him. God help me, I promised him.

For the other two challenges, they have to insult one of their fellow competitors in the most hurtful manner they can muster, and pour cold custard into their underwear while a close-up camera watches for signs of discomfort or embarrassment. Neither present my brother with any problems. While others hesitate or allow their expressions to telegraph their reluctance, Zach just launches straight into them. He leaves the banter for the bits in between, of which there are plenty, because they could get through all three challenges in a matter of minutes. The rest of the programme consists of three things: showing us what's just happened, telling us what's about to happen, and waiting – while an ominous synthesizer drones – for something to happen.

At intervals I glance across at Jodie to see what she makes of all this. When the programme requires her to laugh, she laughs. When she's required to gasp, she gasps. The audience's reaction provides the cues, and as if that wasn't enough, Nat gives additional guidance with leading questions like, 'You must have been really disgusted by that last challenge, Chris. How do you feel about it?' Every aspect of the experience makes my skin crawl.

'Why do they have to go through with any of this?' I ask out loud.

Jodie frowns. 'Those are the rules,' she says, as if I haven't understood what the show's about. But I'm questioning the need for this whole circus in the first place. To her, the show exists, and the rules have been spelled out, and now they must be followed. It's as simple as that.

I'm jealous of her, I realise, jealous that I can't just treat it as a bit of fun.

An array of numbers appears on the screen so the public can vote off the least obedient contestant. At least, that's what they're supposed to do; there's nothing to stop them from picking anyone they like. Or dislike.

Jodie's hand hovers over her phone. 'Should we …?' But she loses confidence when she sees me shaking my head.

Edited 'highlights' are shown for a few minutes while the votes come in. It's a landslide against the poor girl who failed to eat the sheep's eyes. Nat interviews her.

'Gemma, Gemma, Gemma,' he says, 'what went wrong with the first of our little challenges?'

'Eyeballs? I mean, like ... eyeballs,' she says, incoherent with disgust. 'God's sake.'

Nat grins with unconcealed pleasure. 'I wish I could give you a stricter punishment for failing to follow my simple instructions, but unfortunately, decency laws prevent me.' He leers at the camera and the audience jeer their delight, while Gemma attempts to hide her embarrassment. What was she thinking, appearing on a show like this?

'Leave the studio, you disobedient girl!' he crows, and I'm surprised not to see him slap her on the bum as she goes.

The telephone lines open for the selection of next week's tasks and Nat wraps up. 'So, join us on *Obedience* next week, when you can see more of Antonio, Chris, Kate, Latonya, Matt, Michelle, Ryan and ZG.'

The camera stops briefly on each contestant and there's a fresh round of clapping after each name. Except for Zach, who gets an explosion of cheers and wolf-whistles. That's because instead of winking or waving, he's turned round, dropped his trousers and mooned the camera with an arse still slathered with cold custard. Jodie laughs, but stifles it as she turns and sees my look of mortification. The audience love him, and I have to face the horrifying possibility that this might just be the making of Zach. I grab the remote control from the arm of Jodie's chair and switch the TV off.

'He did well,' she says, as if she's trying to cheer me up. 'He's through to the next round.'

My only consolation is that I won't have to endure this again for another seven whole days.

'You just have to see it for what it is,' Jodie says. Bless her, she's genuinely concerned.

'Which is what?'

'A bit of a laugh. It doesn't mean anything.'

It does to me. It feels like a slap in the face, and for the life of me I don't know why.

7

IT TAKES ME UNTIL FRIDAY to track down Trib. He's in the Hog's Head, a traditional pub to the core – dingy and slightly crooked, suffused with heat from a pair of log fires. The wood used to build the place is so old it's almost black and some of the beams are low enough to scalp even someone of my height. The floorboards creak underfoot, but unlike our Portakabin at work, they creak with *character*.

Trib is sitting at one of the tables with a bald man, playing cards. Before going over, before he's even noticed me, I decide a little social lubrication wouldn't go amiss and head for the bar, over which a gigantic model of a pig's head looms. The bartender has extravagant sideburns and a conspiratorial look in his eyes. He wouldn't look out of place on the deck of a frigate, sailing off to fight Napoleon.

'What are Trib and his mate drinking?' I ask, pointing over at them.

'It's the Strathurst Gold tonight.' He's got a thick West Country accent.

'Three pints of that, please.' It's about time I tried some of the local stuff.

'Good choice,' he says, pulling the first. 'Put hairs on your chest, this will. Anything else?'

'No, thanks.'

'Known Trib long, then?' he says.

I calculate. 'About six days.'

'Ah. Forever making new friends, that one.' He finishes the beers, pouring so much that foam spills down the sides. I'm left with three sticky and very full glasses. The first two are a vibrant bubbling orange, the third still hazy as it settles.

'That'll be seven fifty,' he says.

I pay him and wedge all three glasses together to transport them. My hands are wet from spillage long before I get to Trib's table. He looks up as I approach and tries to suppress a smile. His friend cranes his neck round. He's a skinny guy, bespectacled and without a single hair on his head. Younger than I thought too, maybe late twenties.

'Look who it isn't,' Trib says. 'Hi, Olly.'

'Hiya. Drinks all round?' I set my cargo down.

'That's very decent of you, mate.'

I sit down on Trib's side of the table. Better the devil you know. Well, better the devil you've met.

'Where are my manners?' Trib says. 'Olly, this is Mitchell. Mitchell: Olly.'

'Hi. Is that a surname or a first?' I ask him.

'First,' he says. 'Surname's Thomas. Mitchell Thomas, not Thomas Mitchell. Causes all kinds of problems.'

'Mitch does stand-up,' Trib says. 'He's very good.'

I nod towards the wooden pegboard on the table. 'What are you playing?'

'Cribbage,' Trib says. 'It'll only take us a jiffy to finish. I've nearly won.'

'Like hell you have,' Mitchell counters. 'Go on, show 'em. You've only got six there and I'll overtake you on the crib.'

Trib spreads four cards on the table and says, 'Fifteen-two, fifteen-four, two for a pair is six, and …' he taps the upturned three of hearts on the top of the deck '… three for a run is nine.'

He removes one of the pegs from the board and sticks it triumphantly in the hole at the end, then leans back in his chair and puts his arms behind his head.

Mitchell surveys the cards with disbelief. 'You jammy git!'

I take the top off my pint. It tastes of oranges and has a peppery bite that tempts me to chew rather than drink it.

'Good choice.' Trib says, and takes a sip.

'Yeah, err, thanks for the pint,' Mitchell says, 'but it really isn't my thing. Trib keeps trying to get me onto "proper" beer, but the truth is I prefer lager.'

Trib rolls his eyes. 'Philistine.'

'Don't worry, though,' he says, giving Trib a pointed look, 'it won't go to waste. Anyway,' he grabs his coat. 'I'm due to meet Cal in five, so I'm going to shoot off.'

Trib points at the cribbage board. 'And what if I want to call in my debts?'

'You never call in your debts.'

'So, you're refusing to pay me my ...' Trib consults his diary '... twenty-seven pence? I'll send the boys round.'

Mitchell's eyebrows flick up and down.

'Stop it,' Trib warns.

Mitchell looks at his watch. 'Right, I'm out of here. Nice to meet you, Olly.'

It's a shame he's leaving. I reckon I could learn a lot about Trib just from watching the two of them talk. Once he's gone, Trib gathers in the two and a half pints of beer: Mitchell's unfinished glass, plus the two I bought for them. He looks happy as a pig in shit.

'So, you haven't played before?' he says, indicating the cards.

'No.'

'Want to learn?'

'Yeah, why not.'

We play an open hand, so he can show me how it works. He deals us each six cards, but we immediately discard two into the 'crib'. A starter card is then turned over. We take it in turn to play cards while keeping a running total, scoring points for getting to exactly 15 or 31, or for making pairs or runs. After all cards are played, we score again using our own hands plus the starter card. Finally, the dealer scores the crib as a bonus hand.

'So you're trying to put cards with potential into the crib when it's yours, while your opponent tries to throw in crap?'

'You've got it.'

We play a game in earnest. He lets me deal first, and the crib gives me a few points' lead over him. When it's his turn to deal, he turns over a jack as the starter card and says, 'That's two for his heels,' and pegs two points on the board.

'You what?'

'If the starter card's a jack, the dealer gets two points. Did I not mention that?'

I narrow my eyes.

'I didn't invent the rules,' he says.

A couple of hands later, as he's scoring, he says, 'Six for runs, two for a pair, and one for his nob.'

'Beg your pardon?'

'One for his nob, because I've got a jack with the same suit as the starter card.'

I lean back in my chair. 'You're making this up.'

'No, honestly.'

'Okay, I've got a three of clubs here. Three for his chin.' I start to peg three points.

'No, no. You can't do that. Look, Jeff,' he shouts to the barman, 'I've got a jack with the same suit as the starter card.'

'That's one for his nob!' Jeff cries. 'Which means it's Happy Hour! Happy Hour in the Hog's Head, everybody! Strathurst Gold just £2.50 a pint!'

I'm about to accuse them of colluding when something occurs to me. '£2.50 is the price I paid when I came in.'

'Think yourself lucky,' Trib says, 'during some of Jeff's Happy Hours, the beer prices actually go up.'

We continue the game, and I watch him like a hawk for any new and unexpected rules. Despite my lack of experience, I beat him.

Trib looks bewildered. 'That's a real case of beginner's luck. Well, you seem to have the hang of it. Want to start playing for money?'

He must think I've failed to notice how battered his scoreboard is, the legacy of hundreds of games. 'I get it. You let me win the first one, then you nail me to the wall.'

'Has anyone ever said you've got a suspicious mind?'

'More than once.' Kerry used to say it all the time.

'I play for one pence per point difference in score. Cribbage is the only game you're legally allowed to play in a pub for money, so you might as well exercise your civil liberties.'

I count up the spaces on the board. Even if I lose catastrophically I'll owe him less than a quid. 'Okay.'

I beat him again. 'That's fourteen pence you owe me.' I wonder if he's letting me win, and if so, why.

'I'll get the next round in,' he says, and I don't put up any objection.

I don't usually drink with people unless I know them well. Why I've made an exception here is a bit of a mystery. Maybe because I've had a difficult week at work. Maybe because, in spite of the grief he caused me last Saturday, I can't help but warm to him. He comes back with another pint of Gold each and a half of something jet black which he pushes reverently across the table towards me.

'That, my friend, is SAS. A finer beer you'll not find in the whole of the South of England. Of course, in the North it would be a different matter.'

It's thick and delicious, with a taste like a fruit cake made by someone who slipped when adding the brandy. 'That's pretty strong.'

'Six and a half percent. Sample with care,' he warns. 'So, do you want to go for the hat trick? At least allow me some hope of salvaging my reputation.'

I give away a bit too much in the cribs, and he wins by eight points.

'That's a relief,' he says. 'I was beginning to think I'd lost my touch.'

'There's a lot of luck involved, though, isn't there?'

'Less than you'd think. The more experienced player generally wins.'

'Like you're winning now?'

'Well, okay, luck *is* a factor.'

He puts his hands down on the edge of the table. There's a pop from one of the logs on the fire.

'So,' he says, 'we'd better get down to business, hadn't we?'

'Who says I'm here for business?'

Trib smiles, but doesn't answer. 'How did you find me?'

'Since you're ex-directory, I went to Sumi's and asked where you might be. She said you were often at the pub.'

'There are quite a few pubs in Strathurst, and quite a few evenings when I don't go down the pub. So, how long have you been looking for me?'

'Not long.'

'Go on, tell me.'

The beer helps insulate me against a feeling of annoyance. 'Three days. And for your information, there are fourteen pubs in Strathurst.'

Trib cracks up.

'Yeah, all right. Don't rub it in.'

'I do admire your dedication. Well, you found me.' He puts his hands up in surrender. 'Now, what can I do for you?'

I thought he might be rather smug that I've come back after brushing him off on Sunday. But there's no crowing, which makes it easier because I hate needing things from other people; I hate having to admit I was wrong.

'I've been thinking about what you said at Sumi's.'

'Yes?' He leans forwards fractionally.

'I'm ... You know, I think we got off on the wrong foot at Slater's house and I, uh ...' Come on, spit it out. 'I might be more interested than I made out.'

'This is great news.'

'I'm not making any promises.'

'Nor should you.' He sits back. 'What prompted the change of heart?'

Because working at Caduceus is like living in a farce. Because I have no direction in life, something both Zach and Alistair have managed, in their own ways. Because I'm terrified of ending up like Jodie, wallowing in front of the telly, doing nothing. I want to feel that my existence on this wretched planet actually has some value. Even if I only achieve a small thing. Even if it's only getting some kids their footballs back.

Of course, I'm not prepared to tell him all this. 'I kind of like the idea of doing something positive, you know? Something that makes a difference to somebody.' It's a weaker version of what I'm thinking: the truth, just not the whole truth. 'Assuming that's what you really do.'

'Ha! Still suspicious?'

'A bit.'

'Quite right. Never trust strange men. Look, I'll get back to you on this. We shouldn't discuss it now.'

'Because?' I look around at the other customers.

'No, you daft bugger! Because you're tiddly.'

'I am not tiddly! I've only had two and half pints. You've had at least ...' I count them up '... four and a half, including your friend's left-overs.'

'Five and a half,' he says. 'I got one in before Mitch arrived.'

Five and a half pints? There's not a hint of slurring in his voice.

'Here,' he throws a tenner across the table. 'Get us both a final one, will you?'

I grab the note and get up. I have to steady myself on the back of the chair.

Trib points and laughs. 'Not tiddly, he says!'

'Bastard.' But I'm smiling. 'I pity you when you have to stand up.'

As I return from the bar with our drinks, the pub's sound system bursts into life. It's an Arabic tune, heavy on the hand drums and finger cymbals. A middle-aged woman in a spangly skirt and bra bursts out from behind the bar and starts belly-dancing her way around the clientèle, some of whom clap in time with the beat. I turn to Trib for an explanation.

'Jeff's wife,' Trib says above the pounding music. 'She's been to classes and doesn't want them to go to waste.'

Nothing ordinary happens around Trib, I realise. He's a magnet for the unexpected.

8

A KNOCK SOUNDS somewhere below me. I roll onto my back and pull the duvet up to my chin. I'm feeling sluggish, and there's a dull pulse at the back of my skull. A hangover?

Moira's muffled voice floats up through the floor. 'Are you up, Olly? You've got a visitor.'

My lips part with reluctance. 'Mmm-okay. I'll be down in a minute.'

I wriggle back into yesterday's clothes and open the hatch. Moira is worried I'll injure myself if I don't use the ladder, but usually I don't bother: I lower myself through the hole in the floor, dangle from my arms, then drop onto the landing. It's an acid test for the headache, which seems to be manageable. I pad down the stairs, rubbing my eyes and pushing my hair into some kind of order. In the kitchen I see Trib at the table, with Jodie opposite. Moira has just finished pouring him a coffee.

'Er ... hello, Trib.'

'Hiya, mate. Nice place you've got here.' He takes a slurp from his mug.

'Yeah. Yeah, it is. Trib, this is Moira, my landlady, and –'

'He's already introduced himself,' Moira says. 'Very polite boy. But then, he would be, being one of your friends. You two wouldn't mind whisking off my daughter and teaching her some manners, would you?'

'Muuum! God's sake.'

'Shall I put some more coffee on for you, Olly?'

'Yes, please.' I look across at Trib. 'Could you make it a strong one?'

—

Forty minutes later, showered and dressed in fresh clothes, I'm heading away from the house with Trib for reasons unknown. It requires an effort to keep up with him: the guy has seriously long legs. I ask him the question I've been pondering ever since he showed up in Moira's kitchen. 'How did you know where I live?'

He taps his nose twice with a finger. 'Contacts.'

Right. 'So, what is it you want to show me?'

'I want you to meet a friend of mine,' he says.

There's a brittle brightness to the day, cold but cheerful. We're heading down Kiln Street, curving away from the centre of town, where each house's front garden is bordered by an old flint wall. Outside one of them is a pasting table with an array of potted plants. An empty ice cream tub bears the sticker: 'Rosemary 50p'. Behind the wall, a grey-haired woman wearing old jeans, a check shirt and a body warmer is turning over a flower border. Trib picks up one of the pots, examines it and digs in his pocket for change.

The woman straightens as she sees Trib and says, 'I hope you're not putting extra in again.'

'I wouldn't dare, Mrs Selcott,' he replies, dropping a pound coin into the box.

'I'd stop you for a chat,' she says, 'but I've got to get this done before picking up my granddaughter.'

'Right. Give her my best wishes.'

'Will do.'

We carry on walking. Trib rubs the rosemary needles and smells his fingers. 'Goes lovely with lamb, this.'

'You're into cooking, then?'

Trib bursts out laughing. 'Not really. I don't so much cook things as set fire to them and put them out when I think they're done.'

As the housing gives way to shops and car dealerships, we pass a family of four, dressed like clones in cargo pants and tatty jumpers. They all have litter pickers which they use to grab discarded crisp packets or drink cans. Dad wears a collapsible bin on his back and all the rubbish goes into it.

'Morning, all,' Trib says to them. 'Doing sterling work, I see.'

Dad gives a gawky salute and the others say hi.

As we pass them, I turn to Trib. 'Do you know everyone in Strathurst?'

'Not yet,' he says without any hint of irony.

I imagine a vast network of friends and acquaintances stretching all over town, tendrils reaching further over the countryside and up north to the land of his birth. I imagine that no matter where he goes, he'll always have a place to stay, or someone to call on for help. What must that be like?

'Here we are,' he says.

We enter the Hillfields estate, built about ten years ago to meet some quota for affordable housing. It's at the extreme west of town, crammed in between the B3023 and the railway line, hidden behind the big Tesco, as if the core of Strathurst has disowned it. Trib knocks on the door of the first house, one of a row of small, identical residences. I can hardly tell where one ends and the next begins.

A white-haired old lady opens the door. Her cheekbones are high, eyes dark and alert. She wears a white cardigan over a full-length burgundy dress and her elegant black-framed glasses are so fashionable they wouldn't look out of place on someone like Steph.

'Hello, John!' she says with pleasure. I'd almost forgotten Trib has a first name.

'Hi, Mrs Alford.' Trib passes her the plant pot. 'I brought you this.'

'Ooh, rosemary. Lovely!'

'I've brought along a friend of mine who might be able to help with the chair situation. Is now a good time?'

Her face falls. 'Must we?' she says, then answers her own question. 'Yes, of course we must. Come in.'

She opens the door for us. We wipe our feet and enter a small lounge. It's a sparse, neat place with a 60s vibe: warm, earthy colours and modernist furniture. A huge bookcase sits against one wall, stuffed with a mix of new paperbacks and older, well-thumbed volumes. I spot a few of the titles, including *Surely You're Joking, Mr Feynman?*, which I've read, and *Mathematics of Classical and Quantum Physics*, which I very much haven't.

'How much have you told him?' she asks Trib.

'Nothing.'

She looks me up and down. 'So, I'm going to have to explain the whole thing to you as well, am I?'

I open my mouth to say something and Trib says gently, 'I think that's best.'

'I hate this whole business,' she says.

'That's why we're here,' Trib says, 'to get it fixed.'

She turns to me. 'I'm sorry, where are my manners? My name's Ruth Alford.'

'I'm Olly. Good to meet you.' I try to sound at ease, as if this is the sort of thing I do every Saturday morning.

We decline her offer of tea, and she invites us to sit. Her sofa is wood-framed with faded orange cushions that betray a lifetime of use. I might as well hear this through. Like I said to Trib, I'm not promising anything.

Mrs Alford puts her hands in her lap and narrows her eyes. 'They should take them off the streets; they shouldn't be allowed to do it.'

'Who?' I ask. From my peripheral vision I see Trib glance at me.

'Salesmen,' she says with disgust. 'I was sold a chair by a man who came to the door. Tony Summer was his name, about 30 years old, very smartly turned out. It was a special chair. It was, uh …' She flaps her hand, looking for the word.

'Orthopaedic,' Trib supplies.

'That's it. A health investment, that's what he told me. He asked if I'd had any falls, and of course there was that stupid thing back in August; not like me at all. But then …' She pauses. 'He got me wondering about whether this might be the first of many. How on earth do you tell?'

She's stalled, so Trib prompts her. 'What else did he say?'

'Oh, I can't remember it all. He went on forever. He said it was made from the finest materials, approved by doctors, et cetera. He was very persuasive. He kept asking me, "What price do you put on your independence? What price do you put on your mobility?"'

'And what price did he put on the chair?' Trib says.

Mrs Alford's hands, long and liver-spotted, fidget in her lap, like two birds pecking at each other. 'Let me tell you something. I live my life according to a simple principle – if you treat people with respect and decency, the compliment will be returned. Perhaps you consider me naive to think so, but it usually turns out to be true. Trust makes the world a better place.'

I wonder if Trib is going to steer her back to the question, but he says nothing and she volunteers the information anyway.

'It was two thousand two hundred pounds.'

Bloody hell.

'And no, I can't afford it,' she adds.

'But you've paid the deposit?' Trib says.

She purses her lips. 'Yes, I have. I know what you're thinking,

Olly. You're thinking she's a dotty old lady who's lost her marbles and she's a fool for having been taken in.'

'Not at all.'

'Well, I feel like a fool. The next day I realised he'd been playing off my fears, and I got very angry. So I phoned him up at his office and said I'd like to cancel. He said the chair really was the best option for me and that my health would suffer, et cetera, et cetera. I could see he was trying the same tactics all over again, and I told him I was going to back out anyway.'

'And what was his reply?' Trib says.

'That I would be in breach of contract and his company would have to see what their lawyers said.'

Trib leans forwards and puts a reassuring hand on hers. 'There's nothing to worry about, I promise you. He should have given you some paperwork saying you've got a cooling-off period. Seven days, I think it is.'

'Well, he didn't. I went through it all very thoroughly. And it's been more than a week now, anyway.'

'But he's still in the wrong. If he didn't give you that piece of paper, the sale is invalid. He hasn't got a leg to stand on.'

'He'll claim he gave it to me and I lost it. I can see how he works. And anyway, I don't want to have to go through the courts. Why should I? He should do the decent thing and simply let me cancel.'

'Quite right,' Trib says.

'How could he have the nerve, in my own home?' She becomes aware of her fidgeting hands, and plonks them down on the armrests with a thump. 'I don't know anything about the law. Mr Summer is clearly a lot more clever about these things than I am.'

Trib says, 'Devious is the word you're looking for.'

'Don always used to deal with the money side of things. And the difficult people.'

I've noticed the photograph on the mantelpiece of a young

Ruth Alford, resplendent in a white wedding dress, and next to her a lanky man who doesn't quite fit his suit. They look like they've just fallen against each other. Their mouths are open with laughter. Right now, though, Mrs Alford's lips are pressed into a short, straight line. She stares past us, and I can imagine she sees Summer sitting opposite her, all smiles and mock concern.

'What a shit,' she mutters. Seeing my look of surprise, she adds, 'I'm sorry, Olly.'

'Don't be. I think he's a shit too.'

An abbreviated laugh escapes from her.

'So,' Trib says, 'If you don't want to take the legal route, that leaves the matter in our hands. Mr Summer will find us very persuasive.'

'I won't tolerate anything physical,' she warns.

'Absolutely not,' he says. 'Violence is the last refuge of the incompetent. We're simply going to encourage Mr Summer to re-engage with his sense of decency. Just cancel the direct debit. We'll sort out the rest.'

'Anything you can do will be much appreciated, but I'm afraid I can't offer you much in the way of thanks.'

'Oh, yes you can,' Trib says.

She gives him a quizzical look. So do I.

'You could bake us a few of your fantastic ginger biscuits.'

She brightens. 'Well, that's no problem.'

Trib takes a glance through the paperwork regarding the chair, and with a few parting reassurances we leave.

'Now,' Trib says, as we head off down the street, 'you said you might have some misgivings about –'

'I'm in. What's the plan?'

Trib grins. 'Come with me.'

After a couple of minutes I ask, 'Why the ginger biscuits?'

'I'd happily do it for nothing, but Mrs Alford has her pride. She doesn't want to feel like she's in debt. This way she's sort of paid for our services. Besides, they're pretty bloody nice biscuits.'

We walk for more than a mile, through the town centre – which is thronging with Saturday shoppers – and past the Junior School, finally stopping at an unremarkable house in the middle of a terrace, not much bigger than Mrs Alford's.

'This is my humble abode,' Trib says, rapping on a door. 'Number 15. Drop by any time you like.'

I half expect him to invite me in, but instead he leads me a few paces up the road and claps his hand on the side of a black van. In the movies it's the sort of vehicle that's stuffed with banks of electronic surveillance equipment, monitors, operators wearing headphones and other spy stuff.

'You're familiar with the concept of poetic justice?' he says.

'Yeah?'

The doors boom with a hollow, metallic sound as he swings them open, revealing an interior empty except for the world's tattiest armchair. It might once have been green but is now at best a pallid grey, except for the back rest, where something dark has been spilled. Bits of stuffing are visible through the holes worn in the fabric, and a coiled spring protrudes, buttock-threateningly, from the seat.

'This,' he announces, with a flourish, 'is Mr Summer's new armchair.'

9

TRIB STOPS THE VAN just down the road from Tony Summer's three bed semi, turns off the engine and rings his work number.

'Hello, is Mr Summer there?' Pause. 'No, that's fine. I'll catch him later.'

He ends the call and turns to me. 'Excellent. Summer's out with a customer. Pop over to his house and knock on the door, will you?'

'What?'

'We need to know …' he reaches into the back of the van and begins to rummage around '… if anyone else is in.'

'And if there is?'

'Ask them when he'll be back from work. Gives us a bit more information.'

'Who should I say I am?'

He passes me a clipboard which holds several sheets of printed paper. 'You're doing a survey and no-one but Mr Summer will do. Since he's out, you'll call back later.'

I glance at the paperwork. It's a questionnaire about men's magazines from the Margate-Newham Research Group. Real or faked? It's irrelevant. Trib's testing me to see if I've got the bottle to do this. Okay, then. Clipboard in hand, I jump out of the van and close the door behind me. I try not to betray my nerves, walking upright and without haste, and definitely not glancing back at Trib. At Summer's front door I stand on the porch and push the doorbell. It's a newish house, the bricks still orange, the grout still bright and unweathered. While I'm waiting, I read some of the questionnaire. Even if I'm invited inside, I should be able to bluff my way through the encounter.

After half a minute, there's no sign of anyone. I ring again and wait a bit longer, peeking through the window for any signs of movement. Then I go back to the van, looking about casually to see who might be watching. There's a guy cleaning his car a few houses down the road, but apart from that it seems quiet.

'It's clear,' I tell Trib once I'm back in the passenger seat.

'Why didn't you read the questionnaire before you dashed off?'

'I had a look through it while I was waiting.'

'You've got to be more prepared than that.'

This is a bit rich, coming from the man who cocked up the Slater operation.

'I got the job done, didn't I?'

He takes a deep breath. 'Yeah, but … Look, I've got a lot more experience of this stuff, so we do things my way, all right?'

I clench my teeth, release. 'Okay.' But now crunch time is approaching, my bravado wavers. 'What happens if someone comes back while we're in there?' I try to make this sound like a calm and sensible analysis rather than evidence of my fear.

'Look at the front of the house,' he says, pointing. 'If someone comes in through the front door, we go up the stairs, and come out through that window there, down the sloping roof above the garage, then onto the ground and away. But *not* straight back to the van. Now listen, here's what we do: we go up to the house and get inside without taking the chair. I want to be sure there's no-one at home. If we need to make a run for it, we don't want to be manhandling a piece of furniture. Then we make sure we can open that window as an escape route. Only then do we come back for the chair.'

'So our back-up plan is to run like hell?'

'You're good at running; better than me,' he says. 'If it was easy and safe, people would be doing this sort of thing all the time. What you've got to ask yourself is: does the risk justify the pay-off? If the answer's no, then walk away. I won't think any less of you.'

He might not, but I will.

'Last chance for second thoughts,' he says. 'I don't want you bottling out halfway through and leaving me in the shit.'

'You don't need to worry about that.'

'Good.' Trib fishes a notepad out of his glove compartment and reads from a checklist. 'Check the soles of your shoes. Is there anything you might leave on the carpets?'

They're clean and dry. 'Nope.'

'Take everything out of your pockets. Everything.' He's already removed a small mountain of stuff from his leather jacket.

'Including my wallet?'

'Phone, wallet, anything that could be used to identify you.'

It makes sense. I hand over my stuff and he puts it in the glove compartment along with his own. The only thing he keeps on him is the van key.

'Put these on.' He hands me a pair of white latex gloves and we snap them on like surgeons.

He slaps his hands onto his thighs. 'Right. Showtime.'

We get out of the van and stroll up to Summer's front door.

Trib says, 'If I can't get this open in thirty seconds, we abort. Cover me, will you?'

I stand between him and the guy cleaning his car, while he jimmies the lock with two tools that wouldn't look out of place at a dentist. He does it at waist height to look inconspicuous. Meanwhile, I look around to see if there's anyone watching from one of the houses across the street. The sun breaks out from behind the clouds, bathing us in light, and I suddenly feel uncomfortably hot. This will all be much easier if Trib fails to get the door open.

'Stop looking round like you're breaking into someone's house.' His voice is urgent but his body language is relaxed. All the while, his hands fiddle with the lock.

'I *am* breaking into someone's house.'

The door opens. Trib mimes recognition of an invisible someone in the hallway. We slip inside, and I'm about to close the door behind me, but he shakes his head, and pushes it to. He holds a finger to his lips and motions for me to stay exactly where I am, then sets off to check each room for occupants. He moves lightly for a man of his size, even managing to negotiate the stairs silently.

The place smells vaguely of air freshener. The hall doesn't look like it's been repainted from the builder's magnolia and there are no pictures. Through the open kitchen door I can see a stack of unwashed plates and pans on a Formica surface. The lounge door, also ajar, reveals a huge widescreen telly and a rack of DVDs. *Bachelor pad* is my first thought. A click and a hum from the kitchen make me tense, until I realise it's just the boiler kicking in.

When Trib comes back, he clumps down the stairs, as if all his weight has suddenly returned. 'It's clear. I've unlocked the window. It's the first on the right: the bathroom.'

'What if he'd had an alarm fitted?'

'There was no box on the outside of the house. First rule of installing an alarm is to make sure everyone knows about it. Otherwise, what's the point? You'd only be discouraging burglars after they'd broken in.'

I suppose so. He's the security guy, after all.

Leaving the front door on the latch, we go back out to get the chair, which we've covered in black plastic sheeting to disguise its shabbiness. It's the bulk that's awkward, rather than the weight. We manage to manoeuvre it inside and set it down in the hallway without incident. I feel a pang of guilt when I see the rest of his lounge, because if I had a place of my own it would probably look a lot like this. There are racks of shelving full of films, CDs and games. The screen and speakers are aligned to converge on whoever sits in the black leather, pole-position armchair, which is a genuine La-Z-Boy. The decoration is minimal. A glance at the shelves shows me that while much of his taste doesn't match mine, there is some overlap – a Coen brothers box set and a bunch of Radiohead albums. There's a photo of Summer on the DVD rack: a university graduation picture in which he's wearing the full gown and mortar board. A real person owns this house, not just some abstract somebody.

But how has he managed to afford all this stuff? What is he willing to do in order to fund his taste in expensive A/V equipment? I think about how this compares to Mrs Alford's place – what she has after 70 years, and what he has after 30.

'Where should we put it?' Trib says.

I turn without hesitation and point at the La-Z-Boy. 'There. It's the centre of the room.'

'Perfect.'

We shift his prized seat aside and get the armchair from the hall, trying not to chip the door frame as we wrestle it into the lounge. Once it's in position, Trib removes the black plastic and bunches it up in his hands while I watch the street through the net curtains. There is no guarantee Summer won't walk up the drive at any moment. He might have finished with his customer, or forgotten some vital paperwork.

Trib steps back and admires our handiwork. 'Look at that. Magnificent.'

It does look fantastically grotty, like a blob of snot smeared on a pristine white restaurant plate.

'Are you sure he's going to get it? Should we leave a message?'

'No, he'll come to the right conclusion. Never underestimate the power of guilt.'

Trib spots something over my shoulder and his eyes widen. I turn like a startled cat, and there's a figure passing the house on the street outside, just a few metres away from us.

'That's Barry Baxter from the chippy,' Trib says cheerfully. 'I haven't seen him in ages.'

'You are *not* stopping him for a chat!' I hiss.

Trib looks innocent. 'I didn't say I was.'

The man disappears from view and I can breathe again.

'Bloody hell, Trib. Don't do that to me!'

'Sorry, mate.'

'Look, we're done here, aren't we? Let's go.'

'One more thing,' Trib says, holding up a finger. 'Have a good look at that.' He points to the photo of Tony Summer.

'Why?'

'I'll tell you later. Memorise his face while I lock that window.'

Summer has ginger hair and a narrow, pointed chin. His wispy moustache looks like it's been grown purely to make him look more mature, more masculine, but it doesn't really work. He's smiling in the picture, but his eyes aren't involved like the rest of his face is. Or is that my imagination, knowing what he's done? Trib reappears and we make sure we've left nothing behind before escaping into the street. At the door, Trib once again feigns a couple of words with Summer's ghost before we head back to the van and drive off.

He turns to me and grins. 'Not bad. Not bloody bad. So, you survived your first mission.'

'Yeah, it wasn't so difficult.' I could have been calmer, but yes, I did it.

'Now,' he says, 'imagine his face when he comes home and sees that chair in his lounge.'

I get a very clear picture: he stops dead and a briefcase slips from his fingers. His mouth hangs gormlessly open. He nudges the chair from a distance with one shoe to make sure he's not hallucinating, flicks the errant spring with a look of disgust.

Trib pulls the van into a lay-by and applies the handbrake. 'Are you okay?'

But I can't reply. I can barely get a breath in, I'm laughing so hard.

—

My sense of triumph soon decays into doubt. For the rest of the day and long into a sleepless night it obsesses me. Summer will get the police involved and somehow they'll track the chair back to me. I spend a long time figuring out how they might do this, and although I come up with nothing plausible, it's still no consolation. I've broken the law before, but never so deliberately, and never without the prodding of fury's red-hot poker. I fully believe Summer shouldn't be protected from this sort of retaliation – he forfeited that right when he used the hard sell on a vulnerable old woman – so why am I still plagued with uncertainty? Perhaps it's just the vestige of conventional thinking, the result of growing up in a house with Dad and Alistair. Crowning everything is the doubt that this will have any effect on Summer anyway. Assuming he understands the message, he could dump the chair, install a burglar alarm, and still maintain that Mrs Alford can't back out of the agreement.

After a couple of days the memory begins to fade, then to

detach itself from the rest of my existence, as if the whole thing happened to someone else. I feel disappointed. I want it to stay fresh in my mind. I haven't done anything like this since that charity abseil down the side of the Student Union building.

It's a mystery how I can feel so ambivalent about this. I try to solve it, like an equation, but it resists all my attempts at analysis, like those problems in Maths at college, where all I managed to prove was that $0 = 0$. I drift off in meetings at work, drive down the wrong road on the way back home, miss half the plot of a film when out at the cinema with friends. Was I right to do it? Was it worth the risk? I want things to be clear-cut. I want certainty. But I know I can't have it.

Then on Tuesday evening, while I'm in the lounge finishing off *Brighton Rock*, the doorbell rings. I open the front door and there's Trib.

'All right, mate?' he says, his eyes gleaming. 'Fancy a ginger biscuit?'

—

And there they are, on a decorative plate on the coffee table. Mrs Alford pours us Earl Grey from a teapot and says, 'Here's to Mr Summer's change of heart.'

'It's all resolved, is it?' I've been sitting patiently for a couple of minutes and can't hold back any longer.

'Yes. He was very apologetic. He's had time to rethink, and decided that he was being unreasonable. The deposit has been refunded.'

'Fantastic.'

'He also asked me, "Was it you?" and "How did you do it?" Of course, I didn't know what on earth he was talking about.' She takes a sip from her cup. 'So, gentlemen, would you like to tell me?'

We glance at each other.

'Trade secret, I'm afraid,' says Trib.

'Ignorance is bliss,' I add.

'It wasn't anything ... illegal, was it?'

Trib holds up a half-eaten biscuit. 'These really are fantastic. You've excelled yourself, Mrs Alford.'

She gives him a schoolmistress look over the top of her glasses, but accepts she'll get no more out of us. We chat instead, about the weather, about baking, about her career as a physicist. Trib would not, I realise, have simply told me over the phone that Mrs Alford had got her money back. He wants me to see that she's more cheerful, that a weight has been lifted.

Before we leave, while Trib is using the loo, Mrs Alford says, 'Tell me something, Olly. Why did you do this for an old woman you barely know?'

Without Trib to speak for me – and I'm sure he'd know exactly what to say – I have to come up with something of my own. 'I, uh ... well it's the decent thing to do, isn't it.'

'You know, you've done more for me in the last four days than my son has in four months.'

I stare at her, mouth open, every attempt at a reply failing to coalesce in my mind. The toilet flushes, giving me an excuse to shrug off the burden of her praise.

'You ready then, mate?' Trib says, once he has emerged.

'Yeah.'

We put on our coats and shoes.

'You'll always be welcome here,' Mrs Alford says in parting, 'even if I have to bribe you with more biscuits.'

Back home, not even the second episode of *Obedience* can hammer a dent in my euphoria. The programme drifts past my eyes in a kaleidoscope of irrelevance, and the itch of doubt that's been torturing me is gone. The equation is solved.

10

I AM IN SO much trouble.

We're in the pub, clustered round a group of tables we've pushed together to accommodate the ten of us. Overcoming my mild misanthropy, I've met Andy's wife Nigella, Steph's husband Paul and her other friends, and they seem like easy-going people. But my focus never wanders far from the woman behind the microphone. Steph said she was talented, but I was expecting a competent pub gig with lots of covers, not the singer that commands the tiny stage of The Crown.

Rebecca Parry wears a suede skirt, burgundy top and a fitted jacket. The only instruments are an acoustic guitar and her voice. The microphone is set high and she tilts her chin up to sing into it – eyes half closed, as if just waking up – while a tangle of dark hair threatens her eyelashes and her fingers fall effortlessly onto the fretboard. Unlike some pub bands, where there's so much sonic clutter you can't make out a thing, Rebecca's stripped-down sound is remarkably clear, showcasing a unique voice and lyrics you could print as poetry. She has a huge vocal range and uses it to great effect, delivering the words with conviction, punctuating them with stabs at the guitar or playing rippling patterns over a weary monotone. A whisper explodes into a note that makes the whole room vibrate, held over several bars, until it finally cracks and dies.

She pushes at the boundaries of what can be achieved with just one voice and a guitar. The rhythms and chord changes are adventurous, with hints at Celtic music or jazz. The songs – all originals, as far as I can tell – have an honest, home-made quality which couldn't be further from the overproduced crap cluttering the airwaves. Pop is a teenager's game; this is music for grown-ups.

You were given a cliché
and wrapped it in tissue,
and gave it to me as a gift.
I had no heart to tell you
that size doesn't fit me.
It was just what I wanted, you said.

Steph has primed us to clap enthusiastically at the end of each song, but I need no encouragement.

'You like her, then?' Steph says to me.

'Yeah, she's bloody good, isn't she?' I try to make it sound like an appreciation of her skill rather than what it really is: an infatuation, a seduction.

Rebecca finishes her first set. Over the applause she says, 'Thanks. I'll be back after a little break.'

She puts her guitar back in its case and keeps a tight hold of it. As soon as I see she's coming our way, I get up and drag an empty chair over to the table, placing it between me and Dom.

Near the front of the pub a guy in his fifties with a ponytail pushes his chair back on two legs and reaches out a hand to intercept her. 'What a voice!' he slurs. 'There's a spare seat for you here, darling.'

Without even looking at him she nudges his chair so it thuds back onto all four legs and says coolly, 'Save your breath, mate.'

His friends roar with laughter and he disappears sheepishly behind his pint.

I am in so much trouble.

'I think I heard a couple of new numbers this time?' Steph says as she reaches us.

Rebecca nods and takes the chair I've provided but without noticing me. She stashes the guitar case between her chair and Dom's. Her skirt stops just short of her knees. Steph nudges a vodka and orange towards her and introduces everybody in one of those round-table blitzes that leave you unable to remember anyone's name. She ends with me, and I launch into conversation before she has a chance to turn away.

'Is that a real Martin you're playing?' I already know the answer.

'Yes. Which is why I won't leave it on stage.'

'Your songs are fantastic.'

She pauses for a moment before saying, rather formally, 'Thank you.' There is a natural downturn to her lips, a smoky hint of eye shadow.

'Steph said you were good, but I had no idea that …'

She shrugs off the compliment. I've got maybe two seconds before I lose her attention, two seconds to steer her away from the idea that I'm just a more polite version of old Ponytail at the front. So, what can I say? How can I reduce my nervous awe to the point where I can communicate like a higher primate?

Her songs, talk about her songs. 'It sounds like you're using a lot of complicated chords.'

'Yeah, I like to go beyond the usual majors and minors. You know something about music, then?'

'Not much. I used to be in a band at university, very briefly.'

'Oh, yes?' she says. 'What style?'

'We really weren't very good. Erm … we sort of went for punk because none of us could play very well. If you can't be in a punk band at uni, when can you?'

'I suppose,' she allows. 'What was your instrument?'

'Second rhythm guitar.'

'You had two rhythm guitarists?'

'Yeah. Three if Brian turned up.'

'Sounds a bit excessive.'

'Oh it was. "Excessive" was our watchword.'

'Smashing up your instruments? Stuff like that?' She raises an eyebrow, suggesting she doesn't really believe this is a possibility, but I can't leave any room for doubt.

'God, no. We were all well-behaved, middle-class boys, not

exactly committed anarchists.'

'What were you called?'

'Three of the guys were studying Maths, so we called ourselves the Standard Deviations.'

'I like it.' Her lips rise a little and I chalk this up as a minor triumph.

But we're still talking about me, and I have to steer the conversation towards her. 'So, who are your influences?'

She's about to answer, but I hold up a finger to stop her. 'Let me guess.'

She shifts her seat to face more towards me. In doing so, she knocks her guitar case against Dom's chair. Dom looks up from his brand new iPhone, which he's been caressing since the start of the evening. He shuffles up to make a bit more room. 'Sorry if it looks like I'm anti-social,' he says, 'but I am.'

Rebecca turns back to me and I remind myself to thank Dom later. Next to him I must seem like Casanova.

'Joni Mitchell,' I guess.

'Yes, good one. Kind of a safe bet, though.'

I need to think of someone offbeat, sophisticated. Or hedge my bets by mentioning several. 'Sarah McLachlan. Aimee Mann. Maybe someone more folky, like Karine Polwart or Cara Dillon.'

Her surprise at my answer is replaced by a knowing look. 'Ah, but of course, you've been speaking to Steph.'

Steph, who has been listening in, says, 'No. I have told him nothing.'

'I'm impressed,' Rebecca says. 'So you do listen to stuff other than punk?'

'Oh, definitely.' I decide not to mention my fondness for Metallica and Porcupine Tree and we stick to discussing the quieter side of music.

During her break Rebecca chats to everyone at the table except Dom, who has erected an impenetrable barrier of disinterest, broken only by his assertion that music began and ended with

The Smiths. Still, I manage to get the lion's share of the conversation. I keep a close eye on her glass, and as she gets near the end of it I ask if I can buy her another.

'Another one of these? God, no,' she says. 'Are you trying to ruin my performance?'

The automatic answer, the boring answer, would be to deny it. Instead, on an inspiration, I opt for: 'Yeah. Steph put me up to it.'

She glances at Steph – who is busy talking to Andy's wife – narrows her eyes, then turns back to me.

I lean towards her and say, 'She's terribly jealous of your talent.'

'My best friend?' she says with mock surprise. 'Are you sure?'

'Who bought you the first drink?'

Without opening her lips, she emits a low chuckle. 'Thanks, but no. I'd better get back for the second set. Good speaking to you, Olly.'

She remembered my name.

Retrieving her guitar, she heads back to the stage. Even the way she walks oozes grace, but I don't think she's aware of the effect she has on people – well, at least on me and Ponytail. The second set is as brilliant as the first, another feat of hypnotism, and I find myself wondering why she isn't on TV instead of my brother.

When I told you grey's the most beautiful colour
you wouldn't believe it.
When I called you out to the frosted fields
you wouldn't agree to it.
I'll leave you to your lurid dreams,
your bold, unsubtle schemes.
Give me the grey.

This is why: her lyrics are too downbeat, her melodies too intricate. A fingerpicked solo in – I count the beats – 5/4 time isn't exactly making concessions to the mainstream. I find myself wanting to hear each song again, suspecting there are hidden depths, that they will only reveal their secrets in time.

She is, of course, way out of my league, and the knowledge wilts my confidence. Making a first impression on a woman is like unicycling through a minefield. Every guy tries to present his best side, but I've got more to hide than most. Now, depleted with the effort, I can only watch her in wonder.

She prefaces her final song with the words, 'This is the last one. No encores.'

And all too soon it's over, to applause from the pub in general and a wild volley of cheers and whistles from our table, but I know for a fact that no-one has appreciated the evening as much as me.

'I will see you on Saturday!' Steph yells across the pub. Rebecca waves and begins folding up her microphone stand.

What's happening on Saturday? Can't I be invited?

Steph says to the rest of us. 'So, you are all invited back to our place for a little taste of our home-made treats.'

Everyone is agreeable except me. I'm still looking in Rebecca's direction. I have the strong urge to go up there and help her pack away, but … there's something a little guarded about her, and I don't want to blunder in where I'm not wanted. Around the table, people are putting on their coats, gathering up their things. I have no choice. Like a sheep – like a poor, lost lamb – I follow them.

—

Steph puts down a tightly-packed tray of the mignardises, which turn out to be bite-sized cakes, and people dart forward to grab them, like birds pecking at seeds. I sit on a footstool near the door, my plate empty. Steph's husband Paul pours his apricot wine into tiny glasses. Somebody hands me a glass and, seeing that I don't already have one, plonks a cake onto my plate. I try them, and recognise that both are very good, but it's as if a report of their quality has reached me from some far-flung country.

The babysitter, who can't be more than eighteen, looks a bit cowed by the sudden influx of people. She accepts one of the tiny cakes, but refuses a sip of the booze. She gives us all a shy wave and Paul escorts her home.

When Steph leaves the lounge and goes upstairs, I hesitate for a moment, then abandon my plate and follow. I find her in a room with muted lights, leaning over a cot filled with stuffed animals, including an Eeyore and Tigger. She spots me, holds a finger to her lips and beckons me in.

'My daughter, Sophie,' she whispers. Just poking out from under the covers are a shock of blonde hair and a tiny fist. Peering closer I see an eyelid, closed like a tiny smile.

We withdraw and Steph pulls the door to. 'She is so wonderful. A pain in the arse some days, it is true. But still, she is wonderful.'

Her happiness is almost painful to behold. This is what love does to people.

'Are you all right, Olly?'

'I need to ask you something. Is she, uh … seeing anyone at the moment?'

Steph frowns. 'Who, Sophie?'

'No: Rebecca!'

She blinks twice and her voice drops in pitch. 'Olly! You are not …?'

'Yes, I am,' I mutter. Wasn't it obvious to her? Wasn't it obvious to everyone in the pub?

'Oh, dear,' she says. 'This looks serious.'

'Just answer the question.'

Steph bites her lip and thinks for a moment. I wonder whether she feels a duty to protect her friend. But why? I haven't lost my temper at work, despite numerous provocations. I'm just like any other person, at least as far as Steph is concerned.

'She is not seeing anyone,' she says finally.

Her eyes twinkle and she waits for me to say something else, drawing out my agony.

'I was hoping you might tell her that … that …'

'I tell you what.' She takes a pen from a nearby table, grabs my arm and tattoos the back of my hand with a series of digits that might as well be the combination to a bank vault. '*You* tell her.'

—

Twenty minutes later, ensconced in my loft bedroom with the ladder retracted, I know I have to use the number tonight. I can't leave it until tomorrow, I'll never be able to sleep. This has to be timed carefully – too early and she'll still be unpacking her gear, too late and she might already have crashed out for the night. I imagine her travelling back from the pub, tired (what car does she drive?); or at home, putting her feet up after a successful gig (where does she live?); or getting ready for bed (does she wear pyjamas or sleep naked?).

God. *God.*

Deciding that eleven o'clock will be about right, I'm left with nothing to do but itch with anticipation as I wait for the next twelve minutes to crawl by.

What the hell's wrong with me? Why does it matter so much? It reminds me of the terror I felt before asking Sarah out, in my second year at college. There have been a few since then and in each case I pretended I didn't care what the answer was – a self-deception, but enough to get me through the experience. Right now, though, I'm a virginal seventeen again, out of my depth and pinning my entire future happiness on the answer to a single, critical question.

I've changed. I'm getting better. That's what I tell myself. I have to, because otherwise why would I bother? Either my chances with Rebecca will end now in rejection and embarrassment, or they'll end later, sunk by cynicism and anger. Even knowing this as a possibility, even a likelihood, I can't help myself. Hope conquers all objection, all rational argument. I have to ask her out. The thought of her becoming another squandered opportunity appals me. I still wonder about some of the girls I let go, what they might have been like, whether somehow they might have been able to put up with me. Of course, Rebecca is different. Aren't they always? Yes, I know I only met her a few hours ago, but no-one has ever had this effect on me. It's crazy, and I don't care: I'm going to do it anyway. What's the forfeit? Humiliation? Ridicule? Sign me up.

10:56. I dial her number.

From the other end of the line: 'Hello, Luigi's Pizza.'

I look at the phone's display, compare it to what's written on my hand. I see, Steph, that 7 is your idea of a 1, is it?

'Hello?'

I hang up. Do it. Do it now. Do it before you lose the last frayed tatters of your nerves. I dial again, double checking the number. Perhaps she's still out. Some fugitive part of my mind wants it that way.

'Hello?' It's her voice this time, unmistakable.

'Hi, is that Luigi's Pizza?'

'No,' she says slowly.

'Good. Hi, it's Olly. We met earlier in the pub.'

'I remember you,' she says drily. 'As a matter of interest, how did you get my number?'

'Ah, Steph buckled under questioning. Listen, I uh ... never got to buy you that drink.'

'And you feel like you owe me?'

'No. That's not it, I uh –' I'm glad she can't see me wincing. 'Look, what I'm trying to say is: would you like to go out for a drink some time?'

I manage to keep my voice even, but I'm curled over the phone, virtually in the foetal position. I hear that low chuckle again – a Bond villain about to castrate our hero with an industrial laser. And then she says, 'Yes, why not.' Her tone suggests the idea is surprising, but not disagreeable.

'Fantastic! I, umm ...' I realise I haven't thought as far ahead as an actual place to have a drink.

'I'll tell you what,' she says, 'how about going to the theatre? We can meet up for drinks beforehand.'

The theatre? I haven't been to the theatre since school. 'What did you have in mind?'

'I've got tickets for a little local thing opening on Monday. I was going to go with Steph, but she can't make it. Want to come?'

Monday? That's five whole days away. 'Yeah, sounds great.'

'It's at The Mill. Starts at eight o'clock. I'll meet you at, say, 7:30?'

Where the hell is The Mill? 'Brilliant. I'll see you there.'

'Bye, then.'

'Bye.' I hang up and flop back onto the bed, exhausted, content. I still don't sleep.

11

'So,' I ask Trib, 'what's the biggest thing you've done?'

I've accepted Trib's invitation for another lunch at Sumi's.

'The biggest?' he says. 'Why not the most productive or the most satisfying?'

'Because I want to know what I'm getting involved in.'

He wipes his mouth with a paper napkin. 'I don't really like to think in terms of big. The bigger things get, the less control I have over them. I don't have any delusions that I'm curing cancer or solving world poverty. I like things small, manageable.'

'You wouldn't be going after Robert Xavier-Walters, then?'

'Who?' he says.

'That company director who's been all over the news.'

'Ah. I don't read the news much. What's he been up to, then?'

I explain the scandal: the falling share price, the redundancies, the golden handshake.

'There's not a lot you can do about it, though, is there?' he says.

'Which is what makes it so infuriating.'

'That's the problem with the news: you get to hear about all the cruelty, injustice and idiocy in the world, you get to feel responsible for it, but you don't have the power to fix anything. That's why people feel so hopeless, so frustrated.'

'I should probably avoid reading that shit.'

'Maybe you've just got a stronger stomach for it than I have.'

Huh. Or maybe not.

He herds some flakes of pastry across the plate with his fingers. 'You could campaign against that sort of thing, I suppose, but it could take months or years to get anywhere, and you're probably just pissing in the wind. You know what the old boys' network is like. I'm too impatient for all that. I want results. That was the problem I had with my degree.'

'Which was in politics, right?'

'God, no! Politics is dead.' Seeing my look of surprise he says, 'Do you not think so?' He ticks the reasons off on one hand. 'Hardly anyone votes, the politicians are obsessed by self-interest, there's not much difference between any of the big political parties. Can you blame people for not being interested? Politics is about the masses, and nothing's more insulting than treating people as statistical groups.'

'You don't think that man is by nature a political animal?'

'Full of surprises, aren't you? No, much as I appreciate Aristotle's contributions to Western civilisation, I think that these days man is by nature an *apolitical* animal.'

'So what is your degree in?'

'Philosophy.'

'Philosophy?'

'Don't look at me like that. You're the one quoting Aristotle.'

'And your job is?' I prompt.

'Fitting locks and burglar alarms. I did philosophy,' he says, a little defensively, 'because I thought it would be interesting, not because it had great career prospects. Otherwise I would have done accounting. Or dentistry.'

'So, was it interesting?'

'God, yeah. I got a bit frustrated with all the navel-gazing existentialist bollocks, and the lack of practical application, but the ancient Greeks were brilliant, especially Socrates.'

'So what did you get from him?'

He opens his mouth and shakes his head, as if the reply is too big to formulate. 'How to live my life,' he says finally.

'As much as that?'

'Yeah, you cynical bastard.'

'I just can't imagine he has much relevance today.'

'Oh, but he does. Here …' he extracts his diary and flicks through the pages '… try this: "I am certainly wiser than this man. It is only too likely that neither of us has any knowledge to boast of; but he thinks that he knows something which he does not know, whereas I am quite conscious of my ignorance."'

I frown. 'He's boasting about his ignorance? Isn't that a bit arse about face for a philosopher?'

'No, he's saying that acknowledging your ignorance is better than bullshitting. The people who want to look clever are the ones covering up the biggest deficiencies.'

'Huh. My boss is like that. She pretends to know how to run a department.'

He snaps his fingers. 'There, you see: still relevant today. The guy was a moral titan. He died for what he believed in. He was imprisoned and sentenced to death for corrupting the youth of Athens.'

'And is that something you'd risk? Prison, I mean.'

'In principle, I suppose. Although I can't be of much use to anyone if I'm being detained at Her Majesty's pleasure. But who knows? Depends on the situation.'

I could tell him about my own experience in a police cell. It was no more than a few hours, but I know it would get a reaction. It always does. But Trib is the sort of guy people feel they can share their secrets with, and that might be a very good reason for me not to.

As Sumi passes our table Trib says to her, 'Why so glum, Sumi?'

She looks across the café for a moment, as if deciding whether to answer, then leans forward and says, 'They have opened another one of those ridiculous Kafe fantastiK places in the high street.'

'The one next to the bank? Yeah, I noticed. How many is that now?'

'Three. One at the other end of the pedestrianised precinct and one next to the cinema. All prime locations.'

'Why do they need so many?'

'I was talking to a friend in Leicester about this. They open so many KKs that they saturate the market. They lower their prices, even to the point of making a loss, until all of their competitors fail. Then they close down many of their own cafés, letting their own workers go, and become profitable again, but this time with no competition.'

'I've read about this,' I interject.

'And I have experienced it first hand,' she says. 'There was a man in a suit here only yesterday saying this is a KK town now, and I might as well shut up shop.'

'Seriously? That's out of order.'

'I do not understand it,' she says. 'I want to make great food; they want to make money. If I told somebody this, and asked them which approach they like better, I am sure they would say the food comes first. And yet still my business is under threat. Please explain this to me.'

Trib struggles with a reply, but can't come up with anything.

'Have you ever eaten anything in a KK?' Sumi asks.

'I've been to one in Sheffield,' Trib says.

'And?'

'Well, after the vomiting and diarrhoea …'

Sumi sniggers in spite of herself. 'You are too funny.' And then it dies away, and the smile goes with it, and she says, 'You know, they won't stop until I have closed.'

I can see the wheels beginning to turn in Trib's head.

'Ah, but why am I burdening you with my problems?' she says. 'None of this is your fault. You are my loyal customers and I will continue to serve you the tastiest food it is within my power to create.'

'In which case,' Trib says, 'bring us over a slice of that carrot cake, will you?'

'I'll have one too,' I add.

Sumi protests that we're only ordering it out of sympathy, which we both strenuously deny. She caves in and says, 'You are good boys,' like some benevolent aunt.

She leaves us each with a generous slice of cake. It's just as good as her savouries.

'Not fair, is it?' Trib says, sotto voce, so she can't hear us over the conversations of the other customers.

'Life isn't, generally.'

'Don't say that.'

'Why not? It's true.'

'Because it's an expression of defeat. Or worse, people use it as a justification to screw each other over, like that other pitiful phrase they utter just before they shaft you: "it's nothing personal, just business".'

'Thanks for the sermon. Let me write those down and I'll make sure never to use them again.'

Trib puts the brakes on. 'You *have* had a bad week at work, haven't you?'

I let out a sigh. 'Don't even go there.'

'Look,' he says, 'all I'm saying is that if life isn't fair, do we not have a responsibility to make it more fair?'

'Yes!'

'It's just an expression that annoys me, that's all. No biggie.'

I'm being unreasonable and I should apologise. Instead I prevent myself from saying anything else I might regret by stopping my mouth with a huge wodge of carrot cake. Apparently this is comedy gold because Trib starts laughing. So I play up to it, munching away like a cartoon character.

After a concerted effort, I manage to get all of it down. 'So, how do we make things more fair?'

'You're up for more thrills and spills with Trib, are you?'

I shrug, even though the answer is obviously yes.

'Okay,' he says, mopping up the crumbs with a wetted finger. 'There's no time like the present.'

I push back my chair and stand. 'Lead on.'

Before we leave, Trib wedges a tenner under the salt and pepper shakers.

—

The place smells more of fresh paint than coffee or food. The Kafe fantastiK sign is huge, red and unmissable. We're served by a skinny kid with acne and eyelids which are losing their fight against gravity. Pinned to the front of his uniform is a badge with the name 'Brad'. Underneath it, in much smaller print, is a series of seven digits which I assume is Brad's serial number.

'Next-order-please,' he says.

'Have you got any samosas?' Trib asks him.

'Unh?'

'Samosas.'

'Erm ... nah. We have a delicious range of baguettes, pastries and cakes,' he says, in a voice not quite his own.

'I'll just have a small Americano.'

'Same for me,' I add. It's the cheapest thing on the menu.

Brad turns to the coffee machine without saying anything else. To be honest, it looks like every word is an immense effort for him. It's pretty busy in here, but I suppose it is a Saturday. The décor is attempting something between Scandinavian chic and an airport VIP lounge. Looking closer, though, I notice the furniture is shabby, with wear on the simulation leather, loose stitching, screws missing on the chrome and steel tables. This stuff isn't new. After a lengthy twiddle with the coffee machine, our drinks are served to us in paper cups.

'Thank you, Brad,' Trib says.

The use of his first name makes Brad look like he's suddenly been jerked awake. 'Er ... yeah, sure. You're welcome.'

I start heading towards the comfy sofas in the corner, but Trib leads us instead to a table in the middle with high wooden chairs.

'So,' I ask him in a low voice, 'what are we doing funding Sumi's competitor?'

'This,' he says and takes a sip from his coffee.

I give him a puzzled look. He swallows and coughs hard. His face tightens into a look of discomfort and he pats himself on the chest. Ah, I get it.

'Are you okay?'

He shakes his head and coughs again, a wrenching, saw-toothed sound that reverberates off the walls. Several of the customers look round to see what the fuss is. He takes another sip in an effort to soothe his throat, but the coughing catches him at just the wrong moment and he sprays his mouthful over the table. It doesn't take any great effort for me to look disgusted.

'Are you all right?' I use a louder voice, and now we have everyone's attention.

'Urgh! Jesus!' he manages.

I put a concerned hand on his arm, but he shakes it off, grimaces and continues to choke. He slides off the chair and, between bouts of doubling over and looking like he's going to vomit, he manages to dump his coffee cup in the nearest bin. I stand up and back away from my own untouched drink, regarding it with the same suspicion I'd reserve for an unexploded bomb. Brad has come out from behind the counter, but the violence of Trib's reaction has paralysed him in his steps. I thump Trib on the back a couple of times.

'Has he got, like, an allergy or something?' Brad says.

'No! This has never happened before. What the hell do you

put in this stuff, anthrax?'

Brad has no reply. His arms flap, like he's treading water.

Trib stumbles towards the exit and I follow, one hand on his shoulder. 'Should I phone for an ambulance?'

Out of the door and a few paces down the street, Trib clears his throat and straightens. We turn off the pedestrianised precinct and into one of the side alleys. Abruptly he stops and turns to look at me. We both crack up.

'Anthrax?' he says. 'Phoning for an ambulance?'

'You could have told me what you were going to do.'

'And deprive you of the chance to improvise? No way. Did you see the guy in the denim and those two teenagers? They were almost out the door before we were.'

'And what about Brad?'

Trib mimes his paralysed confusion and I have to fight off another wave of laughter.

'Poor guy,' Trib says. 'Still, he'll have a story to tell his mates.'

'We could post something up on the internet; get other people doing the same thing.' I imagine a hundred Tribs up and down the country, spewing their drinks onto a hundred coffee tables. That ought to put a dent in their profits.

'No,' he says, 'you can't do that. It becomes a campaign. As soon as you have an organisation they can point the finger and say: "Look, it's a con."'

I suppose so. 'But this isn't enough,' I protest. 'We need to do more.'

'Oh, yes. Don't you worry about that. There'll be more.'

12

I ARRIVE FIFTEEN MINUTES early at The Mill. It's a modern building of pale stone and glass, with a car park facing woodland. My plan was to get here first so I wouldn't keep her waiting, but I see

Rebecca through the window, sitting at a table in the café. She idly dips a spoon into a broad china cup as she gazes out into the darkness, lost in her thoughts. She looks like she's in a French film, sitting in some Paris bistro while she waits wistfully for her lover – me, preferably – to arrive.

The day after her gig, Steph had asked me within thirty seconds of arriving at work whether I'd phoned Rebecca and what the outcome had been. When I said we were meeting up, Steph had actually squeaked.

'So what can you tell me about her?' I said. 'You know, give me a head start?'

'No, no. That would be cheating.'

'Cheating? There are rules?'

'There is only one rule.'

'Yeah?'

Steph hesitated, fiddled with the network cable she was holding. 'Fais qu'elle soit heureuse,' she said, and turned to go.

'Wait a minute! I'm not having any of that. If you're offering me advice, at least give it to me in a language I can understand.'

'Make her happy.'

I'm glad the waiting is now over. No more meetings where Jane castigates me for not paying attention. No more staring into space while Moira's excellent beef stew cools in front of me.

I sit down opposite Rebecca, catching a hint of citrussy perfume, and say, 'Hi. I thought I'd get here early, so I wouldn't keep my date waiting.'

'That's okay,' she says, 'I like to chill here for a while before a performance.'

I can see why she likes the place. It's spacious and open, with a high ceiling, partitioned by a series of half-walls containing leafy plants. The aromas of home-cooked food and coffee are strong, and the walls showcase paintings by local artists.

'You've foiled my plans to buy you a drink again.' I indicate her cup.

'Let me buy you something instead. The hot chocolate is something else.'

'Okay.'

She goes up to the tiny bar and orders. She exhibits a muted sophistication: a black skirt, thigh-length boots and a roll-neck jersey the colour of slate. I'm glad I vetoed Jodie's overexcited suggestion that I wear my one and only pulling shirt. It makes me look like wrapping paper. Rebecca returns after a couple of minutes with another cup of chocolate.

'Thanks.'

'So,' she says, reseating herself, 'do you always ask women out so soon after meeting them?'

'No. It's not like me at all. But I knew if I didn't leap on the opportunity, some other guy was going to.'

Her brow wrinkles into what could be disappointment, and I realise she's very much testing the waters with this date. I'll have to pass muster if there's going to be a second.

'Like that guy at the front of the pub,' I add. 'The one with the ponytail.'

'You've got to be joking.'

'You never know. He might be rich beyond your wildest dreams; have a flash car, a holiday villa in Spain.'

'And you think those are things I'd be interested in?'

'Judging from your lyrics, not a chance.'

She nods with what I think is approval. 'Anyway, my uncle isn't *that* wealthy.'

I try not to choke on my hot chocolate. 'He's your uncle!?'

Her lips twitch. 'Sorry,' she says, 'couldn't resist.' Christ, she's deadpan.

I ask her to tell me a bit about herself, expecting a treasure trove of fascinating titbits. What I get instead is a bunch of statistics: how old she is (28), where she was born (Dorchester), how many songs she's written (32). Not really what I was after, but she has no duty to reveal anything she doesn't want to. I need to get out of fifth gear and match her speed, because otherwise she's just going to coolly drift out of my life the way she drifted in.

When I ask about her favourite gig, she paints a vivid picture of an outdoor festival in Brighton – low, late-summer sun and an appreciative audience – but she's soon turning the conversation back to me. 'I want to hear more about this punk band,' she says, 'the one you were in at University.'

'You really don't.' But I find myself smiling.

She tilts her head to one side.

'I shouldn't be too critical,' I continue. 'We had some good times in that band. It was pretty short-lived, though. We only played four gigs, all of them at the Student Union, before Scott announced he was embarking on a solo career. As a private maths tutor.'

A tiny lift of the lips, a hint of wrinkling about the nose. Is that a smile? Everything about her is so subtle. Kerry would have laughed out loud, but that's because our sense of humour was the foundation of our relationship, and the reason we still work together as friends. It was the times when we didn't laugh, when we couldn't, that ended it.

'So,' she says, 'were you one of the ones studying maths?'

'No, I did English.'

'But you're in computing now? How did that happen?'

The plan back then was to get a job teaching English. I was going to model myself on Mr Gibson, and the way he taught us during our GCSEs – a magic combination of warmth, enthusiasm and empathy. But at university my anger was always waiting in ambush, triggered by the guy in digs who played techno 'til the early hours, or the bastard head of department who delighted in telling me I'd never be fit to teach. It was a bitter day when I finally conceded he was right: putting someone like me in charge of a classroom full of unruly teenagers would be like trying to douse flames with paraffin.

'Olly?'

'Er ... yeah. I wasn't sure about having to deal with kids all day. Machines care less when you swear at them.'

It's a reminder that I'm bluffing normality; editing out the anger, the self-harm, the therapy sessions with Dr Nylund. While guiding the conversation into safer waters, I pull surreptitiously on both sleeves, making sure they're all the way down to my wrists.

—

'What did you make of that, then?' Rebecca says after the play is over. We've returned to our table in the café.

'It was good.' It was never going to be the main attraction though. I'd been distracted by her proximity, but lacking the courage to touch her hand or put my arm over the back of her seat. I'd been able to recognise that the play – about a family struggling through the Blitz – wasn't bad, but chunks of the plot were missing from my memory, usurped by snapshots of Rebecca in profile: the line of her nose, the gentle double-bump of her lips, those eyes, alert to everything.

'It was pretty sombre,' I add, feeling I've been too vague.

'Mmm. Sorry about that. You know how some films aren't really date movies? That wasn't really a date play.'

I grin.

'Still,' she says, 'it was better than the one I saw last month. Part of the lighting rig failed and they had to struggle through with only half the stage lit. Afterwards, the lead actor ordered a bottle of whisky from the bar so the cast could drown their sorrows.'

'Is that something you have to worry about?'

'What, alcoholism?'

'Ha! No, equipment failure.'

'Well, yes. If a string breaks, that's easy to fix, but if the mixer or the PA go down ...'

'Could you play acoustically?'

'In a crowded pub? Not a chance.' She sips at her drink.

'It would be a shame for the audience to miss such an amazing performance.'

Her lips crinkle as she presses them together; a line appears in her forehead.

'Have I said something wrong?'

'To be honest, I find compliments a bit difficult. If I was that good I'd be signed to a record label.'

'Have you not had any interest?'

'I was approached by a record industry type once, after a gig in a London pub. He said I had a good voice but my material wasn't so hot.

My jaw drops. 'What an ars—idiot.'

'That's exactly what I thought: a typical arsidiot. He said he might be able to do me some favours – and he gave me this suggestive look – but I'd have to let someone else write the hits.'

'And?'

'I said, "I don't do karaoke."'

I laugh, but Rebecca looks pained.

'In retrospect,' she says, 'it might not have been such a good idea. Burning your bridges and all that.'

'No, you did the right thing. When you've written songs as good as yours, you can't just give that up.' I pause. 'That was sort of another compliment, wasn't it? Look, I'm not saying it to flatter you, I'm saying it because it's the truth.'

'Okay ... then thank you.' She shifts on her seat and focuses her attention on her drink, a gin and tonic I bought for her after the play had finished.

'Surely you want people to praise your music, though. That must be part of why you do it.'

'Yes, but I suppose I'm always suspicious that the compliments aren't quite genuine. So much of what I hear sounds empty. "You look pretty on stage", "Your voice is really nice". I mean, pass the bucket.'

'But that's not what I mean.' I avoid the fact that I could, in all honesty, have said either of these things because they're undeniably true.

'No, you're right. It's just … I dunno.'

'What can I say? It's music I want to hear again.'

She nods. 'I'll take that.'

'How often do you play?' I ask her.

'About once a month, on average. In the summer I usually manage a couple of local festivals.'

'Not your main source of income, then?'

'God, no. I wish it was.'

'So what's your day job?'

'I worked in a bookshop until recently, but we had to close our doors. Couldn't compete with the supermarkets' bulk discounting.'

'And now?'

'Ah,' she says. 'This is where your illusions about me being a glamorous singer are shattered.'

'Let me guess. You're a pig farmer? A sewage pipe clearance technician?'

'No.'

'Please tell me you're not a banker.'

Another half-smile. 'No, I work in a supermarket, on the fish counter. I gut fish.'

'Okay.'

'Still want to carry on with the date?'

'Yeah, I might get a good deal on salmon.'

For the first time I get a proper laugh out of her. It seems to escape in spite of her best efforts. Why she'd want to suppress such a thing is a mystery, almost as mysterious as why she would laugh at such a poor joke. But anyway: her cover is blown, and although her reserve is soon re-established, I won't be so wrong-footed by it now.

'Steph was right about you,' she says.

'She's been telling you about me?' I feign surprise.

'Worried?' she says.

'Yes. No. Depends what she said.'

'She said you'd put yourself out for her at work. Her exact

words were –' she adopts a French accent, '"He has been such a darling."'

I start to shrug it off, then bail out halfway through because I don't want to appear ungrateful.

'Aha,' she says, with a little smile of triumph, 'so you're not so good at the compliments either.'

—

I ask if she'll let me walk her home and she agrees. In the subway just before Broad Street there's a homeless guy, all beard and woolly jumper and sleeping bag.

'Big Issue,' he mumbles. I give him some money in exchange for the magazine, despite the fact I've already got a copy of this week's. Of course, I'm doing it to impress Rebecca, to show her what I'm like. It's not completely honest. But on the other hand, this *is* something I do. Otherwise I wouldn't have two copies, would I?

'Bless you both,' he says, with a knowing look in his eyes. It was worth buying another copy just for that.

We get to her house, a tiny detached place near the Tesco Express, and stop under the porch. She puts her key in the lock, and her fingers stay there, ready to turn.

Invite me in. Invite me in.

'I'm not going to invite you in, if that's okay.'

Shit. What do I say? That it's fine? I don't want to give her the impression I'm not interested. I want to be welcomed into the place where she lives and plays music and sleeps. Instead – abruptly, tragically – the whole evening is going to end.

'Do you want to, uh ... do this again, some time?' I suggest.

'Yes. Yes, I would.'

I have passed muster, at least for now. Should I try to kiss her? A peck on the cheek?

'Good night, Olly. I'm ... just going to go straight in,' she says.

'Okay.'

She gives a brief wave, slips through the door, and is gone.

13

EVERYTHING REBECCA DOES has significance. Or rather, I give things significance, trying to divine our future from them. Her wave at the door is a departure, the closed door a barrier. These are precursors to an inevitable ending. Her agreement to another date is reason for hope. Or it's just politeness while she finds a way to break things off. I can't help it: this is the way my mind works.

I decide to leave things for a couple of days, not wanting to destroy the delicate balance between us. I've been too eager already. On Wednesday she phones. Since failing to come up with a simple place for us to have a drink, I've armed myself with numerous ideas for our next rendezvous – Foley's Wine Bar, a subtitled French film at the Regal – but in the event she says, 'How about just coming round?' and I joyfully chuck all these plans out the window.

I bring her purple irises, having rejected roses as too forward and tulips as too ordinary. She looks pleased, and arranges them in the vase on the kitchen windowsill.

'What's in the plastic bag?' she says.

'I thought I'd cook you dinner.'

'Great. What's on the menu?'

'Hoisin chicken.' A dish shamelessly stolen from Moira.

'Mmm,' she says.

I noticed this about her at The Mill: her mastery of the thirteenth letter of the alphabet. She can make it into a yes, a no, an expression of satisfaction, disapproval, interest. It's the inflection, the musicality, that gives it meaning. And she clearly has no idea how sexy it sounds.

She gives me a tour of the house, which is as compact as it looks from the outside, but modern and cosy. Her furnishings are sober and unremarkable, the choice of someone with no interest in interior design. My eye is drawn instead to the many paintings and prints on the walls.

'Your house is like a gallery.'

She looks pleased and I realise I have to read up on art, pronto. The tour finishes at her bedroom, where an acoustic guitar watches over a double bed with a deep, whipped-cream duvet. She turns at the threshold of the room and I feel something is about to happen – a gaze held for a fraction too long, a drawing together, the prelude to a kiss. But before any of this happens Rebecca slides past me, leaving in her wake a smile as mysterious as the Mona Lisa's.

She'll be 30 in a couple of years, but Rebecca displays no sign of ever having been younger than she is now. I can't imagine her as a child. It's as if she was conjured into existence last week, whole and complete, and might disappear just as suddenly. The only indication of her past is the photograph of a woman gazing off into the distance, caught halfway to a laugh. The colours, the focus, are not crisp; the hairstyle not quite modern.

'Your mum?'

'Yes.'

'It's an old photo.'

Rebecca tilts her head, appraising. 'The big C,' she says. 'I was eight.'

I reach out and touch her arm, surprising myself.

'Shall we eat?' she says.

'Sure.'

After this, of course, there is no possibility of a kiss. A whispering propriety demands it. No matter – later will be soon enough. I've been guilty of rushing things in previous relationships, charging in headlong like some kind of kamikaze pilot, aware that I have to enjoy it while I can, before everything goes pear-shaped. This time I'll curb my impatience. If she wants a long, old-fashioned courtship I'll be happy to indulge her. She reminds me that deep down, under all those layers of trash, I am – or at least I want to be – a romantic.

When Trib had first mentioned an astronomy party held in a field, I was sceptical. But he not only persuaded me to come, he got me to invite a bunch of other people. He's chosen a good night. A steady breeze ushers the few low clouds along, leaving a good part of the sky clear for stargazing. Rebecca and I arrive to the sound of chatter and a glimpse of movement through the hedgerow. A five-bar gate opens on to the field and a sign scrawled in magic marker announces:

Astronomy Party
Free Entry
All Welcome!

'Wow,' says Rebecca as we go in, and I can only echo her surprise: there must be a hundred people here.

Just inside the field are a white tent and a big catering trailer with a serving hatch. I poke my head into the tent. On one side are two pasting tables, groaning with bottles of soft drink and orange juice. On the other is a piece of low scaffolding supporting four beer barrels and a canvas banner with the Strathurst Ales logo.

'Straight for the beer tent, eh?' Rebecca says.

'I didn't know there'd be beer.' Although, given that Trib has organised this, it shouldn't come as a surprise.

'Have you got any of the Gold or SAS there?' I ask the guy behind the tables. He's portly, with dark curly hair and a prodigious moustache.

'Of course we have,' he says, 'Trib's very specific with his requirements.'

'What are you having, then,' Rebecca says, digging out her purse.

'A pint of Gold.'

'Make that two,' she says.

He pours the lively beer into two recyclable plastic cups. We sip, make appreciative noises and thank him before stepping back outside.

'I thought this was going to be low-key,' Rebecca says.

'So did I. Trib gave the impression that –' I break off, having just spotted who's in the trailer, preparing food.

'Hi, Sumi.'

'Ah, hello, Olly! And this is your wife?'

'Not quite yet,' Rebecca says drily.

Sumi gives her a knowing look and stage whispers, 'Don't let that one go! He is a good boy.' It's generous, given that she's only seen me a couple of times. 'Now, if you will forgive me, I am nearing readiness here, but I must keep up my battle with this strange equipment.'

'We'll be back for something soon,' I promise.

Sumi looks a lot happier than last Saturday. No-one can muscle in on her turf here.

Further into the darkness, we find clusters of folding chairs and half a dozen telescopes. From behind the electric fence that forms the border to the next field, I can just make out a flock of sheep watching us. They look like clouds grounded for the night.

Trib comes bounding out of the crowd, a half full pint in hand, and says, 'Hiya, mate!'

It seems entirely natural that we grasp each other in a big, manly bear-hug. I try not to spill my drink.

'Rebecca, this is Trib. Trib, this is my ... girlfriend, Rebecca.' I like the way that sounds.

'Lovely to meet you,' Trib says, somewhat formally.

'So, you've organised all this yourself?' Rebecca asks.

'Me and Rob over there. He's the farmer. We did it last year and it was a roaring success. He says he has to ask the sheep for permission, but they're pretty accommodating. Try to avoid the droppings.'

'So, have you two known each other long?' she says.

'Not that long, I suppose.' I do a quick mental calculation. 'Three weeks? That can't be right.'

'It seems like longer,' Trib says.

'It seems like forever.'

'Already we're like an old, married couple.'

'Where did you meet?' Rebecca says.

'Oh,' I try to stall for time, 'it must have been … erm …'

'It was the Hog's Head, wasn't it?' Trib says. 'That game of cribbage.'

We're saved by a deep voice bellowing from the direction of Sumi's trailer: 'Food is up! Come and get it!' Everyone turns to see a formidable Indian man, nearly as big as Trib, with a chaotic black beard. Sumi's husband, I'm guessing.

'I'm starving. Shall I get us something?' Rebecca says.

'Definitely.' I hand her a tenner.

Trib and I both watch her go.

'She's a bit of class,' he says. 'I thought you said you didn't have a girlfriend.'

'I didn't at the time.'

'Early days, then. How did you manage to catch a girl like her?'

'That is an excellent question.'

'You've not told her about our activities?'

I shake my head.

'Are you going to?' It's so like him to give me the option, rather than insisting I keep it secret.

'No.' I'd be stupid to jeopardise what we've got so early on. 'Isn't this a problem you've faced with girlfriends of your own?'

'Not really.'

'How come?'

'I started after my last relationship was over.'

'I thought you'd been doing this for a while.'

'A couple of years,' he says, then adds, 'It's not so easy for a guy like me.'

It takes no great effort to imagine the string of rejections. Trib is clunky, uncool, and a long way from the ideal of male attractiveness. And yet I know he'd treat any girlfriend like royalty.

'I'm happy for you, mate,' Trib says, and nudges me with a shoulder. 'And more than a bit jealous.'

'There's someone out there for you.'

'Easy to say in your situation.'

I'm saved from having to attempt any more clumsy reassurances by the arrival of Andy, Nigella, Steph and Paul. I introduce Trib to them and he greets each of them effusively, as if he's been hearing about them for years. He relishes his role as host, explaining a bit about the constellations, and glancing up every now and again to check the progress of the clouds. Rebecca returns with two steaming polystyrene trays of chicken bhuna and rice.

'That was a great gig the other night,' Andy says to Rebecca. 'Have you got a CD we can buy?'

'Ah, not as such,' she says.

'What she is trying to say,' Steph interjects, 'is that she has a CD, but the sound is very bad. She asked me to help record some songs on the computer, but unfortunately the whole process is much more difficult than it looks. She needs someone with experience. I did my best, but the result is that of an amateur.'

Rebecca looks pained. 'It's …'

'Not good,' Steph interrupts. 'You could not sell such a thing and have a conscience.'

'In which case,' Trib says, 'we should all just go to your next gig instead.' He gets out his diary and pen. 'When is it?'

'November 21st at the Fatted Calf.' Rebecca gives Nigella a sympathetic look. 'Not the best place for vegetarians, I'm afraid.'

'Oh, I'll manage,' Nigella says, 'after all, I've got to put up with this lummox.' She nudges Andy, who flutters his eyelids in adoration.

Adam appears out of nowhere, sporting the same orange top he had worn when I first saw him in the park. Two other boys hang back as he pulls at Trib's sleeve. 'Uncle Trib, can you show us how to use a telescope?'

'Of course. Is there one free?'

The boy shakes his head.

'We'll have to nudge someone else off, then. Come on.'

We drift and socialise, striking up conversations with people we've never met, and I realise how much I'm enjoying myself. Trib has managed to conjure a community out of nothing, here for one night only. Kids leapfrog each other to keep warm. People chat and laugh. The stargazing is just an excuse for us all to be here. We are at one, under the stars.

I end up alone with Rebecca in a dark corner of the field, far from the lights and the chatter. She tilts her head back, and the line of her perfect jaw emerges from the red wool scarf which makes two full circuits of her neck.

'So, show me what's up there,' she says.

I take the opportunity to step behind her and point over her shoulder. She leans back into me, takes hold of my other arm and wraps it around her midriff, just below her breasts.

'The, um … you see the, er …'

'Come on, now,' she says, 'concentrate.'

I am concentrating, on every point of contact between us: her shoulder blades against my chest, the curve of her bum against my upper thighs. Thank God I'm wearing thick jeans.

'You see that bright star?'

'Which one?'

I point her back at the gibbous moon, then track right thirty degrees. 'That's Betelgeuse, and you can see three others – there, there and there – forming a sort of X shape. That's the body of Orion, the hunter. And you see the row of three stars in the middle? That's his belt.'

'Mmm-hm. What's that star in the middle, just below his belt?'

'I think that's Orion's ... uh, sword?' Although I hear nothing, I can feel her laugh.

She rotates in my grasp and my hand falls onto the small of her back. Her fingers brush against my throat, just above the line of my sweater, and pull me magnetically forwards. Her lips part and, without a sound, form the words, 'Kiss me.'

Orion winks.

14

REBECCA NEEDS TIME ALONE to compose, and although my chest tightens with disappointment every time she asks for it, I agree. I'm still in that phase of the relationship where I'll basically do anything she asks, including deny myself time with her. 'Music is who I am,' she says, by way of explanation, and I wonder out loud what it would be like to have that kind of certainty. 'Oh, trust me,' she says, 'there's nothing certain about it.' But she doesn't understand. I've spent my life drifting from one thing to the next, and only with Trib have I found something that feels truly worth doing.

The progress of our relationship remains achingly slow – not the best thing for someone with my lack of patience. But on Tuesday a distraction arrives on my doorstep, all two metres of it, wearing a grin I've come to know well. I invite him up to my room. While I'm pulling the ladder up, I hear a *bonk* as Trib hits his head on the rafters. I try not to laugh. He rubs his scalp and sits down at the desk for safety.

'I had an inspiration yesterday while I was walking past that KK next to the bank,' he says.

'Yeah?'

'They've got a little blackboard out in the street. It used to say, "Try one of our mince pies today!"'

'And what does it say now?'

'I was thinking about "50% off everything! Ask inside!" but although they'd get some annoyed customers, it would also give them more trade. Then I thought of: "Sumi's has home-cooked food and better prices!" and a little map giving directions, but that would look like sour grapes on Sumi's part.'

'So, what did you go for?'

'"Closed for private function."'

'Nice.'

'I've got a much better idea for tonight, though.'

'I'm all ears.'

'There's this little ventilation thingy round the back, built into the wall of their kitchen. I bet I can remove the grill from that.'

'You reckon we could get inside?'

'Oh, no, it's far too small for a person to get through,' he says. 'But it's big enough for a rat.'

—

Where on earth does he get these ideas? More to the point, where does he get a pair of live rats in a cage at short notice? If we needed a snow-making machine or a life-size replica of the Venus de Milo, would he be able to get hold of those too?

The back of the KK is secluded, just a loading area for the various shops facing the pedestrian precinct. We arrive at midnight, after the pubs have closed and the clubs are just getting started. It's mostly quiet, with only the occasional sound of footsteps from the other side of the building to test our nerves. Trib totters on two stacked plastic crates and tries to unscrew the ventilation grill, but the twisting motion of the screwdriver wrecks his sense of balance. He falls off with a deafening clatter.

'You club-footed monkey!' I hiss. 'Are you okay?'

'I think so.' He brushes himself off.

'Here, give me the screwdriver.'

'Mate, even on the crates you won't be able to reach that high.'

'I know. I'm going to sit on your shoulders.'

'Oh, you are, are you? Maybe I should sit on your shoulders.'

'How much do you weigh?'

Trib narrows his eyes. 'Tell you what,' he says, 'why don't *you* sit on *my* shoulders.'

He wobbles a bit, but with one arm clamping my legs against his chest I'm stable enough to unscrew and remove the grill. Trib gets down on his knees so I can dismount, lean the grill against the wall and pick up the cage by its handle at the top. I've heard that rats aren't the disease-carriers they're reputed to be, but I still don't want to get anywhere near those claws or teeth. Trib lifts me up on his shoulders again, grunting with the effort. I tip the cage back so the rats fall against the rear, then open the front, with the intention of rapidly jamming it against the hole, so the rats have no choice about where to go. But tipping the cage has upset Trib's balance, and he takes a step backwards.

'No: forwards, forwards!' I whisper.

He pushes off from his back foot, and I feel myself toppling back the other way. Getting both hands on the cage, I smack it against the vent with a dull clang. The rats waste no time, shooting into the ventilation shaft like a pair of furry projectiles. I see their dark shapes scurrying across the floor of the kitchen, and they're gone.

'They're in.' I brace myself against the wall with one hand and pass the cage down to him.

'Good. You know, you don't balance the way Adam does.'

He gets down on his hands and knees again so I can climb off. I pick the grill back up and turn to see him on all fours, head bowed.

'We've got to screw the grill back on,' I remind him.

He looks up. 'Yes, I'm aware of that.'

'You up for this?'

'Of course. I never pass up a chance to work on my hernia.'

Once we're done, we go back to his house. He phones the environmental health people and leaves a tale of outrage on their answering machine, which, for reasons of his own, he relates in a

Welsh accent. He puts me up in his spare room for the night.

Next morning we decide to pop into the town centre for breakfast, and saunter past the KK. The blackboard outside announces 'Closed Until Further Notice'. This time it's not in Trib's handwriting.

—

Rebecca's small, unremarkable house and clapped-out Renault would be mundane if I didn't know they were hers. But they are, and it's like she leaves a dusting of gold on them.

She is blissfully free of the problems that beset my relationship with Kerry; she's so much more dynamic. I never had a problem with Kerry being a Christian. The problem was that she used her faith as an excuse to do nothing. She never actually said it, but her view of the world was, 'If God wants it to happen, it'll happen.' It was infuriating. I thought Christians were supposed to be tirelessly doing good works. That's what my Aunt Julie did: an endless stream of soup kitchens and fund-raisers and Third World projects that left me wondering how she could still find time for her job. Kerry used to sit on her arse, waiting for God to sort things out.

She was also utterly irresponsible when it came to spending money. And not just her own.

I tried. I really did. Sometimes I'd cut to avoid the more serious arguments with her. I told myself I was taking pressure off our relationship, but it was the other way round – the relationship problems were an excuse to cut. I managed to hide my scars behind the pretence of having gymnophobia, an irrational fear of nakedness, and insisted we only ever had sex in the dark. It had worked, and I hope to make it work with Rebecca too, because in spite of the danger, I still crave that intimacy. My fingers itch to tackle those buttons and zips and hooks.

I invite her up to my attic room, where she runs her fingers along the shelving. 'So many books,' she says with approval, 'so many CDs.'

I've tidied up. The pile of clothes in the corner has been shoved into the bottom of the wardrobe and the PlayStation banished to the cupboard.

'It smells of wood,' she says.

Does it? I've long since stopped noticing. She curls into the easy chair and looks around. I take the straight-backed chair at the desk.

'It's beautiful,' she says. 'I wish I had a room like this.'

'You do.'

'So, why no staircase?'

I tell her about the reduced rates Moira gives me. 'Once I leave, she might get stairs put in for the next lodger, if she's got the cash.'

'Are you thinking of leaving?'

Yes. Then we can get a cottage together by the sea where you'll write music and I'll do carpentry and we'll take walks along the beach together in the morning and make love at night and we'll grow old together and ... and ...

'Not yet.'

She has already made it clear she won't be staying the night, but this doesn't prepare me for the marathon conversation that ensues. We talk into the early hours about books and music and ourselves, while the moon rises and casts its silver light through the roof window. Our talk is as free-flowing and meandering as a stream, and halfway through I realise this might be one of the happiest times of my life. I have to pay attention before it's gone.

At 2:15, bleary-eyed and smiling, she says, 'I really ought to go.' But in defiance of her words, she leans back in the easy chair and rocks slowly back and forwards. She looks like she has always belonged here. This is an entirely different room with Rebecca in it. Her presence and her approval have swept away any notion that this is a lonely bachelor pad. Even the bed, conspicuously single, doesn't seem as sad as it once was. It's inconceivable that this is the place I last cut myself just twelve short weeks ago.

I've worked hard at making a fresh start since then – the new job, those sessions with the damnable Dr Nylund – but all through it I've been dreading a relapse. And yet I survived that disastrous dinner with my parents, and as my internet friend excutter1705 has assured me, it gets easier with time. I'm actually turning my life around. In fact, looking across at Rebecca, rocking in the chair while she continues to survey the room, I think now is the ideal time to make a firm and final promise to myself. I hold on to my left wrist and slip my thumb up the sleeve, feeling the parallel ridges on my forearm. This is it. These are the last marks I will make on myself.

—

Trib makes me realise how cerebral, how theoretical, my life has been until now. I've been exposed to plenty of stories about injustice from newspaper headlines, internet surfing, books, TV. In fact, I've actively sought them out. And yet what did I do about any of them? He makes me realise I've spent years trying to solve the world's problems in my head. Trib's solution – to change the things within your power to change – makes complete sense. Achieving a small thing is far better than complaining about your inability to achieve a big thing. In my own way, I'd become a bit like Kerry.

It gives me the self-assurance to try one of my own schemes at work. I manage to get Andy and Steph signed up without too much resistance. Dom takes a bit more persuading, but eventually relents. He doesn't have the will to resist anything for long. Not when he can moan about what he's being forced to do.

On the morning of Friday 13th November Jane comes into our Portakabin, ready to address the troops. 'Right, team, I've –' She stops dead as she sees the four of us. We're wearing identical black duffel coats, hoods up and arms folded. I've scoured the charity shops of Strathurst to get them.

Jane puts her hands on her hips. 'What's going on?'

We don't say a word. The idea is not to argue with her, because we know it won't work. This is a silent protest.

'April 1st was months ago,' she says.

She could, of course, go to her superior, but I'm betting she won't, because: (a) it will imply she's not in control of her own staff, and (b) she'll have to confess she hasn't done anything about getting us a heater. I notice Dom shuffle a bit, and I wonder if he's going to crumble under the pressure and blurt, 'They made me do it'. But no, he manages to remain quiet, looking for all the world like a depressed monk.

Jane says, 'I'd expected a bit more professionalism from you lot.'

We remain stock still. The only sound I can hear is Jane's breathing.

'If this is about the temperature in here, I've already got a heater on order, so none of this is remotely necessary. In fact, it's very childish.'

On order, my arse. She's going straight back to her office to buy one right now. Which means we've won.

'I'll come back when you're ready to be treated like adults.'

She glides out of the room, trying to retain some dignity. We wait until she's out of earshot, then jump to our feet and come together in a group hug, like a bunch of jet black Teletubbies. Even Dom joins in.

15

TWO WEEKS AFTER our first date, Rebecca takes me to see her father. Isn't it a bit early in the relationship to be doing this? I've decided to leave it a lot longer before risking an introduction with anyone in my family. Maybe decades.

Mr Parry lives in a detached house on the outskirts of Farnham. He's tall and broad-shouldered, with bristly, squared-off hair, a five o'clock shadow and lines around his mouth that remind me of Fred Flintstone. His eyebrows are so big they seem to drag the rest of his forehead into a permanent frown. As we arrive he gives his daughter a huge hug, making me even more determined to make a good impression.

'So, you must be Olly,' he says.

'Mr Parry.' I go for a firm handshake, reckoning he'll do the same. I'm not wrong.

'That's Sergeant Parry to you,' he says.

'Army?'

'Try again.'

'Police?'

'Guilty as charged,' he says. 'But seriously, call me Mike.'

How has Rebecca managed not to mention that he was a copper? Then again, why would she?

'Come through to the lounge.'

My attitude towards the police has never really recovered from my time at university, and one incident in particular. I was outside a nightclub not far from campus, doing the chivalrous thing by trying to stop a guy assaulting Jemma Watkins from Sociology. I pushed him away, told him to lay off, exchanged a few tentative blows ... and the police arrived out of nowhere. What doomed me to a night in the cells was Jemma herself, who was more annoyed by my intervention than the fact that this man – her boyfriend, as it turned out – was giving her a slapping. I lost my temper with her, and the cops lost theirs with me.

I sit and make small talk with Mr Parry while my eyes dance around the room, looking for something to help me in my quest to appear relaxed and confident and worthy of his daughter. I remind myself that I don't actually have a criminal record after the Watkins incident – I was sent on my way with a caution – and there's no real reason for me to be anxious.

The furnishings are bright and modern. An acoustic guitar sits in the gap between the sofa and an armchair, making me wonder if musical ability runs in the family. I spot another picture of Rebecca's mum on a low cupboard. In this one I can see the similarities to her daughter, especially around the eyes, which exhibit the same sardonic humour.

'Rebecca's agreed to cook for us,' Mr Parry says. 'I hope that's okay.'

Rebecca has gone through to the kitchen and is rifling through the fridge and cupboards for suitable ingredients. 'With my dad,' she says from afar, 'there's no middle ground. It's either a takeaway or A&E.'

'I'm not *that* bad,' he protests.

'Let's not risk it. I want him alive.'

'Do you need any help with the preparations, love?' he asks.

'No, I'm fine.'

Before I can offer my own culinary services, he says, 'In that case, Olly, come with me.'

Rebecca appears at the kitchen door, rolls her eyes and mimes 'Good luck' to me. I want to ask what she means, but she's already gone. Mr Parry leads me out to a garden shed with wire mesh against the windows, unfastens two sturdy padlocks and swings the door open. I step inside after him, and he switches on the light, which is a bare bulb hanging on a length of flex from the rafters. On a small workbench are the shafts and heads of arrows. The walls are lined with lengths of wood, each with a slack string attached at one end: unstrung bows. He takes one of them off its peg, places one limb under his foot and with a grunt, bends the thing into a curve, slipping the taut string into a slot so it keeps its shape. He passes it to me.

'Wow.' I twang the string with my thumb, not sure what else I'm supposed to do.

'My hobby,' Mr Parry explains. 'I've always loved archery. Took it up when I was sixteen and never looked back.'

'Do you need a licence for these, then?'

'No. Completely unregulated. Until some nutter decides to go on a rampage.'

He takes the bow back from me, unstrings it and hangs it

carefully back on its hook.

'And what about this one, eh?' He strokes his hand along a specimen that is my equal in height. 'That's a longbow, that is. Hickory and lemonwood. Beautiful.'

'Very impressive.'

'Historically, they'd use broadheads rather than bullet points, which make the arrow much harder to remove and cause massive bleeding. But even with one of these,' he rubs his thumb across the tip of one arrow, 'you're talking about serious damage. Shot from any one of these bows, this would go all the way through you ...' he taps me on the chest with two fingers '... and six inches out the other side. I'd be hard-pressed to miss a major organ.'

Christ. A chilling scenario forms in my head: me and Trib out on a dark night, our plans shot to shit, hiding in a doorway while Mr Parry, in full Robin Hood regalia, stalks us with his hickory and lemonwood longbow.

I snap back to the present, where Mr Parry is finishing a sentence: '... if things were that way. Don't you agree?'

'I, uh ... yes. I couldn't agree more.'

'That's a very refreshing attitude, Olly.'

Has he terrorised all of Rebecca's previous boyfriends like this, or have I somehow earned special treatment? I've got to say something more than just platitudes. How would Trib act in a situation like this? He'd be confident and unflappable; he wouldn't take it so seriously.

So I try to lighten the mood. 'They don't let you use these in the force, then?'

'Of course not,' he snorts, but his attitude changes to wistfulness and he adds with a sigh, 'If only.'

Come on. I'm not expected to believe that he wants to carry a longbow on duty, am I? 'What do the other officers think?'

'Some of them think I'm aiming to transfer to an armed unit.'

'But they're wrong, aren't they?' This is my chance to side with him. 'That's not why you like archery.'

He points at me with the arrow. 'You're exactly right. A firearm is a machine. Whereas a bow is like an extension of your own body: simple, elegant, organic.'

I almost expect him to add the word 'erotic'.

'Do you hunt?' I ask him. I want him to admit that he shoots targets for fun on a Sunday afternoon, nothing more sinister than that. I know he's winding me up. I just want to hear him say it.

'Even if it was legal, what would I hunt?' he says.

'I don't know. Hedgehogs?' If he's going to be silly, I can play that game too.

'What kind of sicko would want to hunt hedgehogs?'

'Erm ... I don't know. It was the first thing that came into my head.'

'Why, have you got something against them?'

'Not really. I'm ... ambivalent about hedgehogs.' Shut up, Olly, shut up.

He carries on with the tour, and I do my best to sound interested in his array of lethal weapons.

'Anyway,' he says finally, with a touch of regret, 'let's go back in. Rebecca will probably be finishing any minute.'

His timing is good. The wine glasses have been filled, and she's just serving up the last of the spaghetti. 'Sit and eat, mighty warriors,' she says.

Mr Parry asks me all the usual questions about work, my interests. I tell him about my love of books and films and music.

'Do you ever go to Rebecca's gigs?' I ask him.

'Ahh, not any more,' he says, glancing at his daughter. 'I'm banned.'

'You're not banned, exactly,' she says, looking uncomfortable. 'It's just ... distracting when you're there.'

He turns to me. 'You couldn't film one of my daughter's performances, could you?' he says morosely. 'I'd so love to see what she's like on stage.'

'Oh, stick a sock in it,' she says. 'You can come along. You just have to act like a member of the audience and not the proud father showing off his daughter.'

'I wouldn't do that.'

'Last time you were grabbing hold of any stranger that came near and saying, "That's my little girl, that is."'

I look at him.

'That was enthusiasm,' he protests, 'pride.'

'It was toe-curling,' she says. 'And the way you check out the crowd like they're a bunch about to riot ... What was it you said? "I'll arrest any drunk bastard who wolf-whistles my daughter."'

'It was a joke!'

She turns to me. 'He's a very protective father.'

'Don't listen to her, Olly. She's exaggerating.'

Ah, like you were in the shed?

'So,' he says, 'did you meet her at a gig? Don't tell me – you were drunk and wolf-whistled her.'

'Dad!'

'I see I've hit the bullseye. And who said romance was dead?'

Rebecca puts her fork down and glares at him. 'Will you behave yourself?'

Mr Parry falls silent, but can't hide the hint of a smile. After another mouthful of pasta he fixes me with an appraising look, one that seems to say, 'I know you're having it off with my daughter and I'm trying to decide whether I approve of you or not'. The irony, of course, is that we haven't had it off. How am I supposed to respond to this? I look down at my plate of spaghetti, and it seems to mirror my thoughts.

'We didn't meet like that,' I tell him. 'I was sober as a judge.' This seems to me a clever thing to say to a policeman.

'Oh, dear,' he says. 'That far gone, eh?'

'You know what I mean,' I mumble. And then, on an inspiration, I add, 'My dad's a judge.'

Mr Parry's smile drops off his face so quickly I expect to hear it hit the floor. 'I'm so sorry, Olly. You can't take everything I say seriously. I just, uhh, shoot my mouth off sometimes.'

He notices his daughter folded over the table, barely able to breathe from laughter.

'What is it?' he says. 'What?'

He has to wait for Rebecca to get herself back under control. 'You've been had,' she says. 'His dad's an intellectual property lawyer.'

He sinks back into his seat. 'Thank God for that. I saw my whole career flash before my eyes.' He points his fork at me. 'You're a sly one, aren't you?'

When he announces at the end of the meal that he and I should do the washing up, I know he's engineering a situation where he can get me back. I walk into the kitchen like a condemned man and catch the tea towel he tosses in my direction. 'I'll wash; you dry,' he says.

From the lounge I hear Rebecca playing a few phrases on the guitar.

'Is that yours, then?' I ask Mr Parry, nodding in the direction of the music.

'The guitar? No, that's Rebecca's first instrument. I bought it for her eighteenth. She leaves it here so she can play whenever the mood takes her.'

'You don't play yourself, then?'

'With paws like these? Good God, no. Although I do credit myself with one thing. I used to take her to folk clubs when she was younger, so I did my bit to spark her interest in music. Now, if I could get her to shoot a bow, she'd be the perfect daughter.'

We lapse into silence again, and I wonder what else I can say to distract him from thoughts of revenge. My mind's gone blank, so I guess I'll just stand here and take it.

When he finally speaks, his voice is low. 'I know I've given you a bit of a hard time, Olly, but that's as it should be. You have to understand that Rebecca is the world to me. I want what's right for her.'

I don't know what to say.

'She looks happy,' he says. 'It's great that you can make her laugh. Growing up, she was always a very serious kid.'

I nod.

He claps me on the back with a handful of washing-up suds. 'That was a compliment!'

'Yeah, now you've really thrown me.'

He laughs.

We go back into the lounge once we've finished, and Rebecca plays us a rendition of 'She Moved Through the Fair'. I've heard a couple of other versions, but she owns it so completely that it sounds like she wrote it herself. Mr Parry sits back in his reclining chair with his eyes closed and his hands clasped behind his head. When she comes to the end of the song, he lets it settle and says, 'Takes you out of yourself, doesn't it?'

I decide that if he doesn't end up filling me full of arrows, I might get to like him.

16

TRIB KNEELS DOWN with his socket set and spanner, and gets to work. Two in the morning and it's utterly quiet. The compound of Grey Owl Security is full of cars and bordered by palisade fencing: two and a half metre steel stakes, each of which splits at the top into a trident of spikes. It's part of a business park, Grey Owl itself a patch of roughly tarmacked ground where cars can be dumped at minimum cost. The nearest houses are a hundred metres away, their windows dark. The air is filled with something between drizzle and mist – fine, almost weightless particles which hang in the air, causing yellow haloes to form around the street lights. Droplets of moisture collect on my hoodie.

Our client, Leticia, is a tall black woman in her late twenties who lives in a small, neat flat crammed with science fiction novels. Trib had already heard about her predicament through his network of contacts. We met her yesterday evening to check the details.

'So your car's been taken away?' Trib had said.

'Yeah, from the street right outside. There's designated parking and I used my permit, but it turns out the council changed the company who manage the scheme. They were supposed to send out new permits to all the residents, but, yeah: didn't happen.'

'So it's their mistake?'

''Course it is, but when I rang them, all they were interested in was whether I had the new permit. I do now, but it's too late, isn't it? I phoned the clamping company – which was hard enough: they never pick up – and they're just not interested in anything I say. Unless I pay up, I'm not getting my car back.'

'How much would it cost?'

She read off a piece of paper. 'Get this: £150 release fee, £95 towing fee, £25 administration plus £30 a day storage for twelve days. Grand total: £630. And it's going up by £30 a day.' Her lips twitched with indignation.

'Have you contacted the police?'

'Yeah. Said it was nothing to do with them. Said I should just pay the fine if I want my car back.'

'Sounds like a scam,' I said. 'They conveniently forget to give permits to a few people in the hope that they pay up just to end the hassle.'

'That's what I thought,' she replied. 'But I don't know what else I can do. I have to walk all the way to the station every day, wait for the train to be late, pay their ridiculous ticket prices ... and if work needs me to go out to a client, what am I supposed to do, take a taxi?' She shook her head. 'I need my car.'

Trib said, 'We can get it back for you.'

'So I hear. But you can't just teleport it back, can you? Look, if this is gonna be like one of Darryl's schemes, I don't want anything to do with it. I'm clean, respectable. Right?'

'We'll have it parked outside your house in a couple of days' time.'

'It'll be locked up. I don't even know where.'

'We can undo locks.'

She lowered her voice, even though we were the only people in the room. 'So, how illegal is this gonna be?'

'No worse than what they've done. No violence or criminal damage, obviously. Nothing they can pin on us. We just take back what's yours. The fly in the ointment is that they'll probably think you did it yourself, but my guess is they'll just let it go at that point. They don't want it to go to court because they know they'll lose. They're chancers.'

She thought about it for a moment and her face hardened. 'Yeah. I haven't done anything wrong. It's their mistake, isn't it? I could claim for all my train tickets, maybe even charge them with theft.'

Trib nodded.

'So,' she said, 'how much is this gonna cost me?'

'Nothing.'

'Nothing? Come on.'

Trib thought for a moment. 'Okay, tell you what: if me or Olly ever need insurance, give us your best deal straight away.'

Leticia tilted her head. 'All right. Sounds fair.' She reached out and dropped the car key into Trib's outstretched hand.

He's a master at this, and I find myself wishing I had his imagination, his contacts, his array of dubious skills. There's a world of difference between buying some duffel coats and stealing a car from a secure compound.

'Two more,' Trib whispers, dropping another nut and bolt onto the grass.

Knowing the entrance is covered by a CCTV camera, he's removing two of the metal stakes just behind it. We lay them on the ground as they come free, and Trib squeezes through the gap, sucking in his beer belly so it doesn't get wedged. The camera sits at the top of a three metre pole to prevent tampering, but that's easily dealt with. From another of his jacket pockets, Trib takes a supermarket carrier bag with a telescopic pointer duct-taped to it. He extends it, reaches up and hangs the bag over the camera. The weight of the dangling pointer will keep it in place if the wind picks up.

'You're sure that's the only camera?' I ask him. I can't see any others – not on the corners of the single, low building or anywhere else along the perimeter of the compound – but I want to know for sure.

'I've checked and double-checked,' he murmurs. 'They're either amateurs or cheapskates. Or both. Now, work quickly and don't look suspicious.'

'I'm with you.'

Trib strides across to the other side of the compound and starts to pick the padlock that keeps the main gate closed. Meanwhile I look along the rows of cars to find Leticia's red Fiesta. In this light everything is a dark grey, so I go by the number plate. There are several dozen cars here and barely any empty space, lending weight to the idea that the company has been overzealous with its clamping.

There it is. I unlock, get in, and adjust the seat and mirrors. The plan is to wait while Trib replaces the fence stakes, then drive out onto the road and keep the engine running, like any good getaway driver, while he re-locks the main gate. Then we remove the carrier bag from the camera, and we're gone. I drum my fingers on the steering wheel. Come on, Trib, get the damned lock open. The seconds are passing so slowly on my watch that I wonder if something's wrong with it. But no, it's just me.

I look up to see that Trib has undone the padlock. He juggles it up and down, as if he's handling an electric eel, then drops it. Clumsy bastard. I wince as the weight of the lock pulls the links of the chain noisily through the bars. Trib turns and runs towards me, batting his hands as if pushing at an invisible barrier. Behind him, on the road, a police car pulls into view. For a moment I'm paralysed, unable to believe what I'm seeing. The car stops in front of the gates, which are beginning to swing lazily open now that the chain is no longer taut.

'Go!' Trib mimes in panic as he passes by the car window and keeps on running. Fear surges through me like an injection of iced water. Torchlight emanates from the window of the police car, and I duck behind the dashboard as it sweeps over me. Knowing I have to move right now, I open the car door and roll out. God knows why I slam the door shut behind me, but I do. I should have used it as cover. Too late now. The light snaps back towards me, but I'm already running for the gap between the stakes, keeping low so the other cars conceal me.

A voice explodes in the night behind me. 'Oi!' The sound of a car door opening. 'Oi!'

I throw myself at the gap in the fencing, twisting sideways and ducking at the last moment so that my momentum carries me through. There's a dull *clonk* as my elbow hits the metal and a brief fizz of pain up my arm. We've agreed to split up in a situation like this and hide in the nearby woods, but Trib has already taken the shorter route, which means I'm obliged to negotiate the other industrial units and double back before I can reach the cover of the trees. I rack my memory for the layout of this place – the satellite picture we looked at on the internet, back when it seemed like pure fantasy that we'd ever have a need for such a thing.

I turn right as soon as possible and it's dark enough here that I risk a glance backwards. The policeman is just coming through the hole in the fencing and I see him turn towards me rather than Trib, who is already out of sight. I imagine being caught and cuffed, taken to the station, facing Mr Parry and trying – failing – to explain myself. And Rebecca? Oh, yes, that'll all be gone, obviously. How did this all go to shit so quickly?

I sprint. The night blurs around me. At the next junction I turn left, then right. I can hear the policeman call out again, but he's some distance behind. I reach the edge of the business park, and only now do I allow myself to double back and head towards the woods. I need to keep plenty of cover between me and the police. I slow my pace until my trainers make no sound on the tarmac.

I'm passing by a health food warehouse when I hear a low purr. The squad car turns round the corner and comes straight towards me. It's a pincer movement. I duck behind a parked van and the torch beam lashes out again. As the light moves, I step round the vehicle, trying to keep every part of myself completely hidden. No, an inner voice says, the driver can't hear my heartbeat. Of course, my panting breath might be another matter. I hear the static from his radio and an indistinct voice from HQ as he draws level with me.

How the fuck did they know we were here? A separate alarm system, linked directly to the police, that Trib missed? He told me – he bloody *told* me – he'd found all their security measures. Isn't this supposed to be his job? There's a stone lodged in my stomach, somewhere between my navel and solar plexus.

The torch beam flicks between both sides of the road. He's assuming I'm somewhere ahead rather than parallel to him and just a few metres away. Then he's past. He turns out of sight at the next left and I continue out of the business park, checking every junction before I allow myself to cross to fresh cover. Finally, I reach the boundary of the trees, vault a low fence and step into the damp embrace of the woods.

—

The van is parked half a mile away in a dirt lay-by. When I get back Trib is already there, waiting for me. I get in, slam the door and start on him: 'So, would you mind telling me what the fuck happened back there?'

He remains facing forwards while he twists the key in the ignition, indicates and pulls onto the road.

'Put your seat belt on,' he says.

'What?'

'Put your belt on.'

I do what he says, jamming the buckle in and thumping it home with my palm. 'Are you going to answer me?'

'Not everything always goes according to plan. You knew that from the –'

'No shit, Sherlock.'

He pulls off the road and switches on his hazards. 'I'm sensing a teensy bit of frustration here, Olly. So, let's have it.'

'What did you miss?'

'What do you mean?'

'Come on. It was a security alarm. It couldn't have been anything else.'

'No, it wasn't. I checked everything. There were no other cameras, no sensors on the gate, no –'

'How did it happen, then?'

'I don't know,' he says. 'Someone must have seen us and phoned the police.'

'Someone saw us in the middle of a deserted business park at two in the morning?'

'Yes. Some people are up at that time.'

'Yeah, right. Who?'

'I don't know. Insomniacs.'

'Bullshit,' is all I've got to say to that.

'You're trying to tell me there's no chance someone saw us and phoned the police?'

'I'm trying to tell you that you ballsed up. Again.'

'I did not!'

'Prove it.'

'You prove that someone didn't see us and phone the police. Go on, ring up the local station and ask whether they got a tip-off.'

A station where, tomorrow morning, Sergeant Parry might be

finding a description of me on the wall. It depends whether they got a good look.

'I don't know why you're so angry,' Trib protests. 'You knew the risks. You accepted them.'

'That's because I thought you were going to hold up your end of the bargain, which was to find all of their security.'

'And I did.'

'Like hell you did!'

'Look, Olly, there's no point getting upset about this. We have to –'

'Why did I ever get involved with this shit?'

Trib says, 'Because it's who you are.'

'Don't tell me who I am! Don't ever fucking tell me who I am!' I have to get out of here now. *Go, just ... go.*

He snorts. 'Maybe you're right. I've certainly never seen this side of you.'

'You don't bloody have to.' A click of the red button sends the seatbelt retracting with a furious buzz and the metal tip hits the window.

'What's that supposed to mean?'

'Find some other poor gullible sap. I'm through with this shit. You think you can stick some half-baked philosophy on your criminal activities and it somehow becomes the right thing to do. And then you have to drag me into it!' My fingers are pulling on the door handle.

'Come on, Olly, calm down and let's talk about this.' He puts a hand on my shoulder and I shrug him off.

'Get your hands of me you stupid, ugly, lard-arsed piece of shit.'

Trib looks like he's in shock. Good. I watch myself get out, slam the door and start walking.

He winds down the window. 'Olly.' He starts the van up and follows me. 'Olly, I'm sorry.'

'Fuck off!'

'It's five miles to Strathurst. Get back in, even if you're pissed off with me.'

'I said, fuck off!'

Turning round and walking the other way doesn't help: Trib puts the van into reverse. As he pulls up level he starts to open his mouth to argue some more. Both of my hands slam into the side of his van. The panels flex under the assault.

'*Go ... away!*'

There's a pause for a couple of seconds, then he winds the window back up and pulls past. The red rear lights of the van dwindle, weave, turn a corner and disappear. The sound of the engine is lost soon after, leaving nothing to hear except for the silent bellowing, bellowing, bellowing.

17

'Olly, stop worrying,' Rebecca says.

'I'm not worrying, I'm just concerned that –'

'You're worrying.'

'Okay.'

'Go and sit with the others. You're making me nervous.'

I've just finished helping Rebecca set up the equipment for her gig at the Fatted Calf. We've had to be quick because there's a covers band on at 9:30. Given the stripped-down nature of her performance, there's a lot of stuff: amplifier, PA speakers, pedals, mixer, tuner, microphones, stands, a spaghetti of cables ... It would be simpler if her guitar was fitted with a pickup, but she doesn't like the sound of them and insists on using a microphone instead. In my band at university the set-up was so much simpler: electric guitar, amp, done. Mind you, we sounded like an accident in a steelworks.

I head back to the table where Steph, Paul, Andy and Nigella are settling in with their first round of drinks. It's an obstacle course to get to them: the pub is heaving. A sizeable part of the audience consists of a gang of young women celebrating something or other. Most of them are already half-cut.

'Is Trib still coming?' Steph asks me.

'He texted me to say he can't make it.'

No-one is aware of our bust-up, and that's the way I want to keep it. After all, when they ask why we fell out, how could I possibly explain? Ultimately I was glad of the walk back to Strathurst by moonlight, because it was long and tiring, a small penance for my behaviour. Trib's brief text – *Not coming tonight. Tell R* – is the only communication we've had since.

'Here,' Steph says, pushing a pint of something jet black across the table, 'I bought you this.'

'Cheers.'

I hear the first few strums of Rebecca's Martin, and the gig begins.

It doesn't go well. The chavettes in the corner guffaw like crows, trip over the furniture and rush headlong towards alcohol-related deaths. In the manner of a car crash, people can't look away from them. Rebecca turns the volume up, but is ambushed by a high-pitched howl of feedback through the PA system. She tilts the guitar and sings over one shoulder, which helps a little, but she can't do this for the rest of the set. At the end of the song she tweaks the settings on the amp and mixer in an attempt to eliminate the feedback, but on the next song it returns, and she decides she has no choice but to take the volume back down. Meanwhile, the antics of the drunkards show no sign of abating.

'Why do people do this?' Steph says. 'They have paid to get in. What are they thinking?'

No-one has an answer, and we all find the experience excruciating. Rebecca plays some of her more up-tempo numbers, and even throws in an energetic – and possibly ironic – cover of The Beatles' 'Help!' to try and win the crowd over. There's applause after each song, but it's muted compared to her last gig. There's a bigger cheer as two girls start dancing on one of the tables near the stage.

A guy in a stripy jumper and baseball cap cups his hands to his mouth and shouts, 'Bring on the real band.'

I am on my feet. My legs propel me in his direction, effortlessly navigating the snaking path between the chairs and tables.

He sees me coming and stands to meet me. 'Yeah? What's your fucking prob–'

My arms fly into his chest, shoving him back against his chair. He stumbles, struggling to stay upright. My right arm goes back, ready for the first swing, which is aimed squarely at that smug fucking jaw. Someone behind me grabs hold of my arm, and another person takes charge of the other. I turn. It's Andy and Paul. They start pulling me back towards my seat. I glare murderously at one, then the other.

Andy shakes his head. 'Let it go.'

My breath is coming forcefully out of my nostrils, like a bull.

'You can't let an idiot like that dictate what you do,' he says.

I say bitterly, 'I'm supposed to turn the other cheek, am I?'

'Exactly. What will Rebecca think if you start a fight?'

Abruptly I'm aware there's no music any more. I look towards the stage to see that Rebecca has stopped playing and is staring at me. A sudden flood of shame rushes into my head where before there was ... what? What was it exactly? I feel like I've been rudely awakened from a deep sleep and I don't know where I am. I allow myself to be guided back to my seat.

Stripy top is pointing a finger at me and saying something, but I don't know what it is. Having saved his pride, he plonks back down and chugs his lager.

I force myself to sit. Rebecca picks up at the last verse, but her eyes don't leave me for a long time. Andy claps a sympathetic hand on my shoulder, and I resist the temptation to swat it away. I take a swig of my pint and wait it out. By the time the end comes, I've managed to haul myself back from fury to a kind of pained frustration. As soon as she finishes, Rebecca starts dismantling her kit. I go up to the stage to help her.

'Rebecca, I'm sorry about that. I –'

'Don't.' She shakes her head, her eyes lost in dark hollows that the pub's muted lighting cannot reach. 'I just want to get home.'

Her mood is thunderous, impenetrable. She rushes between the pub stage and her car boot, chucking the equipment back in like she's about to take it to the dump. I struggle to keep up with her.

Back in the pub, the landlord hands over the cash for the gig and says, 'That could have been better.'

Rebecca fires straight back. 'Yeah, maybe don't keep selling alcohol to people who are already heading for the hospital.'

She snatches the money out of his hand and turns away before he has a chance to respond. I carry on glaring at him, giving him the opportunity to have a go at me instead, if that's what he wants, but he just blows out a lungful of air and goes back behind the bar. Wise move.

The raucous twang of an electric guitar vibrates through the pub as the headline act tune their instruments. We leave.

—

Back at the house, Rebecca sits on the sofa, the large G&T I poured her a few minutes ago untouched on the coffee table. The furious energy that fuelled her back at the pub is gone. Her kit remains in the car, though I've taken the liberty of bringing the Martin back inside.

'I don't know why I bloody bother,' she says.

'I know it was a tough gig –'

'Yeah. You weren't standing up there.' She sits with her hands in her lap, frowning, unreachable. Her hair is knotted and chaotic, as if she's been pulling at it, though I haven't actually seen her do this.

'Rebecca, look, it was a terrible audience. End of story. You can't value the opinion of a mob.'

'No, but you can beat the crap out of them if they don't appreciate the music, right?'

Shit. I was hoping that somehow it hadn't looked that bad.

'You can't do that, Olly. You just can't.'

So I was the worst thing about the evening, was I? Not the crowd; not the technical problems?

'Look,' I say, 'I'm ... I'm on your side, here.'

'You've got a funny way of showing it.'

'He was out of order! I can't just stand by and watch some jumped-up dickhead insult you.'

'He's got a right to say whatever he likes, the same as anyone else in the audience. Do you think I can't deal with hecklers?'

'Please tell me you're not siding with someone who –'

'Oh, just go away, Olly,' she says. 'I want to be alone.'

Her words sting me into silence. I'm arguing with her. I want to carry on arguing with her. How does this happen?

'Rebecca, I didn't mean to –'

'Just go!' she shouts, and there are tears in her eyes. I can see from the muscles in her jaw that her teeth are clenched.

I have done this to her. When we arrived home she wasn't crying; now she is. I hate that I do this to people. I don't understand it. I was worried that getting caught at Grey Owl was going to torpedo my relationship with her. It turns out I'm quite capable of doing that on my own.

I realise my only real option is to do what she says. The Nylund option: run away. And so I leave the house, knowing that anyone else would find a way to make things better, that they would never have got into this situation in the first place.

—

'What's wrong, Olly?' Moira says, from somewhere very distant.

'Nothing. I'm fine.' Automatic, like an answering machine. I go up to my bedroom, haul up the ladder, close the hatch.

I can still see Rebecca's stare from the stage of the Fatted Calf, the furrow of her brow. I can still feel Andy and Paul tugging on my arms. I'm pacing up and down the length of the loft, something I try not to do because it can be heard in both bedrooms below. I sit on the bed, a bed I've longed to share with her, the two of us curled into one another.

The same thing used to happen with Kerry. I would be armed with the best of intentions, but something inexplicable would occur, something I wouldn't notice until too late. And out of it arose the frustration, the shouting, the tears, the slammed doors. And then a confused silence in which I realised, as if it was some kind of new idea, that the problem was me. Bloody hell. At least with Kerry I managed to hide my ruinous temper for more than three weeks. I thought I was getting better at this. What was it Dr Nylund said? His voice is distant now, an echo from a former century. He never really understood this feeling, but how could I expect him to? I was his lab rat, something to which he could apply his textbook theories.

The one thing I know I'm guilty of is hubris – the belief that I can maintain, or somehow deserve, a relationship with a woman. And the cost is that they fall by the wayside, one by one. Or rather I cut them down and pile up their bones like firewood, fuel for my fatal optimism, my insatiable desire for a normal life, this thing that everyone else seems to have, and to take for granted.

My thoughts are so dense they have acquired weight. The inexorable gravity of fate pulls at me, sapping strength and spirit. I know what I will do.

I untape the tiny plastic box from its hiding place on the underside of the bed frame and take the dozen sheets of toilet paper out of the bedside cabinet. I open the box and there is the solution: a bright steel rectangle, bisected with that bumpy slot which provides such an effective grip, even when my hands are sweaty and shaking. Just the one blade left now. I tip it into my hand and the coldness of it makes my arm twitch in premonition. I should have thrown it away when I made that promise to myself. Good thing I didn't.

I roll up the sleeve of my sweater and look at the diagonal cuts in the sensitive skin right up near the elbow – my Kerry cuts, the ones I made when I split up with her. My arms are like history books. I can trace my past right back to the very first cuts, the ones I made after Lambert's betrayal at school, some of the deepest, when I didn't know what I was doing, when I had to staunch the blood with T-shirts and sneak them out of the house to prevent any of my family from knowing.

You promised yourself you wouldn't do this again. Promised for Rebecca's sake.

I hold the razor blade against my arm, about halfway up, and feel the friction of it against the skin. My eyes sting with joy.

If she's never going to see me again, that releases me from my promise, right?

You don't know if she's through with you.

Just a few cuts. It won't be much. I need that searing relief, that emotional scouring.

How would she react if she knew?

She never will. I deserve it after a day like this.

But you don't know for sure that it's over.

I choke down a growl of frustration. I don't care. Just let me do it.

This was supposed to be a fresh start. A promise to yourself. A promise to her. If you're not going to give up cutting now, when will you? There are always going to be hard times. There will always be another excuse to fall back into it. If you split that skin, you've failed.

And the truth is that I can't bear the idea of more failure. I've destroyed my relationship with Rebecca, just like I did with every other girlfriend I've had. I've sent Trib packing. My family endure me with gritted teeth out of some sense of duty I no longer understand. Why don't they just have done with me? Why doesn't everyone? I would.

This is not a good line of thinking. I hear it in Nylund's voice. *What do you have to do to avoid cutting yourself?* Yeah, great question, Dr N. Great fucking question.

I want to achieve something. I want to succeed at something that actually matters to me. I want to be doing something energetic and exhausting and constructive. I want to be out with Trib on some lunatic quest for justice.

Well, perhaps you shouldn't have pissed all over that friendship too. I blink to try and clear my vision.

You self-pitying piece of shit.

I want to go down the ladder and hug Moira or Jodie, just for the human contact, the comfort. But they can never see me like this. Never.

The razor blade is hanging loosely between my thumb and forefinger. I've almost let it slip out of my grasp. I raise it again, and it glints in the light. I adjust my grip, place the sharp edge on my forearm. No: this is my way of coping. Denying myself the relief of cutting is just another form of self-harm.

I grit my teeth. It's bullshit and I know it; it's the worst kind of justification.

And then it comes to me, out of nowhere – why not go back to Trib? What have I got to lose? It's not like I can make our relationship any worse. I could at least find out if that avenue is closed to me forever. Hope – the thinnest of threads – pulls me back from the brink. Maybe I should beg and grovel at his front door. At the very least, I should say I'm sorry.

The thought gives me just a few grams of strength. I'm reminded of an email I once got from excutter1705: 'Every time you manage not to cut, it's a victory.'

I dry my face with the toilet paper, put the razor blade back in its box, and chuck the whole lot into the bin.

I try to feel victorious.

—

It's only after I ring the doorbell that I check my phone and find it's already half past eleven. There's no reply, and I start on a fresh round of doubts. If Trib isn't in, who the hell am I going to turn to? I ring again, and the door opens. Trib stands there, wearing a set of blue pyjamas. His eyes narrow as soon as he sees me. Was this really a good idea?

Then his expression softens, and he says, 'Jesus, you look awful.'

'You said I could drop round any time. I ... took you literally.'

He looks me up and down. 'You'd better come in, then.'

I've been in Trib's house before and it still looks like he's unpacking, even though he's lived here for years. There's no sense of organisation at all, just a random collection of furniture. Books sit in a cardboard box by the window and his television is a tiny, ancient box tucked away in a corner. If Moira saw the place, she'd have a fit. What he does have is lots of chairs, of all shapes and sizes. I take the straight-backed wooden one nearest the door and he sits opposite me.

'So, what brings you here, Olly?'

Huh. Where to start?

'Look,' Trib says, 'I'm sorry about what happened, but I really do believe I had all their security sussed.'

Oh, *that*. Yes, I suppose there is that as well. He's waiting for me to agree with him, but I can't.

After a moment he says, 'You realise we're never going to know the truth for sure.'

I've already accepted that there will never be a neat, unambiguous answer. Perhaps the question is not whether Trib knew everything about their setup, but whether he did his best to try to understand it. And why wouldn't he? Why would he endanger himself?

'You still think it's possible I missed something, don't you?' he says.

'Well ... yeah.'

'Fair enough.'

'You're not going to tell me I'm wrong?'

'I think it's highly likely you're wrong, but I accept your position. Who am I to tell you what to think?'

Yes, this is what I like about him – his open-mindedness, his undogmatic thinking. I take a deep breath.

'I'm sorry, Trib. Look, I trust that you did whatever you could.'

His shoulders lower by half an inch; the frown lifts from his face. 'I did.'

'And I didn't mean to call you –'

'A stupid, ugly, lard-arsed piece of shit?'

I wince.

'I think I'd have preferred a punch in the face.'

I look down into my lap. 'I'd never do that.'

'Oh, I don't know. I'd say it seemed a very real possibility.'

There's no way to answer that.

'Look,' he says, 'it's hard when things go to rat shit, I know, but that's the way it is. As Epictetus says, "Difficulties are things that show a person what they are."'

'Huh. So: I got royally pissed off and insulted you. That's the sort of person I am.'

'No,' Trib says. 'You came back to apologise. That's the sort of person you are.'

I don't deserve praise from him. I really don't.

'Trib, there's something I should have told you right from the start.'

'Yeah?'

I can't believe this. I can't believe I'm actually going to tell him.

'I've got a … a bit of a problem.'

'Go on.'

'With anger, I mean. I've had it for years.'

I'm expecting him to come straight back with a dry remark like 'no kidding' or 'yeah, I noticed that'. Instead he chews it over for a long time.

'Why?' he says at last.

I take out my phone and glance at the time. 'Look, it's late and I've stopped you from going to bed, and … and I should be –'

'Oh, shut up,' he says gently, and it's so unexpected that I do. 'You're not backing out that easily.'

From a cupboard in the corner he produces two shot glasses which he sloshes full of Glenlivet from a half empty bottle. He hands one to me and says, 'Chuck that down your throat and start at the beginning.'

18

THE CHANGING ROOM was a tired old prefab, freezing cold at this time of year and far too hot in summer. In my final year at Kingsmarsh Comprehensive I only ever felt dread in that room: the constant danger that Stendall might choose me as his target for the day. I could only imagine how much worse it was for Duncan Macklin, wedged into the corner nearest the door, as if he might, by some miracle, escape attention. I never looked at him for long. I didn't want any of the other kids to think there was an association between me and the class punch-bag.

Stendall was already starting on him, seizing the opportunity while Mr Crawford was out of the room.

'Hey, Dunc.'

Duncan pretended he hadn't heard.

'Hey, fat boy. You gonna be doing some more falling down for us today?'

Duncan busied himself re-tying his football boots.

'I reckon you are.' Stendall walked up and nudged him hard with one knee, toppling Duncan off the bench and onto the floor, then turned to receive his tribute of laughter from the rest of the boys. I dropped my head and rummaged in my bag.

'I've been looking forward to this all week,' Stendall said. 'I love a bit of exercise.'

He waited for Duncan to get back on the bench, then grabbed his football shirt and pulled the whole thing up over his head.

Stendall pinched the ample flesh on Duncan's belly and looked disgusted. 'Christ, we need to get some of this off you, boy. You're a fucking disgrace.'

I glanced over at Alex Attrill, who had been on the receiving end last week for failing to make an easy save while he was in goal. He laughed with the rest of them. It was the sound of relief, the sound of gratitude.

Our teacher returned, clapping his hands together as he strode in. 'Right. All set, lads?'

Stendall said, 'Duncan hasn't got his shirt on, sir.'

Mr Crawford was already heading out the door. 'Get a move on, Macklin.'

Our boot studs clacked on the concrete and our breath fogged in the air. The grass was more grey than green and the trees at the end of the playing field were like hands clutching at the sky. At this time of year, football was a miserable experience. We started with exercises – weaving a ball round some cones, penalty practice, that sort of thing. After about fifteen minutes Mr Crawford divided us into teams and blew his whistle to start a game. Then, as usual, he left us to it. The hot rumour was that Miss Spinks did the same thing with her netball class and they met up in the windowless PE office for a quickie.

Stendall took over, as was his custom. He was fairly new to the school, but no-one questioned his supremacy. His mum had joined at the same time, teaching History, and although he never relied on the association to get him out of trouble, it was always there, the ultimate backup.

Stendall regularly kicked the ball at Duncan, who was on the opposing team, and shouted something like, 'Shit, I've passed it to lard-face!' then proceeded to trip him up or rugby tackle him. The earth was cold, wet, and churned up by our boots. Soon they were both caked in mud and Duncan was bleeding from both shins.

After half an hour Stendall stopped buggering about and tried to score a few more goals. Duncan had had enough, and started to walk off the pitch. If Stendall spotted him, he'd be dead meat, so I decided to distract him with a reckless run for the goal. Alex Attrill tried to tackle me, but he was a skinny kid, and just bounced off my shoulder. I carried on through their defence. Jonesy – who was a much better player than me anyway – was ready to back me up, but I managed to boot the ball straight past the keeper and into the top right corner on my first attempt.

'Bloody nice one, mate,' Jonesy said, slapping me on the back.

While the rest of the team did victory high-fives and Stendall called his goalie a mong, I glanced in the direction of the changing rooms. Duncan was nowhere to be seen. If he was quick, he could shower, change, and miss the post-match humiliation entirely.

Stendall had spent so much time torturing Duncan that his team lost. At least that's the way the rest of us counted it: 7-6 against him. But when Mr Crawford reappeared at the end of the lesson, it was a different story.

'Good match, boys?'

'Yeah,' Stendall said. '8-7 to my team. I clawed it back in the last minute with a point-blank header.'

He looked round at the rest of us, inviting someone to contradict him. Alex Attrill, new best buddy and champion arse-licker, said, 'Yeah, sir. It was wicked.'

'Well done, that man. All right, back to the changing room.'

—

I was chatting to Jonesy on our way to Maths when Stendall appeared out of nowhere.

'Hello, Griffin,' he said. 'Think you're a bit of a hero, do you?'

Over his shoulder I saw Jonesy turning away, head down. I didn't blame him; I would have done the same. Stendall elbowed me in the stomach, driving all the air out of my lungs. My bag dropped out of my hand and I staggered two paces backwards. I tried to raise my head so at least I could see the next blow coming but I couldn't uncurl from the pain. Now he would knee me in the face. I'd seen him do it to other kids. Shit. *Shit*. I felt his hands on the back of my head and saw his Nikes come into view. I put one hand out to protect my face, keeping the other near my stomach and groin.

He let go and I heard his footsteps receding with the rest of the class. Then, Mr Crawford's voice: 'Carry on, Griffin. You'll be late for your next lesson.'

Mouth open but unable to speak, I stared after him as he walked past. Stupid old bastard. He knew what was going on. A blind man could have seen it. The corridor became silent and I took the time to recover my breath. When I was finally able to unbend I saw Duncan standing there alone, head tilted to one side.

'I saw what you did,' he said.

'What?'

'Distracting him.' His voice was high-pitched and husky, like an old man's, another thing people could take the piss out of.

'I was just trying to win the game.'

'You can't win against Stendall.' He produced a pack of cards from his bag. 'Come here. I want to show you something.'

'Look, I've got to –'

'Come here.'

He backed into an empty classroom. I was pretty sure Stendall had gone, so I followed him in. He fanned the cards to show they were mixed up, then shuffled them some more. He put the deck in his left hand and turned the top card over: the six of diamonds.

'Watch,' he said, and placed his right hand partially over the card. With a circular rubbing motion the card changed into the ten of diamonds.

'What?' I said. 'No way. Do it again.'

He looked me straight in the eyes. I expected him to make some excuse, or lower his head and shuffle off in that way he did, but he just kept staring. The expression was so unfamiliar on his face that it took me a while to realise what it was. Pride. He rolled up the sleeves of his sweater, rubbed the surface of the ten of diamonds, and turned it back into the six, right in front of my eyes. He turned his right hand over to show there was nothing concealed there. He wasn't palming the card. He just wasn't.

'That's impossible,' I said. 'How do you do it?'

'Not telling ya,' he said. This was so unlike him – the skill, the confidence. I realised that no-one in the school really knew Duncan Macklin.

I looked at my watch. 'I'm late for Maths. I've gotta go.'

But it didn't seem like enough, so I turned round at the door, pointed at the cards as he was slipping them back into their box and said, 'You know, that's pretty cool.'

He actually smiled.

—

Having found an audience, Duncan showed me more. We met at lunchtimes in the music room. Cards would disappear and reappear. They would rise from the deck as if they had a life of their own. He would find my choice of card between the pages of a book or hidden in my own back pocket. And the change in him was almost more amazing than the tricks themselves.

Was I Duncan's friend? I don't know. There was no denying he was a strange kid. No-one else at school picked their nose as shamelessly. No-one else had shoved so many empty crisp packets into their anorak pockets that they rustled as they walked. I just didn't think that being different was grounds for the kind of abuse he had to endure. And besides, there were plenty of other odd kids. I mean, Quentin Beezley was caught masturbating behind the bike sheds over a picture of a helicopter. How weird is that?

Outside the confines of the music room, things continued as they always did. Stendall moved on to other victims, but Duncan was never far from the spotlight. I refused to show any sign of approval with the taunts and laughter, and Duncan appreciated it. He recognised that even this pathetic rebellion was a risk. Meanwhile Stendall made even the teachers bow to him. Somehow he managed to maintain a reputation as the school's golden boy while simultaneously executing his reign of sadism. If the teachers saw anything of this, they were unable to reconcile it with their view of him – confident, charming, academically gifted.

—

I was on my way home from school, daydreaming about Vicky Barton and what she'd look like with no clothes on, when I looked up to see Stendall and Duncan a few paces up ahead. To an adult, this scene would appear perfectly innocent, just two friends walking home on a winter's day, exchanging the occasional word. One of them, they might notice, was slouched and spoke in mumbles, but that was just the way teenagers were, wasn't it?

There was a world, an entire world, that adults couldn't see.

Stendall stopped dead and turned to say something to Duncan, too quiet for me to hear. Duncan looked down at his feet. There was no pavement on the other side, so if I crossed the road it would look like I was trying to escape. Instead I decided to walk straight past, hoping his focus was on Duncan. Better for one person to be tormented rather than two.

'… just the natural order of things,' he was saying to Duncan. 'Like Darwin in that Biology lesson. Remember? God, I don't know why I bother.' I thought I'd made it past when Stendall's hand shot out and barred me.

'Hello, mate. Where do you think you're going?'

'Home,' I said, trying to conceal the sting of fear.

'Think again,' he said, smiling. 'I'm out for a leisurely little stroll, and neither of you two jerk-offs are gonna overtake me. Questions?'

We said nothing. He sniffed, stuffed his hands in his pockets and started walking. Duncan looked at me and pressed his lips together briefly – an apology, a commiseration?

Stendall's meandering path was designed to test our patience. He stopped frequently to check for something in his bag or re-tie his shoelaces. Our progress had slowed to a crawl when Stendall got a Game Boy out of his coat pocket and switched it on. Within seconds the dance of pixels and tinny electronic music had consumed his attention and he appeared to have lost interest in us. I decided to push at the boundary.

'One more step and I'll break your face,' he said, without taking his eyes off the screen. I stayed put.

The game took forever, the minutes stretched taut as guitar strings. Other people passed us, adults and other kids from our school. No-one said a word.

Finally he finished, pocketed the Game Boy and carried on walking. I prayed to God, literally, that he would get bored soon and release us, but there could be hours more of this.

We arrived at a bench and he plonked himself down in the middle.

'Sit,' he said, and we did, one on either side of him because it was the only way we'd fit. He slapped his arms down across the back of the bench and we both flinched. Then he decided to get the Game Boy out again.

Something snapped and I found myself saying, 'Why don't you give us a break?'

He looked up, and I heard the tumbledown buzz of a life being lost. Irritation crumpled his face. I expected an instant retort, but he took his time.

'Why don't you fuck off?' he said at last.

I stared. I tried not to stare. Was he letting us go? He made no move to stop me as I got gingerly to my feet. 'Come on, Duncan.'

'Not him. He stays.'

Although his head didn't move an inch, Duncan looked up at me. The orbits of his eyes were haunted half moons and his face sagged with misery. I looked at the empty space on the bench where I had been sitting just seconds ago.

'Go on,' Stendall said. 'Fuck off.'

I glanced towards home. The road was long and straight, a highway to freedom.

I turned back to Duncan and said, 'I'll see you tomorrow, yeah?'

'Not if I keep him here all week, you won't,' Stendall riposted.

Duncan was right – Stendall would always win. It was like a game of poker in which he had an infinite amount of money to spend. He would just keep raising the stakes until no-one could match him. I felt a nausea of self-hatred. So, this was freedom. This was how Alex Attrill felt.

—

'What can I do for you, Olly?'

Half an hour ago I had been stirred up with righteous indignation. Now I was actually sat in front of the headmaster, it had deserted me. Duncan had shown no obvious physical injury when he'd come in that morning, but Stendall's relentless persecution had clearly got to him. He was a snail, retreating into its shell. He didn't speak a word to anyone. When I asked about the lunchtime card trick he just shrugged.

'Erm …' I said to Mr Lambert. No. That was not the right way to start.

Mr Lambert's eyes were pale blue with a border of jet black between the white and iris. His hair was sparse, just a balding fuzz and a hint of beard. How old was he? 50? 60?

'I want to report a case of bullying, sir.' I tried to speak like my dad, that firm, focused tone that made people listen. This had been his idea. I'd told him about Duncan and Stendall yesterday, leaving out my own involvement, and he told me this was the right thing to do.

Mr Lambert smiled. 'We don't have bullying at Kingsmarsh Comprehensive.'

'Yes you do.'

The smile vanished. 'So, who is bullying you?'

'It's not me, sir, it's Duncan Macklin.'

'And the bully?'

'John Stendall.'

'I see,' he said, with a drop in tone. 'And when did this happen?'

I shook my head. 'It happens all the time.'

'All the time? You're suggesting that John is bullying Duncan on a regular basis without any of the teachers noticing?'

'Yes.' It lacked the emphasis I wanted, the conviction.

'And how is it that they haven't noticed?'

My dad said I should always tell the truth, and that was all I could do now, even though my faith in his advice was crumbling.

'Well?' Mr Lambert said.

'They look the other way.' There it was: the resentment in my voice I was trying so hard to conceal.

The volume of his voice halved. 'Be very careful what you say about my staff, young man.'

'Look, I know they can't be around all the time. I mean, he's not going to bully people in plain sight, is he?'

Mr Lambert sat back in his chair. 'Provide me with an example of this bullying.'

I told him about the endless trip home yesterday, a situation where his precious staff weren't around.

Once I'd finished, Lambert steepled his fingers. 'Did anybody else witness this?'

'I don't think so.'

'The judicial system of England operates on the principle that people are innocent until proven guilty. Now, do you have any proof – any real, concrete proof – about this incident, or any other?'

What was I supposed to do? Stick a video camera in Stendall's face and wait for him to abuse someone?

'Neither,' Lambert continued, 'do any of the other students who have made these complaints about John. Now, I understand John Stendall can be a formidable character, but he is an asset to this school. His grades are impressive, he conducts himself with confidence and pride, and he displays all the qualities of leadership. These constant attempts to undermine him have got to stop.'

My disbelief plummeted to new depths. So *I* was in the wrong? I clamped down hard with my teeth, grinding them together to prevent any sound escaping.

'You say the teachers are shirking their responsibilities,' he said, 'and then you furnish me with an example which conveniently happens beyond the school gates. Now, if you came to me with solid evidence of bullying – on school premises, during school hours – I would certainly look into it. But while it's your word against his, I have no option but to dismiss these accusations. John Stendall is one of our best; Duncan Macklin is, sad to say, an underachiever who needs to apply himself more diligently. He's the sort of boy that drags the school down. And you expect me to reverse my opinion of these two based purely on your word?'

But the truth; what about the truth?

'Listen, Olly. I'm going to do you a favour and assume your claims are frivolous rather than spiteful. You're a promising student yourself. Now, I suggest we put this all behind us and get back to what's important: your education.'

The ice blue eyes continued to bore into me and I left without another word. If he'd wanted the meeting to be an education, he'd succeeded beyond his wildest expectations. And the lesson was this: never trust anyone in authority.

—

PE again. Joy.

Duncan hadn't turned up yet. He was increasingly late to lessons, and bore the teachers' scorn with empty eyes, but I didn't think he'd skip PE entirely. Crawford had had words with his mum. We were in the gym this week. Stendall was already gearing up for his favourite lesson, talking the talk, gathering his generals.

'Right,' Mr Crawford said, 'who's going to help with the kit?'

'I will, sir,' I said. It was a way of keeping Stendall at a distance.

He passed the keys to me. 'Drag out the big crash mat, will you, Griffin?'

I unlocked the storeroom door, leaving the keys in the lock, and went in. From one of the white-painted box girders at the storeroom's roof hung a rope. And from the rope, perfectly still and calm, hung Duncan Macklin. The toes of his shoes were only six inches off the floor.

'Jesus,' I heard Mr Crawford say. 'Oh, Jesus Christ!' And then there was the sound of him shutting and re-locking the door behind me, removing the key. From beyond the storeroom, muffled and distant, were the sounds of rising panic. In here, though, it was just me and Duncan together. Just like lunchtimes in the music room. How had he managed to get in here without a key? Another of his small miracles.

Of course, none of this had really happened. Not yet. It couldn't have. I was seeing something that might come to pass. There were still a dozen things that could be done to help Duncan out. Other teachers could be told. There might be a government hotline.

It took minutes standing there, staring, for the facts to bludgeon their way through my consciousness. This wasn't the future. This was already history, gradually receding. The point at which something could be done had already passed. This was Duncan's final trick, and his most audacious: to make himself disappear.

19

I NOTICE TRIB's FINGERS trembling as he pours me another whisky. I chuck it down in one.

'So, then what happened?' he says, and I'm reminded that no, Duncan's death isn't the end of the story.

'I, uh …' I laugh abruptly, inappropriately; I don't know

where it comes from. 'You really want to know?'

'Of course.'

'I decided to kill Stendall.'

I expect this to shock him, but there's no hint of disapproval or judgement. There wasn't from Dr Nylund either, but his reaction was dispassionate and robotic. Trib's is entirely different.

'I mean, I genuinely intended to murder him.' I add this in case he doesn't understand the seriousness of what I'm saying. 'I took a kitchen knife into school and the idea was that I'd corner him in the toilet, or something like that, and just keep stabbing until he was dead.'

'Go on,' he says quietly. There is only empathy from him. This is what I need, not Nylund's analysis, not my own crushing sense of shame.

'The problem was I never saw him again. He wasn't in school the next day. He was off all of that week, and the next. His mum said it was because … the reason she gave was …' and here they are: the words so steeped in bitterness I can barely get them out '… because he was too traumatised by Duncan's death.'

'You are shitting me,' Trib whispers.

'I didn't know where Stendall lived. I suppose I could have found out somehow, but … I just didn't. And that was that. Crazy, isn't it? I dropped the idea of killing him because I didn't know where he lived. And soon after that they left the area. They just started their lives again somewhere else.'

'And what about you?'

'Me? I was in a kind of trance for weeks. Crawford got me to agree that he had been the first person on the scene, that I was with the rest of the boys. He said he would take responsibility for discovering Duncan. I just nodded and did what I was told. By the time I realised he was trying to cover his own arse for locking me in there, it was too late. It had become the official story.'

'Didn't you tell your mum and dad about it?'

'Oh, yeah. My dad went to see Lambert, but it was just like he said: if you're going to accuse someone of bullying a schoolmate to death, you'd better have some pretty serious proof. The school asked kids to come forward if they'd seen anything but, of course, no-one did. None of us knew at that point that Stendall wasn't coming back, so it would have been like informing on the Mafia with no witness protection scheme. The teachers were really just going through the motions; trying to make sure they weren't accused of negligence. Lambert was all over the local press, saying how it was a tragic loss, but that Duncan had always been 'troubled'. Such *bullshit*. But it stuck.

'Lambert destroyed my faith in authority. His version of events became the truth, not because he was right, but because he was in charge. In a way I'm glad, because he showed me how naive I had been. Until then, I'd thought that teachers and parents and leaders always did – or at least tried to do – the right thing. The more I questioned the idea, the more I saw people who were incompetent, egotistical, even psychotic. I began to see it everywhere.

'My parents took me out of Kingsmarsh too. They wanted a new start for me, but everything went downhill anyway. My grades fell. I argued with my new teachers, or skipped their lessons entirely. I could see Lambert in them. A lot of them really weren't fit to be in charge of a bunch of kids. They did it because they wanted to be important, not because they cared about our education. And they thought I was some kind of problem kid, being transferred because Kingsmarsh couldn't cope with me.'

We sit in silence for a while, that profound early-hours silence when everything is still. I could tell him more: about those early therapy sessions my parents put me through, how my dad ignored me because he didn't know how to deal with my mood swings. I could tell him about the arguments I used to have with Alistair, who was setting out to follow Dad into law and, from my point of view, was buying into the whole corrupt establishment. I could tell him that, deprived of the ability to hurt Stendall, I started to hurt myself. I could tell him about my recent success over the cutting and the struggle to stay on the straight and narrow. I could tell him how the anger ambushes me, just when I think I'm doing all right. I could tell him about the daily self-analysis; the strategies for managing my emotions; the endless, exhausting effort to be normal.

I'm too tired. I decide to give him the truncated version instead.

'I was angry with everyone and everything. It became a habit, an addiction. My God, you should have seen me back then, the things I put my family through. I wanted my parents to do terrible things, so that what I did would be justified. It was all so screwed up. But I knew I was the problem. I've got a lot better over the years, but I still struggle to keep a lid on it sometimes.'

Trib says, 'Like at Grey Owl?'

'Like at Grey Owl. Ever since Lambert, trust hasn't exactly come easily to me.'

'And you felt I'd broken your trust by not finding all their security measures?'

I nod.

'Do you still think that?' he says.

'That you broke my trust? No. No, I don't.'

He pours us each a third whisky. The burn of the spirit at the back of my throat gives me the courage to say what I've wanted to say since I got here. 'What I like about you is that although the world is full of bastards, you're actually doing something about it instead of turning a blind eye. You're showing people that acting like an arsehole isn't going to wash. I love that. And I wish I'd been doing the same thing all these years, instead of … whatever the hell I was doing.'

'Hold on a minute. You're angling to carry on? After what happened at Grey Owl?'

'Yeah, because you were right: I *need* the missions. But there's something you need too.'

'What's that?'

'You need someone as angry as me.'

He blinks. 'I'm not sure I follow your logic.'

'We wouldn't have dumped that chair in Summer's house if he hadn't pissed us off. Neither of us would have bothered. You've said how frustrating it is that people won't get up off their arses. That's because they don't have any fire in their belly.'

'There's a difference between having fire in your belly and chewing your mates to pieces.'

'Yeah, I know, I know. But that's why I need this. I need to … turn it into something positive.'

He bites his top lip and sighs. 'Shit, Olly. I don't know. I've got a lot sympathy with that. Really, I do. The problem is, I can't risk you suddenly losing it again during a mission.'

'I didn't lose it during the mission. I followed our escape plan to the letter. I lost it afterwards.'

He's about to reply, but stops himself. 'I suppose so,' he says.

'During the mission I was too busy shitting myself to be angry.'

'Ha. You as well, eh?'

'Look, Trib, what do you need from me? A promise that I won't lose my temper with you again? You've got it.' Am I in any position to say this? The intention, at least, is pure.

He sits back, folds his arms and appraises me. 'Shall I tell you what your problem is?'

He's goading me; I can see that immediately. I will remain calm. 'I'm listening.'

'You haven't learned how to embrace the possibility of failure.'

'Oh, I think we failed all right.'

'That's not what I mean. The stuff we've done … you can't remove the risk. You can minimise it, and we did, but there's always going to be some element of danger. You have to accept that you might screw up.'

'Yeah, of course, but I'd still prefer it if there was no risk involved.'

'No, you wouldn't,' he says.

'Er … I'm pretty sure I would.'

He looks around the room. 'Hand me that pen, will you?' He points to a biro on the coffee table.

I pass it to him, and look round for something to write on.

'How do you feel about that?' he says.

'About what?'

'Handing me that pen.'

I'm not following him. 'How can I have any feelings about that?'

'No,' he says. 'You've not answered the question. *Tell me what you feel about it.*'

'I feel nothing at all.'

'And what were your chances of failing to hand me that pen?'

'Trib, I haven't had *that* much whisky.'

He arches one eyebrow.

'Okay, my chances of failure were basically zero.'

'Right. Now imagine you've just come back from an expedition where you climbed to the top of Everest. How do you feel about that?'

'Bloody brilliant. And –' I'm ahead of him here '– in that case, the chance of failure is high.'

'So, those two things – the chance of failure and the feeling of accomplishment – are related. The possibility of failure is what makes something worth doing. It's a bit like Popper's theory of falsifiability.'

'Popper's what?'

He flaps his hand as if to dismiss it, then changes his mind. 'Popper worked on the philosophy of science. He said that for a hypothesis to be scientific, you have to be able to design an experiment to test it. If I asked you a question like, "Is there a God?", there's no experiment you can devise that will confirm whether that's true or not; therefore it's a non-scientific question. Now, if your scientific theory can be tested, there's a chance it'll be proved false. So, the very thing that gives science its value is, paradoxically, the possibility that any scientific theory might, at any time, be proved wrong. It's the same with our missions. The possibility of us failing is what gives them value.'

'That's some pretty twisted logic.'

'And anyway,' he continues, 'failure isn't as bad as it's cracked up to be. You always learn more from bollocking something up than getting it right.'

'Like trial and error?' I suggest.

'Yeah, that's it – trial and error.'

An idea occurs to me. 'So, if I bollocked things up with you after the Grey Owl mission, and now I've learned from it, then that's just trial and error – it's just part of the process and there's no reason for us not to continue.'

He thinks this over for a moment, trying to find a flaw in my argument. So do I.

'Oh,' he says, 'you're a clever bugger. You should be a politician.'

And, to my amazement, I can see him caving in. 'Trib, look, I embrace the possibility of failure. I trust you. I place my safety in your hands.'

He fights a smile. 'You know, Olly, I've never met anyone quite like you.'

Funny – that should be my line.

'So, if I behave myself, you'll let me back in?'

He laughs. 'Mate, how can I refuse?'

20

'How was your weekend?' I ask Steph, trying to sound as casual as possible as I hang up my coat and switch on my PC. I've come in a little earlier, so it's just the two of us. I want to dip my toe in the water.

'Short,' she says, without looking at me, her fingers clacking on the keyboard.

She's spoken with Rebecca, hasn't she? So this is how it's going to be: terse words and long silences loaded with disapproval. It can only get worse from here. I should have twigged that going out with her friend could backfire. She finishes typing, then swivels in her seat to face me.

'I'm sorry, Olly. Yes, it was okay. We didn't get out much because of the rain. How about you?'

'Yeah, good.' I run the sentence straight into another, because I don't want her asking about Rebecca. 'Listen, is there anything else I can help you with? I can probably spare an hour today.'

'Thank you, but no. I am stuck in.'

So, it appears I'm in the clear for the time being. I'd spent a long time yesterday wondering how to patch things up with Rebecca, even writing several abortive drafts of a letter on actual paper. The idea was to express myself fully without any possibility of being drawn into an argument. But it turned out I couldn't express myself nearly as well as I'd hoped. If I didn't know what mood she was in, how could I know what to write? In the end I'd bought a box of truffles from the specialist chocolate shop on Castle Street and posted them through her letterbox with a note saying, 'Please phone me'. They say actions speak louder than words, but there's been no response yet.

Steph has already turned back to her screen, and as she closes a couple of windows I notice the wallpaper on her PC has changed to a flat, default blue.

'Where's the picture of Sophie?' I ask.

She purses her lips. 'Jane told me to remove it. She said having baby pictures on my computer was unprofessional.'

'Why? Everyone else has pictures of their family.' I glance across at Andy's desk and his framed photo of Nigella. I'm surprised his adoring gaze hasn't bored two holes in it by now.

'Yes,' she says, 'but not my daughter, for some reason.'

The two photographs on her desk are also gone.

'That's out of order, Steph.'

'Yes, but what do you do?'

'Go to HR and file a complaint.'

'It will do me no good to upset the potato cart.'

'The apple cart.'

'Whatever. She will find out I went to HR and then I will be in even more trouble. She detests me.'

It's undeniable that Steph bears the brunt of things. At the rate Jane is going, Steph is never going to have to buy herself coffee again. I think, in a vague sort of way, that something has to be done about this, but my own problems and fixations have soon assumed priority. I can't go beyond tonight without phoning Rebecca. I've given her time to contact me, time to calm down. If I leave it any longer we'll be splitting up by default. I'll plead, if that's what it takes. I'll do penance. Still, there's nothing I can do until tonight. Right now I need distraction; I need ways to occupy my mind. And so I cram every spare minute with extra tasks. I'm constantly juggling things, constantly busy.

'What's got into you?' Dom says just before lunch, having noticed my flurry of activity.

'This shit isn't going to do itself, Dom.'

'Yeah,' he says, 'but here's the problem: the more you achieve now, the more you'll be expected to achieve in the future. You're dooming yourself to a lifetime of hard work.'

'Is this your roundabout way of admitting you're lazy?'

He ignores this. 'I hope you're not naive enough to be angling for a pay rise. Since the Western economy is collapsing, you'll probably never see one again. And the only way you're going to get promoted is if you kill Jane and hide her body somewhere.'

I stare at him, as if I'm seriously considering the idea.

'You're worrying me,' he says. 'Do I need to call security?'

—

I phone Rebecca at six o'clock. She should be home from her shift by now, but I can't get hold of her on land-line or mobile, and I don't want to leave a message. Instead, I sit in front of the TV, having accepted Jodie's invitation of a mindless rom-com. I wonder if it's a good idea to be watching something about relationships, but this idealised Hollywood romance is so far removed from anything in my own experience that I might as well be watching an insect mating ritual.

My phone rings and I snatch it off the coffee table. It's Rebecca.

'Hello?'

'Hi.' Her voice sounds very distant.

I retreat to the kitchen and close the door on the TV. 'Hi. Erm ... how –?'

'Come round?' she interrupts, phrasing it like a question.

'Yeah. I'll be five minutes.' It takes ten to walk to her house.

'See you soon.'

I hang up, go through the lounge to the front door and start putting my shoes on.

'Aren't you going to watch the rest of this?' Jodie says, leaning over the back of the sofa. The DVD is paused, the actors suspended in mid-sentence, waiting for their lives to continue. For the first time since the beginning of the movie, I empathise with them.

'Rebecca,' I blurt helplessly, explanation and excuse all in one word.

Jodie still thinks our relationship is new and fresh and uncomplicated. She rolls her eyes in the manner of a long-suffering parent. 'Go on, then.'

I arrive at Rebecca's house just as the first drops of rain fall. Sheltering under her porch, I ring the bell. I shift my weight from one foot to the other, pull my sleeves down. When she opens the door, she looks different. In part it's the bottle green dress that plunges at the neckline and hugs her figure before flaring out at the waist. Is she wanting to go out somewhere? Her face seems to have changed too, though it's difficult to say exactly how. It's like my memory of her has drifted off course in the past two days. Without a word, she gestures me through to the lounge. At her prompting I take a seat on the sofa, but Rebecca remains standing.

'What do you ... umm ...' she begins, but doesn't finish the sentence. She licks her lips and her eyes dart around, looking anywhere except at me. It's not just her appearance that's changed, it's her manner. Is this really the same woman I saw commanding an audience of a hundred in The Crown? This is her understudy, surely – someone who hasn't had time to prepare for the part.

'I'm sorry for sending you away,' she says.

'You had to. It's fine. I understand.' Of course, it's only fine because she's invited me back.

'That can never happen again, you know. With the guy at the pub, I mean.'

'Agreed.'

'I've already got an overprotective father; I don't need an overprotective boyfriend too.'

Does this mean we're still a thing? 'I promise you – it will never happen again.'

'I was pretty horrified at the time, but looking back, it probably seemed worse than it was. I know you're not a brawler.'

I keep my mouth tightly shut. How little you know me, Rebecca. How little I've really let you into my life. And yet I can't tell her the truth about my anger, about my fears over where it might lead me. She's rationalising my behaviour, and if reconciliation is in the air, I can hardly blow it with a destructive outbreak of honesty. My friendships, my confidences, are gradual things that take months or years of nurturing. And anyway, maybe her assessment of me is more accurate than I realise. The person I was yesterday is not necessarily the person I'll be tomorrow, right? Right?

'I thought it might be over between us,' I confess.

'Would that be such a bad thing?'

'Yes!' I explode. 'At least, from my point of view it would.'

I notice the tiniest contraction of the muscles at the corners of her eyes and lips, an incipient smile. Joy bursts in my chest.

'I just wondered if …' she says, 'maybe you were thinking of …'

Is she testing me? 'What are you saying?'

She shifts her weight, folds her arms. 'I'm not always an easy person to be with – the time for practising, the whole moody musician thing. I guess I just wanted to be sure this was workable.'

'You're kidding, aren't you? How long did we stay up talking the other night? Have you not noticed me following you around for the past few weeks like an adoring puppy?'

'Yeah,' she says, 'but …'

'But nothing,' I insist.

'You …' she says, and breaks off with a tut. She turns to the left, to the right, as if some convenient words might be found in the corner of the room. She leans forwards and grabs the front of my shirt, like a bouncer about to deliver a head-butt. She shakes me against the back of the sofa. At this point I'd be happy for her to slap me in the face, if that's what we need to mark a fresh start.

Instead, she puts one knee on the sofa and leans down to kiss me. I get a glimpse of cleavage just before I tilt my head back and her lips collide with mine. Since I first kissed her, Rebecca's lips have exerted a powerful effect on me, but this time is different: it's a four-minute-warning kiss, the sort of kiss you give someone when the bombs are already falling. She puts one hand on the back of the sofa and one on the wall so she can lean in closer.

She's in the perfect position for me to skirt the hem of her dress and glide my hands up the outsides of her thighs. She inhales in one long breath, as if her breathing is dependent on the height of my hands. I encounter the swell of her hips, then the edge of her knickers.

'Yes,' she says. So vague. So encouraging.

I decide to go for broke. I hook my fingers into the elastic of her knickers, and begin to tug them down. She pulls back and her eyes are wide with surprise. Maybe I should apologise, but the idea comes from somewhere distant, like a voice from the bottom of a well, easy to ignore. I want her, badly. I have done for weeks. She can always say no. Please don't say no. The sound of her breathing is the only thing I can hear – three loud, ragged exhalations before she leans in for another kiss, a nibble of my earlobe.

'Take them all the way off,' she whispers, millimetres from my ear. I slide them down to her knees, at which point she stands and pulls me up by my shirt. The knickers, a virginal white cotton, fall around her ankles. I step on them accidentally, and Rebecca trips. She pulls me over, yelping. My forearms absorb the impact with the floor, and I manage to cradle her head in one hand before it hits the carpet. The entire lengths of our bodies are in contact. Her thighs rise on either side of me.

'Are you okay?' she says.

'Never better.' I can feel the hammer of her heartbeat against my chest. Rain lashes against the patio door.

'Take me upstairs,' she murmurs.

'Let me check my diary.'

'Screw your diary.'

She wraps both legs around me and pulls me down. We never make it to the bedroom.

21

I RETURN TO THE TABLE with two half pints of orange juice and put them down next to the cribbage board.

'Cheers, mate,' Trib says dismally.

'It's good for you.'

'That's as may be,' he says, 'but it's a bugger having to drink this bloody stuff after a hard week's work when they've got Red Plum, Hole Hearted and Sneck Lifter on tap.'

'There'll be another time.'

We're sat in a nook at the Malt and Hops, another busy pub of Trib's acquaintance.

'What's happening with Bruce?' he says.

I glance over at the dark-haired man with the handlebar moustache. He's sitting with three mates at a table in the corner, their conversation inaudible from here. We've dubbed him Bruce because he's drinking Foster's. There's a touch of desperation in his enjoyment, his guffaws abandoned and overzealous. We can only speculate why.

I turn back to Trib. 'He's just starting another pint.'

'His fourth.'

'Yep.'

'We've got a bit of time, then.' Trib fans his cards and squints at them. He's 13p up, because I'm not really concentrating on the game.

I'm thinking about Rebecca, and the abrupt turn our relationship has taken. The urgency of our sex on the lounge floor meant I could keep my top on, and my scars hidden. Since then I've used the phobia excuse that worked so well with Kerry, and Rebecca has accepted it without question. If she gets too near my inner arms, I contrive to wriggle out of her grasp, or pin her arms to the bed. She makes no complaint about this. Quite the opposite. She goads me on. I've never had sex so cathartic, so noisy.

She's different in the mornings: more subdued, quieter. She's definitely an evening person, which is hardly surprising given that at one end of the day she has to get to the supermarket early to gut fish, and at the other she can be playing, or composing, or making love.

'Come on,' Trib says, 'chuck two in the crib.'

The game. Concentrate on the game. I throw in an ace and an eight.

'What's the highest score you can get in one hand?'

'Twenty-nine,' he says. 'You need the jack and three fives in your hand, then you turn over the last five as the starter card, and it's the same suit as your jack. Fifteen-sixteen, twelve for pairs and one for his nob: twenty-nine. I take it from your question that you've got a handful of crap.'

Bluffing and deception are all part of the game. For a while, I thought Trib was scratching his nose when he had a good hand. Now I think he's scratching his nose when he wants me to *think* he's got a good hand.

'A jack and all the fives,' I muse. 'So that's what I'm aiming for.'

'You'll be lucky. The odds are tiny.'

'You've never seen it, then?'

'God, no. Don't know anyone who has.' Trib lowers his cards. 'Ah! I almost forgot.'

'What?'

'I've got some good news. Leticia phoned me up and said she's got her car back.'

'What? Just like that?'

'They obviously lost their bottle. Think about it from their point of view: you're keeping people's cars illegally in the hope that they'll pay up to make the hassle stop, then someone breaks into your premises and suddenly the police are crawling all over the place. That's got to put the fear of God into you. And you realise either the police or the courts are eventually going to make you give the cars back, or someone's going to break in and take them. It's a no-win situation. So you give the cars back and say, like they did to Leticia, that there's been a computer error.'

'Ah yes, that old chestnut.'

'She asked me to pass on her thanks to you. So, you see, even our screw-ups are successes.' He plays with the order of his cards. 'She still asked what she owed me.'

'She's grateful, that's all.'

'And I appreciate that, but why does everything have to be a financial transaction?'

'It's one of the cornerstones of society, I guess.'

'I've no problem with it being *a* cornerstone of society; I've got a problem with it being the only cornerstone. Why does *everything* have to be that way? Why does politics have to be so governed by money when it should be about ideals and policies? Why are schools and universities obsessed by profit when they should be focused on the quality of the teaching? Even the charities are at it now, hiring people, for money, in order to make more money. You know what I'm saying?'

'Yeah.'

'We're going backwards.'

'You sound like a bitter old man, Trib.'

'That's because old men remember a time when things weren't so ... unilateral. I mean, if someone bought you an expensive Christmas present, would you feel you owed them something of equal value?'

'Kind of.'

'There you go,' he says. 'We're all brought up to be accountants, whether we like it or not.'

'That's a depressing thought. But you can balance the books by paying in kind. You know the sort of thing: you fix my central heating; I'll teach you how to play tennis.'

'Sure, and I love that sort of thing. But even better is the idea of doing something as a gift, with no expectation of anything in return. And the only way you can really do that is if the person you're doing it for never knows about it.'

'You don't even want the praise for having done it?'

'Praise is nice, I grant you, but even that's a kind of transaction. I like the purity of doing something only for itself. And if there's no-one to praise me for it, I can always congratulate myself.'

I'm about to tell him it's easy to congratulate yourself. Then I realise it's not true, not even remotely.

Trib carries on: 'Virtue is sufficient for happiness, said our mate Socrates. And he's right: I'm never happier than when I've helped someone out.'

'You like quoting him, don't you?'

'I've got to have something to show for my three years at uni.'

'And anyway, we can always slap each other on the back.'

'There is that. Just promise you're not going to start worshipping me as a hero.'

We both laugh at the idea, but when I think about it, that's kind of what he is. He couldn't be further from the Hollywood idea of a hero – someone with a chiselled jaw and a six-pack who kills lots of bad guys and runs off with the prettiest girl in the vicinity. He's purer than any of those lurid, comic-book sorts. It's easy to fight injustice if you're bulletproof, have laser-beam eyes and can fly. Trib is overweight, clumsy and has a face like a sack of spuds. His only superpowers are a towering sense of decency and cast iron bollocks.

From the table in the corner I see Bruce and his three friends standing.

'He's going.' I start to get up. 'We're on.'

'Not so fast,' Trib says. 'He'll need to go to the loo first.'

'You reckon?'

'Unless he's got a bladder like a beach ball.'

Trib's right. He says goodbye to his mates and heads to the gents, giving us time to pack up our game and walk outside to Trib's van. We get in and wait for Bruce to emerge. I'd spotted him this time last week, when Trib and I had been sampling the delights of the Malt and Hops's bar and their gourmet sausages. We'd watched him slump into his metallic grey Astra, rev the engine far too hard, and lurch out of the pub car park. He'd narrowly missed another guy on the road, who, equally pissed, had slammed a hand on the roof as he passed and said, 'Oi! Watch it!' So, here we are, waiting to see if Bruce does it again.

'It's the Vauxhall, isn't it?' Trib says.

'Yeah.' I read the registration number off the back. '2.0 litre engine.'

'It's not going to be a race,' Trib says.

Bruce comes out of the pub and saunters to his car.

'We're about to find out.'

He gets in, starts the engine, and drives out onto the street. We follow. He's going slower this time, but once he's out on the open road he speeds up. He's heading out of Strathurst and into the country, which is probably why he thinks he's safe from the police. In the manner of drunk drivers everywhere, he keeps drifting towards the nearside, then abruptly straightens up when he gets too close to the hedge. Trib tries to match his speed without looking too much like he's following, although it's possible Bruce isn't noticing a damned thing in his mirrors anyway. The road opens up into a junction with a set of traffic lights, and Bruce sails straight through the red. Luckily for him there's no traffic on the side roads to take him out.

'Arsehole,' I mutter. I'm about to say more when I realise Trib is braking. 'What are you doing?'

'It's a red.'

'But we have to go through. We'll lose him!'

'It's a red!' he repeats, coming to a stop and applying the handbrake.

Bruce's car disappears round the bend.

I turn to Trib and splutter, 'What part of "car chase" do you not understand?'

'I'm not risking an accident.'

'You can get through here easily. The junction's clear. Just do it!' I'm virtually bouncing up and down in my seat.

Trib gestures helplessly at the traffic lights. As if on demand, they turn amber. He drops the brake, stamps on the accelerator and pulls away from the junction with everything his poor van can muster. The engine groans like a wounded animal as he crunches up through the gears.

I slap the dashboard. 'Go, go, go!'

'All right, I'm going!'

We weave our way through the winding roads, left, right, left again, trying to regain sight of him. The hedgerows flow past on either side. Twigs and leaves rustle as they brush the wing mirror.

'That's more like it!'

'Are we having fun?' Trib says, his knuckles white on the steering wheel.

'Hell, yes!'

As we pass a wooden sign for Barfoot's farm the road straightens and the two red pinpoints of light re-appear.

'See,' Trib says, as we gain on him. 'O, ye of little faith.'

I lean forward and squint. 'That's not him.'

'What?'

'Wrong number plate.'

Trib catches up with the car, a Fiat, and keeps a safe distance. 'I can't overtake on a road like this,' he says.

I'd like to tell him to try anyway, but he's right: there are too many tight bends, and double white lines down the middle of the road. We just have to sit behind the guy. He's doing a decent speed, but I don't know if we're losing ground to Bruce. I don't even know how much we've caught up since the traffic lights.

'This may not work out,' Trib says. 'We might have to try again another time.'

'You're not giving up.'

'Not yet. I just don't want –'

'Good. Me neither.'

Leaning over to one side as we go into another bend, I get a glimpse past the Fiat. 'There are two cars in front of him.'

'Are either of them our man?'

'Don't know.' It's impossible to get a good view past the Fiat to see if either is driving erratically.

The cars slow. Ahead of us, the road ends in a T-junction.

'Shit,' Trib says.

The Fiat in front of us indicates right. I see a pulse of white light as the driver in front of him flashes his headlights. The cars peel off in order: left, right and right.

'Umm ...' says Trib and indicates right.

'No. Go left,' I tell him.

'Are you sure?'

'Trust me: left.'

Trib changes his indicator, takes the corner and accelerates again. We gain on the single remaining car, and as we get closer we can see it's Bruce's number plate.

'You're a genius!' Trib says.

We reach the outskirts of a village. Bruce slows at the first row of houses and turns onto a driveway, his car bumping over the higher part of the curb as he cocks up his approach. Trib drives past, takes the next left into a cul-de-sac and parks the van by the side of the road. We wait for a couple of minutes, giving Bruce plenty of time to stagger out of his car, find his keys, drop them, try to insert the wrong one, and eventually disappear into his house. Then Trib starts the engine, does a three-point turn and goes back onto Bruce's road, parking the van a few doors down from his house – inconspicuous but close enough to see that an upstairs light is on.

I sit there, fidgeting, still hyper from the chase. It's eleven o'clock now, and the windows of the nearby houses are dark. After a few minutes Bruce's light goes out too. We give him another ten minutes to drift into an inebriated slumber.

Finally, Trib snaps on a pair of latex gloves and says, 'Right, let's go.'

We get out of the van, closing the doors as quietly as we can. As we approach his house Trib bursts into a grin. He pulls on one earlobe and points up at the window. From behind the pane I can just make out the thunderous rasp of Bruce's snoring.

Trib takes the plastic tub out of his pocket, removes the lid, and with a flick of the wrist chucks fake blood over the radiator grill and bonnet of the Astra. With one gloved hand he smears it around for a more realistic effect, admires his handiwork, and nods. I don't know how it will appear tomorrow morning when Bruce sees it, but in the sickly yellow glow of the street lights it looks like he's run over something pretty substantial. Trib peels off the gloves, shoves them in the tub and puts the lid back on. We go back to the van and drive off.

—

Twenty minutes later we're back at Trib's place.

'Is that stuff permanent?' I ask him.

'No, it'll wash straight off.'

I shed my shoes and we go through into the lounge.

'Now,' Trib says, 'since we've had to sit in a pub without being able to make good use of the bar …' He produces half a dozen bottled beers from his booze cupboard and places them on the table in front of me, along with two glasses and a bottle-opener.

'Have a shufti at them while I visit the little boys' room.'

They're exotic enough that I've never heard of any of them, but they all look intriguing. I pick out the Ceylon IPA, with its picture of a Raj-era moustachioed cricketer, and the Tolstoy Russian Imperial Stout.

The phone rings. I hesitate for a moment, then pick up. 'Hello?'

The toilet flushes.

'I'm after John,' a woman says in a Yorkshire accent.

'He'll be with us in a minute. Who's calling?'

'I'm his mother,' she says, in a tone that suggests I should already know this. 'A friend of his, are you?'

'Yes.'

'Aye? Well, I'd watch me back if I were you.'

'Sorry?'

'Is he there yet?'

Trib walks back into the room and I pass the phone to him. 'It's your mum.'

During the conversation that follows, his face hardens. He doesn't say much more than a 'yeah' or 'okay' every few seconds. He ends by saying, 'I'll be there as soon as possible.'

He hangs up and says to me. 'Sorry, mate. I have to go to Sheffield.'

'Sheffield? What, now?'

He glances at the clock on the wall, a cheap white plastic thing. 'I can probably make it by four o'clock. It's my nan,' he explains. 'She's been taken into hospital and ... it doesn't look good.'

'Then what are you waiting for?'

'I'm sorry to ... It's just ... she always gave me so much support when I was growing up.'

'Don't worry about it. Do what you have to do.'

I follow him back out to the van, give him some more words of encouragement, and see him off.

22

I'VE MANAGED TO STALL her for a couple of weeks, but it was inevitable that Rebecca was going to see an episode of *Obedience* eventually. We watch it at her house, so at least I don't have to endure Jodie's infuriating, if well-intentioned, comments. Increasingly the challenges aren't about allowing slugs to crawl across your face, or climbing into a bath of maggots, presumably because the audience has seen all this sort of stuff before. They're much more interested in things that are embarrassing, shameful or socially questionable, such as stripping off naked in front of the audience. This is done with strategic pixelation, so the voyeurs who have voted for this are denied the very thing they were promised.

Zach continues to spar with the presenter. In retaliation, Nat has started to refer to my brother as 'Zed-Jee', something Zach pretends not to notice. I imagine this is a difficult balancing act for Zach. If he disrupts the programme too much, the director will presumably cut and re-shoot. In fact, what I'm seeing is what they've let him get away with. How much more is there on the cutting room floor? Maybe I owe the director my thanks that this isn't even more cringeworthy. I try to make a comedy of the whole experience because I don't want Rebecca to see how much it gets to me. Predictably, she sees right through it.

'Why does it matter to you what he does with his life?'

'I don't know, it's just …' I have to think for a long time to pin it down. It's not enough to say, 'because he's my brother', nor to say that I don't like the show he's on. I mean, I wouldn't choose to go into law like Alistair, but the fact he's a lawyer doesn't irritate me at a fundamental level. In the end I tell her, 'It's probably because I grew up with him and he used to be so different. He was always a cheeky git, but he was good fun too; we were mates. Now he's so shallow, so self-absorbed.'

She nods thoughtfully. 'Of course, you don't *have* to watch it.'

'Yes, I do. I promised him.'

'That at least makes you a man of your word.'

I like that she's found a positive way of seeing it.

Zach phones me up later that night while we're at Rebecca's finishing off a Thai green curry and says, 'All right, bro? How's it going?'

'Not too bad. I'm going out with this new girl, Rebecca.' I get this in quickly because it might be my one and only chance to tell him.

'Oh, yeah? What's she like?'

'She's wonderful.' I glance over to see her pursing her lips. 'Really wonderful.'

'Cool. Say hi from me,' he says. 'Listen, I'm in *Bonkers*.'

'You're what?' I can't make sense of his sentence.

'I'm in *Bonkers* magazine.'

'Oh.' I've vaguely heard of it.

'You've gotta check it out.'

'Right.'

'You are still watching, aren't you?'

'Yeah, I am.' Just don't ask me what I think of it. But he doesn't, perhaps because he already knows. In ignorance, he can maintain the delusion that we all love him unconditionally.

'Well,' he says, 'I've got to be going. Good luck with the new girl.'

'Yeah, cheers.'

He hangs up.

'That was my brother, Zach,' I tell Rebecca. 'He says hi.'

'Hi, Zach,' she says.

—

I start flicking through a copy of *Bonkers* at the corner shop, but the owner gives me a pointed look and I feel obliged to buy it. I search for the article on Zach as I walk back home. *Bonkers* is a well-named magazine. Half its pages are filled with crazy, laddish stuff that's hard to believe (and therefore probably made up); the other half is devoted to pneumatic women pouting at the photographer with an unhappy kind of lust. The bit about Zach is next to an article on Britain's best snipers, in a section called 'Gone to the Blog', which makes me wonder whether I could have read this on their website instead of having to buy the magazine and finance the people who write it.

> And so we come to *Obedience* (9:00pm Tuesdays, FizzTV) which is car crash telly at its very best.
>
> Contestants have to follow a set of horrible tasks, and the ones who screw up most get voted off. Which is great, and as long as they keep insulting each other and making themselves vomit, I'll be watching. But what *really* makes it is the battle of wills between host Nat and chirpy little gobshite ZG.
>
> Don't vote him off, guys. He's the best thing in the show, and I'll be gutted if he doesn't make it to the final. And talking of the final, I've got my fingers crossed that it involves ZG and Nat sumo-wrestling in a colossal arena of shit.
>
> Who says there's nothing worth watching on the box these days?

There has been other coverage of *Obedience* – Moira has shown me a piece in the paper that asks why, oh why, oh why do we need to see this sort of thing on TV – but Zach has chosen to point me at an article that describes him as a 'chirpy little gobshite'. I don't understand my brother, I really don't.

I take a single page of the magazine and rub it between my fingers. Nope, not even good enough to wipe my arse with. I chuck it in a public bin without even taking it home. I don't want Moira or Jodie – or worse, Rebecca – finding it.

That night I dream I'm in the *Obedience* studio with Nat, throttling the smug little wanker with his own whip. I wake up in a confusion of shame, fear and delight. Why can't I have the same kind of dreams that normal people have, like going to work with no trousers on, stuff I can laugh off in the bright reality of morning?

—

On Wednesday, I turn up at work to find Steph having an argument with Andy, of all people.

'I don't see what your problem is,' Andy is saying. 'It's clearly Jane's responsibility.'

'What is this word you use?' she says, 'Responsibility? Hah! You think Jane is *responsible* for the IT department?'

'Well, yes.' Andy is sitting back in his chair while Steph, who is standing, leans towards him.

'No. She is *in charge* of IT. There is a difference. She has been promoted beyond the level where she is responsible for anything. You need an example? The project plan for the integration work. This is supposed to be something she does, yes? But no, she gives it to me. And when I show her the plan she says, "This is not acceptable. You have to finish two weeks earlier."'

Andy opens his mouth, but Steph hasn't finished. 'This morning, you know what she says? "The plan is failing," she says, "and it is your fault, because you wrote it." So, you see she is not responsible for anything. She enjoys all the benefits of being a manager, but when something goes wrong: bang! It is on me.'

'You've got to stand up for yourself more,' Andy says. Given how red Steph's face is, this strikes me as pretty foolhardy.

'And you will tell me how to do this, please?'

'You could go to HR and tell them –'

'You think I have not tried this? You think I am a pathetic little girl who cannot deal with the stress of work?'

Andy holds his hands up defensively. 'Whoa, I didn't say that.'

'I have already seen the head of HR and told him all about my frustrations. His answer: "If you are unhappy here, maybe you should work somewhere else."'

There's a collective noise of disbelief from Andy, Dom and myself. Andy says, 'You're kidding.'

'Do I look like I am kidding?' she demands. No, she looks like someone about to burst a blood vessel.

'So,' she says, 'I have gone through the correct procedure, but because the head of HR is all chummy-chummy with Jane, he will now tell her about it and she will make my life even more difficult. Do you have any more clever suggestions?' She turns left and right. 'Any of you?'

Far too often I've been where Steph is right now. She's too angry to lose the argument. Stuck in an escalating frustration, she'll get more and more furious until her opponent backs down. Thankfully, Andy has seen the sense to do just that.

'Responsibility!' she says. 'What a joke.'

She sits down and starts to punch keys, as if each one has personally offended her. Once again, I feel I should be helping, but now is not the time. Hers is exactly the sort of contagious anger I need to avoid. There's a problem with the network that I've been meaning to investigate, so this is the perfect moment to slip out and give Steph the chance to calm down.

—

The room with the networking equipment is located just outside Jane's office at a secluded dog-leg linking buildings 4 and 5. It's little more than a closet, containing a pair of two metre high racks of hardware that hum and blink and give off heat. Bunches of multicoloured cables spew out and disappear into the overhead conduits, leaving just enough space for me to get round the back and examine what's connected to what. Not all of the rack spaces are filled. There's a letterbox gap at eye-height through which I get a good view of Jane's office.

After poking around for a couple of minutes, trying not to sneeze from the dust, I spot Steph going in to see Jane, who immediately gets out of her chair and puts her hands on her hips. I can't hear the conversation, but I get the gist of it from Steph's defensive posture and the rapid movement of Jane's lips. I know I shouldn't be spying on them, but I can't tear my eyes away. Steph shakes her head, points a finger at Jane and releases a tirade of her own. Yeah, you tell her, girl. Jane responds by slapping her across the face.

Did I really just see that? Steph is bent over, one hand on her cheek, the other held forward to ward off any more blows. Jane starts to say something, but Steph simply turns and leaves. As she passes the network room her head jerks my way, and I know she's spotted me. She uses a hand to try to conceal the trickle of blood emerging from her nose. And then she's gone, heading off in the direction of the Ladies.

Jane is already sitting back down, as if nothing has happened. I stride the few paces across the corridor and into her office, and as she looks up at me, I belt her across the face.

It's what I want to do, and maybe if I was standing in front of her it would already have happened. But no, I'm still here, trying to extricate myself from the tangle of cables, which seem intent on keeping me immobile. Once I get out, though, once I'm free to go across to Jane, I'll –

Stop. Stop this.

But she deserves it. She's *earned* it.

What was it Trib said? 'Violence is the last refuge of the

incompetent.'

Yeah, screw all that. Justice is an eye for an eye, anything less and they win.

Stop.

I grip the rack's steel frame with both hands and count to ten – no: make it twenty – rooting myself in place while the tidal surge of fury washes around me. Once I'm over the crest of it I'm merely pissed off, and can see how obvious it is: assaulting Jane is not going to do anyone any favours.

I breath as slowly and deeply as I can, and make myself finish the job on the networking hardware. It's a long, methodical task. Several times I lose the thread of what I'm doing while I slide back into fantasies of vengeance, and I have to backtrack to get the job done. I watch Jane while I do this. I watch for any sign of remorse or concern, but she appears to have forgotten the whole incident already.

By the time I've found the problem cable and replaced it, I'm still no closer to forming a practical plan of how to deal with Jane. When I get back to my desk, Steph is the only one in the Portakabin. I sit down and she immediately starts on me.

'Not a word,' she demands, pointing that same finger at me, the one that prompted Jane to slap her.

But something needs to be said. Jane has crossed a line. 'Please tell me you're not going to let her get away with that.'

'I said not a word!'

I place my hands on my desk, palms down. 'I can't let this go, Steph. You know Andy was right, don't you? You have to stand up to her.'

'It is none of your business! None of you!'

'It's my business as a human being, as your friend.'

'If you are my friend you will keep your mouth shut. Or are you determined to ruin everything?'

I feel a contraction of the skin, as if I've just jumped into freezing water. 'Oh, it's *me* ruining everything, is it? Nothing to do with the woman who just smacked you in the face?'

'You cannot see – you are making it worse!'

'Why won't you help yourself?'

'Why won't you help me,' she yells, 'by keeping your fucking mouth shut?'

My vision smears and I bang my fists on the desk three times, causing the whole Portakabin to shake. When I look up, Steph's eyes are wide; her hands are hovering at waist height. I've made her afraid of me – absolutely the last thing I wanted to do. I have to go home, right now. I have to take myself away from the situation. I leave the Portakabin and head straight for the car park, walking past the huge green and white plastic sign at the front of the building which says, 'Caduceus. Tending through technology.'

23

'So, how did it go?'

Trib is back from the North and has asked me round to talk. He sits in an armchair. The curtains have not yet been pulled, and he is framed by the dark rectangle of the patio door.

'She died the night after I got there.'

I'd suspected something like this ever since he phoned. His voice had betrayed a fatigue that was more than just the result of a two hundred mile drive.

'I'm sorry.'

'At least I got to talk to her before she was gone.'

He tells me how she encouraged him to go to university and study philosophy, years after he thought he was done with education. And although I know he's been with the rest of his family in Sheffield, I notice he only ever talks about his nan. There's no mention of his mum or dad, or any siblings.

He runs out of things to say about his trip, and stares at the skirting board. 'How have things been here?' he says.

I don't answer, and after a moment he looks up.

'Trib, there's something that's been bugging me ever since you left for the North.'

'What's that?'

'You know when your mum phoned up and I took the call? She said something.'

'Did she, now? Something about me, was it? I don't know why I'm even asking.'

'She said I should watch my back.'

He turns his face away.

'I'm only telling you what she said.'

'I know, I know.'

'So, should I be worrying?'

'That's for you to decide.' He narrows his eyes, his mind elsewhere, then takes a deep breath and says, 'Well, you've given me your life history. It's probably time I told you about the skeletons in my closet. Crack open that imperial stout, will you?'

I get the bottle opener from the kitchen, take the top off and pour the jet-black beer. There isn't much to divide between two, but my first sip confirms it has a knockout punch, as if someone had distilled Guinness, then dosed it with coffee beans and dark chocolate. If Tolstoy was drinking this sort of stuff, it's a miracle he ever finished *War and Peace*.

Trib makes no comment on the taste of his beer.

'When I was at college in Sheffield I knew this kid, Lee Hinchcliff,' he says. 'We sat together in Maths; helped each other struggle through it, because everyone else was streets ahead of us. I was surprised to find we had similar tastes in music. It was easy for people to recognise me as a rocker – I had the long hair, the ripped jeans, the leather jacket – but Lee didn't fit the mould at all.

'So I put him to the test by asking if he had my holy trinity of favourite rock albums, which at the time were *The Wall*, *Led Zep IV* and the first Van Halen LP. Yes, yes, and yes. I knew I'd found a kindred spirit. Most of the other kids were into Britpop or grunge, and even the ones who claimed to like rock were often fixated on one band, usually Iron Maiden. Like me, Lee had a broader view. We used to go to this pub called The Gravediggers in our free periods – we were under age, but the barman would let us have a half each – and we'd have these long conversations about music.

'Lee reckoned he had every decent rock album I could name. I began to have my doubts when I mentioned some of my more offbeat tastes. *Erpland* by Ozric Tentacles? "Yep." Trevor Rabin's *Can't Look Away*? "Yep." "Bullshit," I told him, so he invited me round to see his collection.

'Pretty nice, his house was. Huge rooms, and there wasn't a carpet in the place – it was all polished wooden floors. His dad was a self-employed builder who'd completed the place a few years before. Lee's mum was diagnosed with cancer just as it was being finished, and she only lasted another four months, so the whole house felt sort of empty.

'He told me I'd to be gone by six because that's when his dad got back from work, and he liked a bit of peace and quiet. That was cool by me. Mum put food on the table at six anyway.

'In his bedroom Lee had three of these racks, packed full of LPs and singles and CDs. Packed with them, floor to ceiling. I leaned in and there it all was, arranged by band, and then in chronological order: complete sets of AC/DC, Thin Lizzy, The Who, Floyd. Endless, endless rows of it. I was too paralysed to choose something, so he plucked the CD of Rush's *Power Windows* out of the rack and went over to the hi-fi.

'The hi-fi. My god. I was pretty chuffed with the second-hand Sony system I'd managed to cobble together, but this was from a different planet: Bang and Olufsen turntable, Denon CD player, Arcam amp, each on its own hardwood shelf. The Ferrari of sound systems. The speakers were these immense things by some company I'd never even heard of, but you only had to take one look at them to know they'd sound amazing. And they did. I'd heard the first track of the album a good few times, but never like this. I'd always known Geddy Lee was a great musician, but there was so much punch from his bass I thought the windows would explode. Neal Peart's snare on the outro was like a machine-gun. My jaw was on the floor for the whole song. Lee looked well chuffed.

'So it became this regular thing. We'd meet at his place every Thursday, and turn the volume up. It was fantastic. It all sounded so clear, so fresh. It was great to listen to this stuff with someone else who appreciated it, rather than having Mum banging on the ceiling and yelling at me to turn the bloody racket down. In Maths I drew this Venn diagram of our record collections – his was a giant circle; mine a tiny speck inside it, a minuscule subset.'

Trib's pleasant reminiscence sours. He opens another beer and sloshes the contents into our glasses.

'In hindsight I suppose the evidence was there, but you have to remember I was only seventeen. This one time he came into college and he had bruising all up his arm. He said he was accident prone, and I just accepted it.'

Under the pretext of folding my arms, I stealthily pull my own sleeves down.

'Towards the end of one of our listening sessions, when he'd just told me again that I had to go by six, I said it would probably be fine if we just turned it down. "No," he said, and it was the way he said it more than anything else. I remember exactly what he was doing at the time: kneeling down in front of the music rack, trying to slide Led Zep's *Physical Graffiti* LP back into its slot. But it was caught on something and wouldn't go in.

'That's when I twigged. I asked him if his dad hit him. Lee pushed at the record, tried to make a bigger space for it with his other hand, but there were too many others crammed in there. He told me not to be a daft bugger and that he'd see me at the same time next Thursday. He tried to sound casual, but made a real hash of it. He stopped trying to get this LP back in, and I knew I'd hit the nail on the head.

'Fuckin' hell.' Trib shakes his head in disgust. 'Lee was one of the most decent blokes I knew. He had a brilliant sense of humour. I never saw him say an unkind word to anyone. And his dad hit him.

'He told me not to spoil our Thursdays, because he looked forward to them all week. I said he had to tell someone, and he said I didn't understand. And he was right, I bloody didn't. He reckoned I'd only make things worse, that his dad had a really stressful job. I didn't care how stressful his job was. He had no right. Finally, Lee threatened me. He told me to get out, said if I mentioned it to anyone, he'd kill me. He was trying to scare me off, but he didn't fit those boots. If he was that tough he wouldn't have a problem with his old man in the first place.

'I wondered what it would be like to live in his world, where every day was a countdown to six o'clock. It was all right for me: I knew what set my mum off, I just had to avoid doing it. But Lee? What was it like for him, spending his life tiptoeing round his father? I said we had to do something about this. And do you know what he said to that? He said he couldn't believe I was doing this to him.'

Trib is incredulous, even years later, and I know how he feels. This is me and Steph and Jane. It's exactly the same.

'It were close to six now,' Trib says. 'I thought I wasn't going to persuade him in the next few minutes, so I told him we'd have to discuss it some more. I promised not to tell anyone, at least not yet, but I decided to go, for Lee's sake. Problem is, his dad comes home early. There's this sound of the key in the lock, just as I'm getting ready to leave. Lee tells me to hide in the wardrobe. He gets his Maths folder out of his college bag and puts it on the desk, along with a couple of pens and a calculator. From downstairs there's the sound of the front door slamming shut, but I'm not moving. Lee has gone pale by this time; he looks like he's going to throw up. I'm furious his dad can reduce him to this.

'From downstairs, his dad calls his name. His voice is slurred, and suddenly everything makes sense. He starts up the stairs – plonk, plonk – really slow. He calls out again, calling his son a little prick, and that decides me. There's no way I'm cowering in a wardrobe while I listen to my mate get the shit knocked out of him. I stand in the doorway to Lee's room which is just round the corner at the top of the stairs.

'It takes his dad forever to get to the top, but I still don't come up with a plan for confronting him. How do you reason with a drunk? He finally comes into view, takes a left turn to go into Lee's room, but I'm in the way. He's wearing faded blue jeans and a jacket, and he's so stocky that if he drank himself unconscious he'd probably stay upright. He squints at me with these eyes like mercury and asks who the fuck I am.

'I tell him if he lays a finger on Lee – but he interrupts, tells me to get out of his house. His breath stinks; it's like a gale-force wind in my face. I look back at Lee and he's wedged into the corner with his knees drawn up to his chin. While my head's turned, I feel Hinchcliff grab the lapels of my leather jacket. Lee flinches, and I can see what's going to happen: once I've gone, one way or another, Lee's going to get the worst thrashing of his life.

'So,' Trib sighs, 'I punch his dad in the guts. Then I clap my hands onto his wrists and break his hold on my jacket. Then I throw him down the stairs.

'It were no accident. He didn't slip, or anything like that. I threw him down the stairs. Loudest thing I ever heard. And afterwards, all I could hear was Lee's breathing, and all I could see was this crumpled heap of denim in the hallway. I thought I'd killed him. And then he lets out this pathetic whimper. I'd reduced this big, tough guy to that. Since no-one else in the house was capable of doing it, I was the one who phoned for the ambulance.

'Afterwards, I waited for Hinchcliff to press charges against me for assault, maybe even attempted murder, but he never did. Of course,' Trib says, 'he never walked again, either.'

I swallow. Trib makes an attempt to meet my eyes, but the shame pulls him back down to a contemplation of the floor.

'The last thing I expected,' he continues, 'was for Lee to stand by his dad and look after him, but that's what happened. I didn't give Lee his freedom. I sentenced him to a lifetime of caring for someone who beat him.'

'But you were trying to protect him.'

'Yeah, well,' he says bitterly, 'the road to hell is paved with good intentions, isn't it?'

'Did his dad still … mistreat him?'

'I dunno. From that point on, I kept well away.'

'But, surely …'

'But what? Do you think Lee wanted me around any more? I'd done enough damage. I did tell my mum, though, and our relationship was never the same again. She knew Hinchcliff, and had a lot of sympathy for him after he lost his wife. She thought Lee needed some tough love and that's what his dad gave him. She never believed he actually hit him, certainly nothing to justify what I did. So, there you go. My mum thinks I'm an absolute sod. If she thinks you should be watching your back, maybe she's right.'

He tosses back the dregs of his beer.

'Violence is never the solution to anything,' he says. 'Never.'

24

THE STORY ABOUT LEE and his dad swirls around in my mind, making sleep difficult. It explains why Trib was reluctant to let me back in on the missions – panel beating his van with my fists doesn't exactly tie in with his ideals of pacifism. I wake early and go into work. Andy and Dom have yet to arrive, but Steph is already there, typing away. She seems determined to work herself to death. As soon as she sees me, she stops and stands up. I brace myself for another earful.

'I am so sorry,' she says. 'It was very unfair of me to shout at you.'

She steps forwards and gives me a hug. My arms hover, halfway to returning it, but she releases me before I come to a decision.

'Let us speak no more about it,' she says. 'There are more important things.'

So, nothing is really resolved. Jane has got away with slapping her, which makes it more likely she'll do it again. I have no choice but to accept this for now. I'm not leaping straight into another argument.

'Now, about tonight …' she says, and I allow her to change the subject. 'I have everything ready.'

'You can drop it off at lunchtime?'

'If I am quick.'

'Okay, good. Good.' I take the key to Rebecca's house off my keyring and hand it to her.

—

The pretext is a quiet night out for Rebecca's 28th birthday. I pick her up at the entrance of the supermarket once her shift is over and drive her back to her house so she can get ready. I've been checking my mobile every time it vibrates, as Steph texts me with updates on how things are progressing.

'So you're not going to tell me where we're going?' Rebecca says as she wipes her feet on the mat and closes the front door.

'I thought maybe we could stay in, instead.'

She looks confused, maybe a little disappointed. 'But haven't you booked –?'

She backs into the lounge, the lights go on, and sixteen people yell, 'Happy birthday!' at the top of their voices. A cannonade of party poppers is unleashed, festooning us with coloured string.

'Bloody hell!' Rebecca says, stepping back as if shot. She looks from face to face, not quite believing what she's seeing. Her mouth opens and closes, but no words come out. I look for delight in her expression, but all I can see is shock.

I try a little levity. 'Looks like you've got squatters. Should we ask them to leave?'

A storm of protest.

'I – I – I'm going to need to change,' Rebecca says, backing out of the room and escaping up the stairs.

I glance at Steph, who bites her lip. The crowd, all ready to celebrate, goes quiet.

Trib offers an explanation: 'Fair enough. No-one wants to party in their work clothes.'

Yeah, maybe.

'While we wait,' he says, 'we can play "name that artist". For example, even I know that is a Picasso.' He points to a Klimt and people are quick to correct him.

It's a whole ten minutes before Rebecca comes back down the stairs, wearing a simple black dress. She flings her arms wide in welcome. 'Thanks for scaring the shit out of me,' she says.

Everyone cheers boisterously.

'I really don't know what to say.' She turns to Steph. 'Have you got anything to do with this?'

'It was Olly's idea.'

'But,' I add, 'Steph masterminded the food.' I push open the kitchen door to reveal the buffet – a panoply of colour that takes up every available surface.

Rebecca stares. 'You devious French cow!'

Steph looks delighted. I clap my hands twice and from the back of the room Andy and Nigella produce trays filled with glasses of champagne.

Rebecca takes one. 'Thank you,' she says, and turns to me. 'This is the best kind of staying in.'

'You're sure?'

'Oh, yes,' she says and draws me into an embrace. My hands fall naturally into the small of her back, and since no-one's looking, I let one hand creep lower, over the curve of her bottom. She grabs the hand and puts it back where it was. I raise my eyebrows innocently.

'Later, darling,' she says. 'Right now I'm going to mingle.' She steps backwards into the kitchen, holding onto my fingers until the distance between us is too great and she has to let go.

I find Trib at the threshold of the dining room, holding his champagne flute like a pint glass. I expect him to be chatting to anyone and everyone in his customary manner. Instead, he's gazing across the room at Philippa, a friend of Rebecca's who works part-time at The Mill. She's willowy and blonde, bookish in steel-framed glasses. Currently she's deep in conversation with Nigella, her hand dipping periodically into a bowl of olives.

'Oh, hi, mate,' Trib says. 'I didn't see you there.'

'Her name's Philippa.'

'Er, what? Who's that?'

'The woman you've been staring at. And yes, she's single.'

His shoulders slump. 'That obvious, am I?'

'Let's go over and chat.'

'I don't think so. She's a bit out of my league.'

'You don't know until you try. Look what happened to me.'

Trib shifts his weight onto his other foot. 'Yeah, but I mean …'

I wait for him to finish. 'Yeah, but what?' I prompt.

'Well … you know.'

'Right. Thanks for making that clear.'

'The sad truth is,' he explains, 'I'm always more comfortable around men.'

'You could always ask Mitch out.'

But he's not listening. His eyes have drifted back in Philippa's direction.

'I thought you could talk to anyone, Trib.'

'Yeah, well, congratulations on finding my weakness.'

'It's normal for guys to be nervous around attractive women.'

'Nervous doesn't even get close to it. She might as well be made out of Kryptonite.'

'Right. Come with me, big man.'

I lead Trib over, like a parent towing a reluctant child. Halfway across he shakes my hand free so he can approach with some dignity. The girls turn, we all say hi to each other, and I introduce Trib to Philippa.

'How's the degree going?' I ask her.

'Pretty good,' Philippa says. 'Still two years to go, though. It's a long haul.'

Seeing his opportunity, Trib gamely jumps into the conversation. 'Oh, you're doing a degree?'

'Yes.'

'I did mine when I was a bit older, too.'

Oh, for God's sake, Trib. Thankfully, Philippa either doesn't notice his faux pas or is too polite to mention it.

'Actually it's my second degree,' she says.

'Really?'

'Yes, I found I missed the academic life. Keep the brain active while it still works, that's what I say.'

'What subject?' Trib asks.

'Humanities. I'm doing it through the Open University.'

'I don't suppose you get to do anything on the ancient Greeks,' he says.

'Oh, yes, quite a bit.'

I catch Nigella's gaze and motion with my eyes. She gives me a knowing look, and we slope off to the lounge, leaving Trib to fend for himself.

—

'My friend,' Steph says, woozy from the fizz, 'my friend over there.'

'Which one?' I ask.

She steadies herself on the door frame. 'Rebecca, of course!'

'Ah, okay. Yes?'

She watches Rebecca, who is chatting to two friends and gesturing with enthusiasm. 'She is changing.'

'In what way?'

'It is you who is doing this, you know? You are changing her.'

Is it true? That was never my intention.

'You know,' Steph continues, 'when we are together she says … No, but I have had too much to drink. You must forgive me.'

'She says what? Come on, Steph, you can tell me.'

She frowns. After a moment's thought, her eyebrows rise. Her expressions are exaggerated, like a cartoon character. 'Very well. She says you are good for her.'

I picture Rebecca slumped on her sofa after the terrible gig at the Fatted Calf.

'Yes, you are,' Steph insists before I can get a word in. 'I can see it. Everyone can see it.'

She leans close and I catch the whiff of alcohol on her breath. 'She says you are so much more plain-speaking than her last boyfriend.'

'Oh, yeah?' I look at my fingernails. 'What was he like, then?'

Steph shakes her head. 'You know they were engaged? Still, it did not stop him from going off with this bimbo. Salaud! Fils de pute! Puh!' She takes a breath and becomes calmer. 'My friend needs to be treated better than this.'

'All I can do is my best.'

'C'est ça!' She taps me on the chest with two fingers. 'You understand.'

Maybe she's right. Maybe it is that simple.

'You know, Steph, I've never thanked you for giving me her phone number.'

'It was nothing.'

'Oh, no-no-no. It was everything.'

She shrugs and looks down at the floor, but can't hide the smile that tugs at her lips.

Andy comes past with the tray again, and she says, 'Oh, there is more champagne?'

—

'So,' I ask Trib, 'how did you get on with Philippa?'

He pulls a face. 'Don't ask.'

'What do you mean? It was going so well.'

'We just sort of ran out of things to say.'

'You were looking at her face, right?'

Philippa is a devotee of the plunging neckline and has the bust to make the best of it. The effect could cause vertigo in a man of Trib's height.

'Of course I was. What else would I … oh, right. No, it wasn't that. I hardly noticed. No, like so many women, she adopted this "I'm happy to be polite until you go away" kind of attitude.'

'Philippa? She wouldn't do that.'

'It's like I've got a huge sign strapped to my forehead that says: "Clueless and Desperate".'

'You enjoyed talking to her, though?' I'm determined he should salvage something from the situation.

'No, I was terrified after you abandoned me.'

'"Only at our most naked can we truly know ourselves or those around us."'

'Oi, I'm supposed to be the one with the words of wisdom.' He thinks for a moment. 'Actually, that's a good one. Nietzsche, is it?'

'No.'

'Kierkegaard?'

'No.'

'Tell me, then.'

'My uncle Barry. He's a naturist.'

—

Steph sways around the house, loquacious and giggling. She continues to knock back the bubbly, and nobody tries to stop her. By the time she and her husband leave – with Paul struggling to get all of her limbs inside the car at the same time – Steph is happily oblivious to just about everything, including the fact that no-one is responding to her conversation, which is now entirely in French.

Having started so early, everyone is ready to call it a night by eleven. Rebecca waves goodbye to the last guests, then comes back into the lounge. She plonks herself down on the sofa next to me, lets out a great whoosh of air, then slides over sideways until her head rests on my shoulder. I reach up and stroke the hair behind her ear.

'I'm going to leave this mess for tomorrow,' she says. The room is littered with near-empty glasses, plates, wrapping paper.

'Definitely. Hey, I've got a present for you.'

She lifts her head and I pass her the envelope I concealed down the side of the sofa.

'Happy birthday.'

'Mmm ... Thank you.'

'Don't thank me yet. You might not like it.'

She hacks the top open with her little finger and draws out the sliver of card. Her eyes scan rapidly left to right, and her mouth drops open. It's a voucher for five hours at a recording studio in London with an experienced sound engineer. Enough time, they told me, for someone who has done enough prep to record a four-song EP.

'Olly, I ...' She bites her bottom lip.

'Is it okay?'

'Yes!' she says, and clasps it to her chest, as if I might suddenly take it away. 'I don't know what to say.'

'Then don't say anything.'

She puts the voucher on the coffee table and throws her arms round me.

Steph was right. All I have to do is my best.

25

ON A SHEET OF PAPER, I've printed the following:

I saw you slap Stéphanie.
You will apologise to her. You will not mistreat her again.
Don't make me take things any further.

I've deliberated over the exact wording, going for short sentences and using Steph's full name, which are both uncharacteristic of my own speech and writing. I cut the unused half of the sheet off, making it A5 size, slip it into an envelope, then put the envelope in Jane's mail slot while the secretary is away from her desk getting coffee. If, by some oversight on my part – or by detailed forensic analysis – she does trace it back to me, the plan is simply to stick to my guns: 'Yes, it was me, and I meant what I wrote. Now, we don't have to get the police involved, do we?' I almost want this to happen; there's something alluring about an all-guns-blazing confrontation.

I find excuses to check the mail slot regularly, nothing more than a glance. On my fourth visit, the note has gone. I can't help myself – I go straight to Jane's office.

'Jane, I need to talk to you.'

'Can this wait?' she says.

I watch her face for some sign of guilt, remorse or fear. She looks irritable, but that's normal. It may be the only emotion she's capable of.

'It's about the incident report spreadsheet. I was wondering whether you wanted it sorted by incident number or user name.'

'Is this really a decision I need to be involved in?' she says.

'The thing is, it's a usability issue.'

She sighs. 'Okay. Take a seat.'

Does Jane not know how easy it is to re-sort the contents of a spreadsheet? It would appear not. I take the visitor's chair. Her hands are flat on her desk, covering a face-down sheet of paper. That's it: that's my note. She follows the direction of my gaze and, without hesitation, opens her desk drawer, drops the piece of paper in and slides it shut.

I try to keep my face neutral. 'Secret stuff, eh?'

'It is not secret.'

'Ah. Private, then. Sorry if I've intruded.'

'It's not private, either.'

I say nothing in answer to this, and sure enough, Jane feels the need to supply an explanation. 'It's the pay gradings for everyone in the department.'

'That's not secret? Can I have a look, then?'

'No, you can't!'

'But it's not secret?' I'm pushing this too far.

'"Confidential" is the word you're looking for.'

Inside my head there is a schoolboy jumping up and down, pointing, laughing. I hope none of this shows on my face.

'Now, this uhh, this spreadsheet ...' she says. Funny, she wasn't interested a minute ago.

Together we make the momentous decision to sort by incident number, at which point Jane glances at her watch and says, 'I have to be at a meeting. Is that all you need from me?'

No, Jane. That's not all I need from you. I nod and stand up. As I head back to the Portakabin, I notice Jane lock the desk drawer before leaving her office. That's it: squirm, you bitch.

—

After lunch, I notice the photographs of Sophie are back on Steph's desk.

I point at them. 'So, you've decided to stick two fingers up at Jane after all?'

Steph has been wrestling with her hangover all morning, but is beginning to look a little less like a member of the undead.

'Not exactly,' she says. 'Do you want to grab a coffee?'

'Sure.'

In the canteen we buy a cappuccino each. Normally we'd go straight back to the office, mindful of Jane's insistence that there's plenty of time to put our feet up when we go home, but instead Steph suggests we spend ten minutes in the comfy chairs.

'This thing with Jane,' she says. 'It is over. It is all resolved.'

'What happened?'

'According to Andy, a miracle!' she says, making an explosion with the fingers of both hands. 'Certainly, I cannot account for it. Jane just seemed to come to her senses. I think she shocked herself with what she did, and has been thinking about it ever since.'

'Go on, then: give me the details.'

'She called me into her office and said, "I have not been fair with you, and I am a strong enough leader to admit it. I would like you to accept my apology and then we can carry on as if nothing has happened."'

'In other words: "Sorry I've been a total cow. Please don't tell anyone."'

'Yes, that is what I thought.' She becomes pensive. 'And then something very strange happened.'

'I'm all ears.'

'She said, "I hope you are happy with your little one. What is her name?" I said, "Sophie," and she said, "Sophie ..." with this sort of distant look in her eyes. And then she said, "I am not able to have children myself."'

Interesting ... 'Do you think it's true?'

'Yes, I do. It was clearly an emotional thing for her.'

'Jane, emotional?'

'Hah! Yes, I did not think it possible either. It was just for a moment, then suddenly she was the old Jane again. She said, "Good, I'm glad that's all cleared up." And that was it.'

'Sacrebleu!'

Steph laughs. 'Nobody says this in France.'

Maybe it's because I haven't been confrontational about Jane, or gone through official channels, but Steph has no idea I'm anything to do with it. This is Trib's pure altruism – a gift for a friend. And he's right, it feels good.

—

'Hello. What's this?' Rebecca says.

We're in my bedroom, and in a few minutes we'll be heading off for an evening of Mitchell Thomas's stand-up at The Mill. I've got one arm and my head into a jumper, and I'm struggling to get the other arm in. I'm sure this thing has shrunk since I last wore it. I turn round and Rebecca is holding a dog-eared blue binder. A sticky label on the front bears the title 'Songs'. Where did she find that?

'Don't look in there.'

'Are these the songs you played with your university band?'

I make a grab for it, but my arms are still entangled. She pushes back on the chair and rolls out of reach. Her lips are shaped into a pout of amusement as she leafs through the dozen or so pages.

'Music,' she says with delight.

'Or some imitation thereof.'

'Ah,' she says. 'I've found one of yours.'

'Don't read that. I'm serious.'

But it's clear that I'm not, because she reads it. I know which one it is: the only one I wrote.

BUNNY
©2004 Olly Griffin

```
E                        A         D
A grope in a club, seven pints of lager:
E                                  A       D
that was the start of our erotic saga.
```

```
      E                         A            D
My friends think I'm living in relationship hell,
      E                         A      D
but what can I do under your witchly spell?
```

Chorus:
```
A                            D   G
Honey, honey, honey,
        A                    D   G
you can boil my bunny,
            A                D   G
and it's a little bit funny
        A                    E   A
that I love you.
A                            D   G
You trash my flat
A                            D   G
and abuse my cat,
            A                D   G
but I don't mind about that,
        A                    E   A
'coz I love you.
```

I should have picked up on your mental disorders.
The clue's in your collection of restraining orders.
The filth they come round on a regular basis,
trying to pin on you all their unsolved cases.

Chorus:
Honey, honey, honey,
you can boil my bunny,
and it's a little bit funny
that I love you.
You treat my like your ho,

```
make me feel so slow.
Well, should I come or go?
I still love you.

I spend my time in court in a romantic daze,
racking my brains to find alibis
that keep you out prison and in my arms.
The judge can't deprive me of your twisted charms.

Chorus:
Honey, honey, honey,
you can boil my bunny,
and it's a little bit funny
that I love you.
You make me want to blub.
So, let's get to the nub.
Are you Beelzebub?
Well, I love you.

Outro:
A         D         G         A
```

Rebecca looks up from the binder. I've decided I might as well be unashamed by my efforts.

'I bet you wish *you* could write them like that.'

'There are only, what, four chords in the entire song,' she points out, 'and they're all majors.'

'Yeah, you don't need any more than that.'

'There's also no melody information for the singer.'

'That's because there was no melody.'

'And you do realise that "daze" and "alibis" don't rhyme.'

'They did the way Scott sang it.'

'Mmm.'

'What can I say? We were young and talentless and having fun.'

'Written about anyone in particular?' she says.

'No, just a general punk rant.' Although five years down the line, and putting my psychologist's hat on, maybe I was expressing my general frustration with girls at the time.

'I can tell you were studying English,' she says.

'Really?'

'Yes. It's not necessarily the words that give you away, it's the immaculate punctuation.' Her gaze falls back to the page. 'I do kind of like it. Will you play it for me?'

God, no; I have to retain some semblance of dignity. I look around my bedroom. 'Oh, what a shame. There's no guitar here.'

She arches an eyebrow. 'Wait till we're back at my house.'

—

After thanking the crowd for their introductory applause, Mitchell takes a few seconds to adjust the microphone stand – the previous act was a lofty Dutchman.

'Get on with it!' a guy in the front row shouts.

'Ooh, a heckler!' Mitchell says. 'And so soon! Tell you what, you can be my straight man if you come on stage. You don't mind coming on stage, do you?'

He imbues these words with every possible shade of innuendo. The guy gives out a nervous laugh, folds his arms and shuffles closer to his wife/girlfriend.

'Sitting comfortably? Then I'll begin. We live, ladies and gentlemen, in a time of great contradictions. Bankers are rich – yes, feel free to boo in a panto style if the urge arises – while stand-up comedians are, lamentably, poor.' He makes a sad face. 'What better expresses this time of contradictions than the humble oxymoron? For those who didn't pay attention in English – and if you were forced to do Shakespeare at an age when you could barely find your own bottom, I sympathise – an oxymoron is a phrase which contradicts itself. What, for example, does "smart casual" mean? Turns out it's not smart and it's not casual. To any sane person, this is clearly ridiculous. Only a lunatic would go into a clothes shop and ask for a "tiny colossal" T-shirt in the hope that the assistant cancels out the two extremes and arrives at a medium. I ask you, what can possibly be both tiny *and* colossal?' He singles out a member of the audience. 'Oh, sir, please don't say it; it's not that sort of show.'

He paces from one end of the stage to the other.

'Airlines are particularly fond of oxymorons. How about "premium economy"? I mean, come on, that's just a failure to make up your mind. And when you think about it, "air field" doesn't make much sense.' He pauses. 'You could even make a case for "airline food".'

He's in his element on stage, relaxed and self-assured.

'If you spot an oxymoron anywhere in my set, I want you to shout it out as loud as you can, okay? Bonus points for volume. Yes, it's like school all over again! We could even bring back the cane if you like. What's that, madam? You *would* like it? Each to their own. Actually, I'm a fine one to criticise education. I thought I was finished with it after college, but a few years later I went back to university as a mature student.'

He pauses, and makes encouraging movements with his hands. When no-one speaks, his shoulders slump. 'Oh, come on, you'll have to do better than that!'

'Mature student?' someone ventures.

'That's the spirit!' He takes a swig of water from a plastic bottle. 'I think the phrase "War on Terror" is almost deserving of oxymoron status. It implies we're trying to make fear itself afraid of us. How do you go about such a thing? I mean, I know it involves bombing people that have failed to learn English – that's a given – but I fear that, linguistically speaking, we're in danger of disappearing into something I like to call "The Twaddle Vortex".'

I glance at Rebecca. She's smiling, but says wistfully, 'Wow, he's confident.'

'On stage, you mean?' I'm puzzled by this. 'So are you.'

'Yeah, but I'm bluffing it.'

I want to tell her that everyone probably is, Mitchell included. I want to tell her that it took at least two pints before I'd do one of our punk gigs. But Mitch's eyes are wandering in our direction, and I don't want to be singled out for talking during his act.

He doesn't swear once. Without this crutch, he has to find more creative ways of telling jokes. There's a political strain throughout, but he skirts round topics that could become rants, and turns them instead into playful ruminations. He drops gay jokes in like grenades, just when they're least expected. Even those lured in on the pretext of seeing a clean comedian – he's anything but – are won over by him. It's difficult to take offence at someone so obviously good-natured.

As his set comes to an end, he wraps up with a real sense of warmth for his audience.

'Thanks for coming to this gig and paying actual, real money to support your humble entertainer. The proceeds will keep me in beans on toast and extra strength condoms. And in years to come you'll be able to say, "I was there. I helped Mitchell Thomas on his meteoric rise to stardom."'

'Meteoric rise!' shouts a woman at the back.

Mitchell points at her. 'Very good. If it wasn't for this gig, I'd probably be forced to take a low-wage job in some dismal government organisation.'

He raises his eyebrows, there's a pause of two seconds, then half the crowd yells, 'Government organisation!' in unison.

Mitchell grins. 'You are my kind of people. I have been, and continue to be, Mitchell Thomas. Good night!'

26

AND SO WE COME to the final of *Obedience*, in which Zach and Ryan battle it out for the prize of £20,000 and the public's undying reverence. At least until the next programme comes on.

I watch the show in the living room with Rebecca and Jodie. I've mentally distanced myself from Zach over the weeks, and can now watch with a sense of numbness which is only occasionally punctured by irritation. He used to be my stupid, embarrassing brother. Now he's just another reality TV contestant: someone I'll meet at my parents' over Christmas and chat with for a while – a newly minted stranger. This is what TV does: gives you the illusion of intimacy while keeping you at arm's length.

But in the final my feelings change. I used to want him voted off, so I wouldn't have to endure any more of it. Now, since this is the last episode, I might as well root for him. So, there's still some part of me that identifies with my brother. And maybe it really is necessary to do an apprenticeship at the arse end of telly before graduating to something better. At least he didn't start in porn.

With only two contestants left, the show has even more filler than usual. Nat plugs the gaps by interviewing Zach and Ryan, which is particularly pointless given that this could be the last time anyone ever sees them. The final challenge is to reveal a secret – the juicier, the better. I've been vaguely aware of this since last week, but now I'm in front of the telly a horrible possibility occurs to me. Is this secret not about Zach at all, but about me? Have I concealed my cutting as effectively as I think? Perhaps the whole family knows. Perhaps they agreed years ago never to let on. Zach wouldn't say anything, surely. Not in public. He's not that desperate for fame.

But I no longer know him well enough to be certain. I have no guarantees.

If he says it, what will I do? Drive up to London and punch his lights out? Refuse ever to speak to him again? I can think of nothing that wouldn't just be indulging my desire for revenge, certainly nothing that would put the secret back in its box.

'Are you okay?' Rebecca says.

'Yes.' Even through fabric she can feel my muscles tensing. I force myself to relax, but my mind has plummeted fully into the nightmare scenario. What will Rebecca say if he drops the bombshell? Will I be able to deny it, laugh it off, convince everyone he just made it up to win the show? I already know the answer to that.

'Sooo,' Nat drawls, 'we come to your secret, ZG. I hope you've thought about this long and hard –' his customary leer lacks any of the warmth or cheekiness of Mitchell's stand-up '– because the final vote is going to depend on just how good it is.'

Zach is trying to look casual, as always, but I notice the quick lick of the lips, the shifting of his weight from one foot to the other. I feel an icicle of nausea stab my guts.

'Right,' Zach says. 'I need to phone someone for this.'

My eyes jerk over to the telephone, sitting in its base beside Jodie, then to my mobile on the coffee table. I'm surrounded by the bloody things. If one of them rings could I demand that no-one answers it? Where's Moira? If it goes to the land line, will she pick up from the kitchen?

One of Nat's schoolgirl blondes dials the number on a phone and hands it to Zach. The ringtone sounds in the studio, but none of the phones in the house make a sound.

'His name's Keith Brinkley,' Zach explains, and I try to conceal my colossal sense of relief from Rebecca. I've never heard of the guy.

Keith picks up after four rings. 'Hiya, mate. Wow. I'm really on telly?'

'Yep. Now, Keith, you know how we discussed that secret we both kept when we were kids?'

'Yeah.'

'Well, I'm not going to use that after all. I've got a better one. Something only I know. Your other friends don't know it; your parents don't know it.' Zach takes a deep breath, 'Mate, there's no shame in it, and I think it's time you told everyone you're gay.'

For a moment there is complete silence in the studio, in the living room and at the other end of the phone line. The delicious, impossible relief I've been feeling curdles.

There's an intake of breath from Keith's end of the line. 'What!?' he says. 'You … fucking …' There's a click as he hangs up. The audience explode into a chorus of boos.

'Oh my God,' Rebecca mutters.

Jodie's head whips round to face me, her hand covering her mouth.

Zach's grin falters. Nat hesitates for a moment, but certainty soon returns. He steps aside and spreads his arms, delivering Zach to the lions with an expression of barely suppressed glee. The camera swivels towards the audience. In the dim blue light at least half of them are on their feet, shouting. I wouldn't be unhappy if one of them bounded down the steps and gave Zach the slapping he deserves, but after a minute or so they yield to Nat's calls for order and sit, grumbling, back in their seats. They might be angry, but they're not going to *do* anything about it. The title of the show has never been more appropriate.

'Do you see?' I ask the room at large. 'This is why I find him so difficult. This …' but I can't think of the words to explain it, and realise I don't need to. They've seen it with their own eyes; what can I possibly add?

'Whew!' Nat says. 'Well, that was quite a revelation, Zach.' He re-establishes his patter and the show continues.

Ryan's secret is tame and forgettable in comparison, but he gets a huge round of applause for it. Nat calls for the lines to open for the final public vote.

Rebecca squeezes my hand. 'It's the last time you'll ever have to watch it.'

'Thank Christ for that. Hand me my phone, will you?'

She passes it across and I punch in a vote for Ryan.

—

The next morning, Moira shows me that Zach has hit the front page of the *Daily Express* with the headline 'Outed by "Friend" on Live TV'. There you go, Zach: fame at last. He may have lost by a landslide, but it's still his photo in the paper, taken from a previous episode and showcasing one of his smuggest expressions. Alongside, there's a blurred picture of Keith Brinkley. So the paper is effectively condemning Zach while at the same time compounding his crime.

Mum phones to tell me their house is surrounded by journalists. Dad has taken the unprecedented step of not going into the office, and has given a very brief statement to the paparazzi: 'I'm not responsible for my son's actions. He doesn't live at this address. Please leave us in peace.' They're now holed up with all the curtains closed, like terrorists under siege, until the men with the cameras piss off. Apparently the press haven't been able to find Zach at his London flat, so they've gone after the next of kin. Will it be me and Alistair next? I wolf down my toast and leave for Caduceus early.

Work is unpleasant. I field the inevitable questions with as much patience and as little emotion as I can manage. Why did he behave the way he did? Have I been voting for him? Did I know what he was going to say?

I don't understand. Do they think I have some kind of control over Zach, just because we happen to share genetic material?

Shortly after I get home the doorbell rings and, after checking through the window that it's not the press, I open the door to a guy in his early twenties wearing jeans and a check shirt. His hair is untidily cropped and his eyes dart around like a junkie trying to find his next fix. It's Zach.

He glances over his shoulder. 'I need your help.'

I close the door on him.

I can see through the frosted glass that he hasn't gone anywhere. He must be able to see that I haven't either. He knocks, and I take three long breaths before opening the door again.

'Please, Olly.' His voice is shaky and desperate. 'I know you must be pissed off with me. Please.'

He's already trying to wind me round his little finger with his tears, and his cow eyes, and his whole 'poor me' act. I open the door wide. He lowers his eyes as he draws level with me. I can smell alcohol on his breath, but he seems dazed rather than drunk. It's impossible for me to smuggle him past Moira and Jodie, both of whom are sitting in the lounge, so I introduce him. Moira is her usual, hospitable self, offering him a cup of tea and a slice of fruitcake which he gratefully accepts. There's no hint of disapproval in her manner, God bless the woman. Jodie says hi, and makes a visible attempt to stop staring.

I lead Zach up to my room. He doesn't bat an eyelid at having to climb a ladder to get there. I offer him the easy chair, pull up the ladder and close the hatch.

'They're really nice,' he says of Moira and Jodie, even though he only met them five minutes ago.

His tone makes me wonder how many friends he has up in London. I picture him in a dingy, cramped bedsit, the antithesis of his showbiz aspirations. To keep himself afloat financially he must have some job other than his paltry TV work, but I don't know what it is. Who is Zach, really? I read somewhere that every cell in the human body is replaced over a period of seven years. Is there anything left of the Zach I knew from childhood?

I'm just about to sit down opposite him when my mobile rings. It's Rebecca.

'Hi,' she says. 'Do you want to go out tonight? There's a band playing at The Green Man.'

'Erm … I can't. Zach's here and he's …'

'Your brother? Why?' The papers have done nothing to improve her opinion of him.

My instinct is to take this call somewhere else, somewhere out of Zach's earshot, but I've only just shut us in here.

'Since when has Zach been a priority?' she says.

I can see her point. I can't let him swan into my life whenever he needs me and sod off for the rest. There has to be some give and take.

'Olly?'

And why should I care what he hears? He isn't exactly sensitive to anyone else's feelings.

'He just turned up on the doorstep.'

Having finished his cup of tea and cake, Zach picks up the small globe I keep on my bookshelf and starts spinning it.

'What does he want?' Rebecca says.

'Forgiveness, by the look of him.'

'And is that something you can offer?'

'I'm about to find out.'

I hear her tut at the other end of the line.

'Look, I wish it wasn't like this, but … he's my brother and he's in a pretty bad state.' Zach glances up, then immediately returns his attention to the globe.

She sighs. 'Okay. Do what you can. Oh, and Olly?'

'Yes?'

'Don't let him make you miserable. You're not responsible for what he did.'

Miserable would be fine; it's furious I'm trying to avoid.

'I'll see you tomorrow –' I look up at Zach '– no matter what happens.'

I end the call and Zach says, 'I … I didn't want to make anything difficult for you.'

'Well, you should have thought about that a little bit sooner. Like a few years ago.'

He looks shocked, as if all that 'he's my brother' stuff meant I was suddenly his mate again.

'Please, Olly …'

'Please what? I can't undo the mess you've got yourself into.'

'The press are after me like a pack of dogs. I can't go back to my flat.'

'So you've come here, to drag all of us into it?'

'No, no. I wasn't followed,' he says. 'You don't know what they're like, Olly. You'd think I was a murderer or a rapist. I haven't even broken the law.'

My mouth drops open. 'You are aware, I hope, that outing your friend on TV was wrong?'

'Yes,' he says in a pained voice. 'Yes, I know. I screwed up.'

'You know he's going to hate you forever?'

'Yeah, probably.'

'So why the hell did you do it?'

'You ...' he shakes his head. 'It's difficult. You can't really understand unless you've worked in show business.'

'Try me.'

'You have to get into their heads – the producers, I mean. You have to predict what they want. If you don't, you'll never get anywhere. They said something controversial would be good for the final challenge, and at the back of your mind is this idea that there's no such thing as bad publicity, and so you just kind of ... go for it.'

I'm shaking my head in disbelief.

'I *know* it was wrong,' he says. 'It's like ... I dunno, I sort of went blind, or something. I told myself he wouldn't mind all that much. Look, if I could go back and do things differently, I would. Trust me, I would.'

'Have you spoken to this guy?'

'What, Keith? No.'

'Don't you think you owe it to him? And while you're at it, how about offering yourself as a punch-bag for the day?'

'I can't.' His voice has dwindled to nothing.

'Why?' And when he doesn't reply. 'Shame, I hope.'

He nods, his lower lip trembling. No, I'm not going to be drawn into sympathy for him.

'I think you need to realise what you've done, Zach. And I'm not just talking about the final of this piss poor game show, I'm talking about your attitude ever since your first TV appearance and all that bullshit you spouted off the back of it. You need to realise how selfish you've been and what effect it's had on Keith and the rest of your family and all the other poor sods who've had to put up with it. The world doesn't revolve around Zach Griffin and you need to wake up to the fact that for the past few years you've been unbearable.'

What a relief to finally say this. Zach stares at me, as if I've betrayed him. He starts to cry, but I'm not backing down. It's the truth and it's long overdue. He's not going to make me feel guilty.

'Do you know what Dad said?' he whines.

'What?'

'I phoned him up after the final and he said, "You bloody embarrass me." Those are the exact words he used. Can you believe it?'

From our dad, the emotional ice cube?

'All these years,' he says, 'I try to get some reaction out of him, and when I finally do, that's what I get: "You bloody embarrass me." It's all right for Alistair, isn't it? Join Daddy's company. Toe the line. Yes, sir; no, sir. Get promoted. I know Dad said we could have a job at Selby and Griffin, but that's not fair, is it? Just because it fits Alistair doesn't mean it's right for us. I mean, even if I started a career in law right now, put everything I could into it, I still wouldn't be as good as Alistair. What's the point of being in a competition you can only lose?'

'This is about Dad?'

'No, it's about being ... something!' he wails. 'I don't want to be laying on my deathbed sixty years from now, thinking I've pissed my life away doing a job I hate. I want someone to tell me I've done okay. I'm never going to be a great businessman, or an intellectual, and I've fucked up my chance of being a celebrity, so what can I do? What can I do?' He bangs his fists on the arms of the chair in sheer frustration. 'I know I've been selfish. I *know*. But when do I get to feel like a success? When? When?'

Just these few words, and I feel closer to Zach than I have in years; I begin to understand. He wants the same thing I want: success on his own terms, not somebody else's. And if he's been hoping to use *Obedience* as a springboard to better things in TV, that dream is now dead.

He wipes his face with his sleeve. 'You hate me as well, don't you?' he says in the voice of an eight year old. 'I thought you might ... you know ... my brother ...' and he ends the sentence with a resigned, 'Ah, well. Never mind. All over now.'

'No, I don't hate you.' I blurt it out. He needs to hear it, and I'm terrified he's going to do something even more stupid, something irreversible. I can't let him leave the room while he's feeling like this.

He sits back in his chair. 'But you do, really, don't you?'

'No.' I need to stall for time; to sift and sort my feelings. 'It's ... it's more complicated than that.'

Not a very comforting thing to say, but I can hardly claim not to be angry with him. I throw him a box of tissues to keep him occupied while I think. He needs me to say something good about him, and that's a problem given that I hardly know him any more. All he's wanted to talk about for the past few years is his singing career, his TV career, his chances of making it big. I can't offer him some vague reassurance that everything will be all right; it's not going to wash. After years of putting up with his vanity, there's no going back on what I've just said. Nor would I want to. What can I say that's honest and true and doesn't amount to another bollocking? He's changed so much since he was a kid, since that blissful time when ... Wait. Yes. Yes.

'Do you remember climbing the oak tree in the back garden?'

He blows his nose noisily. ''Course I do.'

'And there was that time when Alistair didn't know we were up there, and he invited that girl from school to sit under the tree with him, and you dropped an acorn on his head every time he tried to kiss her?'

'Huh. Yeah, I remember.'

'Or that really hot summer, where we had all those friends round and you said the best thing for cooling down was to have a massive water fight?'

'The one where Mum and Dad joined in?'

'Yeah, everyone went mental. Dad connected up the garden hose and Mum was sniping people from the bathroom window with the shower head.'

He bends over double and shakes in silent grief. I give him all the time he needs. I offer him the bin so he can fill it with tear-sodden tissues.

'Growing up with you was great, Zach.'

'Yeah? It's just what I've done since that you don't like?'

'That's about the sum of it.'

After a while he nods. It's something we can both accept. No pulling punches, just the truth. God, it feels good to finally get to the truth.

'It's not you I've got the problem with, Zach, it's that bellend ZG.'

A few weeks ago he would have claimed that's who he was now. Instead he says, 'I think ZG died last night.'

'Good riddance to him. Does that mean I get my brother back?'

Zach's face crumples and a quavering, high-pitched note escapes from him. It's the sound of a dog suffering; a pure, animal pain. I can't help it – I put my arms round him.

—

He stays for the night. We improvise a mattress with a couple of Moira's yoga mats and throw a duvet over the top. I sedate him with a couple of bottles of Belgian beer from a batch Trib gave me, and finish the last two myself. We talk long into the night, and I try to keep him on the topic of the good old days.

When I wake up the next morning, I'm immediately aware that something's amiss. Zach has gone. I know it even before I prop myself up and see his duvet flat and unoccupied. Light floods into the room from the open trapdoor. Somehow, I know he's not in the house either. I get up and pad over to his makeshift bed. He's left a sheet of A4 on it with a scribbled note:

Olly,

I've decided to leave the country for a bit and let everything simmer down. You've given me hope for the future. I won't forget it.

Thanks, bro.

Zach

So, as soon as I get my brother back, I lose him again. I snort with amusement. How typical of him.

I phone Mum and Dad to tell them what's happened. They sound relieved – doubly so, since the gaggle of reporters has already left in pursuit of the next hot-potato news sensation.

A couple of days later, Zach posts a video apology on YouTube. He looks genuinely contrite, and it's a clever way of getting directly to the public without being mauled again by the mainstream media. He's brave enough to allow comments, and they run the usual gamut from uncritical support to foaming hatred.

Deprived of the main focus of their outrage, the press turn on the studio. Thousands of viewers have complained to Ofcom and there are calls for resignations at WTF Productions. Caught outside his office by the swarming journalists, the head of the studio is defiant and unrepentant. He reminds me of Nat, and I wonder if the two are related. Twenty-four hours later, he's resigned. A shareholder revolt? Realisation that the public backlash is too big to ignore? Whatever it is, I'm glad to see him gone. I'm glad to see a line drawn under the whole sordid affair.

27

IT'S THE LAYER OF DUST that betrays her. I can see it on the shoulder of the guitar when I sit in my customary place on the sofa. I reach across and use my finger to paint a line of gloss onto the wood. Perhaps I should write a message to the owner, as people do on the backs of dirty white vans. *Play me.*

On the TV the audience laugh, or at least a recording is played of people laughing. It's a comedy panel show. Rebecca doesn't react to the TV like Jodie does. She doesn't feel the need to emulate the audience's reaction. I've suggested going out for a meal, or meeting up with Steph and the gang, but Rebecca declines all offers. She is, she says, hibernating for the winter. But surely winter is the ideal time to write music and practise the guitar. I haven't seen her touch it since her last gig, a couple of weeks before Christmas. It might have lacked the spark of her best performances, but that wasn't the point. The point was to get back in the saddle after the disaster at the Fatted Calf. There were no technical problems this time, and the crowd were appreciative, even offering some of the wolf-whistles Mr Parry so vehemently disapproves of.

I glance across at my mesmerised girlfriend. 'There's a guitar here that needs some loving attention.' I say this only in my mind. In the interest of balance, I imagine her reply and the conversation that follows:

'What are you trying to say?'

'That you haven't played it for a while, that's all.'

'And you think I should?'

'Given your talent, it seems a shame to waste it.'

'So I have a duty to write songs, do I? And you're the one to enforce it?' (The conversation has to be realistic. She has to give her best argument, otherwise what's the point?)

'No, I just think it would be good if you didn't let everything slide through sheer apathy.'

'Oh, is that what I am: apathetic?'

'Come on, you can hardly deny it, sitting in front of the telly night after night, watching this crap.'

Where does the argument go from here? I don't know. In order to find out, I decide to say it for real: 'There's a guitar here that needs some loving attention.'

'Mmm?' She doesn't look away from the screen. 'Oh, yeah. I've been playing the Epiphone.'

I didn't think of that. The conversation has ended before it's begun, and I'm left wondering whether I prefer my fantasy version, with an ending that includes me winning the argument, Rebecca spending more time with the guitar, looking more happy, more active. Instead, I leave her to it, knowing I can't restart the conversation without giving the appearance that I'm pushing for an argument. And anyway, what right do I have to insist that she plays?

On my way up the stairs, I walk past the rows of Christmas cards attached to the wall by their plastic holders. Twelfth Night has been and gone; I should really take them down.

Rebecca's dad invited us round to his place for Christmas lunch. He was impeccably behaved this time; grateful, I think, that I hadn't whisked his daughter away and left him with only his memories for company. In the afternoon we dropped in on my parents, and Mum offered us an array of food we couldn't possibly do justice to. Of course, Rebecca charmed everyone effortlessly. Alistair was so gobsmacked that his wife had to nudge him and tell him to stop staring. I took a secret pleasure at his astonishment, but when he grabbed a moment alone with me he said, without any hint of cynicism, 'I knew one day you'd bring home a girl like her,' and it was my turn to be stunned.

Zach wasn't there, but he emailed us best wishes from the south of Spain, where he's been travelling for the last few weeks. He attached some photos, and once again he looks like a different person.

The time over Christmas and into the New Year was quiet. The weather was the coldest it's been for years, so we tended to stay in. Mr Parry was more reserved than I'm used to, and they didn't have to spell out that this time of year is when they miss Rebecca's mum the most. The three of us spent New Year's Eve together, neither of them really wanting to go out anywhere. I couldn't help thinking that if Trib were there – instead of up north, visiting friends – he'd have them partying in the streets.

'Any resolutions?' I'd asked Rebecca a few minutes after midnight.

'I don't really believe in New Year's resolutions,' she said, and kissed me.

The Epiphone sits in the corner of the bedroom. I pluck it from its stand, deadening the strings so Rebecca won't hear that I've picked it up. It's even dustier than the Martin. It occurs to me that *I* was probably the last person to play it, bashing out my rendition of 'Bunny' at Rebecca's insistence.

She's becoming like Kerry, that's what scares me. Is this the effect I have on women, leaching the energy out of them until there's nothing left for either of us? Or is it nothing to do with me at all? I really don't understand what's happening to her. If I had a tenth of her talent I know exactly what I'd be doing.

I stare at the unmade bed – the fitted sheet, blue and rippled like the sea, the duvet bunched up in one corner. Rebecca can sit on her arse if she wants to, but I itch to *do* something. I phone Trib, who said he'd be back from his travels at some point today. Sure enough, he picks up after three rings.

'Hello?'

'Hiya, mate. What have you got?'

—

Trib doesn't have anything. Are people less immoral over Christmas? Do they take time off from being bastards? He suggests meeting up at Sumi's on Saturday instead. Recent snow has obliterated features all over town, suffocating everything in a shroud of white, so that when I spot Trib outside the darkened shop, it doesn't look like the right place. Even Trib is unlike himself, wrapped up in a knee-length duffel coat and long stripy scarf. He points wordlessly to a hand-written note taped to the window that says: 'Sumi's has closed. Thank you for all of your custom over the years.'

I'm not sure I can trust the evidence of my eyes. 'She's gone out of business?'

'Looks like it,' he says. 'I had no idea she was in that much trouble.'

We stand there dumbfounded, unsure what to do. Trib puts one gloved hand against the window pane, like a mourner at a funeral paying his last respects. I decide I hate January.

Trib sighs. 'How have you been keeping?'

'Okay.'

'We need to get out of this cold, mate. How about the pub instead?'

I shrug acceptance, and we end up at The Castle, a bright, clean place in the town centre with a roaring log fire. Trib has surveyed the taps and ordered me a pint of some dark winter beer before I can tell him a cup of tea will do. And now I think of it, why shouldn't I have a pint? A hint of liquorice and spice confirms that Trib hasn't lost his knack for sniffing out the good stuff.

He takes a substantial swig and says, 'I went to see Lee.'

'Lee? Why?'

'Unfinished business, I suppose.'

'It sounded pretty finished to me.'

'I used to think that too.' Trib takes another gulp of beer. 'It wasn't exactly a comfortable meeting, but I put the question to him that you put to me.'

'What was that?'

'I asked him if his dad continued mistreating him after the accident. He said no.'

'And you believed him?'

'Yeah, I did. But he also reckoned his dad would probably have stopped anyway, that it was just a phase he was going through.'

'Bullshit.'

'Who's to say he's not right? He knows his dad a lot better

than either of us.'

'You can't honestly believe that.' I'm in an argumentative mood, and I indulge it, since the point is to make Trib feel better. 'Lee might have hoped for it, but that doesn't mean it was going to happen. What you did was probably the only thing that was ever going to stop it.'

'We'll never know, will we?' He stares down at the surface of his beer, black and reflective.

'You were right to go back and see him, Trib.'

'D'you think?'

'Yes. You always do the right thing. It's bloody nauseating.' I'm surprised at how forcefully this comes out.

'If that were true, I wouldn't be in this situation with Lee in the first place.'

'You know what I mean. You know how to make amends. If you cock something up, you rectify it.'

'Yeah, years later.'

I take in a deep breath and blow it noisily out again. 'You're too hard on yourself. It's not like you can turn back the clock and undo what happened, so you did the next best thing. You didn't have to bother doing anything.'

'I suppose. But I've always hated the idea of just taking the path of least resistance. I mean, you have to exercise your free will, don't you? Even if it's hard. Otherwise you might as well be a machine, a cog in a clockwork universe.'

Rebecca springs to mind, and Jodie. At least I have Trib and the missions. There's nothing like a night-time excursion of questionable legality to keep you feeling fresh and vital. And yet, I can hardly claim to be immune from living my life on autopilot at times. When I'm at my angriest, free will seems a distant luxury. The difference, I suppose, is that my autopilot engages due to an excess of emotion, while Rebecca's seems caused by a lack of it.

'Anyway,' Trib says. 'I just thought you'd want to know, since it was you that persuaded me to see him.'

I'm absorbed with my own thoughts and it takes me a moment to realise what he said. 'Me?'

'Yes. You got me thinking about it. I knew it was long overdue.'

'You're glad you did it, then?'

'Aye, I think so. We left with a handshake. That's something.'

We sit there in silence for a moment.

'Have you got your board?' I ask him.

'Mate, when have I not got my board?' He produces it from his duffel coat, along with a pack of cards and his diary.

'According to official records,' he says, 'you're ten pence up.'

—

That night, Rebecca cooks us risotto and we eat it in front of the TV.

'This is really good,' I tell her.

'I should have used more onion.'

I spoon another mouthful in. Tastes fine to me.

'I've been thinking,' she says. 'It's probably about time I looked for a job that's a bit more lucrative and interesting than gutting fish. I might look at college courses, see if I can get some kind of qualification.'

'Good idea.' I pause. 'Will that leave you enough time for music?'

Her shoulders lift and settle. 'I don't know.'

'But what about …'

She appears to know what I'm thinking, because she says, 'Oh, I'll definitely record the EP up in London.'

'And after that?'

'We'll see.'

But the recording voucher was supposed to be a springboard to something better. This is the girl who told me just two months ago that she was born to play music. I use the edge of my spoon to decapitate a prawn. I wonder if I'd preferred it if she'd said, 'I've decided to pack it all in'. At least it would be a decision, something firm and unambiguous. It's the idea that she's going to drift out of music that gets to me.

'Rebecca, you can't just …' I tail off. I have no right to make demands.

'Olly?'

'I just think it would be … such a shame if you stopped.' It's a limp, feeble sentence.

'I don't know,' she sighs. 'It's just so hard. The composing and performing take enough effort, but if you really want to make a go of it you also have to be a businesswoman and a recording engineer and a marketing professional. I mean, screw all that. What's wrong with just making music?'

'Nothing. Nothing at all.'

'But it would be nice if more than a handful of people actually heard it.'

'I'll hear it. I'll listen to anything you write.'

'You're sweet,' she says, and I want to counter by asking how a gifted singer-songwriter can aspire to a desk job.

She goes to bed early, citing tiredness, and although the thought makes me feel sour and mean, I'm relieved. I no longer have to watch her idly retreating from every good thing in her life. I'll join her in bed later, when I'm less annoyed.

I find myself unable to settle to anything. Watching the TV would seem like hypocrisy, my current novel is not engaging, and after a few minutes of *Wish You Were Here* on headphones, I realise I can't listen to music without being reminded of what Rebecca might be about to forsake. My gaze is drawn once again to the Martin, its sound hole an accusing, silent O. I remove it from its stand, nestle it into the crook of my hip and gently strum a few chords. I settle on an E minor seventh – one of those tense, transitional chords that needs resolving. From what little music theory I remember, an A major might do the trick, but I resist the temptation to play it, and keep strumming the E minor seventh, over and over.

Trib has done what I've never had the courage to do: go back and face the defining event of his past. Dr Nylund suggested something of the sort when I used to see him and, of course, I argued against it. What happened back at school happened; life doesn't have an undo function. I was too busy fighting Nylund for us to come up with any course of action. But I have one now.

I thought this whole business was finished a long time ago. I convinced myself it was history, but it's not history until it fails to make my blood boil. Stendall is at the root of my anger and frustration, and you don't chop down a tree by cutting the branches off one by one, you hack through the trunk. I have to do what Trib has done: go back to the source of it all and stare it in the face. But if I can't forgive, what would I gain from it? Understanding, I suppose – a sense of how it fits into my life, how it's affected me, how to neutralise the feelings it still, to this day, produces.

I continue to strum the E minor seventh. No, more than that. Understanding would be good; justice would be even better.

28

NUMBER 121 HAS THE SAME grubby brick and flaking paint as all the other houses in the terrace. I've parked the car some way down the street and on the short walk here I've passed a demolished building on the corner that looks like the relic of a war zone, and a gutted shop which is probably a foretaste of how Sumi's will soon look. Although the snow has largely gone, several piles of it remain on the pavement, dirty and unmelted.

I ring the bell, tug on both sleeves of my sweater. From the safety of my room – sat in front of the PC, looking at maps and addresses – this had seemed like such a good idea. Before the internet, it would have been harder to track Mrs Macklin down. But a Google search shows me she was treasurer of an exercise club in

Reading in 2006. Typing the town and her name into the British Telecom website gets me her address and phone number. I've ruled out the idea of ringing her in case she thinks I'm a nutter.

The woman who answers the door wears a grey tracksuit and an oversized blue jumper that hangs off her frame. Her hair is mousy and sharply cut, her face heavy with disinterest. She's shorter than I expected.

'Donna Macklin?' I ask.

'Yeah?'

My throat tightens and I can't get anything else out. What was I going to say? I prepared some words but they've deserted me.

'Well I know you ain't trying to sell me nothing,' she says. 'They're never lost for words.'

'I knew your son,' I manage. 'We were at school together.'

She stiffens; her eyes narrow. 'And?'

'I thought maybe I could talk to you about …' My voice trails off.

'What makes you think I want to talk about anything?'

My mouth opens and closes like a goldfish. I feel a prickling across my shoulders and back. This was a terrible idea. I could have gone to see Lambert, Crawford, Jonesy. But all of them bought into that conspiracy of silence eleven years ago. I wanted to hear someone tell the truth about Duncan, and only Donna Macklin can do that. But she doesn't want to.

When, after a few seconds, I can come up with no way of salvaging the situation, I mutter, 'I – I'm sorry,' then turn and walk away. It's not like I didn't try. Later, when I'm safely back in my room in Strathurst, I can at least console myself with that.

'Were you his mate?'

Her words stop me. I could debate endlessly in my head whether or not I qualified as his friend, but it's a simple question and it deserves a simple answer. I turn round. 'Yes.'

She jerks her head to one side, more like a muscle twitch than an invitation. 'You better come in, then.'

Am I really ready for this?

'Come on,' she says, 'before I change my mind.'

Inside, the hallway and stairs are a gutted shell, with wallpaper stripped and carpets lifted. A hammer and a scraper lay on the bare boards. She takes me through to the lounge, which couldn't be more different: a new, dusky pink carpet; fresh paint – I can smell it – and a pair of two-seater settees in cream leather that sit at ninety degrees to each other, one of them facing a widescreen TV.

'You're doing the place up?'

'That's right. Have a seat.'

She takes one of the sofas, and I sit gingerly on the other. I feel as much an intruder here as I did when I was dropping off the chair at Summer's house.

She sits back and folds her arms. 'What's your name, then?'

'Olly Griffin.'

I wonder if she'll say that Duncan mentioned me once or twice, but she doesn't. She waits for me to speak.

'I don't mean to intrude or anything. I don't want to … bring up anything you don't want to talk about. I know it must be hard.'

'Love,' she says, 'you ain't got any idea how hard it's been.'

'No. No, of course not.'

My eyes dart round the room. I've already seen the picture of Duncan on the mantelpiece – a schoolkid frozen in time, whose eyes I avoid. There's also a photo of a man with a lopsided smile and a stubble of grey hair.

'Is that Mr Macklin?'

'Christ, no. That bugger fucked off years ago. Left Duncan to it. And look what happened.' Her sudden ferocity scares me, but it's gone as quickly as it arrived. 'No, that's Terry. We've just started going out. Early days yet, but he's a decent guy.'

'That's great. I hope it works out.'

She raises her eyebrows, and I wonder if she thinks I'm patronising her, so I add, 'I've just started a new relationship myself.'

'Yeah?'

I take the photo of Rebecca out of my wallet and pass it to her. She looks from the picture to me and back again. 'She's really pretty.'

'You don't need to tell me she's way out of my league.'

She barks out a laugh and passes the photo back. 'Get what you can, that's what I say.'

Her gaze drifts back to the picture of Terry. 'He works nights. Lorry driver, he is. We don't get to see each other as much as we'd like. Says he'll change to days for me, but since I work at the big Tesco's I might see if I can move to a later shift.'

There's an awkward pause.

'You're sure you were his mate?' she says.

'Yeah. Not for long, but ... yeah.'

'That's the only reason I let you in. Because if he was still here, he'd want to see you.'

'I'd want to see him.'

Another silence. Mrs Macklin is no longer looking at me. She stares into infinity, her lips pursed and brow furrowed.

I have to keep the conversation going. 'I ... don't really know why I came here. I suppose I –'

'It's still difficult, you know,' she says, unaware that she's interrupting. 'You don't ever get over it. Not ever. You wonder when things are gonna get back to normal, and then one day you realise there ain't no normal any more, at least not the way it was. This is your new life and you've gotta live with it. Duncan weren't an easy kid to bring up, that's for sure. Would've been a lot easier if he'd been one of them goody two-shoes who never put a foot wrong.'

'I'm not sure those kind of kids exist.'

'Yeah? What about you, then? Posh accent, well turned out. Bet you got good grades too.'

I laugh bitterly. 'I should have done, but things went a bit ... pear-shaped. I gave my parents a hard time, a bloody hard time. I think all kids do, in their way.'

'Yeah, but there's difficult and there's difficult, ain't there?'

That's a bit of a cop-out.

'How was he at school, then?' she says. 'He'd never tell me. After all, I was just his mum.'

I try to think of how I can put it without being too negative, but there were a lot of negatives where Duncan and school were concerned.

'Yeah,' she snorts after a while, 'well that about sums it up.'

How can she say this about her son, her dead son? I suppose I expected her to love him unconditionally; to have a rose-tinted view of his life.

She says, 'I think he was being bullied quite a lot.'

'He was. I saw it.'

'And?' There's a hint of challenge in her voice.

'I went to the headmaster and told him what was happening.'

She jerks back an inch. 'Yeah? What did he say?'

'He didn't believe it was happening. He said unless I had proof, he wouldn't do anything about it.' Even now, even eleven years after the event, my heartbeat quickens as I say it. Yes, this is definitely unfinished business.

She sighs. 'I went through all this with Lambert years ago. I thought about taking him to court, suing the school, all that stuff, but at some point you gotta let it go. Maybe I could have got some money out of it, but what's the point? Ain't gonna bring Duncan back, is it? It'd be like saying that Duncan's life was worth this or that amount of money. There ain't enough money in the world. He might have been an awkward little bastard, he might have worried me sick and not done what he was told and all that, but … there ain't enough money in the world.'

And this is just what she's prepared to tell me; this is just the tip of the iceberg.

'You know Lambert died last year?' she says.

I shake my head. So, he takes it to the grave. I hope he gave it some thought before the end. I hope he felt some regret, that knot you can never unpick.

'I wish ...' Say it, Olly. This is your one opportunity to tell it like it is.

She waits for me.

'I wish I'd done more for Duncan.'

'Oh, no,' she says. 'You did plenty. You went to the headmaster? That's more than any of them others did.'

Of course, I don't believe her. You can't just hand forgiveness out on a plate like that. My hands start to shake.

A room. A beam. A rope.

'I'm the one who found him.'

She frowns. 'No, it was Crawford.'

I shake my head, not sure if I can speak any more.

Her voice softens. 'They said it was Crawford.'

'No.'

'You poor bastard.'

The threads in her carpet are blue and red and off-white. It's not actually pink at all.

'Look,' she says, 'sorry if I was a bit short on the doorstep. I thought you was another of them people who were gonna say, "I'm sorry for your loss." People still say it sometimes, even after all these years. I know they mean well, but ... No, you're different. You understand it better.'

Do I? Really? I don't know. She's been through more than I ever will. I have no right to break down in front of her.

'I'll make you a cup of tea, shall I?'

I nod, and she retreats to the kitchen, giving me a chance to claw back some composure. I glance up at the photograph of Duncan – freckles and an almost-smile, the grey of the school uniform – and this time I find I can look him in the eye.

After a few minutes, Mrs Macklin returns with two cups of tea and a plate of custard creams.

'You all right?' she says as she sits down.

'Yeah.'

'So, what do you remember about him?'

At last a question that's easy for me to answer. 'His card tricks.'

'Yeah, that don't surprise me.'

'Well, it wasn't the sort of thing you'd forget.'

'Good, was he?'

'He didn't show you?'

'He did at first. I bought him books on magic tricks 'cos he had precious little interest in anything else. He spent hours in his room practising. But that's all he did in them last months. He didn't go out with his mates. I didn't think he *had* any mates. He'd rather stay in and watch his Penn and Teller videos over and over again. He showed me a couple of tricks and they were okay, but, I mean, it ain't gonna put bread on the table, is it? I told him he should be spending more time on his homework. You realise how you could have got a better job if you'd paid more attention at school, so you try and make your kid do it. But they don't listen, do they? Just like you didn't. And after a while he didn't want to show me any more tricks.'

I try to read between the lines, piece together the reality of Duncan's home life. Did she make mistakes, bringing him up? Was he a lazy kid? Does any of it matter?

'You know what I do on his birthday?' she says. 'I buy him a new pack of cards, take them out of the plastic, shuffle them and put them away, ready for him to use to do his tricks. Huh. Stupid, eh?'

'No. No, it's not.'

'I've got them all upstairs in a box. Eleven packs of cards he'll never use.'

'But he would have.'

'You think so?' she says. 'He never stuck with anything, that kid. I know that's my fault. I wanna believe he would've changed, and I might have found the right way to encourage him, but I expect he would've ended up unemployed, like his dad. No qualifications, no energy, no nothing.'

I can't let her say this. 'No.' It comes out with some force. Her eyes meet mine, and again I can see the challenge in them. It's her son we're talking about. Hers.

'He'd be up on stage,' I tell her, 'wearing a tuxedo, performing tricks, amazing people.'

'Huh. You don't need to sugar coat it.'

'I'm not. There was only one thing Duncan was ever going to be. He might not have been any good at Maths or English, but with a deck of cards he was a genius. I saw it with my own eyes. Did you know he could shuffle with one hand? Did you ever see him make cards disappear right in front of your eyes? I've had years to figure out his tricks and I still don't understand how he did them. If that's what he could do at fourteen, how good would he be now?'

Donna Macklin doesn't look defensive or bitter any more; she looks like she'll listen to anything I have to say.

'We used to find an empty classroom every lunchtime and he'd show me what he could do. It was gobsmacking. He could have kept a hundred people spellbound.'

She blinks rapidly. 'You reckon?'

'You gave him decks of cards and books on magic and you gave him time to practice. That's all the education Duncan ever needed.'

'I wanna believe that.'

'Then do. It's the truth.'

Her mouth opens in a yawn of pain. She reaches across to grab hold of my hand and squeezes it with astonishing force.

'I'm sorry, Mrs Macklin. I didn't mean to –'

She cuts me off by shaking her head rapidly. I want to say more, but I know she won't hear it. She stares past me, tethered to the present only by her grip on my hand. Her eyes fill and I lower my gaze to her slippered feet, unable to watch her grief. Still she won't let go. I put my other hand on hers, not knowing what else to do. It's only the urgent need for a hankie that finally causes her to release me. She blows her nose and spends a few minutes calming herself.

'I've blamed everyone over what happened to him,' she says finally. 'I've blamed the headmaster, the teachers. I've blamed them little shits that bullied him. I've blamed God, sitting up there in his ivory tower. I've blamed his dad. I've blamed myself for not being a good mum. I've chased it round and round and round in my head 'til I've gone half mad. And then a couple of years ago I worked out that I'm never gonna get to the bottom of it, and all that blame is just a waste of time. Only one thing makes any sense: remembering him. I've got it all up here.' She taps her head. 'All them memories. All the bad stuff and all the good stuff.' She nods to herself, satisfied that she's done a thorough job of cataloguing it. 'And I thought it was all there, all complete. I never thought that eleven years down the line someone would turn up and add something new.'

—

The streets have changed by the time I leave. The houses aren't so much tired as lived-in. The piles of snow are all stacked up on the pavement, implying that someone – probably many people – went to the effort of clearing the road. When I get back to the car and put my hands on the steering wheel, I find they're still trembling, a combination of emotional fatigue and the fact that all I've eaten today is an apple, a cup of tea and two biscuits.

I get out again and walk to the row of shops. I find a place selling freshly made sandwiches, but opt for the greasy spoon café instead, ordering ham, egg and chips from a disinterested waitress. I chuck the food down like a man just coming off hunger strike, and it has a remarkably fortifying effect. As I mop up the final splodge of egg yolk with my last chip, something occurs to me: Mrs Macklin could have asked me who bullied her son. And she chose not to, for reasons I now fully understand.

But what was it Trib said about the purest kind of mission –

the one performed as a gift for an unknowing recipient? An opportunity has been handed to me. Donna Macklin may not know who to blame for her son's death, but I sure as hell do.

29

THE PROBLEM IS THAT STENDALL can deny any involvement in what happened to Duncan. Does he even think about it any more, or is it all just ancient history for him?

The speedo shows I'm over the limit again. I lift my foot off the accelerator.

Would a judge or jury accept my testimony as the sole reason linking Stendall to the suspended body I found in the sports hall, that image lodged in my skull like a piece of shrapnel? Not a chance. You had to be a kid at Kingsmarsh – eyes open, watching your back, all the time. But I know what I saw.

As soon as I get home I rush up the stairs with barely a hello to Moira and Jodie, and climb the ladder to my room. I look Stendall up on the internet, expecting at best the tiny trail of breadcrumbs I got when searching for Donna Macklin. What leaps out at me instead are articles from prominent business publications and a page on Wikipedia.

John Stendall (born 10 October 1983 in Esher, Surrey) is the CEO of Green Sloth, a British clothing company. He is listed at number 15 in the 2009 Henrikson Hot List, which showcases the 100 most promising young British business executives[1]. His net worth is estimated at £6m[2].

Early Life
Stendall was born in 1983, the son of electrician Barry Stendall and schoolteacher Amanda Stendall (née Thorington). His mother and father split up when he was five years old, and he has had no con-

tact with his father since, stating in an interview that 'I don't need a father figure to look up to. I stand on my own two feet.'[3]

Business Ventures

Stendall graduated from the London School of Economics with a degree in Business Studies. He joined Green Sloth on graduation, and after rising through the ranks, became CEO in early 2008.[4] Under his leadership, the company has seen a substantial increase in revenue and profit[citation needed].

Although he is currently concentrating his efforts on the garment industry, he has expressed a wish to expand Green Sloth into other areas of business[citation needed].

Personal Life

Although he is known for working long hours, Stendall has also found the time to become a qualified pilot. He is the owner of a four-seater Cessna 350 Corvalis.[5]

He is currently single. In an interview with GQ magazine he joked that 'Most of my leisure time is spent trying to avoid gold-diggers.'[6]

Controversy

In May 2009, Stendall was stopped by police after driving at 92mph in a temporary 50mph speed limit[7]. After being breathalysed, he was found to have twice the legal amount of alcohol in his system. Stendall hired celebrity defence lawyer Steve Corrigan and although he technically remains charged with the offence, police have said they will not be pursuing the case any further.

Politics

Stendall is a proponent of free-market capitalism and has been outspoken in condemning government interference in business.[8] In 2008 he made a donation to the Conservative Party, but has since severed all links with them, claiming, 'It was a mistake. Business and politics don't mix.'[9]

External Links
- Official Green Sloth Website

I've heard of Green Sloth. Zach has some of their clothes. I click through the other links, knowing that this isn't doing me any good. I'm directed to an article on the website of a magazine called 'Biz: 21st Century Enterprise'.

John Stendall is the head of Green Sloth, a garment company rapidly accumulating street cred with British fashionistas.

You're known as a CEO who embraces technology. How does this benefit Green Sloth?
'I'm a big fan of telecommuting. People don't do it enough. The technology is there, so why not use it? I don't buy this idea that you have to deal with someone face-to-face to get business done. I encourage people to prefer email to the phone. It stops you being constantly interrupted; you can choose when to read emails and when to respond to them. I'm not saying it isn't useful to hold the occasional meeting, just that there are new methods of doing things which can be more effective than slavishly following the old ways.'

Many executives find email a curse. You wouldn't agree?
'Not at all. They just haven't learned how to use it effectively. I've got two principles regarding email. First, you only send messages that need to be sent, and only to the people who need to read them. Employees who continue to send unnecessary emails are reprimanded because it's a waste of everyone's time. Second, I operate a zero inbox policy. I haven't finished a day's work until all the emails are deleted. Some of that

information will end up on my to-do list, or be sent to my assistant for inclusion on the company wiki, but there will be no emails left. Like all technology, you have to make it work for you, not become enslaved by it.'

What is your working environment like?
'Minimal. I spend a lot of time working from home. I have a study, but it's very sparse. The only tools I need to get work done are a laptop and a mobile phone. This gives me the flexibility to work anywhere I like: the lounge, the garden, my office at work, or at a customer or supplier. Wireless technology has given businesses this kind of freedom. I'm surprised more people don't take advantage of it. You can save a lot of money on office space when most of your staff are hot-desking. It's this sort of smart thinking that has seen us positioned so well to weather the downturn in the economy. Our overheads are very low.'

Speaking of which, your financial results have been spectacular for a small company during a recession. What's your secret?
'Innovation is key to success. It's too easy to fall into habitual patterns that aren't very efficient. If you have a problem it's often lateral thinking, rather than a head-on tackle, that gets it solved. You find ways to make things work. People should never settle for what's been done before. They should never be too busy to invent new ways of competing.' |Biz|

It might have muddied the waters if there was a home page with photos of his wife and smiling toddlers. But it's clear from the evidence that he's an empire-builder: self-promoting, ruthless, and – the acid poured in the open wound – successful. There's not a single sentence suggesting any kindness or compassion. Certainly no mention of any charitable work, but maybe that's something you only do when you've clawed your way to a £100 million personal fortune and need to fish your reputation back out of the gutter. Everything stinks of self-interest. In that, at least, I can recognise the old Stendall.

I go back to the Controversy section of the Wikipedia article, because this, more than anything, is what inflames me. Stendall is now moving in those rarefied circles where he's no longer subject to the law like the average man on the street. He's too important to be held accountable. It's there in his dodging of a conviction for a driving offence just as it was there, years ago, when he terrorised his classmates. How could the school's golden boy possibly be held responsible for Duncan's suicide?

Act like a bastard. Deny all responsibility. Reap the rewards.

Of course, the world is full of these people and always has been: the bankers who destroyed the economy but still receive colossal bonuses, the MPs who claim huge expenses off the taxpayer because they consider themselves more deserving than the rest of us, Jane and her bullying of Steph, Mr Summer and his hard sell. Before Trib, it always used to feel so distant and abstract to me. Robert Xavier-Walters, whose golden handshake caused headlines last year, might as well be a fictional character for all the effect he's had on my life. But Stendall ... Stendall is real. I've seen first-hand how destructive he is.

If I suggested to Trib that we go after him, he'd ask me if this was a grudge, and yes, it is, but I hold it for the best of reasons. Stendall hasn't changed. He admits in the Biz article that he reprimands people over emails. There it is, from his own mouth: he's still treating people like shit. And why wouldn't he? There was never any punishment for Duncan. Stendall must feel unique, special, untouchable.

It's my responsibility to do something about him. But right now, floundering in the fog of my outrage, I can't see what.

—

On Sunday I go round to Rebecca's, aware that I haven't been paying her much attention of late. She's in the kitchen, putting together a falafel, spinach and tomato sandwich. A ray of sunlight streams through the window and onto the chopping board.

'Hiya,' she says.

'I've booked the Star Anise for Thursday night,' I tell her.

She showed an interest in the place before Christmas, but dismissed it after seeing the prices – it's exotic and expensive.

She turns round and her eyes light up. 'Really?'

'Yes. I'll treat you.'

In part it's a guilt reaction, like buying flowers after an argument. Except that we haven't actually argued. Huh. Pre-emptive apologies. I do live a complicated life.

'That would be great,' she says.

She abandons the sandwich and kisses me, then leans back and pushes herself up with her hands so she's sitting on the kitchen counter. At the same time, she wraps her legs around me and pulls me forward. Her hands tangle in my hair as she kisses me a second time, slower, hotter. It's been a long time. Too long. Are we turning a corner? It's like we've been in different countries for a month and grown accustomed to being apart. But now, back in each other's presence, we realise just what we've missed.

My course of action is clear. I'll slip my hands underneath her buttocks, lift her off the counter and carry her upstairs. Once in the bedroom, I can close the door, draw the thick curtains, and in the intimacy of darkness I'll bring us back together.

But before I can do any of this, she withdraws and cocks her head. 'I've been thinking.'

'Yes?'

'There's something I want to do for you.'

I raise my eyebrows.

'I want to help you with your phobia.' She takes hold of my sweater and gives it a little tug upwards.

Light is flooding in from the kitchen window, the hallway, everywhere.

'No. Rebecca, you know I can't …'

She lets go.

'The thing is,' she says, 'if we take it just a tiny step at a time, it won't be so bad.'

Her eyes shine with such kindness, such empathy, that for a second I ponder the heresy of giving in to it. Then my guts tighten. Now, when we are tentatively drawing closer again, is the most dangerous time. I glance out of the window, as if someone might be staring in at us. Rebecca reaches up to the cord, and in one quick movement lowers the blind. It doesn't make things nearly dark enough.

'We can do it together,' she says. 'Look, I'll start.'

She rolls her top up until it's just underneath her breasts, exposing her midriff.

'That's different. You're ... beautiful.'

'So are you. And it's hardly like I'm flawless. Look.' She releases the button on her trousers, unzips and pulls down the fabric, revealing a ridge of discoloured flesh. 'Appendix scar.'

My gaze is drawn to the crease of her hip, which gracefully skirts the side of her belly, before disappearing below a line of black cotton. I lower my head to kiss the pastures around her navel. Cradling my head, she sighs – an expression of pleasure or disappointment or impatience.

She puts a finger beneath my chin and tilts my head back.

'The bedroom,' I insist, before she can say anything. 'I'll be much happier with the bedroom, the dark.'

'It can be the tiniest thing,' she says, taking hold of my left hand and reaching for my sleeve.

I jerk my arm away and she looks surprised by the force with which I do it.

'Please. Trust me, Olly.'

But I don't. My scars are not like hers. They are a window into the worst part of me, a window whose shutters are locked tight, and must remain that way.

'Nothing bad is going to happen,' she says.

She reaches again for my sleeve, slower and more tentative this time, and the panic floods back, trampling all other thoughts. She isn't giving up, is she? I push myself backwards, breaking the lock of her feet behind my back. 'No, look … No!'

Her shoulders drop. 'But if you don't even try, you won't –'

'But nothing! Look, I just can't, all right?'

'I want you to be free of it.' The sympathy in her tone is muddied with irritation.

'It's not that simple.'

I would be delighted to make love to her without all the rules and pretence. But that is not my life. It's the life of Hollywood stars – or rather the characters they play – inhabiting a perfect wonderland of ecstatic and uncomplicated sex. It is not my life.

'I don't understand,' she says. 'Help me to understand.'

'I'm just … I'm just not comfortable with it. Look, I'm sorry if that's a big problem for you, but …' I leave it hanging.

'Oh, Olly,' she says. Her hands fall across her lap, wrists crossed over the fly of her trousers.

It was never this difficult with Kerry; she accepted my 'phobia' and all it entailed without question. But then she accepted everything without question. Rebecca is livelier, more inquisitive, better. And worse.

We face each other across a chasm of misunderstanding, neither of us knowing what to do next.

My phone rings. Glancing at the display, I see it's Trib.

'I've got to take this.'

As I turn away, I see her mouth open in protest, but it doesn't stop me from taking the coward's way out. There was nothing more to say anyway.

'Are you alone?' Trib says.

'Just a moment.' I go up the stairs to the bedroom, out of earshot of Rebecca. 'Okay.'

'Are you up for something tonight?'

'You bet.'

30

AT TEN TO FIVE on the following Thursday, while I'm alone in the Portakabin, a phone call cuts through my workday tedium. Trib doesn't bother with any preamble, he just says, 'Mitchell was beaten up last night. Some bloke ripped into him after his gig.'

'Shit. How badly hurt is he?'

'I've not got all the details.' For the first time I can hear anger in Trib's voice. 'It's nothing life-threatening, but he sounds pretty down. I'm going to see him this evening, try and cheer him up a bit.'

I look at my monitor and decide that completing a spreadsheet of the company's software licences can wait until … well, doomsday, quite frankly.

'I'll come with you.'

'Cheers, mate,' Trib says. 'I didn't mean you had to –'

'No, it's fine; I want to.'

'It'll mean a lot to him. Do you want me to pick you up?'

'Yeah, as soon as you like. I'm done here.'

—

Mitchell lives in a two bed semi halfway between the town centre and Hillfields. When he opens the door it takes an effort to prevent myself from staring. He has a split lip and a black eye swollen almost completely shut. A bruise is beginning to form all the way down one side of his neck.

'Oh,' he says, seeing me. 'Hi, Olly.'

'Hi.' I manage to stop myself from automatically asking him how it's going.

'Jesus, man,' Trib says.

'Yeah, I know. Come in, guys.' Mitchell's voice is muted, head bowed, and he glances down the street before closing the door.

He leads us into the lounge, unable to conceal a limp, and gestures for us to take a seat. He lowers himself into a chair like an old man, hands wrapped like claws around the armrests. I find I have to look away. There's a microphone stand in one corner and a full-length mirror with an ornate brass frame on the wall. I imagine him honing his act here, practising his facial expressions, his timing – the bright, cheeky Mitchell, that is; not this broken creature. This didn't just happen to him; someone actively did it. What the fuck is wrong with people?

Trib says, 'First things first, Mitch: you have to get yourself to –'

'Do either of you want a cup of tea?'

'No, we're fine,' Trib says impatiently. 'Now –'

'Or coffee? I've got some good ground stuff if that's your sort of thing.'

'Mate –'

'There are probably a couple of beers in the fridge as well. Did you drive round, or –?'

Trib reaches out and touches Mitchell's hand. 'Mate, you have to go to the hospital, get yourself checked out.'

Mitchell shakes his head.

'You know it's the sensible thing,' Trib says.

Mitchell turns to me and says, 'I don't do hospitals.'

'Why not?' I ask him.

'Hospital is where you go to be near sick people,' Mitchell says. 'It's where you pick up MRSA; it's where rushed-off-their-feet doctors make mistakes with your health.'

This is what a real phobia looks like, not the fake thing I use on Rebecca.

'Come on,' Trib says, 'those things are rare. Really rare.'

'They happen, Trib. All it takes is a bit of bad luck.'

'But that's not rational.'

'Call me irrational, then. It won't change anything. Tell me this: what's the point of going to hospital if it'll cause me more pain and anxiety than healing at home?'

'Mitch …'

'I'm not going. That's final.'

I see Trib struggling to find a way back into the argument, but I've got an idea that might be acceptable to everyone.

'Mitch, I've got a friend who's a nurse. I can get her to come round and check you out.'

'So *she* can force me into hospital?'

'No, so you can be sure you're going to heal properly.'

His forehead creases. I'm probably tapping into the same fear that keeps him away from doctors.

'Look, Mitch, it'll probably all be fine, but you want to be sure. *We* want to be sure.' I look to Trib for confirmation, and he nods. 'I'll make it absolutely clear you're not going to hospital. I'll tell her it's not negotiable. If I do that, will you agree to let her check you out?'

Trib adds, 'I'll shut up about it if you let her take a look at you.'

Mitchell's eyes dart around the room. 'What if she does find something wrong?'

'Then you'll have to decide what to do. But if she doesn't, you can stop worrying. So, how about it?'

He lets out a sigh and nods reluctantly. I pop into the kitchen to phone Bethan, explain the situation, and ask her if she'll come over.

'Give me the address and I can come round straight away,' she says.

I start to give her directions.

'No need for all that,' she says. 'I took your advice and got a sat nav.'

A good thing too – Bethan's the sort of person who could lose her bearings in her own house. I tell her the address. 'And no mention of him going to the hospital, right?'

'Even I can keep my mouth shut when the need arises, Olly. I'll see you in five.'

Back in the lounge, I tell them she's on her way. They both look round, as if I've interrupted something. I'm about to ask if they want some privacy, but they turn back and carry on their conversation.

'Yeah,' Mitchell says bitterly, 'it was his subtle use of the words "faggot" and "bender" that tipped me off.'

'And you haven't told the police about any of this?'

Mitchell snorts. 'Why? He didn't steal my wallet.'

'Mitch, this is serious. You've got to tell them. You can't just let someone get away with this.'

'Trib, I'm an openly gay man. How do you think the boys in blue feel about that?'

'Oh, come on.'

'The law might have changed in 1967,' he says, 'but the attitudes bloody didn't.'

'You're just thinking the worst.'

'You wouldn't be saying that if you were queer.'

Again, Trib is stuck for words. In the end he settles for a vague, 'What are we going to with you, eh?'

A few moments pass in silence. Mitchell is hunched forwards in his chair, elbows resting on his knees. 'I know who did it,' he says in a low voice, as if confessing a secret. 'Name, address, everything.'

I look at Trib. Does Mitchell know what we do? That's my immediate thought, that he's making a request.

'Go on,' Trib says slowly.

'It was one of the Vose brothers. The younger one: Liam.'

I've heard of him. The Voses are infamous in Strathurst. They're a year or two older than me, and tales of their brushes with the law stretch back at least a decade. How much is true and how much myth, I don't know, but the stories include arson, GBH, drug dealing. They've featured in the local paper several times, under headlines of the 'Why Aren't These Thugs in Prison?' variety.

The doorbell rings and I jump up to answer it. Bethan is standing there, busty and businesslike as ever.

'Thanks for coming.'

'Not a problem,' she says, bustling in.

Mitchell takes a step back when he sees her, but Bethan's bedside manner is as gentle as her appearance is formidable.

'Right. Mitchell, is it? Nothing to worry about, love. Now, let's have a little look at those bruises.'

Trib and I retreat to the kitchen while Bethan examines him. Trib pushes the door to and begins pacing up and down. With his stride, he can only manage three steps before he has to turn. There's a porcelain teapot on the counter, a striking red against the white tiles. I start to make a cuppa for everybody, as much to keep my hands busy as anything else. Trib stops pacing abruptly and strokes his chin. He gives me a sidelong glance.

'Yes,' I say without hesitation.

'Tonight?'

'Yes.'

—

We leave the van in a supermarket car park and head into Stockbank on foot. This is the disowned son of Strathurst, a council estate from the 70s that had a tawdry reputation right from the start and has never managed to shake it. There's no-one around at the moment, but we can hear a dog barking furiously a couple of streets away.

Bethan has reassured us all that Mitchell will heal just fine, 'like a banana ageing backwards' as she put it.

'This is it,' Trib says, leading us towards the end of a terrace of houses with stingy little windows and a row of identically aligned satellite dishes. He rings the bell of number 10 while we stand on a front 'garden' of cracked concrete and weeds. My heart thumps against the wall of my ribcage, twice a second, but I'm contained, in control. I haven't told Trib about the sturdy wooden chair leg I've hidden in my coat. He wouldn't approve, but seeing the damage this fucker did to Mitchell, I want something to fall back on if I need it.

The door is opened by a woman in her forties with straggly blonde hair and a slack jaw. Behind her is a short hallway, a staircase and two closed doors.

'What?' she says, a single percussive challenge, and folds her arms.

Trib shows his faked warrant card and says, 'I'm Inspector Logan and this is my colleague Sergeant Francis.' Yeah, not strictly legal, but then neither is beating someone up.

'And I'm supposed to be impressed by that, am I?' she says. 'You buggers are always giving us shit. You ain't come in uniform this time, have you? Scared you might get run out of here?'

Despite the aggression, her eyelids are low enough to touch the tops of her pupils. It could be drugs or alcohol, or just a lifetime of not giving a shit about anything. How do specimens like this actually attract breeding partners? It's one of life's great mysteries.

'Does Liam Vose live at this address?' Trib says.

'What if he does?'

'I'll take that as a yes. And you're his mother?'

She tries to close the door, but Trib steps forward and it bounces off his size twelve.

'I'll take that as a yes, too.'

She pulls the door back open so she can give us both barrels. 'Now listen here, Mr Fancy Fucking Plod. He ain't done *nuffing*.' She stabs her finger in Trib's face for emphasis. 'You can't prove *nuffing*.'

'Oh, no, Mrs Vose,' Trib says, 'the CCTV images are quite clear. They show your son assaulting another man.'

'He was probly provoked. People are always provokin' him. And you can't see that sort of thing on film.'

'Whether he was provoked or not is irrelevant.'

'Oh, yeah?'

'Yes, because his victim is in a critical condition, Mrs Vose, and if he doesn't last the night we'll be charging your son with murder.'

That causes her eyes to widen.

'Now,' Trib says, 'we can take your son peacefully down to the station, or we can do things the hard way. If we have to, we'll return with a riot van full of angry coppers and tear this shithole you call your home apart until we find him. Which is it going to be?'

I think I like Trib when he's angry.

We hear the rapid pad of feet from somewhere in the house, followed by the rumble of a patio door opening. Mrs Vose casts a damning glance backwards.

'That'll be him, sir,' I say to Trib. I look round the side of the house and can see a figure climbing over the fence that borders the road. The posts must be rotten, because the fence panel collapses under his weight, sending him sprawling onto the pavement. As he clambers to his feet, he spots me and bolts.

'I'll cover this way,' Trib shouts, and heads to the other end of the terrace.

I vault the low brickwork of their front garden and go directly after Vose. Behind me, I hear his mother's nails-on-blackboard screech: 'He ain't done nuffing! You can't prove it was him!'

If Vose does give himself up, the plan is to handcuff him, stick him in the back of the van and dump him in the middle of nowhere to walk home.

He runs like someone who is used to sudden getaways. He pushes off from walls or hangs off lamps posts so he can change direction quickly, but after a couple of these sharp turns, the labyrinthine estate ends. The chair leg thumps against my chest as I pound after him. I adjust its position, but the sodding thing won't stay where it should. I think about pulling it out and abandoning it on the pavement, but the image of Mitchell's battered face is too fresh in my mind.

Vose skirts a roundabout and heads uphill, where the street lights are more sparse. Christ, is he ever quick.

'Give yourself up, Vose,' I yell in the space between breaths. 'We'll get you in the end.'

He cuts through a petrol station – violently bright in comparison to the darkness – and dodges between the cars. The people at the pumps look up.

'Stop him!' I yell, but they just turn their heads gormlessly to watch us pass.

Then we're out of the oasis of light and back onto the street, across the leisure centre car park and left into another housing estate. The gap between us is widening. He's at the point now where he can take some of the corners and I'm not close enough to see where he's gone – I have to look both ways before I continue. More ground lost.

The last glimpse I get, just before he turns and disappears behind a row of houses, is of Liam Vose smirking over his shoulder and flipping a middle finger at me. I slow to a halt and lean against a lamp post to catch my breath. My lungs feel like balloons stretched to the point just before they burst.

'Shit!'

I pull out the chair leg and chuck it into a nearby bush. Once again, a member of the Vose family gets away with it. I have no choice but to walk back to the van. At least it gives me time to cool off. Trib is waiting there and I give him a sanitised account of what happened.

'You made him sweat, then?' Trib says.

'A bit. Not enough.'

'You don't look too happy about letting him go.'

My teeth clench for a second. 'I did not "let him go".'

'Mate, even if he'd come peacefully and we'd got him in the back of the van, we'd still be releasing him at some point.'

He's right. I know he's right. But some part of me still itches for a confrontation with Vose, where he gives me no choice but to use the stick on him. I'd have been appalled with myself afterwards, I know that. But still; there it is.

'It's the best result we could hope for,' Trib says. 'As far as Vose is concerned, he can't go home, he's on the run, and he may end up in prison. He's got to seriously think about what he did, because until he realises the police aren't actually coming for him, his life's going to be very uncomfortable.'

I'm not convinced. Does Vose really think like this, or is he so used to being in trouble with the law that he won't bat an eyelid?

—

Trib drops me off at the Caduceus car park. I sit in my car for ten minutes. Even though I know Liam Vose has gone, even though I saw him disappear, I can't let him go. I drive to Rebecca's and let myself in with the key she gave me a few weeks ago. There are lights on in the hall and lounge, but the house is very still. I wonder if she's gone out somewhere, but as I go through to the lounge, I see her sitting on the sofa.

'Rebecca?'

She doesn't turn to face me. 'So, where the hell have you been?' she says.

'What do you mean?'

'I've been waiting for you. I've been trying to phone your mobile for the past two hours.'

She looks genuinely pissed off. I have no idea why, but it suddenly occurs to me that maybe we need this. Maybe we need to clear the air.

'I switched it off.' There's an edge to my voice.

'Why?'

'Why shouldn't I? Maybe I wanted a bit of a break.'

'Oh, really?' she turns and eyes me with disbelief. 'You picked a good time for it.'

'Well maybe sometimes I don't want to be at your beck and call. Maybe keeping you company while you mope around the house or sit in front of the telly watching crap isn't all that much fun for me. Had that occurred to you?'

Her mouth drops open, and for a few seconds she's too

stunned to answer. 'Shouldn't you have told me, then?' she says in the tone of someone playing their trump card.

'Told you what?'

'That we weren't going to the Star Anise after all.'

No, that's tomorrow. She's got her dates mixed up. I look at my phone and … it's Thursday. We were supposed to be at the restaurant ninety minutes ago. I feel the blood drain out of my face.

'Shit. I … I forgot.' A pitiful excuse, but then the truth often is.

'Did you even bother to book it?'

'Of course I did! You're saying I never intended to take you there at all?'

'That's exactly what I'm saying.'

'I can't believe I'm hearing this.'

'No!' She bangs her hand down on the armrest. 'No, you do *not* get to be annoyed with me.'

I backtrack as fast as I can. 'I'm sorry, Rebecca. I genuinely forgot.'

'I phoned Moira and your mum, but they didn't know where you were, either. How bloody convenient.' Her voice is steeped in bitterness. 'It's all been a big merry-go-round, hasn't it? So, come on, level with me. Where have you been?'

'With … with Trib.' I want to give her more detail, but I'd have to make it up first.

'And you've arranged it so he'll cover for you?'

'Cover for me? No!'

'I think it's time for you to be honest with me.' She folds her arms across her chest. 'Tell me her name.'

'What?'

'The name of the other woman you're seeing.'

I gape at her. 'Don't be ridiculous. There is no other woman.'

'Where did you go on Saturday, then?'

Saturday. That was when I spoke to Duncan's mum, so I suppose I was seeing another woman, but not in the way she means.

'I thought so,' she says, and I realise that my pause has proved fatal.

'No. Just because I don't answer immediately doesn't mean ... Look, there's no-one else. I swear it.'

'Then what were you doing tonight that was so much more important than me?'

Christ, it's all so complicated. 'Wait,' I tell her, 'wait ...' I need to collect my thoughts.

'And what about those phone calls you have to take in private? What is it that you can't trust me to overhear?'

My phone calls with Trib. I thought I'd been discreet.

'You're keeping secrets from me,' she says.

And, of course, she's right. I haven't told her about the missions, the cutting, my sessions with Dr Nylund, about Duncan or meeting his mum. Another hesitation damns me.

'You see?' she says. 'How do you expect this to work if you keep secrets from me?'

'Wait ... Look, I'll tell you everything.' I've got no other choice.

'So you *have* been hiding things from me? Well, I don't want to hear it. That's all I need to know. I can't be in a relationship with someone who lies to me.' She stands up and holds out her hand. 'Give me your key.'

'No, Rebecca, please. I –'

'Give me your key and get out!'

I shake my head, unable to find any adequate words. Her chin starts to tremble, and I realise how hard she's trying to hold herself together. I am despicable. I deserve everything she can throw at me.

'Look, this is all a big mistake. I love you, Rebecca.'

'Blah, blah, blah. It doesn't mean anything coming out of your mouth. It's just words.'

There's a knot of pain in my chest. There's nothing I can say, because she doesn't trust me. And she's right not to trust me.

'Fine,' she says, scooping up her handbag. 'If you're not going, then I'll go.'

'What? Where?'

'What do you care? I'll come back when you've decided to leave my house.'

'No. No!'

She tries to push her way past me, and I find myself grabbing her by the shoulders. Her head bobs on her neck and her eyes widen. What am I trying to do, shake some sense into her? I let go immediately, horrified with myself, and we face each other in shocked silence. I have to show her I'm not a threat, that this is all a big mistake, that I'm sorry. Words aren't working, so I do the only thing left to me: I throw my key on the floor and leave.

31

THERE ARE TIMES, sitting in the passenger seat of my car with a laptop, when I wonder what the hell I'm doing. But then another flurry of activity comes through on the screen and I'm mercifully absorbed again. Seeing what text might appear, nestled in all that data, is something I cling to like an addict, the same sort of compulsion I imagine a gambler might get as the roulette wheel spins. I leave the car only to get fish and chips from The Crispy Cod in the village and to relieve myself in the nearby public toilets. And this is what I've done for the last four days, from seven in the morning until seven at night, shivering in a few cubic metres of icy, fetid air. I've told Moira not to make me an evening meal, that I'm really busy at work. She has no reason to doubt me.

A copy of *The Lord of the Rings* lies in the driver's footwell. I've been meaning to read it for years, and it's more likely to take me away from the real world than any other book I can think of. But I find myself unable to concentrate on it. I couldn't give a shit about Bilbo Baggins's eleventy-first birthday party. Worse than that, it reminds me – in spite of the fact that Bilbo is half her height and 83 years older – of Rebecca's 28th, the high-point of our relationship. After several failed attempts to find Rebecca at her own house, I'd gone to her father's and begged to see her. Mr Parry stood there with his arms folded. He didn't raise his voice, nor did he admit that she was staying with him. He simply stood firm until I left. Rebecca might as well be locked behind the gates of fucking Mordor.

She's right, of course. I should have been more honest. But how? The only thing I'm certain of is that it all stems from my anger. Without that there would have been no need for the cutting or for any of my numerous deceptions. This is why I need to face Stendall. This is why every time the self-pity comes knocking – every time I feel the need to cut – I turn my thoughts to him instead.

Trib is not involved; I haven't even told him about it. This is something I have to do alone. Only once I'm done with this can I allow myself to think about Rebecca, Trib, my job, or anything else in my life.

Avoiding Steph on the Friday following my bust-up with Rebecca was impossible. But again she showed no sign of having received the phone call that would turn my working life into an ordeal of poisonous glances and mutters of disgust. Still, I could see it approaching fast, so I decided to dodge the consequences entirely. I finished work on Friday, and on Monday I phoned in sick from the car, already ensconced in my new work. But there was one other thing I did before leaving Caduceus. I waited until the others had left the Portakabin, then sidled over to Dom and said, 'Could you spare a couple of hours this evening to explain some networking stuff to me? I'll buy you some ... whatever it is you like to drink.'

'Yeah, okay.' He thought for a moment. 'Scotch. A peaty single malt. None of that blended crap.'

When he said, 'Come through to the server farm' he wasn't kidding. Most people who work in computing have a fairly powerful PC or two at home. Most of them don't have their own rack, stuffed full of enterprise-grade electronics. It looked more professional than work. He was generous with his time, spending the whole evening explaining what I wanted to know about cracking wireless encryption and analysing network packets. Not once did Dom question why I might want to know this. To him it was a purely technical exercise.

Stendall's home address wasn't difficult to find on the web. Although tempting, I rejected the idea of confronting him immediately. I needed to find out more about him first, so that when I faced him it would be with the support of some hard facts, not just a festering, decade-old hatred. And, if I'm honest, there was an element of fear. I still remember vividly how he was in those days: the iron-grip control, the sudden bouts of violence.

I experienced a perverse kind of pleasure whenever I re-read the articles about him, like picking at a scab. It's the same toxic compulsion I used to get from arguing on internet forums or picking fights with my brothers. One sentence from the Biz article sticks in my mind: 'your financial results have been spectacular for a small company during a recession'. I want to know why. I want it to be for some reason other than his performance as a businessman. I can't stand the idea that he might be brilliant. I want to catch him doing something wrong, cooking the books, or sacking staff without reason, something I can use as evidence and justification for ... whatever it is I'm going to do. I want the evidence that Mr Lambert demanded at school, but I was never able to provide. I want Stendall to finally be punished for what he did.

It's true what he said in the article: he does work from home a lot. Over the last four days he's barely left the house. When I started this on Monday, I only had access to the resources on my own laptop: the software I'd downloaded, plus a few articles

Dom had pointed me at. I managed to get a signal from Stendall's wireless router only by parking uncomfortably close, on the road immediately outside his sprawling, chalet-style house. From there I could see his swimming pool, covered for the winter, and the windows of the kitchen and one bedroom. His house is set back from the village, on a road where nobody would normally park. Staying there would arouse suspicion before long.

After a couple of hours thrashing away with the software, I managed to break Stendall's wireless encryption. I then piggy-backed his broadband connection, so I could surf the web using his equipment and his account. For a while, I wondered about downloading the foulest porn I could dredge up, and tipping off the authorities. Sadly, I only had access to his internet connection. I couldn't actually plant evidence on his computer.

However, the network analyser made it easy to capture everything he was sending or receiving. It was then a case of finding the nuggets of useful information in amongst all the gobbledegook the computer used to enable communication over the internet. By sifting and filtering the data, I could see the emails going to and fro, and get some of the text from the websites he was visiting. Much of it was disappointingly dull and businesslike, but there was the occasional message that stirred me up.

From: johnstendall@greensloth.co.uk
To: vickyfoster@greensloth.co.uk
Subject: Christmas Meal Cost

Vicky, I see you've finally put your claim in for the Christmas meal. Now I know why you left it so long. Given the economy I thought I was generous in allowing £20 a head. Your department averaged £27.82 a head. Not acceptable. And don't give me that 'Phil said it was okay to go a bit over' bullshit. I've heard that one before.

Let me remind you of a simple equation: Profit = Revenue - Cost. Didn't they teach you this in your Economics degree? The Christmas meal is a COST. I don't care that you've only been with the company for six months. This should be ingrained from day one.

Perhaps you'd like to stand up at the next board meeting and announce that any time the company gives you a budget, you're going to overspend by 40%.

Profit = Revenue - Cost.

Don't make me tattoo this on your forehead.

This was the old Stendall, all right, hiding his sadistic streak behind a veneer of respectability.

On Monday he was using his internet connection up until one in the afternoon. After that, I saw the garage door open and he drove out in his Audi. I snapped the laptop shut but continued to look down at it, hoping that from his point of view I might be reading a map or a newspaper.

Out of the corner of my eye I caught his spiky blonde hair, the same style he'd had at school. He drove straight past without any display of having noticed me, but if he came back and I was still here, it might be a different matter. If he got a good look at my face, he wouldn't fail to recognise me.

This wasn't good enough. I drove straight to the local computer parts supplier and bought the most powerful wireless aerial they sold. While I was at the shops, I decided to make things a bit more comfortable for my second day. I bought a thick fleece to put over the one I was already wearing, some fingerless gloves, two packs of sandwiches and a Thermos to fill with strong black coffee.

The next day, using my new aerial, I found I could get a signal from the next road up. After logging in to his router (username:

'admin', password: 'admin' – ha!) and tweaking the settings, I found I could retreat even further. A convenient lay-by up a slight rise on a country road proved ideal, giving me line of sight to his house, a reliable wireless connection and very little chance of him noticing me. If anyone else questioned what I was doing, I'd say I was measuring electromagnetic pollution levels for the Environment Agency and watch their eyes glaze over.

Since then, things have been frustratingly quiet. It's now Friday, I've spent a week on this, and I still haven't found anything to justify the vast amount of time I've expended. Nor have I gained any appreciable insight into Stendall apart from the fact he's still a bastard. I'm not delving deep enough. If only I could snoop the actual contents of his PC. But that would mean getting into his house, which simply isn't happening.

I can only spend so long at this before Jane realises I'm not off sick. All it takes is one phone call to Moira's house and I'll be looking for another job again. I decide to see this through to the end of the day, then pack it in. There have to be other strategies.

While I'm pondering this, the laptop leaps into life again. I use a familiar string of keyboard shortcuts to get to the payload of the email message. Now, this is more interesting. Another email comes through: Stendall's reply. Then a reply to that. This carries on for several minutes, messages ping-ponging between them, and with each one I sit up straighter in the seat, my hands moving faster over the keyboard.

The messages end, and after a few minutes waiting for another, I see Stendall's garage open and the Audi edge out. This is my opportunity. I clap the lid of the laptop shut, toss it on the floor and leap over into the driver's seat, almost castrating myself on the gearstick in the process. The engine growls into life and I drive after him.

32

A BLACKBOARD OUTSIDE the Hog's Head announces:

> Monday – Quiz Night
> No entry fee
> No prizes
> Forfeits for wrong answers
> Enter if you dare!

That's one way for Jeff to economise during a recession.

After my week of solitude, the noisy clatter of people enjoying themselves reassures me that I'm not the lone survivor of an apocalypse after all. Trib isn't here yet, so I make my way to the front of the crowded bar to get a couple of drinks in.

When my turn comes, Jeff raises an eyebrow and says, 'What the hell happened to you, then?'

'Eh?'

'You look like a bulldog with a pineapple jammed up his arse. Bad week?'

It's very difficult for me to express just what on earth my week has been.

'What'll it be, then?' he says.

'Two pints of the Gold, please.'

He starts to pull the beers. 'Waiting for Trib, are you?'

'Yeah.'

He plonks the two glasses in front of me and starts to serve the next customer. I'm stalled with a bunch of pound coins in my hand, ready to pay. 'Jeff?' He's already pulling a Guinness for the next guy. 'Jeff, I haven't –'

'What are you waiting for,' he says to me, 'the second coming?' He winks, and his attention is back on the pump.

Funny how a little thing like that can brighten your day. I pocket my money and head for a table in the corner just as Trib appears at the door.

'Hiya, mate,' he says.

We sit, and I push one of the pints towards him. 'Here, I saved you a trip to the bar.'

'Marvellous.' He takes a substantial swig and smacks his lips before removing his coat and hanging it on the back of the chair. 'How's things, then?'

'Okay.' What more can I say? A week of computer hacking and arse cramp isn't going to make for scintillating conversation. 'How are you?' I ask him belatedly.

'You don't look your normal perky self, Olly.'

'Huh! I was perky? When was this?'

'How's Rebecca?'

'Fine. Get your board out, will you?'

He extracts the cribbage board and cards from his voluminous jacket and we begin a game.

'Do you want to score your crib too?' he says after a couple of hands.

He's right. My mind's not on the game. Trib idly rotates his pint glass on the table, an eighth of a turn. Another eighth. Another.

He says, 'Do you want to talk about it?'

I'm not discussing Stendall, which leaves me with the other problem that's been preying on me, Rebecca, and I realise that, yes, I do want to talk about it. I've never met anyone so capable of extracting the truth from me. Nor anyone I'd rather tell it to. The comforting rhythms of the game make my confession easier; I parcel out the information in little bits. He looks shocked. The only part I skip is that tricky little detail about her dad being a police officer. I tell Trib that Rebecca knew I was concealing something from her. To him, this means the missions. For me, of course, there are even more complications, layers upon layers.

'How can I be honest with her when I'm doing all this stuff

with you?'

He shuffles on his chair. 'I'm sorry, I really don't know how to answer that. You did appreciate what you were getting yourself into.'

'Yeah, I'm not blaming you. I take responsibility for everything I've done. I suppose I was just focused on the danger of the mission rather than the … romantic consequences. I wasn't even going out with her when we delivered Summer's new chair. How could I have known this would happen?'

'So it was the Vose mission that did for you? You didn't have to come along with me, you know.'

'Yes I bloody did. There's no way I was going to let him get away with that. My crime was doing it on Thursday, when I should have been going out with Rebecca. Seeing Mitchell in that state blasted all other thoughts out of my head.'

Trib deals another hand.

'She was furious,' I tell him. 'She thinks I'm seeing another woman.'

'And are you?'

'No, I am not!'

'Just checking. It does happen, you know.'

'Not with me, it doesn't.'

He ponders this. 'No, you're not the sort, are you? But anyway, you don't want to take relationship advice from me.'

'Don't do yourself down, Trib. It helps to talk about it.'

He nods. After a couple more hands he excuses himself and goes to the loo. When he returns, he scoops up two pints that have magically appeared at the edge of the bar. When did he order those?

'So,' he says, 'are you not going to ask me whether I've got anything in the works?'

'No, I'm okay for the moment.'

'I guess the Vose thing and its consequences has kind of put you off, eh?'

'A bit.'

'That's the excuse you're sticking to, is it?'

'What do you mean, "excuse"?'

He conjures a dramatic pause by taking a slurp from his pint. 'Might you be up to something independently?'

'What? Why would I be up to anything?'

Trib sits back in his seat. 'I thought so. Come on, then – 'fess up.'

'You're a blunt bugger, aren't you?'

'Yup. It wouldn't have anything to do with this John Stendall, would it?'

'Are you frigging psychic or something?'

'Seeing you talk about him … it's obvious that it still gets to you; that things aren't finished.'

Yes, the meeting with Duncan's mum made that clear. I thought for years that it was all over, but it's as much a part of me as my heart and lungs. Or perhaps, more appropriately, my appendix – something that can be excised.

Trib says, 'Not thinking of doing anything stupid, are you?'

Oh, I've fantasised about what I'd like to do to John Stendall, but there's no way Trib's prising any of that out of me.

'No.' At the same time, I can see that having Trib involved might stop me from doing anything too crazy. He could be my safety valve.

'So what are you doing?' he says. 'Partners in crime, remember?'

'It's a … personal thing.'

'That's my speciality. Look, you don't have to share it with me if you don't want to. I won't be offended.'

Oh, what's the point? He already knows I'm going to cave in. And so I tell him about Stendall's business, about monitoring his email. He looks impressed at what I've managed to achieve.

'So what did you find out from all this snooping?'

I've printed out the emails and have been referring to them frequently in an effort to tease out more information. Is it just coincidence that I happen to have them with me now, so I can pass them straight over to Trib?

> From: edlacey@greensloth.co.uk
> To: johnstendall@greensloth.co.uk
> Subject: Site 15 – Urgent
>
> The situation with the kid I mentioned is getting worse. We need to see to him. Phone me.
> Ed

> From: johnstendall@greensloth.co.uk
> To: edlacey@greensloth.co.uk
> Subject: Re: Site 15 – Urgent
>
> No. I will not phone you. I want YOU to sort out the problem.
>
> Anyone below you in the organisation is not my concern. I won't be dragged away from important work to micromanage your part of the business. The Site 15 crew are YOUR responsibility, not mine.
>
> You said you could keep this watertight.

> From: edlacey@greensloth.co.uk
> To: johnstendall@greensloth.co.uk
> Subject: Re: Site 15 – Urgent
>
> I never said anything about 'keeping it watertight'. This whole scheme was your idea in the first place. I never liked it. I always thought something like this might happen. If we separate him from the others for any reason, they'll start talking.
> Ed

From: johnstendall@greensloth.co.uk
To: edlacey@greensloth.co.uk
Subject: Re: Site 15 – Urgent

Ed Lacey wrote:
> This whole scheme was your idea in the first place.
But I pay you to manage it!

I don't care what you do with the others. Print some more money. Whatever. Just stop bothering me about it.

From: edlacey@greensloth.co.uk
To: johnstendall@greensloth.co.uk
Subject: Re: Site 15 – Urgent

John Stendall wrote:
> But I pay you to manage it!

And I should never have let you persuade me. You can't start something like this and then just wash your hands of it. There is only so much a guy like Ibrahim or Darren can do. They are not equipped to deal with this. As the CEO, the buck stops with you. You need to come to Site 15, see what the situation is and make a decision. This is not something that can be resolved over email.
Ed

'What do you think?' I ask Trib. I want his opinion, untainted by any of my own bias. Check and balance.

'It sounds pretty dodgy.'

'What do you think he's doing?'

He shakes his head. 'There's not enough here. Anything I say would be a guess.'

'Then guess.'

He reads them again. 'It sounds like he might be involved with counterfeit money, and maybe he's having problems with one of his workers. He might be facing a whistleblower, which would imply he's doing something immoral or illegal. I don't know, it's just a theory.'

It's a pretty good theory. The same things have occurred to me.

'What you really need to do,' he adds, 'is go to this Site 15 and see what you can find out there.'

'You mean, go *back* there.'

Trib leans forward in his seat. 'You've seen it?'

'A few minutes after the emails ended, he left the house. I assumed he was going to Site 15 to sort things out, and it looks like I was right.'

'What did you find out?'

'He went to this big, ugly building on an industrial estate just inside the M25. There wasn't much I could do while Stendall was there. He went in, and after about twenty minutes he came out and drove home.'

'Can you get back to it?'

'Yeah, no problem.'

Trib scratches one eyebrow. 'So, why didn't you tell me any of this before?'

'You'd think it was too much like revenge.'

'And is it?'

'Maybe,' I admit. 'I don't know. I knew you wouldn't approve of me going after him.'

'Why not?'

'It isn't small enough, local enough.'

'No, you've got it wrong. The idea is that you don't take on things if you have little influence over them. You pick your battles carefully. Stendall still matters to you, whether you like it or not. If you think he's doing something wrong and you can do something about it, that's fine. Drop him in it. Grass him up. There's only one condition.'

'What's that?'
'I'm coming with you.'
'It could be dangerous.'
'I'm a big boy.'
'I'm serious, Trib.'
'So am I. Our little spat with Liam Vose wasn't exactly free of risk. Listen, you say you take responsibility for your involvement, well so do I. I'm coming with you, mate.'

I shrug. 'Okay.'

It was always going to be a token protest.

33

'No windows,' Trib says, as we drive past in the van. 'Not one.'

Site 15 is a huge, stained, concrete structure that was obviously not built with natural daylight in mind. Even the few windows it once possessed have now been boarded up. The only other interruption to the stark expanse of concrete is an industrial roller shutter which looks like it's used as a loading bay. There is no company name, nor any other signage. It looks even more sinister at midnight, brooding at the edge of the industrial estate like some disused cold-war barracks.

When I followed Stendall here two days ago he'd parked his car outside and gone in through a side building, connected to the main structure and about half its height, featureless except for a single door with peeling red paint.

'Look,' Trib says, pointing at the security cameras with one hand while he steers with the other.

'I parked a good distance away last time.'
'How many have you counted?'
'Five. One on each corner and one overlooking the door.'
'Snap.'

He pulls up outside another industrial building a hundred

metres away and kills the engine. We're completely hidden from our objective.

'So,' he says, 'we've got a few problems. There are no windows to look in through, and there's precious little chance of getting through that steel shutter. I think the door's our best bet, but we'll have to deal with that camera first.'

'There might be another option: looking in through the skylights.'

'If there are any.'

I produce the satellite picture I printed off Google Earth earlier this evening. Site 15 appears as a dull, beige rectangle with a grid of sixteen grey squares on top.

'We can disable this camera here,' I mark it with an X on the map, 'go up this ladder and we're on the roof.'

'Escape routes?'

'Either back down the ladder, or we can jump down onto the side building's roof, and from there onto the ground.'

Trib looks up from the map. 'Are you sure you need me?'

He has no idea how much I need him.

We stow our wallets, phones and other stuff in the glove compartment. Trib pockets the van key and gives me his spare. The only other things we take with us are a torch, Trib's telescopic pointer and a plastic bag. We'll come back for the screwdrivers, spanners or crowbar if we need them.

After planning a route to the building with minimum exposure to the cameras, we leave the van and head out into the night, heads down. On CCTV we should appear as two anonymous guys taking a short cut through the industrial estate, hunched up against the cold. Although there are still people working a little way off, loading lorries for some overnight delivery, this area is quiet.

As he approaches the camera, Trib turns his back to it, extends the pointer, looks up, and expertly places the billowing plastic bag over it. The movement looks strangely graceful, like some basketball manoeuvre. Having passed under the camera, I turn back and start up the ladder, which consists of metal rungs set straight into the concrete. I place each foot carefully to minimise the noise. About half way up I become aware of a sound: a high-pitched hum, the whir of a motor perhaps. I climb past the camera, a tamper-proof two metres away. The plastic bag moves in the breeze, causing the telescopic pointer to swing like a pendulum. I hope they're well attached. A strong gust of wind could cause us problems. Trib follows me up, quiet as a cat. I climb over and onto the roof. There's a squat air conditioning unit and light floods from the array of skylights. The sound has changed to a low hiss, like steam escaping from a pipe.

Trib appears next to me. It's exposed up here, and we stay in a crouch as we make our way to the nearest skylight. Our footsteps make no sound on the concrete. The glare from inside is blinding, and we have to wait for our eyes to adjust. When they do, the source of the sound becomes immediately clear: it's the chattering of sewing machines. They're crammed in, row upon row, a worker hunched at each. From here, all we can see are the tops of their heads – black-haired, every one of them – and pairs of arms, working furiously.

Trib rubs some grime off the window. I put my hand on his shoulder in alarm.

'They won't be able to see us,' he murmurs. 'If they look up, all they'll see is the lights.' He indicates the rows of fluorescent tubes hanging from the ceiling. 'And they won't hear us. This is double-glazed.'

I peer back through the dirty glass. Stacks of clothes fill one corner, but the rest of the floor space, as far as I can see, is devoted to labour.

'Why are they working now? It's past midnight on a Sunday. In fact, it's Monday.'

'Early start?' Trib says darkly.

My eye is caught by one of the workers putting his hand up,

half-mast at first, then fully raised. A huge man in uniform gets up from a chair and approaches. The raised hand falters, falls. My perspective shifts: it's not that the uniformed man is a giant, it's that the worker is a child. His head bobs a little as he talks. His hands, clad in fingerless gloves, are held out, palms up. The guard draws a stick from his belt, prompting a sharp intake of breath from Trib. The stick is pointed directly at the boy, who adopts a position of surrender, his fingers shaking rapidly. I haven't heard his voice, or even seen his face, but how eloquent those hands are. The worker turns back to his sewing machine and the guard returns to his chair with a contemptuous glance over his shoulder.

'They're kids,' Trib mutters, his eyes darting around. 'They're all kids.'

It wasn't obvious at first, because they wear jumpers and coats as they work, but their jerkiness, their nimbleness, betrays them. A girl traverses the aisles with a trolley almost too big for her to manoeuvre, collecting piles of disembodied sleeves to take to the next station. There's not a patch of white skin in evidence. It's as if the skylight isn't just a window into the building, but into a different country entirely.

'It's a sweatshop, isn't it?' I whisper.

'Looks like it. They must be working shifts. Maybe all round the clock.'

'Why here and not some country with cheaper labour?'

We look at each other, both remembering the same line in the email, both coming to the same conclusion.

'He's not paying them with real money.'

I knew Stendall was up to something. Profit = Revenue - Cost.

And here it is, the ruthlessly logical conclusion to his theory: sweatshop workers paid in faked banknotes.

'The walls must be soundproofed,' Trib says. 'That's why there are no windows. From the street you can't see or hear a thing.'

'Well, someone's seen it now. We need to –'

I break off. Feet on metal rungs. We look at each other. I point to the air conditioning unit as our only real hiding place, and start to get up, but it's already too late. A man's head appears above the edge of the roof – a buzz-cut and a bouncer's build. He spots us and pauses to mutter something into a walkie-talkie.

'Shit,' says Trib.

'We've got to go.' I run to the edge of the roof. The drop to the side building can only be about three metres, but looking down from above, it seems much more. I glance back at the guard, who is now clambering over the edge and will be able to run over to us in a few seconds. I hold my breath and jump. The air rushes in my ears as I accelerate, and I make sure my legs aren't locked when I hit the roof. They absorb most of the impact, and I roll on to my side, leaving my hip and hands to take the rest. I stand and look up at Trib. He's peering over the edge, his face betraying a serious doubt. He's got five seconds if he's lucky.

'Come on! Look, it's fine. I'm fine.'

He bites his lip, shakes his head.

'You've got to!'

He turns his back on me and moves away from the edge, disappearing from sight.

'Get back here!' I nearly break a cardinal rule by saying his name.

I hear his voice above me, reasoning with the security guard: 'Now, look, this is not what you –'

His cry of pain rips the night, echoing off the sheer-sided industrial buildings. I realise with a bubbling panic that Trib won't try to fight back. The guard has already failed to prevent us from seeing what's going on here. How far is he willing to go in order to silence us? What orders has Stendall given him?

I jump up and try to grab hold of the edge to haul myself back over, but there's no chance of reaching it. I hear scuffling above, another grunt of pain. The only way up is the ladder. To reach it

I would have to get down to ground level and go all the way back round the building. It would take forever. But even that isn't an option. Two men have come out of the building below and they turn and spot me. One is dark-skinned, with a full, black beard, the other white, whippet-lean, moustached. They both draw their sticks.

I turn and take a running jump off the opposite side of the roof. I've acquired so much momentum when I hit the ground that I have no choice but to roll. The world inverts. Hard tarmac presses against my neck, back, the base of my spine, then I'm up again, staggering for balance and sprinting for the nearest cover. I need to be out of their line of sight before they get round the side of the building. Weaving round a rubbish skip I make for the side of an industrial unit and take a hard right. A quick glance backwards and there's no sign of them.

Circling round in a wide arc, dodging from building to building, I approach Site 15 from the opposite direction. I'm relying on my pursuers to assume I'm still running directly away, so they'll be searching the wrong part of the industrial estate. Meanwhile the minutes are passing, minutes in which I'm unable to help Trib. I find my way to a vantage point where I can see both the ladder and the door to the side building. Two guards are at the bottom, arguing with each other. My breath catches in my throat. Trib is leaning against the wall, holding one hand up to a head that glistens with blood. They must have chaperoned him down the ladder somehow.

I should never have jumped off that roof. I should have made Trib go first. Idiot. Fucking *idiot*.

The two guards who chased me return, and the argument intensifies. I can't hear what they're saying because they keep their voices down, but the body language is unmistakable – fingers pointed in accusation, defiant stances. Abruptly, Trib makes a run for it. Perhaps he isn't as seriously injured as he's been making out. If I rush them now, it might give him a chance to get away.

But Trib is slow, far too slow. He gets no more than a few paces before the thin guard with the moustache catches up. He grabs Trib by the scruff of the neck, draws his stick, and breaks one of his legs.

I rush from my hiding place at an impossible sprint and bowl into the four guards, scattering them like skittles, tearing through them like a tornado. If only it were true. No, instead I watch impotently as they guide Trib back to the building, supporting him by his shoulders, one of them clamping a hand over his mouth as he howls. I itch to stop them, but there's no way I can close the distance fast enough, and even if I did, I can't take on all four. They disappear inside, and the door slams shut on the sounds of Trib's pain.

This is all so fucked up. My fists ache from clenching. I want someone to tell me what to do – someone with certainty, someone with a plan. I could phone the police, but how long would it take to convince them, to explain things? And while I wait for them to arrive, what's to stop these bastards bundling Trib into a car and driving him off somewhere else? There is no time, and there is no relying on anyone else. It all comes down to me.

They want both of us silenced, but they only have Trib. They need me too, and they'll try to get to me through him. They'll have no qualms about torturing him, because they're definitely going to prison if any of this ever gets out. And once they've extracted the information, what then? Will they turn up at Moira and Jodie's house in the middle of the night? How far is this going to go?

It all comes down to me. I remember how I felt about Stendall at school – that he would always raise the stakes beyond the point where anyone else could follow. That's what I need to do. I have to ditch the fear, stop thinking about the consequences, and do whatever it takes to get Trib out of there. These fuckers are not going to give up until I make them give up. Will I risk my life for him? Yes. Am I going to wimp out when he needs me most? Not a chance.

There it is. *There*. The kernel of anger I need. The honed, focused needle of fury. I'm not used to nurturing it, but that's what I do now, and a strange sensation washes through me – a cold, purifying sense of freedom. I can do anything. In what way am I not every bit as dangerous as they are? I swallow down great gulps of air. No more procrastination. It has to be done now.

I jog back to the van, get in, and drive it round onto the road bordering the factory building. I adjust the headrest so it has solid contact with the back of my skull, and make sure the crowbar is to hand. Then I reverse at full speed, lining up the red door in the wing mirror and hoping my aim is good. The edge of the van strikes the door at 45 degrees, just as I intended, with an orchestra of splintering wood, screeching steel and the splash of broken glass as the van's rear light cluster explodes. I'm ready for the impact that pushes me back into the seat, but wasn't counting on the sideways wrench that sees the van end up square to the building and tears my hands off the steering wheel.

Half of the wooden door has broken off, the other half hangs from its hinges. I grab the crowbar, jump out and squeeze past the van. Inside there's a waiting area. Blocking access to the rest of the room are a glass door and the cubicle of a security station. Beyond, in an area with seating and a couple of desks, I can see Trib, hunched over in a chair, and the four guards.

Holding one arm above my face for protection, I hammer the crowbar into the glass door and it becomes a waterfall of tiny cubes splashing to the floor. The guard closest to me, the one with the moustache, unzips his jacket and reaches inside for something. My shoes crunch on the glass fragments as I surge forwards, and I break his arm with the crowbar as he draws … fucking hell: a pistol. It clatters to the floor and he staggers back, howling. I scoop the gun up and point it at him. He back-pedals until he hits the wall and slides down into a sitting position, his face contorted with pain.

There follows a profound silence. The pistol weighs heavy in my hands.

One of the guards takes a tentative step forwards, arm extended. 'This has gone far enough,' he says, as if talking to a child.

I pull the slide back, simultaneously cocking the hammer and putting a round into the chamber, then I thumb the safety catch off. Who says video games aren't educational? I aim at him. 'I will shoot you in the face if you come any closer.'

The gun shakes more than I'd like, but he draws no confidence from it. The opposite, if anything. His hands carefully assume a position of surrender. His chest rises and falls. I point the pistol at each of them in turn, like an invitation. No-one takes me up on it.

I get each of them to throw their stick in the corner, and to demonstrate to my satisfaction that they carry no other weapons. A glance at the monitors in the security station suggests there are no more guards in the main part of the building. Only now can I allow myself to look at Trib. He's been tied to the chair with duct tape, the roll still hanging off where they haven't bothered to cut it. Half of his face is covered with blood from his head wound. His hair is matted with it. Although his eyes are half-closed, they drift towards me in recognition.

I turn back to the guard with the buzz cut, the one who hit Trib while he was on the roof. He takes a step backwards and his head vibrates rapidly from side to side. I give him the space of a few heartbeats to luxuriate in fear, then say: 'Untie him. If you hurt him any more I'll put a bullet in your leg.'

He unwinds the tape carefully.

'We've given him something for the pain,' he says.

'What was it?'

'Ibuprofen.'

'How compassionate of you. Did I tell you to stop untying him? Get on with it.'

When he's finished, he steps back out of the way.

I put one hand on Trib's shoulder. 'I'm going to get you out of here.'

'No more violence,' he mutters, slack-jawed. He's groggy with pain.

'These fuckers deserve everything that's coming to them.'

'No –'

'Shut up and stay put.'

Turning my attention to the guard with the broken arm, I instruct him to put three chairs together in the middle of the room. I order his three colleagues to sit, and for broken-arm to run several loops of duct-tape around them, fixing them, in one block, to the chairs. He winces while he does it, tears squeezing out of eyes which are narrowed to slits. I am beyond sympathy.

When he's finished, I get him to sit on a fourth chair and I lash him to his colleagues, ignoring his strangled moaning. I know this is the point of maximum danger, the point where he might make a move, but the pistol – which I press up under his chin – holds an astonishing power over him. All four of them sweat like they're in a sauna. They are absolutely obedient. There's no attempt at heroics, none of the calm confidence in the face of death you see in action movies. I tape their mouths shut. Their eyes are jittery and blink often, but none of them choose to meet my gaze.

In the security booth with the monitors I rummage around under the desk. There's a single PC, its hard drive light pulsing like a heartbeat. This is where the CCTV footage is being stored. It's a removable hard drive, presumably to make things easy for them to archive. I pull it out by its handle, causing the pulse to die, and shove it into my coat pocket.

On my way back to Trib I catch sight of the steel door leading to the sweatshop. Behind it are a hundred fearful kids. I haven't seen a single worker's face, and for some reason I feel I should. For a moment I consider getting the key off one of the guards and going through, but what would I achieve? I'd probably start a riot. No. The police have to see this as it is.

Trib hasn't moved throughout any of this. I flip the pistol's safety back on, gently lower the hammer and stick the gun down the back of my jeans. Slinging Trib's right arm over my shoulders, I take him out to the van. His left leg dangles uselessly and he has to lean on me. It takes a couple of minutes for us to manoeuvre him into the passenger seat and fasten the belt, but at last I begin to feel something like relief.

As soon as I drive off – and thank God the van is still in working order after what I've put it through – I start to shake uncontrollably. I manage about half a mile before I have to stop, get out, and vomit onto the pavement. I give myself a couple of minutes. We're out of it now.

'Phone police,' Trib murmurs as I get back in.

'After we've got you to a hospital.'

'Now,' he insists. 'Use phone box … not mobile.' He nods at one nearby. 'Don't give them … chance to cover up. Don't make this for nothing.'

When I make no move to get out, Trib begins to take off his seatbelt and fumbles for the door handle.

'What are you doing?'

'Phone police.'

'Stay put, you stubborn bastard! All right, I'll do it.'

Thankfully, the phone box hasn't been turned into a library or defibrillator, and it still works. I punch in the three nines and leave a succinct message with the operator – I need police and ambulance, I've found evidence of a sweatshop. I give details of the location and the building, then hang up before she can start asking questions.

When I get back to the van, Trib's eyes are closed.

'Trib?'

One eyelid climbs reluctantly upwards.

'I've done it, Trib. I've called them.'

The eyelid sinks back down. Something is wrong. Surely the

pain should be keeping him awake.

I drive flat out. Thank God there's so little traffic at this time of night. A mile from the hospital, Trib mumbles something.

'Say that again.'

'Phone ... police.' He's barely conscious.

'I've already done that, Trib.'

I drive into the hospital car park and stop right before the main doors. I have the presence of mind to hide the gun in the glove compartment before I go round to Trib's side and attempt to get him out of the passenger seat.

'Come on, you need to help me here,' I tell him as I try to support his weight.

'I was ... hit by car,' he says.

'No. We were at the factory, remember? We were –'

He grabs me with his right hand. The grip is tight, but the weight of the arm drags at my sweater. He fixes me with a hooded, bloodshot gaze. I think his nose is broken.

'Hit by car,' he insists.

Yes. Yes, of course. 'I'm sorry I didn't get the bastard's number plate.'

The hand falls away.

We shuffle through the doors into the glare of the reception area and for a moment I seem to forget what I should be doing. A porter comes over with a stretcher. He helps me get Trib onto it, and soon he's being wheeled into the hospital.

'You can sit down,' says a woman who has materialised next to me. 'It's all right,' she says, 'the important thing is that he's here, where he can be looked after.'

Her tone is slow, patient; she thinks I'm in shock. Maybe I am.

I sit on a chair in the reception. An old lady with curly white hair stares at me. I want to ask her what her problem is, until I realise that my coat, head and hands are smeared with Trib's blood. My knuckles are grazed. When did that happen? Someone comes through the doors and asks if the owner of the black van could kindly move it, please. It takes me a while to realise this means me.

I go out and move it.

—

The doctor finally comes out to see me, interrupting my continual pacing, my inability to sit down for more than thirty seconds. He's young, sober, and projects an air of confidence bordering on the arrogant. I couldn't think of anyone better to deal with Trib.

'How is he?' I ask.

'Your friend has a serious head injury.'

Shit. Doctors never use the word serious lightly.

'We've brought his intracranial pressure under control,' he continues. 'He's stable now, but we ... uhh ... we can't tell if there's going to be any lasting damage.'

I have to swallow. 'Lasting damage? You mean brain damage?'

'At this stage, we can't tell. There's no fracturing of the skull, no blown pupils. Those are good signs, but we won't know until he wakes up.'

I had the chance to shoot them.

The doctor says, 'He's also broken his nose, two ribs and his left leg. The bruising is very localised. You say this happened as a result of a car accident?'

Brain damage. Christ, not brain damage, please.

'I don't suppose you got the number plate.'

'No.' Of course, the guard was just doing what he was told. The order came from higher up.

'No,' the doctor repeats.

'I want to see him.'

He shakes his head. 'He needs rest. We're going to keep him in for observation. There's nothing more you can do here. You might as well go home. Come back tomorrow.'

Time passes, and I'm aware the doctor has gone, that maybe he left quite a while ago. How many minutes have passed? What has happened during that time? I don't know. The doctor is right, there's nothing more I can do here. Having put Trib into the best possible hands, it becomes clear there's more for me to do tonight – another path stretches out, arrow-straight. It's been there for years, hidden from me; only now is it revealed. Clarity. Blinding clarity. Where there should be fatigue, there is instead a thumping, urgent and powerful.

It's too bright in here.

The van keys are in my hand.

34

A DRIVE-BY OF SITE 15 and the place is silent and still. There's no evidence of the police having turned up. Typical. So, that settles it – onward to Stendall's. On the third ring of his doorbell, an upstairs light comes on. By the sixth, Stendall is opening the door in a dressing gown, looking tired and pissed off.

'Have you got any idea what the time –' he begins, but the appearance of the pistol silences him. A kick of the door sends him staggering backwards.

He retreats through the hallway, the gun a constant two metres from his chest, pushing him back as if by magnetic repulsion. He staggers past modernist paintings and doors of solid oak, into an enormous open-plan kitchen. His back hits the cooker door and he continues to slide along the kitchen units until he comes to rest in the corner. He has nowhere left to go. His eyes are as wide as a panicked horse, dark corneas completely encircled by white.

'Is there anyone else in the house?'

He shakes his head rapidly. 'I've got money,' he blurts. 'I can give you money.'

'It's not about money.'

His expression changes. 'I know you ... from school,' he says.

Astonishing that he could ever have forgotten, but then his priorities over the last few years have been a world away from Kingsmarsh Comprehensive.

'Yes, you do.' And it's like sunshine breaking through a bank of cloud: this is how Duncan finally gets his revenge, eleven years down the line and from beyond the grave. 'This is about Duncan. Duncan wants his life back.'

His mouth hangs open, as if his jaw muscles have failed.

'That wasn't ... I wasn't ... It was such a long time ago,' Stendall says, as if this somehow excuses him. 'No, wait – I was stupid, I know. I admit it.'

'You were stupid? *He died.*'

'I didn't know he'd do that,' he whispers. 'How could I have known?'

'You tortured him.'

'No! No, that's not –'

'That journey home, when you stopped us from going past. You remember that, don't you?'

His eyes flicker as he casts his mind back a decade and more.

'Don't you?'

He bows his head. 'Yes.'

'So, what did you do to him? When it was just you and him. What did you do?'

'He ... he had this pack of cards on him –' so he went through Duncan's pockets; effectively, he mugged him '– and I'd heard he did card tricks, so I asked him to do one for me.'

Asked? Stendall never asked for anything in his life. Reading between the lines: Duncan holds the cards, terrified, while Stendall slaps him on the chest and demands his best trick.

'And?'

'He – he – he tried to palm one of the cards and dropped it.' He stops there, as if the story is complete.

'Tell me what you did.'

He doesn't want to, but the gun demands an answer.

'I ...' He swallows. 'I dropped his cards down a drain. That's all I did, honestly. Look, I know it wasn't a nice thing to do, but it was only a cheap pack of cards.'

No. He didn't just take away the cards, he took away Duncan's confidence, ruined the only thing he was ever any good at.

'Look, I regret what happened. You do realise that? I think about it every day.'

Bullshit. Just seconds ago he was struggling to remember it.

'I ... it was ...' he sputters. 'I bullied him, I know. I didn't have any guidance, growing up. My dad left us when I was six – just six.'

'Oh, so it's all his fault?'

'You don't know what it's like, having to grow up without a dad.'

'Duncan did. But then you didn't know that, did you?'

He shakes his head. 'I'm not like that any more.'

'So you've learned from the experience, have you?'

He nods, falling neatly into the trap. 'I run a business. Successful. Employ lots of people. Look ... I'm sorry for who I was and what I did, but I've moved on from all of that.'

'Captain of industry? Pillar of the community?'

'I'm a completely different person. You can't ... you can't judge me for what I did when I was a kid.'

'Right. So, what about the factory of slaves you've got working for you? What about the guy who's in a critical condition in hospital after having the shit kicked out of him by *your* security guards?'

'I don't know what you're talking about.'

'Plausible deniability, is it? You don't know what's happening in your own organisation? Don't lie, you piece of shit. Maybe you should beef up your email security before discussing Site 15 with Ed Lacey. Don't even think about denying it. You want the power and the riches and all that other shit, but you won't take the responsibility, will you? It's Ed Lacey's fault, it's your dad's fault, it's Duncan's fault. The time has come for someone to *make* you take responsibility.'

Stendall's legs buckle, and he ends up sitting in the corner, his knees drawn up to his chest. He starts to cry. Where's the bolshy son of a bitch from the emails? Where's the tyrant of Kingsmarsh Comprehensive? The great man is brought low, and now a real difference can be made. It's not like he even has a wife or children to miss him.

'You haven't learned shit. What you learned is that you could get away with it. Did you get off on Duncan's death? Made you feel powerful, did it? You should see Duncan's mum and how it's still killing her, eleven years later. You should see the conditions your slaves have to work in. But you don't want to be involved with those little details, do you? Too comfortable in your ivory tower. Too special. Too fucking important.'

He's trying not to hyperventilate. Given these facts, given the destruction of everything he is and has, maybe he wants to die. The seconds stretch taut. A clock on the kitchen wall ticks, ticks, ticks, counting out little parcels of time that can never be recovered.

What now? The words are all used up. Everything that needs to be said has been said. What now? The pistol sweats.

'Olly,' he says, remembering suddenly, grasping at anything to keep the conversation going, anything at all.

It's a shock to hear my name, and for a moment I think he's got it wrong. But no – that's me, that's my name.

'Oh, God,' he says. 'Oh, God. Look, no-one has to know. I won't tell anyone.'

He thinks that now he's identified me I'll have to kill him, that I can't leave him alive to phone the police. So I shoot him in the face, destroying his mind, his memory, his malice; blowing the back of his head off and smearing his brains across the kitchen cupboards. Then what? Simple: I get arrested, and I go to prison. Just by coming here, I've sealed my fate. I'm threatening a man with a gun. I've broken into his house, broken into his business premises. In the eyes of the law, I'm the criminal. It doesn't matter what Stendall has or hasn't done, what he can or can't deny. I'm the criminal.

The hopelessness of it all descends, like a curtain at the end of a play. What am I doing? Where did I think this would end up? I can't kill a man. It's against everything I believe. Even here, at the end of things, brimming with hatred for Stendall and pushed to the ragged edge of my fury, I can't kill a man. It's strange where you find your comforts.

I sit down on the kitchen floor, my head humming with fatigue and despair. I should be furious at my own stupidity, but all I can muster is a deep disappointment.

'Look, it's ... it's not how you think,' Stendall says slowly.

'Oh, really?'

'Olly,' he says, holding onto my name like a life raft, 'Olly, you're right – I do know about Site 15. And I know it's illegal. But you should see the conditions in their own countries. These kids come from war zones. They're safe here. It may not look like they have much, but it's a lot better than what they're used to.'

So, he's like me and Trib, is he – righting wrongs even if it goes against the letter of the law? He's doing it out of a moral conviction, a desire to help people out? No, he's doing it because it's profitable. The anger comes surging back, carrying me inexorably forward again, and a tiny voice somewhere in my head says, *Oh, God. Not again. I am so tired of this.* But it won't be denied.

I look up at him. 'What are their names?'

'What?'

'Give me some of the names of your workers.'

He pauses for a moment. 'Ibrahim.'

'Second name,' I demand.

This time the pause is too long. 'That's one of your guard's names.' I recognise it from one of the emails.

'It's a common name. Look –' he says.

'You're bullshitting. You're trying to justify what can't be justified. What does "print more money" mean? My guess is that you're paying them in faked bank notes to keep your costs down. Is that close to the mark?'

He swallows.

'You've brought them to England for your convenience. Am I right? It's easier to control them if they're just down the road, rather than in another country. That's what you always wanted: control over people. And you've got the nerve to tell me that you're doing them a favour?'

I point the gun at him again. The back of his head thumps into the kitchen cupboard.

'You know where I got this? I got it from one of your security guards. I broke his arm to get it because he was about to shoot me. He was about to shoot me because I broke into Site 15. I broke into Site 15 because my friend had been beaten and captured by your men. My friend was captured because you gave them orders that no-one must ever find out what went on there. It all comes back to you. The buck stops here.'

'No, no –' he says.

'You started Site 15. It was your idea. Don't even try to deny it. I've got the evidence.'

'Please …'

'So, this –' I wave the gun '– is your doing.'

'Don't kill me,' he says in a tiny voice.

'Shut up.'

'Don't … please don't –'

'Shut up! How many peoples' lives have you fucked up? How many?'

I can *see* my pulse. The hammering of my heart is so strong that the veins in my eyes are visibly throbbing. Is it possible to have a heart attack at the age of 25? I can believe it.

I'm going to prison, that much is clear. I have only one chance to make him see the consequences of his actions, and suddenly it's so obvious what I have to do. If not now then when? This is a once in a lifetime opportunity. I wedge the gun back into the waist of my jeans, where it presses hard against the base of my spine. The creases in Stendall's forehead relax for a moment, an impossible hope dawning, but it only lasts as long as it takes me to free one of his kitchen knives from its wooden block. Stendall brings his arms up to his face for protection.

'This is what you do to people.' I roll up the sleeves of my sweater and draw the knife across my left forearm.

He tries to push himself further into the corner.

'Look! For the first time in your miserable life, look at what you do to people.'

He watches from behind the cage of his arms, unable to turn away.

'This is your fault. Yours!'

I continue to cut. My hands are shaking, my jaw clenched like a vice. God, it feels good. Stendall keeps his kitchen knives very sharp. For that, if nothing else, I can thank him. My eyes sting with tears of joy, of shame, of relief. I switch the knife to my left hand and start drawing the blade across my right arm. I can't stop myself. Each cut helps relieve some of the pressure in my head, bringing me closer to sanity. Finally I reach the point where the physical pain outweighs the anger. It flips suddenly, like a see-saw, and I realise I've finished. I look down at my arms. Blood oozes out of the cuts and down towards my elbows. I roll both sleeves carefully back down to absorb it.

Stendall remains in the foetal position, tear-streaked, petrified. He might suffer years of trauma after what he's seen tonight. One can only hope.

35

I wake from dreams of torture in which I can't tell whether I'm the perpetrator or the victim. For a moment I wonder where I am – in my bedroom at Mum and Dad's house, or the grey-walled digs of University, or maybe a police cell. No, I'm in my loft bedroom in Moira and Jodie's house. I experience a couple of blissful seconds of calm before the memory of yesterday returns to swamp me. There's no getting away from what I did last night, or what I have caused to happen to Trib.

When I arrived back home, the house was dead and still except for Moira's soft snoring. I cleaned my arms as quietly as possible, took two ibuprofen and climbed the ladder to my room. My blood-encrusted hoodie and long-sleeved T-shirt went into a plastic bag to be cleaned or disposed of later. Putting on pyjamas took the last of my energy before sleep engulfed me.

I shift in the bed, and find the pyjama sleeves are stuck to my arms with dried blood. Fortunately the sheets have escaped contamination, so I won't have to clean up any further.

What have I actually achieved? Stendall will never forget what happened, but it will be easy for him to rationalise: 'A lunatic came to my house and threatened me with a gun.' Now that the storm of last night has blown itself out, I feel a deep resignation. When the police come, I'll offer no resistance. I'll tell them why I did it, perhaps even try to convince them it was the right thing to do. They'll have to take me away, of course. That's their job. But maybe they'll understand.

Although I'm still tired, I know I won't get any more sleep. I want to stay in my room, cocooned, until someone drags me out, but that would be pathetic and I can't handle any more self-hatred. I have to face the world and keep up the pretence that I'm a normal human being. I get up and shower, leaving the pyjamas on so

I can get them clean and peel them off with less chance of reopening the cuts. Back in my room, I apply a couple of plasters to the worst areas, then put on a long-sleeved T-shirt and a sweater. I make my way downstairs.

'You're going to be late,' Moira says.

I look at the kitchen clock. 8:56. Of course, it's Monday. Moira's day off, but not mine.

'I've ... got some holiday I needed to use up, so I booked today off.'

'Ah, that's grand. What're you going to do with it?'

I'm going to see my seriously injured friend in hospital, then come back and wait for the police to arrest me. 'No real plans. I thought I'd just chill out. Can you let me know if anyone wants to get hold of me?'

'Sure.'

I hover at the threshold of the kitchen. 'Moira, I don't suppose you could do me one of your cooked breakfasts, could you?' She does an epic full English on Saturday sometimes.

She looks surprised, but says. 'Yes, why not? No point rushing into the day, is there?'

I have to turn away. I don't want her to see how pathetically grateful I am for this little act of kindness.

—

They've given him his own room. I knock before I open the door.

'Trib?'

He's in a semi-reclining position, supported by pillows. His head is partly bandaged and they've shaved his hair down to stubble. There's bruising all over his face, his left leg is in plaster, his eyes are closed and his mouth hangs open. He wears faded, hospital-issue pyjamas. The room's sky blue paint suggests he's ascended halfway to heaven already.

'Trib?'

His eyelids flutter open. The shape of his mouth changes, but it's in his eyes that I see recognition. I look for signs of disgust, fury, even fear, but under the swathe of white and the bruising it's impossible to tell what he's thinking. In the absence of any unambiguous sign that he wants me to leave, I make my way closer. He's connected to some kind of monitoring device. I move the visitor's chair next to his bed and sit. His mouth moves. There's a croak. I offer him the glass of water on the bedside table and he takes a tiny sip before handing it back. The doctor said his nose was broken; even something as simple as drinking has to be done carefully.

'How are you feeling?'

'Never ... better.' His voice is nasal and slow, and he tries to move his jaw as little as possible, like a ventriloquist. The nurse had said he was doing reasonably well, all things considered.

'One problem,' he says. 'Long words. Can't ... find them.'

'You can't remember them?'

He nods. 'Doctor says it should clear up. Need to see ... other doctor.'

'A specialist?'

'Yeh.'

'Okay, good, good. Do you mind if I ...?' I indicate the glass of water.

He gestures for me to go ahead and I take a sip. 'Listen, Trib. I, uh ...' I what? Where do I start? What do I say?

'Thank you,' he says.

'Don't say that.'

He lets out a tiny percussive breath.

I lower my head. 'Don't thank me.'

'You got ... me out of there.'

'I got you into it.'

'No,' he says. 'Got myself into it. My choice.'

'I'm the reason you're in hospital.'

'You're not the ... one who hit me.'

'No, but it was my ...'

He shakes his head, a tiny movement, maybe all he can manage.

'... it was me who ...'

He shakes his head again.

'... if I wasn't so furious with Stendall, I wouldn't have ...'

He puts his hand on mine, and I clamp my jaw shut, force the emotion back down my throat and into the pit of my stomach.

'Not,' he says, 'your fault. Now, I don't want ... to hear any more about it.'

I lean forward until my head is on the bedsheets, next to his good leg. I close my eyes and try not to make a fool of myself. He moves his hand to the back of my head, like a dying relative showing one final act of fondness, or a priest offering absolution. I take a few minutes, but there, in that simple darkness, with the softness of the sheets against my eyes, I find a sense of calm.

'You okay?' Trib says, when I finally emerge.

'Yeah.' And in order to steer the conversation back towards more prosaic things, I add, 'I'm afraid I've battered the van a bit.'

'What is it with you and my van?'

A laugh bursts out of me like a sneeze: there, and then gone. 'I'm sorry.'

'Worth it,' he says. 'Thought you were the fuckin' Terminator.'

A rampaging, unstoppable angel of destruction? Yeah, that was the idea. Nothing else was going to get the job done.

'You wouldn't have ... shot them,' he says.

'I don't know. Maybe in the leg.' I'm not going to apologise for what I did. They deserved everything they got.

'They could have bled to death,' he says.

'So could you.'

He thinks about this for a moment. I can hear his breathing. He reaches a hand up to his bandaged head, as if he wants to scratch it but has been ordered not to.

'Trib, I ... I thought you might die.'

'Don't be daft,' he says. 'You still owe me 8p.'

Yeah. And the rest.

'Do you fancy winning it back, then?' I ask.

'You've not got …?'

But I have. I take the board and deck of cards out of my coat pocket. I rescued them from the back of the van this morning.

He laughs weakly. 'You're a life saver.'

I make a pretence of shuffling the cards, then deal six each. Trib picks his up with a little difficulty and fans them. He stares for a moment before throwing two into the crib. I do the same, then turn over the start card: the five of clubs.

Trib says. 'You sly bastard.' He throws down his hand: the remaining three fives, plus the jack of hearts. 'Twenty-nine!'

'I wanted you to see it, just once.'

'Mate,' he says, 'I'm not goin' anywhere.'

No. You're not, but I might be.

'What have you got, then?' he says.

I could have fiddled the deck any way I wanted, but I was focusing only on giving Trib the highest possible score. I throw down my cards. 'I gave myself nothing.'

He scans the cards. 'Nineteen,' he says.

'Uh? How do you work that out?'

'You can never get nineteen points. So … if you score nothing, you say, "nineteen".'

'Another arcane bit of cribbage lore?'

'Yeh.' He leans back against his mountain of pillows, exhausted. 'You don't look so happy,' he says.

'It's hard seeing you like this.' I won't tell him any more than that, not yet. He's in no fit state to hear what happened at Stendall's house. What he saw me do with the guards was bad enough.

'We … did it, though,' he says. 'You phoned the police. Watch the papers. See what happens.'

I don't want to give him the bad news: that the police weren't there when I passed Site 15; that all Stendall has to do in order to carry on with impunity is shift his operation somewhere else, tighten up security and make a call to the boys in blue. It could be a shock when Trib does read the paper. Strange that I'm resigned to being arrested, but I can't bear the idea of my friend's disappointment. It makes me wonder how many stories in the press are as simple as they make out. How much of what's actually reported as a crime started out with good intentions? The media want straightforward stories for their readers to believe in: good and evil; outrage, terror and justice. Something to fill a bit of spare time. Why do court cases take so long to resolve when Joe Public can reach a firm conclusion after a few paragraphs or a sound bite?

The door opens and the nurse comes in. 'Come on, now. You've had more than a few minutes. Mr Tribbeck needs his rest.'

'Thanks, nurse.' I get up and put my coat on. 'Look after him.'

'Oh, you don't need to worry about that.'

I take one last look at my friend, beaten and bloodied, but undefeated.

'Goodbye, Trib.'

—

I drop in on Mum before returning home. She's surprised and delighted. We share a pot of tea and engage in our usual, slightly awkward conversation, talking about nothing of any importance. I leave her with a kiss on the cheek, something I haven't done for years.

'Has anyone called?' I ask Moira as I come in through the door.

'No. Are you expecting someone?'

'Not particularly.'

'You can leave me with a message for them if you like.'

'No, that's fine.'

So what now? I spend half an hour wandering around the house, doing absolutely nothing. I'm consumed by my thoughts, and it's only once I catch myself pacing up and down the bedroom for the umpteenth time that I lose patience with myself. If this is my last day of freedom, I ought to be *doing* something with it. So I go to Giuseppe's for lunch, then catch the matinee of a half-decent comedy at the Regal. After that, I start phoning around. I can't do this with any of my friends from work because they still think I'm ill, but I manage to entice three mates out, including Ed, who comes all the way up from Southampton. The fact that I insist on footing the bill for the evening might have something to do with it.

We meet up at the Hog's Head for a couple of beers and a chat, move on to Strathurst's finest curry house – where Ed lives up to his reputation by scoffing a chicken phal without rice – and finally hit the Duke of Wellington so we can work our way through their collection of single malts. An evening of guilty pleasures.

They ask me what the celebration is, and I tell them I just feel like it. They won't settle for that, of course, and come up with ever more exotic reasons as the evening, and the alcohol consumption, progresses. Ed speculates loudly that it's my last day as a man before the operation.

The evening was a great idea. It's difficult not to enjoy yourself when surrounded by half-cut mates. They have to leave before the last train, so I'm back home by quarter past twelve. Moira is still up.

'A late one, then, Olly?' she says, then adds, 'Have you been drinking?'

'Yup.' I give her a big grin.

'If you're sick in this house you'll be cleaning it up yourself.'

'I'm not that far gone,' I assure her, and immediately blow it by stumbling over some non-existent obstacle.

'Up to bed with you. You're a disgrace.' But she's trying to hide a smile.

I stop after a couple of steps and turn around.

Moira says, 'I'll save myself the trouble of trying to decipher your drunken slur: no, nobody called for you.'

'Okay.' I continue to negotiate the stairs.

Come on, boys. Don't you know there's a nutcase on the loose? Maybe they're waiting for the wee small hours, so they can bust down the door and scare the shit out of me, although the shock value will be lost when they have to wait for me to lower the loft ladder. Then again, it might not happen at all. Maybe the police won't believe Stendall's story of the madman with the gun, and refuse to investigate further. Maybe Stendall thinks he has too much to lose by exposing me and would prefer to lie low while he relocates his business.

Whatever. I hit the sack.

36

THE POLICE ARRIVE AT 8:00 the next morning, just as I'm finishing a slice of toast. Or rather I should say: *he* arrives. It's Rebecca's dad. I open the door and there he stands in full police uniform, hands clasped behind his back. How perfect that it should be him.

'You'd better come with me,' he says.

Moira, who is just coming down the stairs, pauses at the end of the staircase, her hand hovering halfway to her mouth.

'Don't worry,' I tell her, 'it's Rebecca's dad.'

'Oh, right,' she says, but still doesn't move off the final step.

I don't know why I tell her not to worry. Because I still want things to be all right, I suppose. Because after all this time living with her, I still want to maintain the illusion of being a clean-cut, respectable lodger and all-round good egg. Ah, well.

I put on my shoes and coat, and let him take me out to the car. At least it's his own Ford Focus, not a squad car. He points me at the passenger seat. Once we're both in, he starts the engine and pulls away. I look back to see Moira framed by the door, receding from view. He drives us to Forest Road, over the railway line and into the countryside. He pulls the car up at the edge of the woods and turns off the ignition. Everything is quiet except for the slow ticking of the engine as it cools.

'Why have we stopped here?'

'I wanted us to have some privacy.'

What's going on? He continues to face forwards, hands resting on the wheel, as if he's still driving. Is he going to let me have a ten second head start, then take his longbow from the boot, fill me full of arrows, and apologise to his superiors for cocking up the arrest?

God knows. Life has gone off the rails; anything is possible.

'I've been talking to Rebecca,' he says.

So, he's going to use some kind of emotional leverage to get a confession out of me. I'd prefer to skip all that.

'Isn't there something more important we should be talking about?'

He frowns. 'More important than my daughter?'

I hesitate. 'Of course not. That's not what I meant.'

'Then what did you mean?'

'I … nothing. Bad choice of words.'

We stare at each other. He doesn't seem to understand me any more than I do him. Is it possible that he's not here to arrest me? Or is this another mind game, putting me at ease before he slaps on the cuffs?

I gesture with one hand. 'Carry on.'

'Look, if you don't want to hear it, then –'

'No, I do want to hear it. There's nothing I want to hear more.'

'Huh.' He takes a deep breath. 'Rebecca has told me some things about you.' It's clear from his tone that not much of it was complimentary.

'There is no other woman, Mr Parry, I swear. Everything else she's said about me is probably true, but there isn't another woman. You can tell her that.'

He fixes me with a look of irritation. 'I'm not here as your go-between, Olly.'

She doesn't know he's here, does she? He's taken this step on his own.

'So what are we doing here, then?' I don't care if I sound confrontational. It's irrelevant anyway, because he doesn't seem to hear the words.

'I had such high hopes for you,' he says. 'And you've let me down.'

I've let *her* down, surely.

'What you really need is an excuse to put me in prison, don't you? Then I couldn't possibly pester your daughter any more.'

'What are you saying?'

'Just trying to see things from your perspective.' He really doesn't know about Site 15.

'If you hurt her again, I'll …' He trails off.

His intimidation irritates me. 'You'll do what? Beat the crap out of me? You can't do that – you're a police officer.'

'You, young man,' he points for emphasis, 'don't know what I'm capable of.'

I hold my arms out in invitation. 'Get stuck in, then.' I'm not going to be cowed by him, but if he does decide to take a swing, well, I've probably earned it. He lowers the finger, shakes his head. He's here to bollock me, not to arrest me. This is a massive improvement on what I was expecting a few minutes ago.

'Mr Parry, I want to be completely honest with you –'

'That would be nice.'

'– I never intended to do anything to hurt your daughter, I promise you that. I confess to being an idiot, but I've always tried to do what's best for her. I hope she also said I made her happy sometimes too. I just didn't always know what she needed from me. What can I say? I'm a man; I can be a bit thick when it comes to relationships. And if you want remorse from me, you've got it, because I'm sorry. I'm truly sorry.'

For a few moments he gives me a searching look, then he twists the key in the ignition and the engine growls into life.

I'm bewildered. 'What? Is that it?'

He doesn't speak another word until he's dropped me back at

Moira's house.

'Consider that a warning,' he says as I get out of the car.

I go back in and pop another slice of bread in the toaster. I've been sitting at the kitchen table for a few minutes, pondering Mr Parry's words, when the headline on Moira's newspaper registers on my consciousness: 'Vigilantes Reveal Britain's Sweatshop Shame'. My hand hits the table with a thump, and I draw the paper closer.

> They're the sort of working conditions you might expect to see in a sweatshop in the Far East. But these pictures come from a West London factory owned by a British company, and exposed by a mysterious vigilante group.
>
> Police raided the sweatshop during the early hours of Monday morning after an anonymous tip-off. They found over a hundred children, some as young as twelve, being kept in captivity and forced to stitch together T-shirts and hoodies for exclusive fashion company Green Sloth.

So they *were* there. They must have arrived at Site 15 after I drove past on my way to Stendall's.

> The children, mostly from war-torn Somalia and Darfur, were told they would be deported if discovered. They lived in squalor, with no heating, poor facilities for preparing food, and toilets described by police as 'disgusting'. Most were in a poor state of health, with some requiring immediate medical attention.
>
> Detective Chief Inspector Bill Hallett, leading the investigation, said, 'These children have been treated abominably. Many of them show signs of having been beaten.'
>
> When police arrived at the factory, they found all four of the site's security guards tied up. Hallett said, 'Evidently someone had been there before us. Let me make it clear to the public that we do not condone vigilante behaviour. The correct

procedure in these circumstances is to inform the police and let us deal with things.'

Police are conducting a full investigation to discover the extent of the operation. They have seized computers at Green Sloth's head office, and are interviewing members of staff. They are keen to speak to managing director John Stendall, 26, who left the country in his own light aircraft early on Monday morning. According to aviation records, he landed at a rural airfield near Zagreb, Croatia, but has not been seen since. Police are appealing to the Croatian authorities to help locate him.

I put the paper down and stare into the distance. He fled the country. He fled the country and he never phoned the police. He could, of course, still phone from abroad and tell them what happened, but in order to press charges against me he'd have to come back. I'm in the clear. I sit there, stunned, trying to absorb the news. My toast pops up and I jump, then laugh out loud, as if the emergence of hot bread from a kitchen appliance is a cause for celebration.

'Vigilantes Reveal Britain's Sweatshop Shame.' How's that for fame, Zach? Of course, the irony is that he'll never know who did it. No-one will.

Moira comes into the kitchen. 'What was that whole thing with Rebecca's dad, then?'

'Oh, he just wanted a chat about something.'

She raises her eyes at this, but doesn't pursue the conversation. 'So, after last night's excesses, how are you feeling this morning?'

'Wonderful. It's a new day, a new world.' I leap to my feet and hug her.

She steps back in surprise. 'Are you on the happy pills or something?'

I go into work, knowing I can tackle anything. Jane is not happy that I've taken so much time off; Andy and Dom are continuing an argument they started a month ago; there are mountains of work caused by my absence and by Steph's epic three-week holiday, which she's managed to extract from Jane by threatening to leave the company. None of it matters. It's all trivial.

At lunchtime I pop out to an internet café and send all of the emails I intercepted from Stendall's wireless connection to *The Independent* for forwarding on to the police. I give no hint of my identity, and make it clear that I want things to remain that way.

When I get home I connect the hard drive from Site 15 to my PC and erase all the data. Then I disassemble it, scratch the disk surfaces with a screwdriver blade and put the bits in a bag to take to the recycling centre as scrap. The pistol gets similarly dismantled, and I go out after dark, drive a few miles up the A3, and toss the pieces into the river Wey. Maybe not the most environmental option, but anything else seems too risky.

—

'I told you we'd make the papers,' Trib says when I show him the headline story.

The Independent has taken my anonymous emails very seriously. They run a long, investigative piece on the sweatshop, profiling some of the workers and turning them from faceless immigrants into human beings. They interview Haben, who was trying to earn enough money to move his family out of Mogadishu and across the border into Kenya to start a new life, free from the civil war that had claimed the lives of his uncle and two sisters. He shows no surprise at having been betrayed, and I experience a fresh wave of shock that any fifteen year old should be that jaded.

It's strange. I freed them, yet I've never seen any of them face-to-face. I still regret not having stepped through that door. The article details how the workers were betrayed by people in their own country who claimed to be helping them find work, how compliance was enforced with 'pay rises' for exceeding targets, and the threat of beatings for underperformance. I'm astonished that Stendall ever thought he would get away with it. But then he has always been driven by an arrogance I find impossible to understand. He and I think in fundamentally different ways, like we're members of different species. He abstracted himself from the idea that his workers were anything more than resources to be used up and thrown away, like batteries.

The police don't find him in Croatia. This leaves a very sour taste in my mouth. By going to his house I tipped him off and gave him the chance to escape. But my opinion changes over time. Stendall is now effectively living in exile, and could be caught at any time. He will live in daily fear, like his sweatshop workers, like Duncan. It's a kind of justice.

Trib improves each day, and the longer words become easier to recall. The police come to interview him and he fobs them off with our vague hit-and-run story. I bring in magazines and books for him to read because he's bored out of his wits most of the time. But the thing that brings the biggest smile to his face is also the shortest. It's a business card:

Sumi's Home Cooking Service
Authentic Indian food
in the comfort of your own home!
Let me be your chef, waitress and washer up!

'I knew they couldn't keep her down,' he says.
'I asked her how it was going.'
'And?'
'Early days, but she sounded very fired up.'
'She doesn't need any practice, does she? We could get her to take over the hospital kitchen.'

It's a relief to see him on the mend, both physically and mentally, but it's going to be a slow process. His fractured femur will take months to heal.

'No more football with the kids for a while,' he laments. 'I'm going to miss that.'

'And no more missions.'

'But I think we both know it's the end of all that, don't we?'

I'm surprised to hear him say it, even though my own thoughts have been heading in the same direction. It was always going to be unsustainable in the long run. I'm ready to move on. I once asked Trib about his biggest mission, and he managed to wriggle out of replying. Now I know the answer. I was there. It's a fitting place to end.

'What are you going to do instead?' I ask him.

'Oh, don't you worry about that. I've got plans.'

And yes, I believe him.

'You know, Trib, in a way I'm glad you're giving up the missions. You *were* using them as a bit of an excuse.'

'Excuse? For what?'

'Not getting a girlfriend.'

'Oh,' he says, 'you reckon, do you?'

'Yeah. Now you've got no reason not to phone Philippa.'

'Philippa?'

'The bespectacled blonde Valkyrie you met at Rebecca's party.'

'Come on. You know that didn't work out so well.'

'What do you mean? You only spoke to her for thirty seconds.'

'It was more than that! And anyway, I might not fancy her.'

He stares at the hospital wall. There's nothing remotely of interest there, although I suspect Trib might be seeing something more, possibly a plunging neckline.

'You do fancy her.'

'Maybe a bit,' he confesses.

'I think you've lost your bottle now the missions are over.'

'Up yours!' he says.

'Prove it to me, then.' I pass him a piece of paper. 'Here's her phone number.'

He recoils, as if I've just offered him a hand grenade. 'You're a bastard, do you know that?' But his annoyance evaporates as he ponders the idea. 'What would I tell her?'

'I dunno. The truth?'

'What, you mean: "Hello, I quite fancy you and I thought you might want to go out for a drink some time. Please excuse the hideous scarring."'

'Yeah. Why not? Women love scars.'

He looks at me dubiously, and I realise this may be the single most hypocritical sentence that has ever escaped my lips.

'What's the worst that could happen, Trib? She might say yes.' I pause, then add, 'I think your problem is that you haven't learned how to embrace failure.'

'You're a git,' he says, 'a bastard and a git.'

He snatches the piece of paper out of my hand.

37

I COULD MAKE THIS so much easier for myself. I could phone her mobile, or drop off a letter asking her to meet me somewhere. I'm sure her dad isn't vetting her post. I toy with the idea of bypassing Mr Parry by putting a ladder up to her bedroom window and climbing up to woo her, like Romeo. Suitably theatrical, but maybe a little creepy. And, of course, Romeo and Juliet doesn't exactly end well. Ultimately I reject all of these ideas. No deception, no clever plan, I simply decide to storm the gates.

'Hello, Mr Parry. How are you doing?'

He folds his arms. His frown alone could deflect bullets.

'Would you mind if I apologised to your daughter?' This is a carefully chosen phrase, something difficult for him to refuse.

He begins to open his mouth, but is cut off by Rebecca's voice from somewhere inside the house: 'Who is it?'

'It's Olly,' he says over his shoulder. 'Do you want me to have him arrested on some trumped-up terrorism charge?'

After a pause she appears at the door. Her gaze is direct, chin tilted up a little, but I'm not so easily fooled. Her defiant posture can't hide the pallor of her skin, the expression of fatigue that haunts her eyes. But nor can I deny the lurch I experience at seeing her again, like a sudden stumble into a body of water. Just the sight of her, this fraction of a second, is enough to flood me with hope. I must hold on to my strength, my sense of purpose.

'What are you doing here?' she says.

'I ... um,' I glance briefly at her dad. 'I think we need to talk.'

'I'm not so sure that's a good idea,' Mr Parry says.

'Look, if you don't want me in your house I can take Rebecca out to my car and discuss it there. Surely there can be no harm in that.'

He narrows his eyes. Yes, he hasn't told his daughter about our little talk in his Ford Focus, has he? And he knows I can reveal all if I choose.

'No, we'll talk in here,' Rebecca says. 'Come in.'

Mr Parry doesn't look at all convinced. 'Rebecca, are you sure that –'

'We'll be up in my room,' she says.

He wants to argue further, but I can see him put the brakes on. I wipe my feet on the doormat and follow her up the stairs. Rebecca's bedroom is like a B&B before the guest arrives. She hasn't made this space her own. The only things rescuing it from complete anonymity are the objects on the bedside table: a Stephen Fry novel and a mug featuring a treble clef. In a way this is good; it means that moving back in with her dad is temporary. She offers me the solitary chair and sits on the edge of the bed.

'I don't understand why you're here, Olly.'

I launch straight in. 'There is no other woman. I said it before and I meant it.'

'Huh!' she says. 'You'll forgive me for wanting some proof.'

'How am I supposed to provide that?' Surely it should be her responsibility to prove I *am* cheating on her.

'You tell me,' she says.

'I can tell you where I was on that Saturday when you thought

I was seeing someone else. I can tell you what the secretive phone calls were about. I can tell you … look, I can tell you everything. You were right that I wasn't being honest with you, and I want to tell you the truth.'

'But you know it's too late for that.'

'Too late for the truth?'

'The damage is already done. Nothing you can say will undo it.'

'I know, but … but I can at least give you an explanation.'

She shakes her head wearily. 'You might be able to give me an explanation, but you can't give me a justification.'

She has the power to deny me, the same way she has the power to silence someone as big and tough as her dad with just a couple of words. If she asks me to leave – and she could say it in the space of a breath – then everything's over.

'Maybe I can.'

'Oh, really?' she says.

'But in return, I'd want the same thing from you – the truth.' My heart is beating faster now. What I'm about to say is dangerous; it's all or nothing. 'I'm not the only person who's been hiding things in this relationship.'

Her pause is no more than a second, and I think, *Yes, I'm right*. I'd figured it out yesterday, during a conversation with Trib. Even while incapacitated in a hospital bed, he's still busy helping people out.

'Listen,' she says, 'I've got a very good reason –'

I interrupt: 'So have I.'

She frowns. 'Are you angry with me?'

The truth. That's what I'm committed to. Only the truth. The same way I did with Zach. 'A bit, yes.'

'Let me get this straight,' she says, '*you've* come here to be angry with *me*?'

'Given that I'm not the only one keeping secrets, yes. I've got as much right to be cheesed off as you. This is not a one-way street.'

'You have no idea what you're talking about.'

'So you can keep secrets, but I can't? Is that what you're saying?'

'You have no idea.'

'I came here to tell you the complete truth, which is that I'm angry with you. And you're angry with me, and we both owe each other an explanation.'

'I don't owe you anything. The relationship's over, Olly.'

The words are like a slap in the face, and before I've got time to think, I'm saying, 'No, it's not.'

Her mouth drops open. 'If I say it is, then it is. It takes two people to make a relationship work.'

'Of course it does, but neither of us have given it a fair chance. The truth is, I don't think it's over and neither do you.'

'I beg your pardon,' she says, with the same sort of emphasis people use when swearing. 'Don't tell me what I think.'

'Then why did you invite me in? Why didn't you turn me away at the door?'

'Olly, has it occurred to you that I might have moved on?'

'Moved on? Bull*shit*. Look at you. You're stuck in your dad's house, looking like you've been run over by a steam roller.'

'How dare you,' she says, but it comes out as little more than a whisper.

I'm doing it again: I'm winning the argument, the way I always do.

I take a couple of deep breaths, try to moderate my voice. 'You ... have depression, don't you?'

A moment's silence is all the answer I need.

'I want to help,' I tell her.

'You can't. It's in my head. You can't reach it.'

'I don't believe that. People affect each other's moods all the time. Otherwise I wouldn't have been able to piss you off so thoroughly, would I?'

'Huh. This is different. You don't know what it's like.'

'I have at least *some* idea. I've already been through it with you: the bad gig at the Fatted Calf, that time over Christmas. Just because you haven't told me doesn't mean I haven't seen it.'

Her chin trembles. She glances towards the bedroom door and I rise halfway out of the chair.

'Please don't get him involved. This is our one opportunity to be honest with each other. Let me tell you the whole story, and then you can either agree to give this another chance or tell me where to go. But until then – until you know the truth – you can't make a proper, informed decision.'

'You think you've got something that justifies your behaviour? Something that's going to explain away all the ... Oh, Christ.'

She stops dead because I've rolled up both sleeves and held my arms out to her, wrists facing upwards. What little fight she has goes out of her. She looks afraid of me, the way my family did when I lost control.

In this moment I'm more naked than I've ever been in front of another human being, but now the sacrilege is done, the panic hits hard. Although my hands are unfurled, the rest of my body is clenched like a fist. I stamp on the carpet a couple of times and force myself to take in some air. My entire body shakes, as if I've been teleported to the Arctic, and a violent prickling sensation reaches all the way down my arms and into my fingers. My vision blurs. I blink to try and clear it. My heart-rate is absurdly, dangerously fast. I'm going to die. This is it, here, in this bedroom, right now, I'm going to die.

But the torture continues and I realise that, no, I don't get to bail out that easily. I force myself to breathe more slowly, more deeply: the exercise Dr Nylund taught me.

I know what I need to do, in the abstract at least: I need to get myself back under control, pull myself back to my reasoning, persuasive best. But I can't. Something has fallen out of reach, out of my control. Her dad is only meters away. I wait for her raised voice, the pounding of feet on stairs. Assuming my body is up to it, escape will be my only option. I need to clear my eyes enough so I can see where I'm going as I run past him and out of the door. I need to be quick enough to outrun the shame.

'Olly,' she says.

I'm still trying to hold my arms out, but my elbows are against my chest and I'm bending over double on the chair. My body is still insisting that I hide the scars. Too late now, of course. Far too late. That was the whole idea – to give myself zero chance of bottling out.

'Olly,' she says, and I feel her fingers on my shoulder, hesitant.

If this is the last time she touches me, I'd better make sure I appreciate it. I hear the bedsprings creak as she gets up, and all too soon the fingers have gone. This is where she leaves the room, gets her dad, phones the men in white coats. This is my chance. If I go now, it can be as swift and clean as the escape from my parent's dinner party last October.

Rebecca's hand is on my shoulder again; she hasn't left the room after all. She puts something into my hands – a toilet roll.

She says, 'I'm afraid we're all out of tissues.'

—

And so I tell her everything. It takes a long time – school, Duncan and Stendall, my history of self-harm, the missions with Trib, the discovery of a sweatshop. I surprise myself with the story of my own life. Rebecca hangs on every word, fascinated and horrified. Again, I wonder whether this ruthless dedication to the truth is a wise move. All or nothing.

I finish, in shame and trembling, at the episode in Stendall's kitchen.

'Shit, Olly,' she breathes.

'Yeah.'

'I mean … shit.'

'I know.'

'So, you hurt yourself rather than Stendall.'

'Yeah. Not much of a choice, really, was it?'

'I know what that's like.'

'What do you mean?'

'To always be harder on yourself than anyone else.'

So, does this bring us closer together, is that what she's saying? I'd like to find a way to articulate this, but all the words seem to be used up. We sit in silence for a while.

'This is, uh ... quite a lot to absorb,' she says. 'Maybe you should, you know, leave me to think things over.'

Is it an excuse to get rid of me, now she knows what a maniac I am? It's irrelevant. I have no strength left to argue. I've made my plea, and nothing will sway the jury now, one way or the other. The defence rests.

I allow her to lead me downstairs. Mr Parry springs up from his seat in the lounge, but he loses confidence in whatever he was intending to do, and gets no further. I know how he feels.

'Mr Parry,' I say in acknowledgement.

'Olly,' he says neutrally.

Just before I close the door and set off for home, I use my last reserves of energy to pass Rebecca a business card for the Star Anise. On the reverse are the words I wrote hours ago in honest black biro, back when I was cresting a wave of hope.

7pm, Monday 8th.
Please, please, please.
Olly

It's done now. I trudge back to Moira's house, to my cosy loft bedroom and the enveloping numbness of sleep.

My phone reads 19:10 and I'm beginning to feel nervous. A waiter arrives at the table and asks if I would like a drink while I wait. I decline. The Star Anise is beautifully decorated, with stiff white tablecloths, muted lighting, and an eight-pointed star motif that extends to the lampshades and the salt and pepper pots. The chairs are elegant constructions of polished wood and oxblood upholstery. They're not comfortable. The napkin, once fanned like the tail of a peacock, has long since been reduced to a knot of cloth in my lap. The place is beginning to fill up – white-haired men with pressed suits and women in bright floral dresses, bohemian types wearing glasses that make a statement, families out for a significant birthday.

19:15.

She's probably spending a few extra minutes getting ready. Or she could be coming by bus, in which case there may have been a delay. I find these scenarios comforting. The more of them I can come up with, the better. A woman in a black, knee-length woollen coat appears at the door and is immediately met by a waiter. He takes her coat, and beneath she is wearing a strapless red dress which he does his best not to notice too obviously. She exchanges a couple of words with him. He bows a little and makes a gesture in my direction. Her hair has more volume. She's applied a little make-up. It's her.

'Hello, Olly,' she says as she reaches the table.

'My God,' I say in reply, running my eyes up and down her.

She takes the chair opposite.

'Would you mind not sitting there? I'm waiting for a depressed woman.'

She smiles and in the depths of my mind a voice says, *Yes*.

'It's all still in here,' she says, 'don't you worry about that.'

'Well, it looks like you've made some pretty fantastic progress.'

'You and your compliments, eh?'

'You'd better get used to them.'

She bites her lower lip and picks up the wine list. 'This is nice, isn't it? I tried to eat here once before, but my date kind of stood me up.'

'I wouldn't have missed this if the streets of Strathurst were running with lava.'

Her expression becomes serious, and she lowers her voice. 'Olly, just because I'm here doesn't mean that what you've told me isn't worrying. I mean, you threatened a man with a gun.'

'To save Trib.'

'Yes, but even so …'

'It won't happen again. I swear it. And anyway, I can't: I don't still have it.'

'You're not packing heat tonight?'

I spread my arms wide. 'Pat me down if you like.'

'You wish.'

'I do.'

'All I'm saying is … don't have too many expectations, just because I've turned up.'

'You're here. That's enough.'

'Sweet,' she says. I can't tell whether she's being genuine or subtly mocking. Either's fine, I guess.

We order a Merlot and choose from the à la carte menu.

'Giving things another chance like this,' she says, 'you do know what you're letting yourself in for? I haven't stopped being the person I was.'

'Honey, you can boil my bunny.'

She laughs. 'I'm adding that to my set list.'

'Not while I retain copyright.'

'But seriously,' she says, 'there are no guarantees this is going to work. We are a bit of a pair of screw-ups.'

'Well, I certainly am.'

'Er, hello? Crazy depressive bint who goes running back to Daddy at the first sign of trouble.'

'Er, hello? Gun-toting maniac who gets a bit too familiar with a kitchen knife.'

She starts laughing.

'It really isn't funny, Rebecca.'

Oh, but it is. She only manages to bring herself under control because the waiter arrives with the wine. He pours us two glasses and retires discreetly.

'So what are your plans for the future?' she says. 'What are you going to do instead of your moral crusades?'

'I want to go into ... management, I suppose.'

She takes a sip of the Merlot. 'Mmm. Tell me more.'

'I need to devote myself to something worthwhile – not just a job or a pastime, but something I believe in. So, I'm going to offer my services to this musician I know.' Rebecca's wine glass stops halfway to her lips. 'She wants to get on with writing and performing, and it's outrageous that she's not better known, so I thought I'd take care of the bookings, marketing, promotion, website, all those sorts of things. If she wants me to.'

She puts her glass back down on the table. 'Why do you do this?' she says.

'Why do I do what?'

'Insist on believing in me?'

'Because you don't have enough belief in yourself. I'll supply the shortfall.'

For a moment she stares at her napkin, unable to look up. Then her hand snakes blindly across the table towards mine. I give it an encouraging squeeze.

—

The meal is every bit as good as we'd hoped. She lets me walk her home, and we stop under her porch. She puts the key in the lock, and her fingers stay there, ready to turn.

Invite me in. Invite me in.

'I think I'm going to invite you in,' she says.

We go through to the lounge and sit on the sofa. She pours us each an amaretto and we sip them while we sit in companionable silence. *Don't have too many expectations.*

Rebecca says, 'Roll up your sleeves.'

It's so much easier this time. I hold the material away from the cuts, because they're still sensitive. She takes my right arm by the wrist and elbow, very delicately, then leans forward and brushes her lips against the scars. I can feel the sensation all the way to the base of my neck, the nerves aligning.

'You,' she says, 'have to stop doing this.'

'I will if you will.'

'Ah. That's not so easy.' She taps her head. 'My scars are in here.'

I lean forward to kiss her on the temple.

'I've missed you,' she murmurs. 'Sorry I've made things so difficult.'

'Ditto.'

'You were right to suggest we try again,' she says.

'I didn't have any choice. I'm catastrophically in love with you.'

'Huh. It may be a catastrophe at that.'

'Then let's go down in flames together.'

One side of her mouth curls upwards. 'You can be so romantic.'

'Yeah, well …'

'No,' she says, 'I mean it.'

Her lips find mine, and soon Rebecca is whispering, 'I think I'm going to take you upstairs.'

—

I wake abruptly. Low sunlight filters through the curtains and I'm aware that Rebecca's side of the bed is empty. I sit up and find that she hasn't gone far. She's on the edge of the bed, naked, looking straight ahead.

'Are you okay?' I ask her.

'I … I think so. I was just getting up.'

I reach out to stroke her shoulder. 'Tell me.'

'That offer of yours – to be my manager. You really mean it?'

'Of course I do.'

She reaches behind and squeezes my hand. 'I want to make a go of it – a proper go of it – but …'

'But what?'

She shakes her head. 'You know. The usual reasons.'

I slide out of bed, pluck her Epiphone from its stand and place it on her knee. Then I sit behind her, my thighs encompassing hers. Sweeping the tangle of her hair aside, I place my lips next to her ear.

'Give me your left hand.' I place it on the guitar's neck and mould her fingers into a simple A major. 'Put your right hand here.' I arrange her fingers on the strings. 'Now: play.'

She strums the first chord.

ACKNOWLEDGEMENTS

THANKS TO THE FOLLOWING people for feedback during the very long gestation of this novel: Loree Westron, Scott Smyth, Joan Smith, Gail Loose, Neil Edmunds, Chris Hammacott, Wendy Metcalfe, Carol Westron and the late Eileen Robertson.

Thanks also to the Arvon Foundation and their tutors, who commented on parts of this novel or on my writing in general: Naomi Alderman and Joe Dunthorne, Ed Docx and Alice Jolly, Jon McGregor and Helen Oyeyemi.

For help with French, merci beaucoup to Martine Egan.

All errors are the author's responsibility.

Biggest thanks, again, to my wife Helen – consultant, editor, proofreader, shrink and provider of 'writing chocolate'.

With the environment in mind, I've typeset this novel to use 20-25% fewer pages than most equivalent books.

The wonderful cover design is by Chris Hammacott from The Art of Communication: book-design.co.uk

No AI was used at any stage in the writing of this book.

To be first to hear my (admittedly infrequent) writing news, you can bypass the social media moguls and sign up to my newsletter: www.richardsalsbury.com/newsletter

If you like this novel, please recommend it to (or buy it for) a friend. A personal recommendation is still the surest, warmest, truest way of finding a good book.